# Tourist in Bohemia

Elizabeth McKellar

ISBN 978-0-9547488-2-1

First published 2011 by Mark Argent, www.ma-books.com

Typography by Silverfen, www.silverfen-type.com

Printed by YPS Publishing Services

*Typographic note*: this book is set in the typeface Utopia, designed by Robert Slimbach. This is one of the Adobe Originals range of type-faces, which is a project begun in the 1980s. Utopia itself was released in 1989, a year before the story of *Tourist in Bohemia* ends.

For Catherine and Julian

# ACKNOWLEDGEMENTS

I started writing *Tourist in Bohemia* in January 1999 and it was completed by 2001, so if anything in the novel seems prophetic it is not from hindsight. It has taken a decade to see it in print after a couple of near misses with mainstream publishers. So my thanks go to my publisher Mark Argent who believed in it, took it on, edited it, then designed and costumed it perfectly.

Gray Watson was my knight in shining armour in 1979. Tim Pearce was there too. Neil Roberts replied with a "keep going and send me more" when I first started writing. Peter Middleton encouraged me and brought contact with writers Peter Gutteridge, and Amanda Boulter who generously gave up time to write to me.

I'm grateful to all those who cheered *Tourist* on — Jan Vaughan, Jim Sherlock, Ewan Smith, Mary Chadwick, Les Brookes, Trudi Tate, Geoffrey and Jennifer Pawling, Ben Duncan and Dick Chapman, and David and Caro Fickling. Special thanks go to the poet Tony Mitton from whom I learned about sound, precision and that every word counts, and to our children Doris and Guthrie and my lifelong friend Kate Baker.

*Tourist in Bohemia* is dedicated to Catherine Dawson and Julian Pritchard. They accompanied the book from the first lines through countless drafts and rewrites. My thanks to Catherine for her meticulous proof-reading — any mistakes are my own or where I have ignored good advice. And finally, my thanks to Matthew Pritchard for the memory of his playing of the Chopin E minor piano concerto in Jesus College Chapel.

EXULTATION is the going
Of an inland soul to sea,—
Past the houses, past the headlands,
Into deep eternity!

Bred as we, among the mountains,
Can the sailor understand
The divine intoxication
Of the first league out from Land?

Emily Dickinson (1830–86)

# CHARACTERS

ELEANOR (ELLIE, NELLY, EL) *a dressmaker*

GRENVILLE *a rich toff*

YASMINE (THE WITCH) *theatre costume-maker and Grenville's friend*

SANDRA *theatre costume-maker and Yasmine's partner*

GAIL AND ZEB *married couple (LUCY their baby), artisans working for Theo*

THEO *Grenville's architect*

MARTY (MARTIN) *a tranny*

ARCHIE *a civil servant and Grenville's uncle*

RAJIV *a maître d' and Uncle Archie's young partner*

DAVID *a journalist friend of Grenville's*

TINKER (BELLE) *a rent boy*


AUNT POD *Grenville's aunt*

OLLIE *Grenville's old school friend*

BAPTISTE *Grenville's lawyer*

LAUREN *Grenville's agent*

IMOGEN AND CARLO *Theo's sister and her husband*

RON *Marty's dad*

NATASHA *journalist*


And many hangers-on, relations, party-goers, friends, drifters, gatecrashers, dropped-names and one night stands.

# *London — May 1979*

## i

## DIRECTIONS

"So how does this clitoris thing work, then?" Grenville shouted above the roar of the Underground.

"I'm not giving a demonstration here," Eleanor said.

"Pity! It's not just poofters like me that need education, my dear. There is too much secrecy and confusion in the world. Provincial prudes who feel shame and run away are giving in to the hideous forces of repression," Grenville's ranting voice was ground up in the clatter of the train. Eleanor, not wanting to be lumped in with the provincial prudes, nodded her head.

"I am determined to stay in the vanguard of sexual politics," he went on. "Despite my great age I'm still a radical, I still believe in the war against guilt and censorship!"

Though Grenville moaned about being over thirty, there seemed to be an endless supply of sex. Eleanor put this down to him being gay, upper class and the most gorgeous man she'd ever seen.

"Your hetero world is a dreadful mess," he said. "The pursuit of erotic pleasure as part of the great quest for enlightenment is virtually forbidden. Why is that, d'you think? Women are so peculiar. What, in Heaven's name, d'you want? Do you want sex?"

"Not just at the minute."

"There you are! It's inconceivable! Perverse, when one thinks how much you girls are lusted after. What do you want?"

"What I'm after is —"

"I know a little ditty and it goes like this," Grenville began,

"*Nimini pimini Boys like polygamy!*"

The train was slowing to a stop as Grenville finished,

"But…! *Nomini pomini Girls like monogamy.*"

They picked up Eleanor's bags, left the train, walked off the platform and onto the escalator.

"All the same," Grenville announced, "I think it's time to diversify. Try the other side —"

"Have a go at women you mean?"

"Jolly exciting, uncharted waters. New adventures! Which is why I will need you, my pet, to give me directions, provide a map, tell me how it all works."

Eleanor looked up at him as he slouched on the moving handrail, sounding off from the step above. Unlike her, he was bold and promiscuous. She was timid in bed. Thought maybe love should come into it somewhere. No point in saying so. He'd think it was pathetic.

"There is a leetle button, yes? We press, yes? And *wheee!*" Grenville rolled his eyes.

"Got your sex education from a comic, did you?"

"All right, all right. Seriously. I mean, women are different aren't they?"

"Have you someone in mind, then?" Eleanor really, *really* hoped it wasn't her. Was this why he'd offered her a room in his house? Yes he was gorgeous but she hadn't come all this way to be a guinea pig.

"Someone in mind? Not quite. But I'm preparing myself. So what will I do? Advise me, my dear. I should take it more slowly? More… whatyoumacallit?" Grenville juggled with invisible body parts. "Foreplay!" he shouted as he went past a startled busker. "I've been reading all about it in a magazine."

"A magazine?" Eleanor repeated and cringed as Grenville yelled at her over the heads of the crowd,

"*Bottoms* or something! I don't know. It was full of women anyway. Perfectly filthy! I've obviously been missing out. What d'you think?"

Eleanor had never been on the London Underground before and had to concentrate on keeping up. Her pack bounced on her back as she hurried after Grenville, down the tiled tunnels and out onto another platform.

"How do you know which way to go down here?" she was out of breath.

"Aha!" Grenville pulled Eleanor over to the curved wall of the platform, "Now, my young friend, pay attention. Here we are in front of Beck's brilliant map. A piece of genius. Beck of the tube and Bazalgette of the sewers, unsung heroes of our beloved city. Gods of the Underworld, guardians of the trains and drains —"

There was a hot blast of wind and a train rushed into the station.

"The London Underground map is a perfect system based on colours and cardinal points," Grenville shouted. "Even the most mundane journey on the tube has a mythical quality for we are always *bound* north, south, east or west like the migrants of the Blues or the travellers in a tale —"

The train doors parted and they pushed into the crowded carriage.

"I like to think that we are hurtling through the city's body in a cell of warmth and light," Grenville's voice was still loud as everyone, pressed together, waited in silence for the doors to close. "And I like to think of the superb sewage system too of course, only it's not so much fun imagining oneself as a turd."

Eleanor looked down and let her hair hide her face. Not long now, surely. But she must think of something to keep him off sex and sewers. Two stops and the journey was done but as they walked away from the train towards the exit, Grenville started up again,

"A new direction for the libido is —"

"Grenville, I haven't come to live off you and what I'm hoping —"

"Really? I'm sure I shall find having you around tremendously pleasant and I know I intend a heterosex recce but I think we'll keep *our* relationship platonic, don't you?"

"Oh, definitely!" Eleanor tried not to sound too relieved as it might be insulting. "I think just friends is best for us, I do. What I'm after is a job and —"

"This venture into fannydom," he said, steering them towards the news stand at the station exit. "My friends are not at all supportive. Think it's queer. But," Grenville waved at the kiosk plastered with pictures of Mrs.

Thatcher, "I am merely responding to these radical times. Our new Prime Minister has a handbag, blouse and bouffant —" he said as he bought a paper. "A break with tradition, wouldn't you agree? Change is in the air! Fannydom is in the ascendant and 'Enterprise' is the watchword."

## ROOM

They emerged from the Underground and after dodging fast moving traffic, turned into a quiet square of delapidated grandeur. There were dumped cars and basements full of trash. A dusty wind blew newspaper across the square and splayed it onto gap-toothed railings. Up some steps, under a pillared portico, Grenville unlocked one half of a massive door. Stepping over the junk in the hallway they carried Eleanor's luggage up a wide marble staircase to a spacious landing on the first floor. Grenville started stabbing the air with his newspaper, saying,

"Loo, kitchen... bathroom... up here... my room, library —"

Eleanor, ducking away from Grenville's waving arm, caught glimpses of scruffy, book-filled rooms furnished with stunning untidiness.

"And at the top," Grenville led her up futher flights of stairs, "are your quarters." Putting down her suitcase he muttered, "First-night-at-boarding-school-awfulness for you, I'm afraid,"

Never having slept away from home but wanting to get away from it, Eleanor didn't respond. Instead, she looked round, trying to orient herself.

"I've put out some pillows and sheets and my tartan rug which I thought might comfort —" Grenville cocked his head at a distant ringing sound, "There goes the phone!" he said as he rushed away down the stairs. "Come to the front when you've settled in," his voice receded.

Eleanor stood still for a moment and then eased her backpack off her shoulders and put it beside her bookbag, coat and suitcase.

The attic was long and low, with a firedoor opening onto a roofscape of chimneys and high parapets. The viewless windows made the space feel private. There was a large brass bed, antique furniture, piles of books, boxes and half-sorted jumble. She didn't mind Grenville's clutter; the miracle was that here, in the middle of this great, chaotic city, she had a room of her own, quiet and safe.

Eleanor slumped down on the bed. She felt shaky. Maybe she was in shock. Couldn't get over it. What she'd done. How she'd had the nerve to come all the way from her hometown to London, a place she'd hardly ever been in her life. And as if that wasn't scary enough, she'd come invited by a loony toff she hardly knew, whose world was more weird than hey-diddle-diddle. She had a moment of white panic. How was she going to manage?

She must stand up and force herself to do something. Make the bed. Use the clean sheets Grenville had provided. It was a choice: risk this or go back to life at home. Being nagged. Being compared to her big sister. Having a nothing job at her Dad's works. Come on... tidying, sorting things out... it always calmed her.

When the bed was made, Eleanor began to unpack. She cleared a shelf and claimed it for her bag and sketchbooks. Her nightdress and shawl went on the bed. She pulled over a flat-seated chair to use as a bedside table. A lamp was wanted. She'd feel more settled tonight with a light at hand next the bed. Maybe there was one... somewhere in all the junk up here.

At the other end of the attic there were storerooms, one with a basin and toilet. Like the rest of the place they were untidy with boxes and lumber. Eleanor spent some time exploring cupboards and looking for a lamp. She found one. More rummaging turned up a dusty packet of bulbs. They fitted. Was the lead long enough? Eleanor put the lamp on the chair, crouched down and plugged it into the socket near the bed. She knelt on the floor and pressed the switch. Yes! Never mind the smell of hot dust, she felt pleased with herself. Looking round the room, it seemed more familiar and cosy. She'd have a pee and a wash now.

Eleanor glanced in the mirror as she rinsed her hands. She didn't wear makeup and her clothes were simple. The girls' fashion for black trousers, white shirt and boy's lace-up shoes suited her flat figure and the need to travel light.

The rest of her unpacking was done in no time. Clean underwear went into an emptied drawer. Four coat hangers on a curtain pole dealt with the rest of her clothes. Eleanor took a deep breath. She should go and join Grenville.

He wasn't in any of the rooms she passed on her way back downstairs. But off the first floor landing there was a large double door. Closed. He must be through there, then. She hesitated as she worked out which side of the double door to open and felt nervous as she tried a handle. The heavy door opened slowly, along with her mouth.

*Woooh!* The room was vast. Enormous. It could have swallowed her Mum and Dad's house whole.

"You are amazed?" came Grenville's echoing voice.

Eleanor looked down from the white plasterwork figures on the ceiling to search for him among the scaffolding and chaos below. The whole scene was backlit by three floor-to-ceiling windows. The sun, shining through the trees in the square beyond the balcony, filled the space with flickering shadows and reflections. Eleanor was too dazzled to move,

"You know, you never said —!"

"Didn't I? Yes I did. Surely. I can remember warning you that I was restoring a room. Builders in the ball-room! Noise. Mess. Pong. Hoped you could cope and so on." Grenville was in front of the central window, his studded leather jacket catching the light like shining armour.

"But I just thought you meant putting in a few Victorian —"

"Victorian? How nasty! No, no, no! Please can we not call it Victorian. Such a ghastly period of spiritual and moral darkness, don't you think?" He had come across the room to stand beside her, "Here's your tea."

Eleanor took the mug. The vulgar design was so shocking it made her blink. It had a shiny pink penis for a handle. She looked up at the ceiling,

"That's beautiful though, isn't it? What are those figures up there?"

"Nymphs and muses. And over here," Grenville pointed, "a rout of fauns and rustics. It's Apollonian

Dawn at one end, and Dionysian Dusk at the other, d'you see?" He turned round to look straight at her, with head on one side, eyebrows raised, "All right, my dear? You know, it's so very *good* of you to come."

As if she was doing him a favour. It was that lovely way he had. His manners. That's what had won her over from the start. That promise of something personal behind all the noise. Even though she could hardly understand a word he said, it was as if he really liked her. Needed her, even. Wanted to know everything about her. Yes her, plain, ordinary, nowt-a-penny Eleanor.

They picked their way over builders' rubble and sat on either side of a silver tea service which had been plonked down on a packing case among a mess of over-flowing ashtrays, magazines, books and record sleeves. Grenville sprawled with one leg flung over the arm of a decrepit club chair and talked to her. She leant her head back on the sofa and felt herself open up to the space. She'd never been in such a big room before, not in this way, not to belong in it herself, all private like. The effect was amazing. It was like having huge lungs and being able to take in lots of air and feel light. Set free.

"...what d'you think?" Grenville's voice brought her back to earth.

"About what, love?"

"Sex. What else is there?"

There was having to get on. Make a life. Sex was for afters. And more than anything there was not wanting to go back. Go back to the family, dead-end grotty jobs and "told you so." Leaving home, coming to London to live with a barmy sex maniac like Grenville was enough excitement to be going on with. She must get Grenville off sex and onto helping her find a job.

"I need to get work —"

"It's all in hand," Grenville said. "I've arranged for you to meet the Witch of Wandsworth."

"Y'what?"

"My friend Yasmine. Marvellous woman. Has a workshop. A factory of enchantment where she makes costumes for the theatre and so on. All right for you?"

"The theatre!"

"Yes, I thought you liked it."

"I do, I do, I love it!" Eleanor said. "But I only ever did dressmaking at college. I've not done theatre costume and I've not even got the full certificate in —"

"Oh pooh to certificates! It's all sewing and snipping, isn't it? Pins and needles and so forth. We should start thinking about what we might have for supper —"

"But I've never done —"

Grenville raised a finger,

"I have an important truth to impart and it is this: certificates or no certificates, most people are hopeless." Then he pointed at her, "But not you, I think. More tea?"

"Yes," Eleanor said.

"Good. You won't turn down the Witch. You've got a few days to settle in here, then she's taking you on trial, starting next week."

"You mean she'll give me work?"

"Absolutely. She's got a lot on and needs a skivvy. I expect she ate the last one." Grenville got up to put a record on the stereo, leaving Eleanor gawping into space.

She looked up at the dancers on the ceiling...

They brought back a memory. A memory of a school trip to an exhibition of theatre costumes... lifesize models... proper settings. And the best... a night scene where stars twinkled in a dark blue sky and there, suspended above the windowsill, with one arm out to his side and a finger to his lips... *sssh*... had been the moonlit figure of Peter Pan. Eleanor loved Peter Pan. She would sew on his shadow and be taught to fly. Fly away. The theatre... it was magic... magic made real. She had studied the gauze leaves and petals of Peter Pan's tunic and lost herself in drawing. Drawing and sewing. The only things she could do at all. Eleanor wanted to get into that moonlit world. But it had always been a hopeless notion, what with her being such rubbish at everything. Might as well think of flying to Neverland.

And yet... here, now, just like that, thanks to Grenville, she had arrived right at the edge of her dreams.

## APPRENTICE

Eleanor was let in by an entryphone. She looked up and down uncarpeted stairs and wondered where she was supposed to go. This was like the first day at Grenville's all over again. Another test already. Another venture into the unknown. She sighed. Just getting here across London on her own was enough work for today. What she really wanted at this moment was to bolt back to her safe attic room. She waited inside the front door but no one came to meet her so she went down some steps to look into a basement. She could make out all the equipment needed for dyeing and distressing fabrics, including a huge vat. Maybe that's why Grenville called Yasmine "the Witch". But there was nobody there cackling and flinging bat's blood into a cauldron and by now Eleanor would have been glad to find a troll, a goblin or anyone to tell her where to go and what to do. She pressed her lips together. She was the heroine in this story and heroines were never put off. They did not go back. The studio is not down here. It must be up. Eleanor began to climb the stairs until, pausing on a landing, she heard from somewhere above, the stabbing whirr of a sewing machine and the scrunch and click of scissors. She wiped her hands down her coat. Would she be able to hold a needle in her sweaty fingers? Forcing herself up the final staircase, Eleanor emerged into a long room full of skylight.

"So," came a voice, "we wait long times for you Eleanor. Creepy creepy on the stair, eh?"

Yasmine came round the high cutting table. She was a mature woman, exotic-looking with a thick length of white hair, contrasting black eyebrows and eyes so dark they looked purple. Yasmine took Eleanor's hands and turned them palm upwards,

"Ouf! Sweaty sweaty. You frighten of the Witch, yes?" She helped Eleanor out of her coat, saying, "Not worry. I not eat you yet. You too much bones," Yasmine patted Eleanor's cheek and smiled. Eleanor felt like a child. A favourite. It was a new feeling and she liked it a lot.

"What can you do?" Yasmine asked.

"Anything, anything you need, Miss. I can do all the basics and I'll do the clearing up and —"

"So! You will be the little slave for Yasmine and Sandra. There is Sandra. You will do wave."

Eleanor smiled at a young woman with spiky, blue-tipped hair who waved back.

"Now you go and do wee-wee," Yasmine ordered. "You hang coat, you wash all away the sweaty and you begin. No shilly-dallies. We have much works."


Eleanor's first job was to learn where everything belonged. Sample books, dressmakers' dummies and adjustable hat stands were kept in a walk-in cupboard to protect them from dust. Two plan chests contained trays of threads, pins, needles and every kind of haberdashery. Glues, staple guns, punchers and tape measures were kept on wheeled trolleys. Just like at college, little sharp scissors were attached to the trolleys on long ribbons. The studio was strewn with gaudy materials and fancy trimmings, but underlying the finery she could feel the iron grip of discipline.

Round the room hung cork boards on which were pinned designer's drawings along with little squares of fabric and all kinds of pictures for reference. Eleanor stopped to study the designs and repin a sketch that had slipped sideways.

"You like tidy," Yasmine said, stroking Eleanor's shoulder.

"Yes, yes I do."

"I like also. Everything in my childtime is mess. We are always hiding... running away. Trying to escape the pigs."

Eleanor was curious about this funny foreign game. She would please the older woman by getting her to chat about her childhood.

"Pigs?"

"Porno pigs!" Yasmine hissed. "Soldiers! They kill my father and brother, they burn everything!"

Eleanor put her hand to her mouth. The shock filled her eyes with tears.

"Ai, sweetie! Not cry for Yasmine," she hugged Eleanor. "Is all far away now. Look! no more mess," she pointed round the studio, "Grenville, he help me get. He is so good man. Even he is not the tidy one!"

Eleanor swallowed. She was never going to speak again.

"Grenville give to me the money for starters. But I do good for many years now. No more hungry!" Yasmine opened her arms to show off her curvy figure.

"How did you meet?" Eleanor could not resist.

"You will not ask this question. You work now."

"Sorry —" Eleanor closed her mouth. She *must* shut up and stop rushing about like a puppy, all piddly and waggy-tailed.

"Today, you finish with Romeo," Yasmine gave instructions. A new actor taking over a part meant costumes came back to the 'shop for refitting. Eleanor, as a beginner, would do the boring job of alterations.

Before taking up her work, Eleanor looked over to Sandra and tried a friendly question. Sandra ignored her till she was nudged by Yasmine into producing a reply. Eleanor soon learnt that though Sandra rode a powerful motorbike and wore leathers, she was obsessed with the kind of women's clothes she never wore herself. Yasmine did not allow radio or music but as the three of them worked, Sandra droned in her strange, affected voice about the female stars of old Hollywood movies; she knew what they had worn, in every take, down to the last marabou feather.

Unsure of herself, Eleanor decided to leave the talking to Sandra but worried that Sandra was trying to make trouble, always watching the effect of her innuendos and saucy remarks as her eyes flicked from her work to Yasmine, to Eleanor to Yasmine and back to her work. As the day went on, Eleanor began to wake up to something else. Yasmine and Sandra touched each other a lot. Before speaking to Sandra, Yasmine always stroked her face or body and Eleanor took this as a lover's tenderness. Would just have to be adult and get used to it. But Eleanor wished Sandra would leave her out of it. The way Sandra stood so close and stared into Eleanor's face whenever she spoke, made it difficult to know where to look. And it might aggravate Yasmine who seemed like the temperamental, jealous type. Eleanor could not afford to get caught up in some tangle between these women. She needed the *work*, needed it to lead on to more. Work. Yes. That was the road to freedom. None of this traipsing after the lads or getting married as a way to leave home; that was just one prison into another.

When the day ended and Eleanor was leaving, Sandra made ready to go out too, saying she wanted to catch some experimental film show. Sandra had promised Grenville details about the venue and said to Eleanor,

"Tell Grenville I'll bike round with the info —"

"Or you'll just ring him up? Here's the new number —" Eleanor edged away from Sandra's staring face to write the number on a bit of paper.

"Can't do that. Can't use the phone," Sandra said.

"Whyever not?"

"I'm a bit Mutt n' Jeff." Sandra's voice was flat but her face was angry.

"Y'what? A bit...?"

"Deaf," Sandra shoved her face at Eleanor and made a jabbing sign with her hand.

"Deaf!" Eleanor was so embarrassed she began to babble, "I'm sorry! Honest to God, Sandra, I didn't realise. You're so —!"

"What. Normal." Sandra stood over Eleanor.

"No! You're not normal, you're both bloody terrifying. But I never noticed you were deaf and that's that!"

"No use shouting," Sandra said. Yasmine made a hissing sound in the background that might have been laughter. "So I'll come round." Sandra reached for her leather jacket and prepared to leave.

"Yes! Fine! And Sandra I'm —" Eleanor bit her lip.

"Nah, don't you worry," Sandra put an arm round her waist. "Not notice is not so bad. I forgive you. You can have a lift on my bike..." she flicked her wrist as if revving up.

Seeing a suggestive smirk pass between Sandra and Yasmine, Eleanor tried not to look as young and gormless as she felt.

# iii

## CRAFT

Grenville's balcony doors were propped open with jugs of yellow lilies. The breeze ruffled their petals and brought the hum of London into the ballroom. Eleanor was sitting at a table, sewing, finishing part of a costume Yasmine had made for an avant-garde film. Grenville, coming past with a big plate of toast in one hand and a mug of coffee in the other, paused to say,

"Very punk. The Witch likes punk."

"I can never thank you enough," Eleanor said, "for getting me a job with Yasmine and —"

"I did very little. Come and have breakfast, pet lamb. The Witch is ruthless where her craft is concerned —" Grenville picked his way over toolboxes and builders' debris. "You must be good or you wouldn't have lasted two minutes."

The ballroom was still full of scaffolding and specialized plasterers' tools, handmade wooden things that looked to Eleanor like mystery objects from a museum. It was strange to think that until recently the ballroom had contained apartments. Strange to imagine those rooms, in midair now, where people had come home to have supper and go to bed. Peculiar rooms they must have been, with great slabs of elaborate plasterwork running along one wall and then vanishing into a corner or plunging through the floor — cheap bedsits where dancers and cherubs struggled to emerge out of the edge of a ceiling. The most damaged piece of stucco had been the central ceiling medallion. Now it was finished, Grenville liked to lie on the floor and look up at the white mandala.

"Do come! I've put your favourite French apricot squidge on the toast," Grenville called out from the floor. "Fresh coffee in the kitchen! I would have brought you some, only I ran out of hands. The four handed Shiva Nataraja is what we need —"

"Or a tray."

"Too *bourgeois*. Shiva, Shiva, yes…" Grenville got up and put a record on his stereo. One speaker was on the edge of the mantlepiece and the other at the top of the decorators' platform. "*A Morning Raga…* just the thing."

Eleanor went to the kitchen and put the coffee pot, milk bottle and a mug onto a tray. She returned to a room that was full to the brim with the soft flow of sitar and tabla. The sound was like an element. As she passed through it, the music poured into her ears and nostrils, drenching her hair and the pores of her skin. She glanced up at the dancers on the ceiling, white and innocent in the cool morning light.

Eleanor exhaled a *haa* of happiness.

"You like? Marvellous isn't it. I'm taking you to an evening of Indian dance and music tomorrow. I should have made more coffee, our plasterers will be here soon."

Gail and Zeb's restoration of the plasterwork was nearly done. An uninterrupted cornice rimmed the huge room. Friezes and cartouches which had been destroyed by partitioning had been repaired. The dawn nymphs and the evening maenads floated free on the ceiling, their trains of creatures, their rising sun and crescent moon restored to them once more.

"Zeb. He's from from Wales. Is Zeb a Welsh name?" Grenville wondered. "Zebadiah? He was *victorious over the Philistines.* Very auspicious name for an artist."

"It might be short for Zebedee," Eleanor said. "He was a character on kids' television when we —"

"Never watch television — too corrupting!" Grenville jumped up to answer the front door and let them in.

Eleanor was not due at work till later so while the plasterers were on their scaffolding, she asked to come up for a closer look. Eleanor felt at home with Gail and Zeb. It helped that they were ordinary. A married couple even. But really it was because like her, they lived through their hands and eyes.

"Lovely, it's been," Zeb said, as he rolled some baccy. "Taught us a lot, working with Bert and Ernie."

"Bert and Ernie?" Eleanor had not noticed any assistants.

"They were the masters working here when this room was first done —".

"Long gone, I get it. Famous, were they?"

"Dunno," Zeb shrugged. "What I'm saying is, you can tell by just looking, see. Different hands. Different ways of doing things."

"How's that, then?"

"Bert's really clever the way he compensates for flaws in the mould or where joined sections can't quite meet," Gail said. "Because no space as big as this can be completely, completely regular, can it? Bert's botches are really artful. They're as clear as if he'd signed his name. Look at this —" They took her to the far end of the platform. "Look how he turns the corner here. Really difficult. It's miles out of true but you'd never realise. See how he's done it? Crafty, that is!"

"And Ernie?" Eleanor asked.

They moved along the scaffolding again and Zeb pointed,

"I'm working on Ernie's swan, look. Deep relief here, which he knows will catch the light and give a good shape. But not too fussy. And look at these ribbons, all freehand. He's working close up but knows exactly the effect from a distance," Zeb stroked the swan's curved wings, "beautiful, that is!"

"Where have they left their names?" Eleanor wanted to see.

"Oh no," Zeb said. "We call them Bert and Ernie but don't know their real names at all. They don't need to sign their names, we know them by their work."

Eleanor was impressed by all this attention to detail that would never be noticed by anybody. "Those poor workers in the past," she said, "going to all that trouble just for a bunch of idle rich who'd have taken it for granted and never even looked up! At least Grenville will appreciate it."

"It wouldn't matter if he didn't," Zeb drew on his roll-up. "The point is, it was a livelihood for the worker, as it is for us. Bert and Ernie did a beautiful job for it's own sake. And for their sake, we'll do the same."

"So you don't sign your work..."

"Well, just maybe..." Gail said, "there's two little plaster sparrows that weren't there before..."

# *Five months later*

i

## SHOPPING

"I'm not bloody going in there!" Grenville stopped before the supermarket's windows. They could see the shoppers being shunted through the checkouts and hear the piped music, "Let's go to Jamal's."

"Jamal's?" Eleanor said. "Buying all the food for tonight's dinner party at the corner shop will cost the earth."

"But that's what money is for! Buys you the real thing. Proper people." Grenville had turned and was walking towards their corner shop.

"But it's late," she tried to resist. "The supermarket is much quicker."

"Nonsense. Lets go and see Jamal and his boys."

Eleanor remembered then, that she was Grenville's sidekick. She was not responsible for his friends or his party. She did not have to care about the state of the living room, the pubic hairs in the soap or the timing of the food. She skipped along beside Grenville, nudging him.

"Got a new girlfriend coming tonight, have you?"

"*Nein!* I'm still searching for my *schweifende blonde Bestie.*"

"Y'what?" she said. "Sorry, I know I'm ignorant."

"Never apologize. We all have the knowledge appropriate to our culture and circumstances. I want a splendid blondie beast. I gather women like talk."

"She'll get plenty of that."

Grenville didn't like being teased. "Here we are!" He opened the door of the shop for Eleanor. "Hello! Good evening," he called over her head.

"Ah! Yes. Yes. Good evening, sir!"

Eleanor admired the way Grenville never changed to suit people. With royals or rentboys he'd be the same person. He never toned down his toff's accent or his manners. But then, he was never rude or sarcastic either. It was like he was innocent, the way he found everything fascinating and went on as if everyone was equal and meant well and liked him. Which they did, mostly. She, on the other hand, couldn't help trying to fit in by smoothing out her northern accent. She could do it, had a good ear, but it made her feel a fake. No better than a parrot. Eleanor envied Grenville's easy way through the world and wondered how much of it was to do with wealth and privilege and how much was down to him just being born confident. And a boy.

Mr Jamal interrupted the argument he was having with his sons and cronies to come and give Grenville a wire basket and gather him into the discussion about a new road scheme. "What I am saying is this, you see, that it will interfere with my deliveries altogether —"

Eleanor picked up a basket and started to squeeze round the aisles which were like narrow canyons with goods packed high and tight up the sides. The shop smelled of spices. Indian music wavered in the background, topped by the sound of men's voices.

Grenville came up behind her, his basket already half full of titbits.

"They say women like presents, compliments on their appearance. What are we going to feed these people?"

"How about pasta with ratatouille —" Eleanor said.

"Ratatouille? Too mushroomy. Cosy chats, they say. Ugh! Mushrooms… like slugs somehow. Turn everything grey. Can't do cosy. That's not your scene surely? Tea for two? Friendly fucks? Terminal boredom?" Grenville added some poppadoms to the assortment of exotic starters in his basket. "I suppose since it's an Indian shop we ought to do curry. Well, you're a straight woman, what do you like?"

"Can't make curry for eight people in half an hour. I need to relax a bit, feel safe —"

"Safe! Safe is no good. Risotto? I must have some danger, dirt, filth and fetish." Grenville lifted a jar off the shelf. "I say, Lime Pickle! Must have some of that. Are presents a good idea?"

"Maybe. I don't like them much. Not what I really want —"

"Nuts and honey and Greek yoghurt for pudding. Which is?" Grenville asked, poking about among packets of sweets.

"Intimacy, closeness is what I like —"

"Closeness? I think it's time to expand, experiment, explore! Highland Spring water. Exotic Tropical Juice. We'll need veg, old fruit."

"But there's women's lib now, Grenville. Are you prepared for that? They've got onions and peppers —"

"The political stuff? You mean relationships with women are conditioned by their social and cultural oppression and are therefore inherently sado-masochistic blah blah blah?"

"I see, I suppose it must sound quite inviting to you." Eleanor wrinkled her nose.

"Absolutely! As a sado-masochist I might be expected to find all that very interesting. Submission. Control. Power and pleasure! *Copulation is the parody of crime* and so forth. Fresh ginger?"

"Oh no! No. Horrible."

"Oh yes! Yes. Peps things up no end. Well, at least the *theatre* of it, uniforms, leather, whips, etcetera. Come to think of it, old bean, I'm not really in a risotto mood."

"I don't understand," Eleanor whispered, hoping Grenville would take the hint and lower his voice, "how anyone can want to be hurt. It doesn't make sense. Noodles, then."

"Noodles! Terribly good. The *thwack* focuses the mind, releasing one from the tyranny of desire. Complete surrender. A few moments of blissful freedom. Do you know, I think we should have pasta, with a vegetable sauce, oodles of garlic, no slugs. A ratatouille sort of thing. What d'you think?"

"All right then. With lots of grated cheese —"

"Bringing freedom from the quotidian and freedom from the awful responsibility of being *one*. What sort of cheese?"

"Make the best of what's available," Eleanor said. "But why —"

"We must get a move on, dearest. I told my guests to come at eight and it's past that now."

Grenville went over to the till and rejoined the roadworks discussion while adding Indian sweets and packets of trailmix to a basket already full of treats.

Eleanor put together the ingredients for the meal and after another ten minutes of town planning, paying, bagging up, answering questions about the party and being helped out of the shop with calls of "good night!" and "cheerio!" she and Grenville were on the way home, though he was walking backwards and shouting to the shopkeeper,

"But Jamal, dear man, it sounds like you might get some parking space! Yes! Think of it! Private parking in central London! You and the Queen! Thanks! Bye-ee!" He spun round and Eleanor had to hurry to keep up with him as he went on, "Jolly good! That's done. Couldn't get Jamal to see that a new bus lane might actually benefit him. Fear of the new! Fear of the future! What d'you think?"

# PLAYERS

Two of Grenville's guests were waiting at the top of the steps under the mansion's portico. He was still explaining to Eleanor how the transport system of the metropolis would be reorganised if he ruled the world, when one of the guests called out,

"In your Mussolini mode this evening, Grenville! Yet late, as usual."

"But worth waiting for," Grenville put down the shopping and embraced the man, kissing him on the mouth. Eleanor had met this friend before and knew his name was David.

"Eleanor," David brushed her cheek with his own. "And this is Marty," he turned towards the newcomer, a slender young man with a shoulderbag.

"Hi," Marty gave Grenville a sideways glance. "I'll take the shopping for you, shall I?"

"Yes, thanks. Absolutely lovely. Yes." Grenville gazed at Marty before unlocking the door.

The dinner arrived out of a muddle of talk and help from some of the guests. The wheeled scaffolding, planking and ladders were pushed to one side of the ballroom. Plastic sheeting remained over the floor and furniture but a dining table was uncovered and put in the centre of the room in a cleared space among the tools and workers' gear. Sections were added to the table, which was spread with a white bed sheet for a cloth and laid with a mixture of family silver, cheap canteen cutlery and plastic picnic spoons. A random set of chairs of moulded plastic, regency hoopback and tubular steel were gathered round the table. Grenville busied himself with lighting the room. This was what interested him. He adjusted lamps, asked for advice, changed his mind, adjusted some more. He brought antique silver candelabra to the table. Eleanor watched as he lit them; it was unusual to have him so quiet and concentrated. Before returning to the kitchen she looked up at the ceiling where the pulsing shadows of the candlelight made the bacchantes sway and dance.

On one of her journeys to the table with bowls of food, Eleanor was surprised to see a woman, a complete stranger, come down from upstairs. It took a moment for Eleanor to realise that the glamorous creature was male. The feminine gear brought him down to her level, so she didn't feel shy,

"Hello, I'm Eleanor. I don't think we've met."

"Yes we have, darlin'," he said, puckering his glossy lips, "I'm Marty. Here, let me take those." He walked expertly on very high heels.

Marty's flirty style created a permissive atmosphere. "She" was happy to play along with comments about waitresses, nibbles and maids of all work which would have disgusted Eleanor had they been tried on with her.

The remaining guests had arrived, among them Grenville's Uncle Archie and his quiet young partner, Rajiv. As they all settled round the table and began to eat, David addressed the older man opposite him,

"Come on Archie, indulge my journalist's lust for insider info: what's the new woman at Number Ten like? Do tell!"

Everyone at the table turned to listen.

"Bloody terrifying, my dear. She's everywhere! A whirlwind. But," Archie said, "extraordinary thing is, her private secretaries adore her and there is definitely a little frisson —"

"A frisson! Whatever do you mean?"

"Well, of course you can't expect an old woofter like me to find her a turn on but —"

"A turn on!" Grenville shrieked. "Impossible!"

"Oh yes. She's quite a flirt in her housewifey way."

"Yeuch! Stop! Archie, stop!"

"Come, we need some good housekeeping. The country's a mess," Theo, Grenville's architect, spoke up.

"But she's only been PM for two minutes," Archie went on, "and its already clear she will brook no disagreement. Scepticism is treated as disloyalty and, as you know, we at Whitehall feel being sceptical is a sacred trust." Archie took a mouthful of wine and savoured it. He reached out a fleshy hand and tilting the claret bottle, peered down through his lunettes at the label while he spoke, "God knows, parliamentary morality has always been rather primitive, prep school stuff but now we're down to street gang level — kiss my arse or I'll kick your head in!"

"Perhaps it's Freudian, Archie," Grenville said. "Personal. She reminds you of horrid old Nanny —"

"Nanny was a sweetie, as it happens. No, no," Archie insisted, "it's not personal. It's that she's completely intractable and —"

"Desperate not to get bogged down in endless counter-arguments," Theo interrupted. "Specially after all these years of paralysis. A kick start! That's what's needed for the economy —"

"Ah! But word is..." Archie plucked up a spicy poppadom with his plump fingers.

"Go on. Go on!" David poured Archie another glass of wine.

"There hasn't been a single economic discussion in the Cabinet since this government came in," Archie said. "They're obsessed with ideology. They're zealots. I don't like it. All this talk of *believers*. I find it sinister, actually."

"Archie, you're just an old leftie-over."

"Old leftie? Old leftie! Grenville, do I take you to mean that I'm old enough to have fought in the last war? A war against Fascism indeed and waged by well-known lefties like... ah... Churchill? Don't you think, dear boy, you're getting a bit old yourself for the part of *enfant terrible?*"

"Never too old to be a radical," Grenville said. "And I don't see what's wrong with an ideology of more freedom, more individualism —"

"It's an ideology of selfishness. Greed will not be frowned upon," Archie said. "It's ugly and all dressed up in things you won't like at all, Grenville, like the sanctity of the family and down with the sixties."

"As an old hack," David said, "I quite like this government's populist approach but I don't like the fundamentalism. I think they're a bit sinister, actually. Though not as sinister as the Ayatollah. Now there's a beast, a *rough beast!*"

"Ah yes, *Its hour come round at last,*" Archie said.

Eleanor couldn't follow this. All she knew about those foreign places was that women were lower than the animals.

The talk turned to the spread of Neo-fascism.

"O God! Do stop rattling on! Serve yourselves, pass the stuff about," Grenville waved his hands.

"Nazism is a very serious subject," David said.

"Of course, of course. But..."

What *but?* Wasn't David Jewish? Eleanor tensed.

"— such a *splendid* uniform!" Grenville hissed.

Eleanor was amazed to see David snort with laughter at this outrage.

As the food was eaten and more wine drunk, the conversation became lighthearted and switched to the art of importuning.

"Bet you've had offers, doll," Marty spoke to Eleanor.

"Oh yes. I had an offer only the other day, as it happens." Where Eleanor came from, the women didn't say much in mixed company. The men did the talking. But since living with Grenville, where everyone turned to any novelty, Eleanor had found a talent as a comedian. Even though she was putting on funny voices and making most of it up, she could let go and be herself. To encouragement like — "Go on, go on! Do tell! What was he like? Or indeed, *she*, my dear!" Eleanor began,

"I was in the Cromwell Road, waiting ages for a bus and three turned up at once, you know how it is..." Her audience groaned. Eleanor flattered them by playing the country bumpkin dazzled by pleasures that cityfolk take for granted. She described getting on the nice empty bus and the thrill of sitting right at the front on the top. She went on with a story about a tramp who had come to sit behind her. How she'd tensed up but did not want to be seen showing contempt for unfortunates by moving away. Luckily, hers was the next stop.

"I was very fed up though. The whole of the top deck empty! Why did he have to come and sit right behind me? I soon found out."

Eleanor paused and felt them all lean towards her. She lowered her voice,

"He shuffles about a bit, right? Then he taps us on the shoulder. I get a horrible waft of dog's breath and then, do you know what he says? He says —" Eleanor put on a voice of exquisite gallantry,

"*I dare say a fuck is completely out of the question.*"

There was an explosion of laughter, Archie's the loudest. He asked, wheezing, "What did you do, Eleanor? What did you do, my dear!"

Eleanor, inspired by the response, held up her hand for attention,

"I gets up, and for once, I give a brilliant answer by just blabbing the very first thing that comes into my head..." Eleanor opened her eyes wide and lisped,

"*Oooh! I'm ever so sorry but I'm getting off now!*"

Among the laughter she caught Theo's eye.

She left the table to more applause. As Grenville followed her, Archie held him back saying,

"She's an absolute poppet. Well done, Grenville."


## BACKSTAGE

"Uncle Archie adores you —" Grenville said to Eleanor as he came into the kitchen. She found Grenville's instinct for spreading good feeling among people very endearing.

"Another one for your fan club, my pet and Theo too, ho ho. Yes, you were divine out there at the footlights," he hammed. "Simply divine, darling! But now there's a cutlery crisis —"

On cue, Marty came in, carrying empty dishes and a bunch of used spoons. He put them down by the sink, saying,

"That Theo, he's ever so dishy but gawdelpus he's dead heavy, I've got stuck in the seat next to him and something tells me I'm not his type of girl."

"You'll have to pinch someone else's seat then, won't you," Eleanor said.

"Oooh! 'Ark at 'er," Marty put an arm round Eleanor, lifted her chin and ran a red painted fingertip along her jaw. "She does learn quick!" It was like being fancied by a man and a Madam. Eleanor tried not to look put out.

Marty went back to clearing dishes, saying, "I reckon you could have that Theo, Eleanor. It's you he fancies, doll, not me."

"What a good idea! Do let me pimp for you," Grenville offered.

"You'd be wasting your time, love," Eleanor said as she prepared to wash up. "He'd want something classy and I bet he thinks I'm a peasant."

"Quite. He's a brilliant architect but the most ridiculous stuffed shirt. But being as he's an old chum and one of the few personable heteros of my acquaintance, I could fix up —"

"Tell us about your Uncle Archie and Rajiv," Marty interrupted.

"Boring *nomini pomini* couple," Grenville began slamming drawers and cupboard doors in his search for clean cutlery. "Rajiv was one of my discoveries. Beautiful, isn't he. Picked him up in Queensway. Early hours. Dark back alley. Among the bins. God! I was terrified. Thought he might pull a knife. God! It was exciting! Went back a few times but he turned out not to be terrifying at all. He's educated, respectable. Wanted lurve. Security. Quite hopeless." Grenville picked up the used spoons Marty had brought from the ballroom and went on, "So what to do? Set him up for Uncle Archie! Archie is a child of the Raj and has a passion for it all — Sanskrit poetry, sitar music, temple dancing. Speaks Hindi and Urdu. But they go too far!" Grenville flung the spoons into the sink. "Years and years Archie and Rajiv have been together! The whole thing is totally beyond me."

"It's called love, Grenville," Eleanor frothed up hot suds.

"No it's not," Grenville sounded angry. "It's called safety! *Nomini pomini*! It's monogamy and deeply perverted."

"Well, perhaps it's the old colonial rip-off —"

"Spare me the commi-rot. Haven't you any idea of Rajiv's power? At twenty, he was underage so —" Grenville picked up a grubby teatowel and began drying spoons and throwing them onto a tray where their crashes punctuated his speech, "all Rajiv has to do is lift the phone and he could have Archie's whole life and career in smithereens —"

When spoons missed the tray and clanged to the floor, Marty picked them up.

"And he could earn himself a fortune selling his story to the vile tabloids. Top Civil Servant in Queer Sex Horror!" Grenville ranted. "Absolute Drivel! Read all about it in *The Double Standard* or *The Daily Hypocrite!*"

"Not so safe then, is it," Marty said.

"Come along girls! The show must go on!" Grenville patted Marty's bottom. "Onwards and *upwards*... Ungh!" He picked up the tray of clean cutlery and left.

Eleanor washed up some plates while Marty lit a cigarette and leant on the worktop next to her.

"Like a drag?" Marty offered Eleanor a puff, holding it for her because her hands were in the sink. Eleanor drew on the cigarette and again felt confused by intimacy with this funny lad. Didn't know what to make of him. Her. Both. Neither...

"What's Grenville to you?" asked Marty, drying dishes and squinting through the smoke of the cigarette in his mouth.

"I'm his lodger. I pay rent, not much I know but... we're just good friends."

"Come on, doll, I've caught you peeking at that Theo... you're no dyke, are you."

"Nope. But I don't sleep with Grenville."

"That's not what I asked," Marty stubbed out his cigarette. "Lets get this lot to the table. Or they might start wondering what we're up to, eh?"

They returned to the ballroom where David, Archie and Theo's girlfriend were discussing air travel. Theo and Grenville were standing up, conferring about the ballroom restoration and Rajiv was sitting on his own so Eleanor and Marty joined him, making a group of young ones.

"Rajiv is a chef," Eleanor said.

"Blimey! What does a professional make of a shambles like this, then?" Marty made Rajiv laugh and soon had him chatting about the London scene.

Rajiv is another one like me, thought Eleanor. Has a new life... thanks to Grenville. She smiled at Marty, who was looking at her. So here we all are... three curiosities... a girl-boy, a gay boy and a lass from the back of beyond...

They sat in a pool of candlelight. Far above their heads, plaster cupids glimmered in the night sky.

## LATE

At around midnight, Rajiv made a move to leave. He fetched coats, helped Archie on with his and prepared to drive them home to Holland Park.

Archie kissed Eleanor on the cheek and swaying slightly, repeated the tramp's words from her story, *"I dare say!* Did the old boy really say that? Dear girl, you're such a scream." Archie's guffaws, goodbyes, and *awfully sorry, I'm getting off now!* boomed up the staircase while Rajiv tried to shush him and make sure he didn't break his neck. Theo and his girlfriend left at the same time.

A while later, as Eleanor was on her way to bed, the front door sounded. She went down and let Theo back in.

"Sorry to drag you away from the party. Girlfriend has mislaid her bag," he said.

"I guessed it was you. I found it after you'd gone." She handed over the bag.

There were distant yelps from the ballroom where Grenville remained with David and Marty. "And you didn't drag me away —" Eleanor wanted Theo to know that whatever Grenville got up to, she wasn't part of it, "I'd already left the men to their fun and games and was away to the attic with me teddy and hot chocolate."

Theo was looking at her. He would see she was slender and neat. Direct. No pretty dress, no jewellery, no deference. A man like him, he'd be irritated that she'd not made any effort to be alluring. To be pleasing and feminine. What use was a girl if she wasn't attractive? Eleanor smirked at him, seeing a tall, dark, bearded man holding a woman's handbag. He frowned at her, tucked the bag under his arm and grunted goodbye.


## THEO


He got into his car as his girlfriend was saying, "I couldn't face going back in there. Those dreadful people. No proper couples. No real women, just perverts. I can't stand men in women's clothes, it looks so disgusting! And Grenville's girl, looks like a schoolboy with a put on working-class accent. What's her name?"

"Eleanor," Theo made the mistake of remembering. "And I don't think the accent is put on, it's the way they speak where she's from —"

"Well, you can't deny she's very common. And I really can't see what's so hilarious about a woman using swear words. But you all jollywell laughed at that vulgar story. Which I've heard before, I'll have you know!" She had noticed Theo's amusement. "And that place is a mess.

How you can bear working for people like that is beyond me."

"I like restoration work," Theo said. "I was at Cambridge with Grenville and he's extremely well connected with old and new money. If I do a good job he'll circulate my name. Keeping in with him is very much in my interest. And Archie's all right, surely? A gentleman of the old school, rather like your old man —"

"Daddy is not a queer with a Paki boyfriend, *if* you don't mind. And I heard him say he hated the police. What sort of attitude is that from someone who's running the country? The only normal person was that journalist, though he's Jewish."

"David? And how do you know he isn't one of... those?"

"Because he's married! He told me. His wife's out at the ballet. She's that woman who writes in the Sunday supplements. So!"

Theo thought it easier to change the subject.


## ELEANOR

She lay in the warm lamplight of her attic, looked round and felt at home. She had tidied up. Most of Grenville's lumber had gone into the storeroom: papers into files, books onto shelves, porn mags neatly stacked.

If she strained to listen, she could just hear the distant goings on in the ballroom. No use getting upset about it. Though it was creepy. But it was Grenville's thing. Nobody was doing anything they didn't want to. And nobody was trying to get her involved. Better to remember that ever since coming to live with Grenville, she'd felt free. Happy. Maybe sometimes she felt over excited like a kid at the circus. Or just dog-tired and weepy with trying to keep up. But then she'd come to her attic, go to bed and sleep and sleep. And she'd get up after, no bother, always in a good mood, always out the right side of the bed. The past, the old frustrated Eleanor had melted away. It was like her head had emptied out and she didn't know who she was or what she thought about anything. Just that she had work, a room of her own and Grenville for a friend. There was nothing more she wanted.

Eleanor turned off the lamp and went to sleep.

## MARTY

He reclined in the passenger seat of David's car. Before leaving Grenville's he had changed out of his femme clothes and makeup and was back in his jeans and jacket. All the same, he went on enjoying the feel of being passive. Submissive. Being driven home by a big dark man in a posh motor. It had been a good session. He felt complete. For a while there, the forbidden Marty had come out to be admired. And had given satisfaction. He and David had no need to talk. Sex was their intimacy. Of their other lives they knew nothing, except sometimes Marty would see a piece by David in the newspapers or catch sight of him on television. "I know you" Marty would smile to himself. "I really know you, honey!"

David drew up by the entrance archway of the council tenement where Marty lived, "All right?"

"Yeah. Thanks."

"You'll let me know if you... need anything," David said.

"Yeah, I will."

"I'll be in touch."

"Sure. 'Bye."

Marty crossed the dark yard, guided by the bulkhead lights over the staircase entrances. He climbed the concrete steps to the second level and let himself in.

"Is that you, son?" Marty could hear the relief in his Dad's voice.

"Yes Dad." Marty stepped into the bathroom, switched on the light over the mirror and searched his face for any signs of makeup. "How've you been? All right then?" Marty called out as he put his bag down, put the plug in the bath and turned the taps on.

"Oh, mustn't grumble. N'you?"

"Fine," Marty put his head round his father's bedroom door. "I won't come in and chat. It's late and I'm knackered. Must have a wash and get to bed. School tomorrow."

"That's right. You get your kip!" Now Marty was home his Dad would switch off his bedside light and go to sleep.

"Goodnight, son."

"N'night, Dad." Marty pulled his father's door to nearly shut. That's how his Dad liked it... a bit of light from the corridor and the comforting sounds of movement around the flat to send him off.

After a bath and hair wash Marty put on a towelling robe, made a hot drink and unpacked his bag. He knew he would not be disturbed. His father was disabled and could not leave his bed without help. Marty was sure of total privacy even though he could hear his Dad's breathing.

He sponged and dried the leathers and shoes. The underwear, lace gloves and stockings he examined for tears or ladders before dropping them into the suds he'd prepared in the bathroom basin. After hand washing, he laid them flat on a towel which he rolled up and wrung gently. He had seen this trick when, as a child, he had watched his mother looking after her "fancies". The artificial satin dress washed out easily and wouldn't need ironing. He took the damp clothes and put them on hangers to dry in an empty section of his wardrobe. After lifting out the combination lock suitcase from the bottom of the cupboard, he put away his wig, his makeup bag, canes and stiletto shoes. As Marty blow dried his short fair hair, he ran the heat over the seams of the dress and underwear. They would be dry by morning. Before he left for work and the homehelp came for his Dad, everything would be locked up and hidden away, out of sight, at the back of his cupboard.

Marty lay on his back in the dark of his room, hearing his father's soft snores. He shifted on his buttocks, which still smarted from the evening's session. He was going to be a bit strung out in class tomorrow but he'd got lessons prepared to give himself and the kids a low-key day. His sandwiches were ready in the fridge and, as usual, he was all organised. Had to be. Not like that chaotic Grenville. Talk about how the other half live.

His work drab was on a hanger on the back of the door. Marty looked at it suspended in the gloom... the spectre of his everyday self... sober suit, plain white shirt, narrow tie. Just what Grenville's fag hag Eleanor had been wearing. Wonder what's going on there? She had sleek, dark, shoulder-length hair. Hers was real. Marty fell asleep remembering the warmth of her smile in the candlelight.

# SET

Eleanor watched Theo, Grenville's architect, walk across the ballroom. His manly style was very attractive. The formal suit looked good on him, at any rate. Grenville was speaking to him as they came towards her,

"...Eleanor, the Rapunzel I keep in my attic, is here today." She smiled but there was no response from Theo. Just a nod. She felt put down and wished she didn't smile so much.

"This rapunzelment of Eleanor is entirely voluntary, you understand. I will not be jealous if I come back and find you... *compromised*," Grenville ignored their embarrassment. "I might insist on joining in by way of rent, that's all. Colour charts!" Grenville helped Theo lay them out on the table. "Maps of Heaven, are they not? It's so miraculous, this infinity of difference from just three primaries! Spunkingly good, wouldn't you say?"

"Can I get you some coffee?" Eleanor asked Theo. She could tell he didn't really want any but accepted it all the same. Likely he didn't approve of mixing women with work and wanted her out of the way.

"Be quick, pet lamb!" Grenville called out. "I shall want your advice."

When she returned with Theo's coffee, Grenville said,
"Good. Eleanor understands colour. Very important in the theatre. Mood, symbolism and so on. The decorative plasterwork should be white, that's right for the period

and we'll stick with it. But mustn't be slaves to tradition. So what would you do for the rest?"

Eleanor said, "How about some sort of yellow? It's the best —"

"Aargh! Yellow. Impossible," Grenville waved his hands. "It's the colour of disease and madness!"

"There are the blues," Theo tried showing Grenville a colour sample. "Can't go wrong —"

"Not blue. One does not want to inhabit a Wedgewood soup tureen, does one. Though blue is very cool and spiritual, it's true. The colour of transcendence. That's what religion should be, transcendent. The revamped communion materialises it all, which only makes it ridiculous, an insult to reason."

"There are lots of blues to choose from here. How about —" Theo pushed the chart closer to Grenville.

"The liturgy should be, above all, poetic. Perhaps if it wasn't soup tureens. Can one have a different sort of blue?" Grenville wondered. "Blue can be very chilly. Religion should affirm certain possibilities. Can't one warm it up a bit?"

"Warm blue?" Theo sounded unsure. "You start moving into lilac and mauve, Grenville. You can't want that, surely."

"Mauve? Very mysterious. The colour of Fannydom! It should assert something 'beyond'. There is more to life than meets the eye. Ye-es, mauve."

"You can't be serious. It musn't be allowed to predominate," Theo said.

"Why not? There really isn't enough of the feminine in religion. The *Virgin* Mother. Really! A prudish and revolting perversion of parthenogenesis. What more proof do you need that Christians are barking. If only there was a decent religion. There must be a life of the imagination, of the soul, some alternative to grey materialism and —"

"Greys?" Theo said. "Here's a whole section of mushroom shades —"

"Don't like mushrooms!" Grenville frowned. "Too like slugs. I have not learned to *bless them unaware.*"

"What about green?" Eleanor suggested.

"Green?" Grenville shook his head. "Too swampy. Red. We haven't thought about red. Blood. Redemption. Lipstick! Might be a bit much on this scale though…"

"Consider the cost," Theo was getting impatient. "You must settle on a colour —"

"How about all of them at once. Take the bits you like and make a completely new religion," Grenville said. "Or do you think that's too garish and hippyfied? Pro sex and with no deity. A pleasuredome. There again, having lots of deities might be fun…"

"Don't you think there is a —"

"Not really," Grenville interrupted Theo again. "If there is a God you'd think He'd have made sure Freud got there before St Paul and Odo and all those early Christian lunatics. Yellow. I like the association with Zen, with contemplation, with conscientious objectors. Yellow is warm and life affirming. Goethe's light, Wordsworth's daffodils —"

"You must decide which yellow," Theo pointed. "Look, here, there are hundreds —"

"Yes, one must be very careful. Wouldn't do to end up in a custard pie after all, would it? Where shall we start?"

"I have to go, Grenville, I'm due with clients in Hampstead —" Theo said.

"Because the Word made flesh —" Grenville went on, "is a wonderful idea. But what if the Word is *guilt*?"

"How about gilding some of the plasterwork, then?" Eleanor put in, hoping to bring Grenville back to the point.

"Gilt! How very amusing, my dear —" Grenville raised his hands, "*I believe in —*"

"I've got to go," Theo snapped. "I'll leave the charts with you." He shut his briefcase and made to leave.

As Eleanor saw him out, he spoke to her, "Try and get him to come to a decision by Monday. I want to book the decorators and the paint will have to be specially mixed. It all takes time, money and organization, you know."

Eleanor did not like being made responsible for Grenville and resented being bullied on his account. "It's not my problem," she softened her words with a smile but Theo had already turned away down the stairs without looking at her.

"You gave Theo a hard time," Eleanor scolded Grenville on her return to the ballroom.

"Not at all. The old fart needs livening up. I chose him because he's brilliant at restoration, I've known him for years and he cares about money. Rent boys ripping off the odd shirt or rifling my wallet is to be expected. But for this, I need someone I can trust. There are family funds involved. Fancy him do you?" Grenville waggled his eyebrows.

"I don't think so, love. He's right out of my league. He ignored me and anyway, I think he's another of those blokes who think women are just decoration. He's too old fashioned —"

"Well, the patriarchal beard is a bit of a problem," Grenville said. "But it does signal he's hetero: really likes girls and so on."

"I don't understand —"

"Rarely in the history of pooftery have men had beards. And certainly not in the present climate of American hearty homos or London pansy punk. Anything goes, from moustaches, muscles and check shirts to kilts, earrings and purple lipstick but beards, no. Can't you fancy poor old cuntface then?"

"I like his beard. I like manliness and —"

"*Vive la différence!*"

"Difference? That's just another word for inferior, isn't it? An excuse for you blokes to keep women down —"

"Stop it!" Grenville raised his voice. "Spoiling feminism! Making it into another set of *mind-forged manacles* —"

Eleanor began to feel weepy. It was all too much. Feeling put down by Theo and now being shouted at.

"Twisting it into another of those fucking awful religions! Redemption —" Grenville stood as if crucified then shot his arm round into a Nazi salute, "becomes tyranny! Institutionalised neurosis. And I won't be called a *bloke* under *any* circumstances. Shall we have some more coffee?" He went on speaking as Eleanor wiped away her tears. "Or is it time for lunch? That's Marxism's fatal flaw, *Liebchen*, conflating equality with the elimination of difference. Don't cry, old thing, it's confusing."

"Sorry!" she sniffed. "It's just you're all angry. Like my Dad. Sorry."

"And don't apologize. Angry? I'm not angry! We're only batting ideas about. Pub lunch by the river?" Grenville reached out his hand but did not touch her. "Putting the ideas into practice is when the trouble starts," he said. "That's the time to cry."

"Let's get out —" Eleanor started to leave but instead, she took a breath and turned back, determined to stand up to Grenville. "So you think there's a big difference between men and women?"

"Shall we put the top down on the car?" Grenville picked up his keys. "There is no culture without the ability to discriminate, to make, destroy and recreate categories. But we'll need to keep warm."

"So you think there are two distinct and different genders," Eleanor persisted as they left the room. "You don't think gender is just..." she tried to remember the proper phrase, "— socially conditioned?"

"There are two genders and they are absolutely different," Grenville said, helping Eleanor on with her coat,

"There's the people we fancy and there's everybody else."

# iii

## TRANSPORT

Eleanor jaywalked the traffic and jumped a slowly moving bus in Knightsbridge. She gave the conductor a cheeky look as she swung up the stairs. Leaning into the sway of the bus, she dropped into an empty window seat. She was getting to know London. And to love it. Outside the bus, the weather matched her breezy mood. An empty sweet wrapper twirled past the window. She looked down from the top deck at the crowd of people passing in and out of South Kensington station. Wonderful how they didn't know or care who she was and how she'd never see any of them again.

"Wotcher!" Marty sat down beside her.

"And here was I thinking how wonderful it is to be alone in the big city!"

"Well, at least I'm not a niffy old tramp," Marty looked coy. Eleanor nudged him,

"And I'm not getting off at the next stop!" She could relax and flirt, he was a tranny and it was all a joke. Marty smiled and offered her a cigarette,

"Going back to Grenville's?" He held out his lighter. She nodded and pulled on the cigarette as he lit it. "Looks like I'm going *all the way* with you, then!" he said. "How's things? All right, mate?"

"Mm, I'm so happy!"

"Blimey, you don't often hear that! What's the secret?"

"Grenville." Seeing Marty go all wide-eyed Eleanor said, "Not like that! What I'm saying is, he rescued me."

"Rescued you from what?"

"From under a stone. Home," she said.

"Bad was it?"

"Well, not a nightmare or anything. My Dad's done really well... come up from nothing. He set up his own business." Eleanor exhaled. "And they get on all right, Mam and Dad. No screaming matches or booze trouble or owt like that —"

"So the problem is... ?"

"I don't suit, somehow. Never have."

"They're idiots, eh? How's that then?" Marty's interested voice and direct look made Eleanor talkative. Grenville would never discuss families or the past or anything personal. And Marty was on her level. It was great, for once, not to be struggling to keep up.

"Well, I've never been right for them. My sister is the one they like. I was useless as a kid. So I got nagged at home and picked on at school. Were you bullied?"

"Yep. Didn't you get away to college?" he asked.

"No, worse luck. Did my dressmaking course down the road at the local tec. And nearly messed that up n'all, on account of my boyfriend. What a disaster that was! He'd never spend time with me, apart from... you know. Then he couldn't wait to get back to his mates in the pub. And he was cheating on me but muggins here," Eleanor pointed to herself, "was too gormless and lovesick to work it out. Love's young dream? *Psss...* I'm not going down that road again in a hurry. What about you, Marty. Do you live at home? Have you been away to college?" His skinny build and fair hair made him seem young but Eleanor reckoned he was at least five years older than her.

"I like travelling, seeing other places," he said, "but I couldn't stand to leave London. At least there's a scene

51

here. A bit of tolerance. But, come on, how did you get to meet Grenville?" He turned the talk away from himself.

"Oh Marty," Eleanor clutched his arm. "What if I'd never met him? Oh! It doesn't bear thinking about! There are such a lot of 'what ifs!' " She counted them off on her fingers: "What if I'd not agreed to stand in for a mate, pulling pints in the theatre bar that evening? What if Grenville hadn't come up from London for that studio drama? What if his boyfriend hadn't been in it? What if his boyfriend hadn't stood him up? Oh God! I'd have been stuck, forever... under that bloody stone..."

"Never mind that! Go on. What happened?"

Eleanor remembered Grenville coming and going, standing at the Star and Garter bar, sighing, flipping the beermats, looking round all the time,

"So there's this gorgeous feller, right, and he's obviously waiting for his date, girlfriend, as I thought. Well, I took the money for his second vodka and knowing all about being stood up I said, to be sympathetic like, *No luck?* He misheard me! Or pretended to. D'you know what he said?"

Marty shook his head.

"He said —" Eleanor imitated Grenville's upper class accent,

"*Fuck? 'Fraid not. Ei'm a faggot. But thenk you.*"

Marty grinned, "That's better than your tramp story!"

"That's cos this one's true. And you know how polite he is?" Eleanor waved her hands like a fop in a play and did him again,

"*Ei'm freitfully flehttered, all the same.*"

"That's typical," Marty said. "I think he plays the innocent so he can be shocking. So, what did you do?"

"Us went red as a ripe tomato and run away t'till."

She'd understood that word "faggot". She'd heard it at football matches, sing-songed, with the other "f" word, as an insult. So that's what they looked like. She'd never have known. He was refined. An upper-class twit type. From another planet. Except for his clothes, mind. Eleanor knew all about the cut and cost of that leather coat.

"But I forced myself back to him," she said to Marty. "I wasn't having him think I was some ignorant clod-hopper in a huff."

And, she'd thought at the time, being "one of those", he wouldn't give her any bother about leading him on if she were friendly.

"So we got chatting and he said he might as well go back to London but that he was starving and well over the limit. Needed to wait and eat and could he take me out for a meal? So I rang my Mam and told lies by the yard. Then went out with him."

"And you got on, that's easy to see."

"It was wonderful, Marty! It was like coming home. I told him all about my boyfriend trouble. He told me all about this lad he'd been after. I moaned about my family. He moaned about some book he was writing and the people who wanted him to do something else or other. I didn't understand the half of it but I didn't let on. Then at one point he said, *and you, Eleanor*, he remembered my name, *what do you want?*"

"Ah, yeah," Marty nodded. "He likes to ask that. What did you say?"

"Well, I'd never been asked what I wanted before in my life, but I knew the answer, straight off. So I told him, I said, *I want out of here. Out, out, out!* By now, I'd had some wine and got very bold. I said, *I want London. A job. Me own life and me own money.* And I can remember saying, *Pigs might fly n'all!*"

"But they have!" Marty said.

"Aye, they have! Thanks to Grenville —" Eleanor, playing the rescued damsel, clasped her hands and sighed, "— my knight in shining armour!"

Some of Grenville's friends ignored her, treated her as an enemy alien or made fun of her accent. But not Marty. In drag or in drab, he took notice of her. It occurred to Eleanor that he might be very in love with Grenville so when he asked, "And in this fairytale, does the knight in shining armour get the damsel?" she took the chance to let him know that they were not in competition,

"Oh no! In this story they stay good friends while the knight goes off after other dragons!"

"That sounds like Grenville, all right," Marty said.

Eleanor felt she'd been the centre of attention long enough, "Now, come on Marty, tell us about you. What do you —"

He nudged her and pointed out of the bus window,

"But we're getting off here!" he said as they got up to leave the bus. "Looks like my story will have to wait."


## VOICES

At this hour the house was noisy with people coming and going. The bathroom and Grenville's bedroom were strewn with clothes and makeup. Look fab or die. Primpers jostled in front of every mirror, making sure they would not be refused entry to the voguish clubs.

Grenville was in the ballroom unpacking a cardboard box and Eleanor was in the kitchen making a pot of tea. All the lights were on, techno jerked from the sound system and the rooms were full of voices:

— If you want tea, Eleanor's your man

— set up a line on there

— Thatcher's the one who's really queer not me. You've heard about this government's latest idea

— I'm not going there. Last night it was full of 'orrible boys from Balham

— my Mum cried buckets when she heard. She'd always fancied Lennon the most

— my Mum won't speak to me

— full of Herberts what spent all night cadging poppers off of me

— so, Grenville, you get a television at last

— I hate punk and them clubs with nothing but pogoing yobbos

— this is not to be thought of as a television. Nothing so vulgar, my dear. It is a VHS recorder and for showing art

Look fab or die, unless you're famous or friends of the famous. The famous came to Grenville's too. Eleanor had learned not to gawp. Mostly, they ignored her and she didn't mind being an audience. And big Rosa, who sang gospel while she worked cleaning bathrooms, toilets and kitchens, had come today. She saw Rosa got paid. Eleanor enjoyed the clean, quiet order of the house. It never lasted long. Disco music pulsed in the

background, the front door thudded, the telephone rang
and the rooms were full of voices:

— We'll try this porn film I've borrowed with a
promise of squalor and depravity

— but have you seen them new Walkman things? I
want one

— 'snot a very good film is it? Look! he's wearing
a tanktop

— fuck the police

— yeah fuck'em, do 'em good

— it's all blurry innit n'gone into black and white
now

— that's a big cock in any colour, though

— What we need is for everyone to shag everybody
else. There'd be no wars then

— no whores! Where would you be, dear

— has he had you, Frankie?

— I won't answer that

— We'll take that as a yes, then

— You try getting makeup for black skin


Outside it was getting dark. Through the busy reflections on the glass, Eleanor could make out other lives in
the windows opposite. Lives stacked up like the silent
screens of televisions left on all night in a shop. Below,
invisible in the darkness, could be sensed the dank,
unused spaces between the buildings where the rubbish
was put out. But up here, all the lights were on and the
rooms full of voices:

— no fighting, no killing, no being beaten up by
Skins

— you want makeup with lots of glitter. Here, have a
go with this, Bambi

— 'make love not war'... ah yes... the dear old hippies of yesteryear

— This film is so bad it must be art. Oh God! It is art. I'm supposed to review it

— this new Green movement thing sounds like a jolly good idea

— no being spat at. I hate it when people spit at me

— Eleanor! Ellie! Come and sit next to me, doll

— why do they hate us so much?

# Six months later

i

## WITCH

Eleanor left Grenville's house in spring sunshine but came out of the station south of the river into a different climate. Rain had polished the pavements and the traffic hissed by as Eleanor decided whether to walk to work or wait for the 189 bus down Nightingale Lane. She was looking forward to work, she had been there long enough for Yasmine and Sandra to start trusting her with more interesting jobs.

Arriving at Yasmine's, her bright mood dimmed when she realised that Sandra was away. Although she'd worked with them and they were regular visitors at Grenville's, Eleanor had never been alone with either. She had just about learned to cope with the emotional turbulence of the studio when here was another, nerve-racking set of rapids. Yasmine was bending close to examine her stitching,

"Your fingers love the stuffs. The sewing is good."

Eleanor was pleased to be praised by someone with such high standards but tensed as Yasmine stroked her neck.

"Touff! So tight up!" Yasmine sniffed, "who make the love for you?"

"No one at the moment," she tried not to sound embarrassed. "I don't have a *boy*friend at the moment." Eleanor went on inserting tufts of lime-green net into the seams of a costume.

"What happen to the last one? Tell me you shoot him." Yasmine moved back to the cutting table. Eleanor laughed,

"I wish I could! But I were the one as got dumped."

"What for?"

"Another girl."

"But you are so young! You not want more than him also? You want more, yes?"

"Ye-es but it was such a mess. He left me feeling so useless."

"Sss! I shoot him for you. Who is he, this porno?"

"In my home town."

"Ouf! He is the country pumpkin. Not worth the bullet! And he is porno in bed. I know. Disgusting chauvinist pigs. Men and this fucking. Uh! Uh! Uh! Like dogs!" Yasmine tossed her hair over her shoulder, raised her eyes and gestured with both hands. "And the taste! Yeach! No good for nothing. Just for make bebe." Yasmine looked back at a length of hand-dyed gauze, picked up the scissors and swooped onto the material. "So you live with the poofty. For safeness? Eh?"

Eleanor let her work drop into her lap while she watched the speedy precision of Yasmine's cutting.

"Well, I don't want romance just now, anyway. *Work* is what I want," Eleanor hoped Yasmine would hear the emphasis. "Romance is not the way to get on. It's not safe."

"Grenville not safe, Eleanor, you know he fuck everything now. His stupid stick girl. All bone, no boobz." Yasmine whirled the lengths of fabric over to the basque on the dummy and whisking pins from the cushion strapped to her wrist, began moulding and pinning it into place.

"Thin is the fashion —"

"Pah! Fashion is porno! All poofties! All poofties make girls to look like pretty-pretty boys! No boobs. We want fashion for push up the big boobs and stick out the big bottoms. Eleanor!" Yasmine wagged her finger. "Not stop the work, please."

"Sorry, I just couldn't stop looking at the fantastic way you've interpreted that design. It's perfect!"

Yasmine pouted her lips and wriggled her shoulders, "I teach, you learn. Good! Where you go out for tonight?" she demanded.

"Nowhere, I don't think Gren —"

"You stay here. I cook for you. Relax! We tell all about our lifes and the porno fuckups."

Eleanor was caught. Nervous but flattered. To be cooked for by Yasmine was a great honour. Her dinner parties were famous.

"Is good. I like alpromptu."


Having taken a glass of wine on an empty stomach, Eleanor was sunk into a wicker armchair in Yasmine's warm kitchen. Eleanor watched while Yasmine prepared food with the same passion as she cut and pinned materials. She seemed to have two minds, one to cook and one to keep up a stream of outrageous gossip and sex talk,

"I live in many city. I am in Trieste. I have friend, a stupid country pumpkin but she has bebe so the big boobs. I love her. I look after bebe for her to go out for the work. Yes? I love bebe. He is magnificent, so fat! Big legs. Big bottoms. I give bottle and she come back and bebe asleep? Full, yes? Not want boobs. She is so angry with me because her boobs full, hard, very hurting. Hurt! She cry for desperate. So I suck to stop her pain. So big her nibbles with pretty-pretty hairs all around. I drink! I die of heaven!"

Eleanor, half way down her second glass of wine, giggled at Yasmine's hysterics.

"What did it taste like?" she was always curious.

"Sweetie-water. O so sweetie-sweetie! I have orgasms to think of it."

After eating, Yasmine led the way to another room. Eleanor had a blurred impression of a *boudoir*, womb-like, with rich, dark colours, sumptuous fabrics, and huge cushions. There were no tables, sofas or armchairs, the whole room seemed to be a soft surface to lie or recline on.

"Grenville said you had a wonderful sitting room," Eleanor managed to say.

"This not sittingroom. No mens in here, never. You want for wee-wee?" Yasmine nodded at a door hung with glass beads before putting down a plate of her handmade sweets and a pot of tea.

The bathroom had no window but was lit with a soft light reflected in flattering mirrors. Eleanor, brought up to hygenic lino and tiles, was amazed by the deep carpet, the silk drapes round the bath and bidet, the midnight blue, star-studded ceiling. She tried to clear her head by washing her flushed face in cold water and looking at herself in the mirror. She had to get out of this.

"Look Yasmine, I'm not a lesbian —" Eleanor began after sitting down a little way from Yasmine who was lounging, her head resting on her elbow.

"Lesbian? Lesbian! What for these stupid words, Eleanor, eh? Not use porno talk to me, please."

"Well, what about Sandra?"

"You will say no things to Sandra." This was stated as a fact. "I love Sandra for always. But sometimes we want different. More. Sandra also. But we do not rub it in our noses. Open for mama," Yasmine ordered. She dropped a marzipan apple with chocolate leaves into Eleanor's mouth. "It make you not so tight up."

"What is it?" Eleanor asked with a flicker of anxiety.

"Is good for relax. Hash. I make. Eat is better than smoke. Smoke bad for body."

Eleanor had a moment of worry before the chocolate melted in her mouth. She loved marzipan too. "Iss rully yummy," she mumbled.

"Yummy!" Yasmine laughed and said, "I want to brush your hair now. You like? Is magnificent, your hair. Sandra say also. And so black with so white skin! You shave arm under?"

"Not really..." Eleanor answered in a drowsy voice. The hair brushing was so comforting she was beginning to relax.

"Is good hairs. Arm under is like little pubies." Yasmine put down the brush. "Take this away..." She helped Eleanor out of her shirt. "Show Yasmine? Hm? Lift up the arms for me? Over your head, like slave girl." She looked at Eleanor and stroked the dark fur of her armpits with the back of her warm hands.

"I like," Yasmine murmured.

Eleanor hung her head, feeling shy.

"You are so pretty-pretty. So white like the spring onions."

Eleanor apologised for her small breasts.

"Is true. I like big boobs. More woman," Yasmine said. "But I like you so much. Your nibbles so soft, like apricots."

Yasmine pushed Eleanor gently onto her back,

"I eat you now. Is yummy."

## COSTUME

Eleanor had got used to coming down from her attic to find lads, often with nothing on, in the kitchen and bathroom or strangers asleep on the sofas of the ball-room. She'd put a warm blanket over them if they were asleep or have a chat and give them breakfast if she had time. But today, Grenville and Eleanor had the place to themselves. Eleanor, in bedsocks and pyjamas was putting bread in the toaster when a naked Grenville wandered into the kitchen. The clothes were over his arm.

"Which shirt, d'you think? It all depends on one's mood. Which do *you* prefer, girls or boys? Who one wants to impress. This pink one or the blue with stripes? Which do you like? I'm giving a lecture at the RCA and then going to see my agent. You're making toast? Goodoh. Tea for me. And then I must sort out my trip to Berlin…"

Grenville left the kitchen and shouted down from his bedroom,

"I've got a pale yellow shirt. Girls are very lovely in many ways, of course. But I can't cope with them. Can't make them out. Come and advise me, *carissima*. Is it a bow tie day, d'you think? My Aunt Pod says bow ties are worn by cads and bounders."

"What's a bounder?" she called out. "A class jumper, is it?"

"Jumper? I'll be boiled! I'm giving a lecture not grouse shooting. Pay attention, do. Ah!" Eleanor had come up to his bedroom with their breakfast. "Raspberry squidge! Put my tea over there. What about this red shirt?"

She began, "I think the red shirt with —"

"This white tie? It's all so confusing. Women are so terrifyingly time consuming. Too mafioso? I'm lecturing on postmodernism so they're getting a massacre anyway. Women need so much attention and admiration and endless reassurance. Ties are very, very tricky. Too wide and you look like a gigolo, too narrow and you look like a folk singer."

Eleanor settled herself on Grenville's untidy bed.

"I like to be with women. I do," he insisted. "I deeply approve of fannydom. Check shirt? The meaty macho look?" He held the shirt against his naked body and faced Eleanor as he went on, "Women's bodies are more mysterious, more subtle, more pornographic and frightening. I haven't really got anything..." Grenville flung the shirt aside and rummaged in his cupboard, slamming hangers this way and that, "...with gravitas and academic probity. What shall I put on? Help me, for Heaven's sake!"

"You could start with some underpants."

A still-naked Grenville came out of the cupboard, reached over to the chest of drawers and bit off a big piece of toast before going on with his mouth full,

"And the cunt, the taboo, the holy of holies... what an extraordinary orifice! I'm very curious about that. But my curiosity may be a consequence of culture rather than nature."

Eleanor got off the bed, picked up the red shirt and handed it to Grenville who put it on as he talked,

"I'm putting on the red shirt. What next? I must have a swig of tea. Some of the time I just need to get my cock out and into something. What now?"

"Underpants, Grenville. Underpants."

"And you, my dear old duck? There's always the possibility of a suit. Girls or boys for you?"

"I've had the best time with women," Eleanor said, expanding her night with Yasmine into a wealth of experience. "But I fancy men. I just do —"

"Thing is, does this grey suit make me look like a foppish fuckwit? A ball-less boffin? They'll just think I'm a frightful fogey trying to look subversive." Grenville put the suit back in the cupboard, complaining, "I still don't know what women want."

"*Women search for the one. Men want the many,*" Eleanor had read this in a women's magazine.

"*Nimini pimini.* Not a suit, then."

"*Women need to feel loved to have sex. Men need sex to feel loved,*" Eleanor quoted from the same article.

"How is this to be reconciled? It's hopeless! So much of what I like, women find insulting," Grenville sighed. "And there's so much hanging about! A lot of it fairly boring because the sort of women I find sexy don't have anything to say of much interest." Grenville held up two pairs of trousers, "Which ones do you like? Come, my angel. Speak unto me. We must get on."

"Black," Eleanor said before explaining, "Well, in the end I think it comes down to this… I prefer boys' bodies and their clothes and… I don't know. Sometimes I'm with a lad and I get to wishing he'd reach out and… well, you know, kiss me and that, but with women I never —"

"Yes! *the colour is black, the material is leather, the seduction is beauty!* Black leather! Pretty boys, naughty and cruel. Where are they? Yes. Yes. Such a turn on! I'll have anything in leather, male or female!" Grenville found his leather trousers and put them on while Eleanor argued,

"Well, if you can want someone for their leather trousers I don't see why I can't want someone because they're... interesting or... or... loving —"

"That's *friendship!* What's *that* got to do with sex? A tie. Need to choose a tie. Black bow tie after all?" Grenville held one under his chin. Eleanor shook her head and did a thumbs down. Grenville checked in the mirror. "Quite right. They won't listen if I look like a pizza waiter —"

"My Mam would love it, mind," Eleanor said, "just her style, Italian waiters."

"Tut, my dear," Grenville lowered his eyelids. "Nothing wrong with Italian waiters. And, what's more," he picked up another piece of toast and pointed it at her, "one must never judge people by the objects of their desire. Actually one must never judge people at all. The New Testament was right about *that*, at least."

Eleanor, remembering religious assemblies at school, asked, "Do you mean the 'forgive your enemies' number? Turn the other cheek?"

"Ah no. Self-defence is tedious but absolutely necessary and revenge is one of the great pleasures. All too rare, unfortunately. Socks are a minefield. And shoes? I don't believe in forgiveness. Atonement perhaps. Yes. A little *punishment...*" Grenville's eyes narrowed as he moved towards Eleanor with a fixed look on his face.

Oh no! What was this? She tensed as he approached. Had Grenville suddenly turned psycho on her? Frightened, she scrabbled across his bed to get away from him. He dropped down on his hands and knees and ducked under the bed, muttering,

"I think those shoes… with buckles… if I can find the other one. What d'you think?"

Eleanor flung herself back onto the pillows, laughing.

"What! What?" came Grenville's muffled shouts from under the bed.

## SOLO

Eleanor wasn't needed at work till the afternoon but Grenville shot off, leaving a back-draught of shouted reminders, questions, exploded newspapers, burnt crusts and blown kisses. When he'd left, she tidied the kitchen, reassembled the newspaper and made herself another cup of tea. After fetching her shawl from the attic and taking the phone off the hook, she went into the ballroom to read the paper.

With a recommendation from Yasmine, Eleanor had been taken on for a production of *Oliver!* Even though she called herself a sequin stitcher, Grenville always asked after her work, taking it seriously, wanting to know what she was making of it. As she moved a pile of Grenville's books, which he'd dumped on her favourite sofa, she caught sight of her name in his handwriting,

*Eleanor — it's a ghastly period but jolly filthy, I suppose? Onwards and upwards anyway, old fruit. Best swishes ho ho. G.*

She examined the pile — *Oliver Twist* and illustrated books on Dickens and Victorian London. Eleanor arranged her tea and books within reach. She adjusted the nest of cushions, wrapped herself in her shawl and settled into the sofa. Taking one of Grenville's books into her lap she was soon cocooned in reading and pictures.

Sunlight and shadow moved across the floor. After a while Eleanor got up, stretched and taking some of the books, propped open the ballroom door so that the shimmer of sunlit trees, warm air and light could reach down the landing towards the back rooms.

Then she ran a bath and stepped into the midmorning quiet of the house.

Shaking a few drops of Grenville's bath essence into the water she tossed it into a froth around herself and inhaled the steam. It smelt like him, sharp and clean of lemon balm.

She looked down her body. Depressed is how it would have made her feel, not so long ago. The small breasts, bulgy thighs, furry shins. She dressed herself in foam. Men are so lucky. They don't have to spend half their lives in front of the mirror, putting slap on, taking it off, plucking their eyebrows, waxing their legs. Lovely clothes too. They don't have to go half naked or wear uncomfortable clobber to be fancied. Itchy brassieres, torturing high heeled shoes, cold sweaty tights... she was having a rest from all that. A rest from sex and worrying about her body and men. Work, that's what mattered at the moment.

Eleanor shifted, raising the island of her tummy out of the foam. The pink tide-mark left by the hot water made an O on her belly. She watched her pubic hair spring up as the water drained out of it. Froth remained like snow on the treetops. She sank the island under the water.

Sex was such a disappointment. Got more out of smutty daydreaming and doing for herself than from the real thing. Except Yasmine. It would be lovely to have that with a lad. The time, the care, the affection. No hurry to be rid of you afterwards and get back to the pub. Granted, she'd only been a top-up for Yasmine. But still, she'd been made to feel special, wanted for herself. Not felt so tense about her looks and whether she was odourless enough, attractive enough. Perhaps it was the dope.

Eleanor sighed, causing a flurry in the froth under her chin. Or was it because Yasmine was a woman like herself?

Sitting up, she chose a rose-scented soap and turned it in her hands. She creamed her neck and armpits and crouched to lap soapy water between her legs, round her fanny and bum. With men, it was so embarrassing being touched in an intimate way, humiliating really. Because it wasn't so intimate after all. More like you could be anybody.

She lay down again and put her head under the water, wetting her hair. Funny how being miserable and lonely made you feel randy. Only it didn't do to give into it. That just made you feel worse, like the time she'd gone with that man she'd got talking to in the dole queue.

Eleanor heaved up with a rush of water, her sliding body making a rubbery sound on the bottom of the bath. Kneeling, she reached down Grenville's shampoo, lifted the lever for the shower attachment and enclosed herself in the drumming spray and lather of hair washing. Afterwards she ran some more hot water into the tub and paddled it round before sinking back into the warm.

Since coming to live with Grenville she had not been miserable or lonely.

She lay still and listened. The suds fizzed softly as they rose and fell over her breasts with her breathing. She could hear the tank filling somewhere and, coming from the street, beyond the sunny ballroom and the balcony, the distant sound of an idling taxi.

Solitude was another new pleasure.

# iii

## VISIT

Eleanor was being driven through the outskirts of her hometown. Grenville had offered to come with her for the weekend to satisfy her family. She had managed to impress them, for once, by having a rich, upper class boyfriend. More than a year it had been now, and they wanted to meet him. Eleanor had tried to explain that Grenville was not exactly her boyfriend but her Mam wasn't having it. Trouble was, Eleanor could not let on that Grenville was gay, there was no knowing what her Dad might do and to say that Grenville had other girlfriends would mean more questions and arguments. Eleanor had to keep on the right side of them. Her Dad was giving her handouts that made it possible to hang on in London while she made her way. Her earnings from costume making were still low and on-off.

As they left the main road and drove through the suburbs, Eleanor said,

"I wouldn't care if I never saw them again. I come home for the money. I feel despicable —"

"We all have to compromise, my dear. In deference to your father's royalist sensibilities, I have eschewed my copulating corgis tee shirt —"

"It's all right for you, you're rich, independent. You can cut free."

"Don't be ridiculous! Independent? Where do you think my money comes from? Families are perfectly awful but there is nothing to be done about it. I can as soon 'cut free' as change the colour of my eyes."

73

As Eleanor directed Grenville through the housing estate she began to feel more and more wound up, "I'm dreading this. It's going to be bloody terrible. I'm sorry to drag you —"

"Never apologise. I'm delighted to dabble in a little social anthropology. And, rest assured, I do know how to behave among the savages of suburbia —"

"Grenville, you mustn't —"

"Play with my food or warble on about flagellation."

They turned into the close.

"It's not just about offensive clothes and shutting up about sex, love," Eleanor said as they drew up outside her house. "It's about... you'll have to... you know, pretend and that."

"How so?" Grenville looked out of the car at the crazy paved driveway, replacement windows and hanging baskets.

"My father hates gays."

"How queer of him."


Eleanor's mother had sent Grenville and her husband to the lounge bar of a nearby hotel while supper was got ready. Eleanor was fed up because it had meant that she was left to lay the table and make a display of all the best china while her Mam went off to beautify herself. Like the wicked witch, she had always played "who's the fairest of them all" with Eleanor's boyfriends. Grenville, Eleanor noticed, was going to get the usual treatment: her Mam had changed into a shorter skirt, higher heels and a more revealing top.

"Your property in London will be worth serious money soon," said Eleanor's Dad between mouthfuls of *coq au vin*. "Prices are set to rocket. This chicken's done to a turn, Missis. Being an owner occupier round here, like what we are now, is a good thing. I'll have you know, houses in this location are coming up fast. A better class of people are moving in. Getting too expensive for scroungers and suchlike. We have a connection, you know, in the estate agent business, being my son-in-law that is. And he had a word in my shell-like and said to stop renting, borrow money and buy up. So I did. Bought this house off the old woman who owned it. Didn't know her arse from her elbow. She was easily persuaded. I got it for next to nothing. It's wonderful what this government is doing. Cutting red tape. Creating wealth. Letting people like me, get on."

"We're doing the house up now it's ours," Eleanor's mother said, "central heating, nice décor. But we don't think much to DIY. Like you, Grenville, we can afford to have it done proper like, by professionals. The upstairs bathroom has just been finished —" she ate primly, not wanting to disturb her lipstick, "and I've been ever so busy choosing a colour match for the Austrian blinds."

"Absolutely!" Grenville agreed. "Choosing colours is very difficult. The most infinitesimal gradation of shade can be the difference between right and wrong. But with the bathroom there's at least the certainty that the porcelain and tiles must be white. I suppose blue might be allowed in the tiles if they're Delft."

"We've had a new suite put in. Top of the range. And I spent a long time, I can tell you, choosing between *Champagne* and *Avocado*."

"Avocado? But that's all black and knobbly surely," said Grenville.

"It's a green colour," Eleanor put in.

"Green? In the bathroom? That would never do. Like lying in a swamp and so unflattering for the poor ageing bod —"

Grenville, warmed up now, talked with his mouth full. Eleanor had always admired his disregard for prissy table manners but here, it made her feel jumpy.

"I made the mistake of buying a pair of dark green silk knickers once but I found the green set off my varicose veins. So I gave them to a young renter. What is it old bean?" Eleanor had nudged him under the table.

"Oh God ah! A young um passing... ah?"

"Jumble sale," Eleanor said.

"Yes! Jumbo thing."

"Oh, we're always giving away mountains of clothes to charity," Eleanor's mother said. "The lady down the Oxfam says she relies on me. Well, they can charge more for the designer labels so I'm very popular. Would you like some more? My hostess trolley keeps everything piping hot!"

"Herself's second helpings are just as good as her first. Not often you can say that about a woman, eh Grenville?" Eleanor's father winked.

"What? Right ho! Delicious."

"I left the mushrooms out of the recipe because I know you don't like them. So can I tempt you to a teensie-weensie bit more, Grenville?" Eleanor's mother's gold bracelets clashed on the table as she leaned towards him.

Grenville held out his plate, saying,

"I'm very wild. I never resist temptation."

After supper Eleanor's father moved to the lounge to watch TV while her mother insisted on a tour of the "stately home". She was keen to show off the improvements.

"I've done yours up too." Her mother opened the door to the room that Eleanor had slept in all her life.

It had vanished. All the precious clutter of her child-hood had disappeared. On the pink repapered walls hung pictures of thatched cottages and cats, bought ready framed from a department store. Her old bed had been replaced with matching twin beds and one wall was made up of a fitted wardrobe suite. On the display shelves were gift shop novelties, glass animals and a wicker basket of dried flowers.

Eleanor had been swept away. She stood confused as her mother darkened and brightened the room, showing off the dimmer switches for the built in spotlights.

"You'll have the room when you visit. I put my grand-children in here when they come. I've got some of their things in the drawers." Eleanor's mother turned to Grenville and prompted, "People say I don't look old enough to be a Nana."

"Well my Nanny was very young. Looking back on it I think she was probably one of my aunt's little fancies."

"Our son-in-law is doing ever so well," Eleanor's mother said. "He's very enterprising so our married daughter lives in the lap of luxury... she was always the bright one. You'll like your new room, won't you, Eleanor."

"Where are all my things?"

"You don't want any of that old rubbish. Your sister didn't want it, not even for the kiddies. They have such lovely clothes and things nowadays."

"I don't care about the clothes, Mam, but what about the little dolls' teaset Uncle Arthur give us and the ark he made and his photo...?"

"It were just trashy stuff, all chipped. They weren't antiques or anything. I checked. You wouldn't have got any money for them. This room, now, it's an investment. I had a design consultant —"

"But my photo of Uncle Arthur. I loved him. We got on and —"

"Our other daughter loves the new look. What do you think, Grenville?"

"It's certainly *pink*."

"It's all completely colour coordinated," her mother said. "So you must like it, Eleanor."

She didn't like it at all. To her eye it looked like one of those stuffy hotel rooms. A room without a memory and all for show. She opened her mouth to protest. And closed it again. So what. Couldn't be bothered. She took a moment to register the change in herself. How she felt no need to argue. No need to resist or fight her corner any more. In that second, without any fuss, without cake, champagne or celebration, Eleanor cut the cord and left home,

"It's great, Mam," she said. "Yeah. Great."


Eleanor and Grenville were leaving for London after breakfast but Eleanor's hopes of the visit passing off without drama began to fade as her Dad saw the head-line: "Gay Sex in School Storm" on the front page of his newspaper.

"There's going to be a clamp down! And quite right too." Her father shook the paper. "The idea! Teaching kids at school about filth. It beggars belief! It's high time these shirtlifters got the message — we don't want to know. They're not wanted."

Eleanor went hot and gripped her chair, waiting for Grenville to make his *Bang goes Shakespeare! Off with Michaelangelo!* speech. But her Dad ranted on, unchallenged. Eleanor was relieved but half disappointed to see that Grenville wasn't listening. He seemed to have switched off.

"Weirdos! I hate them. I won't have them working for me. If I find they're that way, they're out!"

Eleanor felt she had to object. She reminded her father about the equal opportunity laws. Her Dad put the paper down and stabbing it with his finger, used the bullying voice that had always shut her up,

"There's ways around that, my girl. I wouldn't be where I am today if I bothered with all that red tape. That's why this government gets my vote. People have to please me and look sharp if they want a job in my firm. Look what's happened to the police, they have to take any old rubbish now... women... wogs... Don't even have to be tall anymore."

Eleanor looked over to Grenville but he was yawning as he buttered his toast.

"Why should I pay good money to defectives and perverts? That's what I'm asking!"

Eleanor's mother interrupted her husband to ask Grenville if he'd slept well. Eleanor's heart sank again; she knew Grenville was an insomniac. But he looked up from his breakfast plate and answered,

"I slept very well indeed. Extremely well. Thank you."

Eleanor had never heard Grenville lie before and felt sorry he'd done it on her account.

"And I won't have pansies anywhere near me," her Dad was sounding off again. "The wife wouldn't like to think of it, would you, Missis. And I've a responsibility to my young office girls. It's a bad influence, giving them all the wrong ideas about men…"

As Grenville drove away, Eleanor smiled and waved out of the car window. As soon as she was round the corner she began to cry with relief. Grenville puffed out his cheeks and said,

"Fuck a duck!"

Then he started to laugh. Grenville hardly ever laughed or smiled yet Eleanor had never seen him so helpless. Soon she was crying with laughter as well. Grenville stopped the car by the kerb and banged the steering wheel as he whooped and rocked. Again and again they started to speak, they clutched each other and were off again. For Eleanor, a whole lifetime of anger and frustration seemed to pour away with the laughing. In the end, they had to get out of the car to get some air and break the spell. Eleanor slipped her arm through Grenville's and pressed herself against his side,

"I do love you," she said.

"Well, I love you too old thing, absolutely." His voice was absent minded. He was becoming aware of his surroundings: the deserted, tree-lined streets, the tidy suburban driveways. He turned himself and Eleanor back to the car, muttering,

"God ogod ogod, it's terrible out here. Is this the real world? There is no hope. We're going back to London, *now.*"

"How did you survive that?" he asked, when they were on the motorway.

"By believing the stork made a mistake."

"The stork?" By "that" he had meant the weekend. "Aha, put you with the wrong people, you mean?"

"Yes. I just don't belong there —"

"Hm, you look like your mother. I rather like her."

"I don't! You can't!" Eleanor said.

"Yes I can. I like ambitious people."

"She's a horrible tart."

Not horrible at all. Grenville did not say this out loud. From his point of view, Eleanor's mother was a splendid woman, absolutely on his wavelength. Dirty in thought, word and deed.

He'd been trying to sleep and finding it difficult, as usual. Agitated, restless and trapped. Couldn't get up, creep out and go cruising. Hated wanking. Found himself thinking of Eleanor's mother. She'd flirted with him at dinner so he'd tried holding her gaze and giving her that slight toss of the head he used as a signal in the clubs, when he wanted to pull. No mistaking her smile of triumph.

He'd just got back into bed from stripping off and turning down the heating when his door opened and Eleanor's mother slipped in.

"Eleanor's told me you don't sleep very well. I can hear you moving around." She put two glasses and a brandy bottle on his bedside table. "I've brought us a little nightcap, love. The others are fast asleep." She poured a measure into the glasses, "Would you like me to stay and have mine with you?"

"Yes. Indeed. I certainly would. How delightful."

She'd drawn up a chair close to the bed and sat opposite him allowing her gown to fall open. She was not naked. Much better than that. She'd been fully dressed in something really rather provoking. When she leaned towards him to put her glass down on the bedside table, Grenville had reached out and taken her wrist.

"Are you up for it then?" she'd asked.

"What d'you think?" He'd pulled back the bedclothes.

"Oh aye, that'll do," she'd said. "Pity to waste it."

And it had all been jolly filthy and instructive. The condom thing had been a bit of a bore, but she'd done all that. Other girls he had tried, always wanted to chatter and tease and play silly games, even *after* sex, just when there was a chance he might get some sleep. She, on the other hand, had patted his cheek saying, "Eleanor doesn't know what she's missing, does she, pet?" before gliding away to let him sleep. Which he had, brilliantly. And she wanted no strings. No repercussions. Excellent woman.

Grenville tapped the steering wheel and glanced over at Eleanor. She was dozing. He didn't seem to be telling her of this adventure. Though he'd avenged her... cuckolding her awful father. And he'd never kept anything from her before. Grenville looked at the fuel gauge on the dashboard. He believed in openness. The smashing of taboos. The way to wrest sex from the icy grip of religion and morality was to tell everything. Come out. Shame and repression were an abomination.

It wasn't urgent but he could do with some petrol, a pee, a coffee and some more food. Eleanor would probably want a chocolate bar.

Sex was sacred. Above and beyond the mundane calls of love and friendship. But this business with Eleanor was complicated. He'd crossed a boundary there. It had been a splendid act of Oedipal revenge... poking the Bad Dad's woman. Come to think of it, he had not only avenged Eleanor but himself and all his kind. Pleasuring the Patriarch's wife. Brilliant. He'd surpassed himself. So why didn't it bring the full thrill of transgression?

Grenville thought about the answer as the central reservation barriers of the motorway streamed past him. Chances were that Eleanor would be fantastically upset, actually. Accuse him of going over to the enemy. He didn't want that. She might hate him. Very disturbing. Go off. Leave him. Not good. Not good at all. A motorway mileage sign passed. He read the distance to the next service station. Quite a way yet.

Living with Eleanor, he realised as he glanced at her again, had brought a great improvement in his life. He was far less lonely. Enjoyed himself more. Someone there to talk to when he came back from his adventures. Someone to come home to. Someone certain to be on his side. And he slept better; the nights were less of a long ordeal.

The sign for the Services exit came up. Grenville manœuvred into the inside lane and slowed, subliminally registering the countdown bars till the turnoff.

He had always felt angry at the thought of secrecy, of protecting people's idiotic sensibilities. And lying to people made one despise them. But he did not feel angry, he felt unusually serene and far from despising Eleanor he felt... responsible. Grenville drew up under the service station canopy and switched off the car engine. He reached out and touched Eleanor on the cheek. She woke up.

"Chocolate? Coffee? Sandwich? What d'you think, dearest?"

# PROPOSAL

Grenville and Eleanor were standing on Waterloo Bridge. Whenever possible on Sundays, Grenville liked to take Eleanor streetwalking, as he called it. This meant a stroll through a park, a visit to a gallery or a walk round an interesting corner of the city. The walks always included a view from a bridge because, as Grenville was explaining, he wanted the feeling of suspension, of transition between two worlds. They leaned on the parapet with the breeze in their faces and looked down the wide road of the river, watching its traffic: water buses, police launches, tourist boats and barges. Grenville pointed out buildings and changes in the skyline, telling her the names of Wren and Hawksmoor churches.

"How can people *bear* to live in the country?" Grenville shook his head.

"Well, its escapist isn't it. But you were brought up in the countryside, weren't you? Your parents...?" Grenville would talk about everything, nothing was private, not even the most depraved notions or shameful ideas, except, Eleanor had noticed, he hardly ever talked about his childhood or his parents. "What was it like?" she fished, always curious about people.

"Very lovely. But no good after the age of ten. One needs culture. Civilization. These are not to be found at the hunt ball. The country makes people potty. Absolutely. The city's the thing."

They came off the bridge and walked along the Victoria Embankment towards Whitehall and St James's

Park. Eleanor liked Sundays in London. They had a muffled quality. Because all the shops and offices were closed, the traffic noise died down, the streets emptied and the pace slowed.

When they reached St James's, they strolled past the duck pond and along the path under the trees as Eleanor pointed out to Grenville how, for her, a park in London on a sunny Sunday was just like one of those theatre scenes where the stage is set with stock characters which come to life as the curtain goes up. There was the uniformed Nanny with her Silver Cross pram, the embracing lovers, the old woman on the bench feeding the birds, the kid pulling a clacking plastic toy, the couple with their dogs. In the distance, a group of the homeless looked like a picnic party. They sprawled in the sun, passing round a smoke, a can, a bottle. A pair were coming across the grass to join the group, the girl trailing her blanket like the train of a long dress.

"Those sort of people worry me, though," Eleanor shook her head.

"Politically? There's certainly getting to be an awful lot of them. Or morally, are you prejudiced in some way?"

"No, I feel sorry for them and everything but —"

"Dear old Ollie is no trouble, is he?" Grenville referred to his old schoolfriend, "been doing heroin and dossing about for years. And Mad Jasper is always fascinating to me. Oh yes! *Must* tell you. He was up before the Beak recently for smashing up a lover's flat and when —"

"Spare some change?"

Eleanor brought her gaze back to the lad who had appeared in front of them. Dirty army surplus jacket, sore at the corner of the mouth, bloodshot eyes, blinking. She glanced away, too ashamed to look for longer.

"Yes. Hang on." Grenville searched through his pockets. As usual with strangers, he was friendly and unafraid. Eleanor saw a crumpled pound note in the change Grenville handed over.

"Blimey! Thanks, mate!"

"Not at all. Are you interested in this?" Grenville held out a chocolate bar he'd found in his coat pocket. The boy caught Eleanor's eye and winced. He spoke to Grenville,

"You sure?"

"Actually, I prefer Lion bars myself, with the rice-krispy bits. What d'you think?"

"Nah, these's great. Marathons. Got nuts. Yeah, I like these ones."

"Jolly good."

"Ta mate, ta. Cheers."

"Cheerio." Grenville turned back to Eleanor, "And when Mad Jasper was asked what he pleaded, d'you know what he said? He said, I plead *true love*, Your Honour!" Grenville snorted.

"But when you give them money you're just supporting a habit," Eleanor said. "They are wasting their lives. Escaping. They have no reason to take drugs —"

"Good Heavens! How do you claim to know that? It's a short but viable way of life with moments of bliss. What else is there? Terrible boredom or perhaps unhappiness. I will always contribute to the fulfilment of desire, where I can."

"But it's not real. It's escapism and —"

"What d'you mean *not real*."

"Well, it's just chemicals," Eleanor said.

"Chemicals are very real. That's what we may be after all, an intricate organization of chemicals. Real. Escape. These words you use, old fruit. Living in the country isn't an escape, either. The country is very real. Flies. Cowpats. The awfully mad. It's so real it's insupportable. Quite, quite dreadfully real. I'd take you but..."

Eleanor and Grenville had left the park and were taken up with negotiating the traffic and discussing where to go next. They decided on an exhibition.

In the gallery, Eleanor was enjoying the paintings, finding the colourful portraits and Omega fashions useful reference for a costume drama she was involved in at work. But Grenville let rip,

"God! I can't be doing with all this self-conscious, cosy Bloomsbuggery. Retrochic for the oldies, the one-eyed and the blue-rinsed. Art should be a sacrament, it belongs in church, it should change the way people think. This stuff exists to match the curtains."

"They were innovators in their time," Eleanor defended them.

"Not really. The Woolf woman was the only one with fangs. These daubers are imitating Cezanne, or worse, copying banal totties with tits and tulips by boring old Matisse."

"Well, sexual innovators —" she tried.

"Faggotty cliques there have always been. Not at all radical. Absolutely safe, upper-class, immune —"

"What about Oscar Wilde, then?" she reminded him.

"Ah! St Oscar the Martyr. He brought that on himself. No no, my dear, what is terrible about Wilde was the hideous, hideous hypocrisy. The hatred the case exposed. And that has not changed one little jot."

"Just a minute!" Eleanor had learned how to argue with Grenville, "How can you say nothing's changed when there are orgies every night and Terry was round yesterday bragging he'd been fucked over a bar stool, in front of everyone, in the —"

"Schoolboy pranks. Cock fun. Which will be tolerated until something, another *Wilde* thing, who knows what, unleashes mass hysteria. It's only just under the surface."

"Well, these people seem to've had very nice lives," she said. They had stopped in front of a richly coloured painting of a young girl in an armchair, reading in a booklined interior. Next to this was a lighter scene of a group in deckchairs, splashed by the mauves and greens of sunlight and shade. "Look Grenville, I'm sorry, but from where I'm coming from it looks just great. What I see is intelligent company, nice houses, nothing to do all day except write and paint and go abroad when the mood is on. And the women could have children and take lovers if they wanted. Seems like bliss to me."

"Ye-es," Grenville said. "One wants to keep a group round one. Some sort of family. As long as they are not *really* family. One's foul relations, I mean. The life of an ageing queen doesn't bear thinking about, it's true. We could get married, for example. Do you want to have children?"

Eleanor was scribbling a quick sketch and making colour notes as she answered,

"I don't know. My life started when I met you so I'm still in the nursery… too young to have children! I hated being a kid. By 'eck, how I hated it! Bullied, hopeless at everything. Mum and Dad doting on my sister, sly cow, and wishing I'd been a boy."

"Me too. So you got off on the wrong gender from the start?" Grenville pointed at her sketch, "You should make a note of that flesh pink next to the lemon yellow. Very characteristic. D'you wish you'd been a boy?"

"Thanks, yeah. Sometimes. For the freedom. The respect."

"And a nice big *willy!*" Grenville blared.

"Nope. Never wanted one of them."

"Bang goes Freud, then."

Eleanor, by now immune to the outraged looks that came Grenville's way in public, went on as if they were alone,

"But yes, I do want kids someday. I should like to be a good Mum. Love my kids as people, for themselves. It's an important relationship which —"

"I'm not really interested in people or relationships," Grenville interrupted. "I'm interested in poetry, *real* art and sex. Do lets leave this rubbish, dearest. I need to go to the tearoom and eat enormous amounts of cake. Or cream tea? What d'you think?"

# A year later

## JOURNEY

At Christmas, Eleanor and Grenville expected to go to their own homes but this time Eleanor's family were going to Las Palmas. She used the pantomime season as an excuse to drop out.

"That was a fib*elito*. Actually, *querida*, that was a mega-fib*erama*." Grenville looked up from his desk and wagged his finger at Eleanor who had just put the phone down on her mother. "You are not involved over Christmas and New Year, are you. You haven't taken a job in Wardrobe anywhere —"

"No. But bloody hell fire! I'd rather be turkey stuffing than spend Christmas, spend ten seconds, in the Tropicana hotel with Mam and my sister and that lot!" Eleanor flung her arms up, tossed her head and did a few stamping steps across the ballroom, "Aye! Watching Mam do fucking flamenco with the waiters! *Ole! Ole!*"

91

She finished by leaning over Grenville's desk and leering at him.

"I do believe you're a snob, my dear, but I am impressed and not a little alarmed at your abilities in the porkies department. I'm a hopeless liar. Who will you go to?" he asked.

"I'll stay here. Do wicked, forbidden things while you're away, Grenville. Like, oooh, eat mushrooms and watch television!"

As usual, he did not respond to her teasing.

"Seriously though," she perched herself on the edge of his wide desk, "I could do with a nice quiet time before the rush. Starting in January, I've been promised some cozzies on a big job for the RSC and I'm hoping to hear from the BBC 'shop about a classic serial that's in the pipeline."

"But you can't spend Christmas on your own. That's dreadful!" Grenville said.

"I don't understand you, pet. You don't give a bugger about Christmas. You hate it. Always threatening to dress up as Santa and commit mass murder." She leafed through one of his art magazines.

"Yes yes, I want an end to *Kitsch*mas. All that abominable ho ho ho and humbuggery." He threw his pen onto his desk and leaning back in his chair, went on, "It's vile! Shameful! Not the right sort of buggery at all!"

"So why get all sentimental about me being on my own? Since you don't care about it?" she said.

"Ah, but I *do* care about it. That's what's so painful."

"Come off it! You don't believe all that nutty stuff about mangers and angels and —"

"Yes passionately," his voice was fierce. "It is the one really, really good bit."

"You're kidding!" She looked up from the magazine. "Like, let me see... Once upon a time there was this unmarried mum taken on by this sad old geezer and they get caught short, right? So she ends up producing..." Eleanor had rolled up the magazine and waved it like a conjuror, "Hey presto! A boy! It has to be a *boy*, from under her blue nylon nightie, in the straw, with a whole lot of royals and peasants in tea towels looking on?" She laughed at her own performance. "It's loopy! And you don't believe it for one minute!"

"Oh but I do."

Grenville turned away from her and said,

"Now and always the longing for a better world, for light..." He gazed at the winter sky outside the balcony window, "and understanding. Wisdom for the powerful and an end to want and suffering for the humble shepherd. The intersection of the human body and the divine spirit..." He spoke quietly. "And all, all are represented — male and female, black and white, high and low, all classes, all ages. Outsiders and travellers. The fertile woman and the sterile ox. Angels, humans and the silly creatures. There, together. *All in one country*, gathered round the newborn."

Eleanor put down the magazine and sat, biting her cheek.

"It is a great moment," he continued, his voice still low, "I long for it. Yes, I must believe it. What else is there? And it cannot go unmarked." He swung round and pointed at her, "So you will come and be frozen to death and petrified with boredom at Wyvernden!"

"Well, I'll admit, love, I'm fascinated. I've always wanted to know what —"

"At least you'll be sponging a good dinner. Food's excellent. Aunt Pod sees to that. The sickening siblings will be there, I'm afraid and…" He looked away again. "And Mummy is a bit diff um diff… hm." He reared up from his desk and went over to the windows.

"Different?" she suggested.

"Ah yes, a bit different, certainly." He rapped on the glass. "Could never take people um home and so on because ah because…"

Was the door to the secret chamber creaking open?

"You were ashamed of her?" Eleanor, projecting her own feelings, thought she'd help him confess.

"Certainly not!" Grenville said. The door slammed shut.

"Worried for her, I mean," she tried to take back her mistake.

"Yes, always that."

Eleanor decided to say nothing and rely on his usual talkativeness to take over. It didn't. After a long silence in which she stared at his back and he looked at the dead pot plants on the balcony, he said,

"So you'll come. Keep me company. I think you liked it when I came home with you…"

Emotional blackmail? Today had brought her a Grenville she'd not met before.

"Yes, all right love," Eleanor said, full of curiosity.


## BAGGAGE

"No need to pack fetish gear, Wyvernden is absolutely bulging with it, that is if your scene is whips and riding boots —" Grenville was by the shelves in the ballroom

94

throwing the extra books he might need during the four-day Christmas visit into a cardboard box.

"Or we can rustle up a rusty suit of armour. A blunderbuss or two? I never finished Foucault's *Surveillir et punir*. Chuck that in." He flung another volume into the box. "Or there is always Aunt Pod's bee-keeping tackle if your taste runs to net veils, hive tools and puffer gun thingummies. I've just bought John Ashbery and this Rilke. Bung them in."

It was Christmas Eve and Eleanor had been ready for ages. Grenville had insisted he wanted to leave for the country by midday but it was past that now and he was still packing. She knew that one way to keep him on task was to stay close and prod him into decisions.

"I don't remember this book on sadomasochism..." Grenville flipped through its pages. "Good Heavens, it offers a cure! In the form of a religious conversion. That's just opting for another form of sick, wouldn't you say?"

He threw the book towards the box, it fluttered open and landed with a thud like a shot bird.

"Missed!" he crowed, "I'm not meant to read it! Too corrupting! You have remembered to take every single warm garment in your possession? De Sade claimed that cruelty was a force of nature," Grenville picked another book off the shelf, "and accuses us of hypocrisy for pretending that it doesn't govern social relations as well. Layers is what we need. Keep out the cold. Vests. Viyella shirts. Pyjamas, even! Never mind fashion. Celine. I shall take his *Voyage au bout de la nuit*. I might have a chapter on him in my book. Perhaps cruelty could be thought of as a form of intimacy, what d'you think?"

Eleanor didn't answer. She lit a cigarette to blow away images of torture. Grenville was too much sometimes. She wanted to get information about his family not listen to upsetting theories about all that stuff of his,

"So what are your —"

"For me, sadomasochism is the ritualization of a perpetual conflict," he began. "On the one hand, desiring the enshrinement or confirmation of the self in the death of the other. Have we remembered to pack the presents? And longjohns, thermals, legwarmers? Will you cope with the sight of me with my trousers tucked into my socks? Masochism, on the other hand, offers total surrender, freedom from responsibility, a willing abdication of the self. Specially when you wrapped the presents so beautifully, pet lamb. We musn't leave them behind."

"I've already put the presents and my bag in the car, Grenville. What are your sisters like?"

"Incest! Awfully naughty. Worth doing because it's so wicked. I shall even wear a hat, can you bear it? But the idea of fucking any of my three sisters is too, *too* —" He opened his mouth, rolled his eyes and dragging his hands down his cheeks, made his face into a horror film gargoyle. "Don't know how their hubbies managed! But there is repulsive proof enough. It's a tweed deerstalker sort of thing with earflaps. I hope you won't be too ashamed of me."

"There are kids?" Eleanor had never heard of any nephews and nieces.

"Even wickeder. Though I can't say it ever did me any harm. I rather liked being molested."

Eleanor felt nauseated for a moment, as if she had inhaled too deeply.

"Yes," Grenville insisted, "pity the poor paedophile. Now *there's* a love that dare not speak it's name."

Eleanor shuddered and stubbed out her cigarette, "They do so much harm, Grenville! I really can't —"

"They might do less harm if they were allowed to *speak*. Out in the open with it! Fortunately, I've never fancied children myself. Horrid things!" He held up two books, "Which shall I take, d'you think? Celan? Heidegger?" he tilted his head from one to the other.

"Both." Eleanor said, to be rid of the question. "How many kids —"

"Of course, I care about children very much, in a general way, they come trailing clouds of glory and so on. Those plaster ones up there," he looked up at the ballroom ceiling, "are very lovely indeed, its true, but I've hardly met a real child I liked. Both books? That's preposterous! You can't think I'll ever manage to read *both*."

Eleanor looked at the box, which already contained enough reading for a month, and sighed, suspecting that he would hardly glance at a single page of what he was taking, "You don't need —"

"Absolutely! Children are useless. Since I don't fancy them I find them dreadfully inconvenient and tiresome. Snow is predicted. Might be fun as long as we don't get stuck. I think I'd better take both these books, as you suggest." Lobbing them in, he began to drag the box out of the ballroom and onto the landing.

"Christmas dinner, will be awful," he panted, "children whingeing, whining, fussing, having nothing to say but interrupting continually so no one else can speak either. Mind you, not much wasted since their parents are all blockheads. The children will refuse to eat the delicious food and sneer at each other's presents. One can't even enjoy their barbarian talent for subversion and anarchy because it's all driven by greed and spite. Is that our luggage?" He looked at his bags piled at the top of the stairs, "It's rather a lot, old girl," he complained. "There may not be room for it all in the car, you know. Let's make some more coffee. I could do with a squidge fix, breakfast was ages ago."

Eleanor wanted to know what she was in for. She needed some preparation if only to be free of fantasies of Dracula's castle, Bates motel and madwomen in the attic. It seemed safest to try with what she knew about the aunt.

"So your Aunt Pod is keen on fox hunting," she said, as Grenville stood drinking coffee in the kitchen doorway.

"You could say that, because horses are what she's about. Though the stable has become rather a school full of old ponies since my father bought it."

"Your Dad bought a school?" Eleanor was lost.

"He was killed." He put down his cup and wandered away to rummage through the coat cupboard, "This waterproof horror, I think..." He pulled out a dark green jacket. "Fortunately, no one of our town aquaintance will see us."

Eleanor knew he'd lost his father when he was thirteen, "How did he —?"

"Riding accident."

"Really! Out hunting, like?" Eleanor was following Grenville around the house.

"No. Raging drunk. As usual. Mounted a hard-mouthed old hunter. Forgot he'd asked for the horse to have a snaffle. Yanked about in his usual furious way and it threw him. Onto the cobbles. Smashed his skull. Serve him right."

"So you didn't get on with him?"

"Our relationship has improved enormously since his death."

Eleanor and Grenville started to carry suitcases and coats downstairs.

"Grenville, I'm worried about my clothes. Where I come from, women have to drag up. Will your family mind if I'm not in a posh frock and half a ton of makeup?"

"Completely different set of sartorial rules for life in the country: everyone looks perfectly awful all of the time. Except Aunt Pod in full hunting rig. That's a super sight. You'll see it on Boxing Day. Otherwise it's all a terrible turn off. Town's the place for sex. I've never been able to enjoy *country pleasures*."

Pausing on the stairs to catch his breath, he put the bags down and turned to Eleanor,

"But I worry too, old thing, always have ghastly nights beforehand. Last night I dreamt that my father's on his horse. I roar past in my car, which one should never do. Horse rears up. Throws the old bastard off. He lands in my passenger seat, shouting as usual. I manage to ignore him. He sort of dematerialises or perhaps I push him out of the car? He leaves his whip on the dashboard. Terrible, frustrating, wading-through-treacle traumifications as I try to track him down and give it back to him. One doesn't have to be the Doctor from Vienna to interpret *that* now, does one!"

He hauled his bags up and continued down the stairs, "There's this idea that dreams are the truth you can't face. But, there again, they could simply be an alternative picture produced by a different part of the mind or indeed just another stratum of self deception. The idea that they can be prophetic is even more interesting. Makes you realise how little we know about the mind."

They piled up his luggage on the pavement.

"So your dad was a sort of lord of the manor?" Eleanor was still trying to get a grip on this period-play world, where people went hunting, had titles and were waited on in their own homes.

"Sandhurst man. Left the army when he inherited Wyvernden."

"And a loud, violent type like my Dad?"

"Your father is a dead bunny by comparison."

Grenville opened the boot of the car. It was half full of plastic bags, wellingtons, old blankets and trashed umbrellas.

"Father had this detestable habit of punching. Stopping a hair's breadth from one. Liked to see one flinch. Very proud of his accuracy." Grenville tumbled the rubbish to one side, "I was determined to learn neither to flinch nor to cry. By the age of seven I had mastered the crying but not the flinch. Still, I won in the end."

He lugged his book box across to the back of the car and heaved it in. "Baulked him. Leaned into the punches. Lost his confidence, then. Nyah."

"Didn't it hurt?"

"Nothing to the pleasure of spoiling his beastly fun." Grenville wedged in two more suitcases.

"It must have been difficult for your mother," Eleanor said. Perhaps he was going to explain about her, at last.

"Adored him. Upset her terribly that I hated him. Never got over his death. Always was a bit fragile."

"Fragile? She has some illness?" Eleanor asked, imagining a *Dame aux Camellias* or Mimi from *La Bohème*. She had learned to make suggestions when trying to get things out of Grenville, knowing that he could never leave a subject if he thought his listener was misinformed.

"No-oo not ill in that way. Just... um... fragile."

He pressed down the lid, lifted it again, shoved, rearranged. "She was, is, very beautiful, very sweet. But always found it difficult to cope. And then his death took what was left." Squeezing and squashing the baggage in, he puffed with effort but his voice was steady as he said,

"Really, the truth is old thing, she's absolutely bonkers."

Leaning his full weight on the car boot lid, he finally managed to force it shut.


## RELATIONS

Having stopped for supper on the way, they arrived at Wyvernden Hall after dark. Eleanor had an impression of stone gateposts, headlit flurries of snow, a bridge, then crunching gravel under high walls. Too late to ask Grenville how to address his aunt and mother. Madam? My Lady? Your Ladyship? They all sounded daft, like playacting.

Grenville had been tooting the horn as they came up the avenue and, as they got out of the car, a door opened in the blackness, dropping a drawbridge of light and releasing a pack of yelling dogs. Eleanor's worries were exchanged for a turmoil of flailing paws, wagging tails, barking and shouting,

"Get down! Down Turpy! Dido! At once! Nipper! Nipper, stop it! Damned dogs! Pay no attention, Eleanor ducks! Giddy! Giddy, darling!"

She could see that aunt and nephew were very alike, that Aunt Pod was a tanned, middle aged, tomboy version of Grenville. Tall and lean, she carried a cigarette and glass of spirits in one hand and tried to calm the dogs with the other.

"Sorry there's no Christmas tree," she shouted over the tumult, "Dogs go mad peeing up it!"

Learning the names of two labradors, two terriers, a three-legged collie and realizing that "Giddy" was Grenville got Eleanor over the threshold, through the long tapestried hall and up the stairs to a panelled room with a log fire.

Grenville's mother greeted him as if his coming was a complete surprise. A petite woman, she clung to her son, laughing girlishly and wrinkling her nose at him. She ignored Eleanor who took the chance to look round, registering how many painted portraits and photographs there were of Grenville's mother in the room and how her beauty had contributed to the refinement of his face.

"Darling, it's so cold, which is why I'm in these dull things," his mother simpered. "So you musn't be cross with little me."

"You look perfectly lovely, as always," Grenville's voice was tight.

"What a sweet, naughty man you are," she flirted. Taking his hand, his mother made him sit beside her while she chattered to him, all the time patting her hair and wanting compliments on her appearance. Grenville's language was effusive but the delivery, Eleanor noticed, was mechanical. After a few moments he extricated himself in order to show Eleanor to her room.

Wyvernden Hall felt like a huge deserted hotel where she might have a whole floor to herself. She was relieved to have been put in the room next to his. As they left after settling in, Grenville turned the key in her door and gave it to her, saying,

"Keep it locked."

"O my God! Why? Will I be raped by a barmy butler?" she joked to cover her jitters.

"Nothing so thrilling, I'm afraid. It's Mummy," he frowned, "she'll come in and steal your things. Bit of a klepto, that's all."

"But she can afford to have anything in the world! What does she want to steal my mingy bits for?" Eleanor regretted her nervous babble when she saw Grenville's frozen face and had to go all the way back to the sitting room with him in silence.

In Grenville's family, the adults exchanged presents on Christmas Eve. When the drinks had been topped up, the presents were handed out by Aunt Pod. In spite of the distractions of unwrapping and saying thankyou, Eleanor noticed that her present to Grenville's mother was put unopened into a large bag she kept by her side. Then, whenever Grenville looked away from his mother, she would tug at his arm or take his hand. Her voice seemed to trill on and on but sometimes, Eleanor saw, her face went blank and she sighed with the effort of it all.

"Maybe you'll think it's boring," Eleanor tried speaking to Aunt Pod, "giving you socks, like. But when we're dressing actors who have to wear riding boots for a part, we give them these new popsox things. Makes the boots go on ever so much easier."

"Right-ho!" Aunt Pod heaved up, just like Grenville might have done, and rushed off with all the dogs skittering after her. In a few moments, escorted back by the dogs, she returned with a pair of boots. She plumped down in her armchair and lodging her cigarette in her mouth she changed into the knee-length stockings and boots. Jumping up, she stamped about saying, "The girl's an absolute genius. Look Giddy!"

She turned to Eleanor, "That is absolutely marvellous, ducks! Mind you, the proof of the pudding is getting the damned things off. Give the old trout a hand."

Realizing that Eleanor was the centre of attention Grenville's mother began calling and beckoning as she rummaged in her bag.

"You there! Eleanor!"

Eleanor felt flustered as she knelt and pulled off Aunt Pod's boots.

"Well I call that *really* cutting the mustard!" Aunt Pod smiled. "Best damn Christmas present I've had in years. Thanks tons and tons! You will let me give you a peck?"

Eleanor flushed as Aunt Pod kissed her on the cheek.

"Thingummy! Eleanor!" Grenville's mother kept calling, "I'll find you something nice, dear."

As Eleanor went over to her, Grenville took the chance to escape and get another drink.

"Have this," his mother held out a necklace. "My dear husband won't mind," she waved a hand in Grenville's direction, "if I give it to you. You should make more of yourself, you could be quite pretty if you tried. I don't need it anymore, I never really liked those beads, I liked them for a bit, I don't think those beads suit me, do you? But they will do for you." She patted her hair and fidgeted with her clothes. "You see that picture over there? It was taken by Cecil Beaton, he's in love with me, says the girls are going to have a terrible time with such a beautiful mother, I have so many admirers, even after I married, Daddy got dreadfully jealous." She fiddled with her wedding rings. "Daddy gets angry with them but I can't help it, you see, they are so in love with me, but my dear husband can't bear me to look at anybody else, so very, very in love with me —"

Aunt Pod interrupted this monologue,

"Time for Scrabble, Fifi!" she spoke to Grenville's mother as if to a deaf child then turning to Eleanor said,

"Pay no attention, ducks. It's all bilge. She's as tight as an owl."

A table and game were put out. Drinks were topped up again. Eleanor would have preferred some tea but did not know how to ask. Where was the kitchen in this huge place? Was it over in the sister's wing of the building? Could she get a hot drink for herself or did it have to be done by some poor Cinderella? Or a creepy Mrs Danvers person? She could have asked Grenville but he was out of reach, back beside his mother again, being stoned to death with confetti.

His mother was allowed to play as she liked and when, after a lot of fussing, she produced words like *aabfmno* and *hikopru,* they were accepted without comment.

"Damned mouldy lot of letters I've turned up!" Aunt Pod complained.

"At least it's proof you don't cheat," Grenville said, "I'll never understand how you can be better at this than I am, Podkins, when all you've ever read is *Horse and Hound* and *The Racing Post.*"

Grenville bantered, but to Eleanor his voice sounded sedated.

"He's such a rattle!" Aunt Pod addressed her remarks to Eleanor, "He may be 'the most brilliant man of his generation' but you'd go off him if you saw him on a horse. This is how Giddy rides —" She did a demonstration, bouncing in her armchair. "Elbows out, flapping like a farmyard duck!"

Caught between his aunt's teasing and his mother's demands for admiration, the Grenville Eleanor knew seemed to retreat. He made her think of a hibernating creature curled into a tight ball. Ticking over. Waiting it out.


## COUNTRY

It was Christmas day. There had been a walk through the snow to church in the morning, followed by a big family lunch party back at Wyvernden Hall. After this, Eleanor had retreated to her room and was sitting up on the uncurtained four-poster bed, wrapped in her coat. She looked round at the panelled walls and over to the criss-cross leaded windows casting cold snow-light onto the dark furniture and wide, uneven floorboards. A set for a Jacobean play.

"Open up old thing!" Grenville called, rattling the latch. Eleanor let him in and bolted back to her territory on the bed.

"Don't blame you wanting a rest from it all. Aunt Pod sent me to get you. It's freezing up here." He went over and turned up the dial on the convector heater.

"I'm not coming down to be made a mock of!" she said.

"Do come and have some cake and kümmel —" Grenville stopped on his way back to the door, "What! That's a bit steep! I know they're all frightful but nobody has actually insulted you, have they? Anyway, one lot have returned to their quarters and the rest of the foul relations and their vile sprogs will be gone —"

"Your sister kept asking me, *do you know so and so? Do you know them and them? Were you at such and such?* And all the time I had to answer no and no and no!"

"*Certainly not* is what you should have answered. For Heaven's sake! She's a clot. This is one of my favourite views..." He leaned down and looked out of the window at the snow-covered hills, "West Field, Church Knoll, Coppice Hill and —"

"It was obvious they all thought I should be *serving* the dinner or lunch or whatever you flaming well call it, and not sitting at the table with —"

"You must stand firm and not be ashamed. No retreat, pet lamb. Remember..." Still gazing at the view, Grenville went on, "you're frontline troops in the fight against snobbery and —"

"Aye! I see," Eleanor raised her voice to get his attention. "That's why you asked me to come isn't it! I'm just cannon fodder to you, Grenville! Just like my class have always been, eh? It's all right for you —"

"D'you think I'm immune from attack?" Grenville snapped. "The grievance is always against my race, my class and my gender. I represent the enemy for many, many people. People whose radicalism I admire." He leaned his head on the window's stone lintel. "It may surprise you to know, that despite my fascination with fascist fancy-dress my politics are —"

"Your brother-in-law asking me what my father does. What business is it —"

"Precisely to put business his way, probably. Look out here at the snow," Grenville tried again. "When I was a boy the moat —"

"*Wheah d'yew geo skiing, Ehleneagh?*" she waggled her head in mockery.

"O God!" Grenville turned away from her as he spoke. "This obsession with obsolete categories of class, gender, race and sexual orientation is *so* boring I can't bring myself to argue about it any more." He waved dismissal. "It's such a distraction from what's really important about people and *so* unsexy!"

"*D'yew rayd et awl, Ehleneagh?*"

Ignoring the interruptions, he reminisced,

"Lots of pretty people in gay lib in the 60's but since then…" He raised his hands. "At the last political meeting I went to, I looked round and, d'you know? The most apalling thing! There wasn't a single person in that room I wanted to put my cock into. I gave up being an activist there and then. I resolved to write —"

"I wish I hadn't come!" Eleanor shouted, wanting to make him apologise for the way she felt.

"Aren't you curious?" His voice was tired. "New places, new people? Who knows what adventures one might have? Anyway, it's worth coming for this, surely —" Pointing out of the window, he appealed to her, "Don't you find the snow very beautiful? Please don't sulk any more."

There was a moment of quiet in the room.

"Come, dearest!" Grenville turned towards the door, "Let's tog up, stuff some cake and go out, what d'you think?"

Eleanor had to shade her eyes to see Grenville who moved darkly against the low criss-crossed light of the winter sun. She could swallow her anger or, if she persisted, Grenville would leave the room and she would be stuck up here, alone.

"All right," she said, shuffling to the edge of the bed.

"Good girl! Well done," he said. "Onwards and upwards!"

Grenville pulled a sledge as they walked up the road from the Hall to the church for the second time that day.

"Snow is so lovely…" he looked round. "But for Aunt Pod and the Hall it's a disaster… the livestock, the birds, the oldies in the village, the frozen pipes at the stables. *And* it will mess up the Boxing Day meet. Can't be sorry. I'm on the side of the fox." He snorted, "Always was a class traitor!"

The church was at the top of a wooded rise and Grenville explained to Eleanor that the hill had been a sacred site ever since a pagan hero had vanquished a wicked wyvern there. They paused by the war memorial where he pointed out the dragon's head on his family coat of arms. It matched the one on his signet ring. Here it was carved above the names of the fallen in the Great War.

"I like the old-fashioned names," Eleanor said, "Ernest and Cedric —"

"Yes, so many, just from this estate. John Jarvis was my grandfather's coachman and those Baileys there? That means Ada Bailey, Jarvis' wife, lost her brothers as well."

"But it's all *years* ago, Grenville."

"Not to me, it's not!" he said. "I remember Ada. And her son John, whom you met in church this morning, has only just retired from the stables. And, you know, one of my very earliest memories —" his voice softened, "is being given strawberries, in his cottage garden, by old, old Grampey Turner. Look here! Robert, Harold and Alfred Turner. All his boys killed. It's... it's insupportable! And you seem to think that life in the country is some sort of escape? The country fills me with —" He shook his head and walked away, the sledge's steel runners grinding on the gritted stone flags of the path.

"But I'm glad to know where I shall come to at last!" His voice lifted again, "They will take me back, that's the greatest comfort. In death, I know exactly where I'll be..." He pointed to a wrought iron grille set into the dry sandy walls of the church, "Through there, in the family vault."

"Oh aye, with the upper classes. Out the wet and doing nowt, as usual," she said.

"Hm. Not so harmless," he muttered. "They're mostly soldiers... killed while urging ploughboys to their deaths."

"So you're a pacifist," Eleanor said.

"Well, that's a bit tricky. The defence of the realm against the Crown's enemies is the ancient role of the nobility. It satisfies honour and justifies our power and privileges. But a world *without* boundaries, there's a wheeze! I'd be prepared to die for that."

This morning, after Christmas service, Grenville had been so busy greeting people he had not had time to show her the new carving of a dragon in the niche above the south porch. He pointed to it now, squatting in its nest of snow, its head arched back, breathing flames of stone.

"There's the wyvern again," he said. "Symbol of greed, pestilence, darkness and untransmuted matter. That's the hero's sword you see through it's neck. Spunkingly good, don't you think? We finally managed to fund its restoration, along with the lychgate. No thanks to the present vicar. That awful, happy-clappy dimwit taking the service today. He disapproves of this 'image of the devil.' Imagine having to deal with such people!"

They moved down the path.

"What does the lettering say on this gate thing?" Eleanor asked.

"*Semper ad lucem.* Always towards the light."

"And all this will get you to heaven faster, will it?" she said, as they passed through the lychgate.

"I doubt it very much. Not with all the responsibilities I've shirked. And who knows what *sins of the fathers* I shall have to atone for."

Eleanor still felt fed up and refused to be moved by his subdued manner.

"Shouldn't the cost of it have been spent on the workers' cottages instead of on all this? Hardly anybody goes to church any more, anyway," she said.

"The cottages are much more comfortable than the Hall —"

"And there's you people at dinner," she interrupted him, "complaining about the rise of house prices in your village when you're coining it from rents on your London properties."

"The point is, my precious, that everything is done, not for *money*, but to preserve a way of life. Doomed, in my opinion, but there you go..." Grenville started to caper round her. "A way of life, I might add, that involves a large number of working class people!" He struck a fencer's pose. "Who now can't afford to live in their own village because —" he feinted and lunged at her, "it has been bought up by new-rich townspeople like *your* family, Eleanor dear. Nyah!" he shouted. "A hit a hit! I win I win!"

"Piss off! You're just a clever clogs. Talk your way out of everything, you!" What was left of her anger ran out, like the last grains of sand through the neck of an hourglass. Till the next time.

They sledged gently down from the church along a wide path towards some trees. The snow was well trodden and packed hard. On either side there were toboggan tracks, paw prints, trampled snowmen and the abandoned drift-trenches of a snowball fight. But the sun was setting and the warriors had all gone home for tea. In the hush, Grenville and Eleanor were the only disturbance apart from the startled call of a bird and the soft fall of snow from a branch.

As they started going up Coppice Hill, Grenville began to explain,

"What you have to understand, old thing, is that the wyvern, the story, the name, the motto, are all good for business. All summer, visitors come in coachloads to the Hall and farm, to feed the animals, buy fluffy things made in Taiwan and watch medievilly weavers, farriers, falconers and fuck knows what craftifying like billy-oh. It's an obsolete way of life, full of pomp and campery, maintained as a circus for townees and tourists."

Grenville was ahead of Eleanor, dragging the sledge through virgin snow, looking about him all the time, checking and treading the ground.

"I know I'm the rightful heir" he said, "but I can't be doing with it. I will write my books and stab at a dragon or two that way. My last article caused a gratifying amount of hoo-ha. That must be my contribution, what d'you think?" he paused to look at the view.

Eleanor could only grunt because the climb was steep and in spite of the freezing air, she was getting hot.

"Even *landscape* as an idea is a completely dead duck..." He ploughed on, "Bit tough on those of us left by our education with a Wordsworthian attachment to it. Like the dinosaurs we're dying out —"

"Lots of people care about the environment," Eleanor said.

"That's a necessity. I mean the world will belong to a new species: people who have never heard the dawn chorus and for whom *landscape* is a few sooty shrubs

113

on a roundabout. Where will they find their spiritual sustenance one wonders?"

By the time they stood together at the summit, the sky had been painted bright blue fading to pale green. The red sun, setting among orange and purple clouds, had cast a glaze of pink over the snow-covered landscape.

"Oh, it's such a beautiful place!" Eleanor said, the words vaporizing in the cold air.

The Hall, the church on its hill, the woods and fields lay below them.

"Would you like it?" Grenville turned to her, "I can give it to you. All we have to do is babble some drivel and sign a few papers making you my wife and it's yours. Run Wyvernden for me. It's a big job, of course. Pure theatre. You'd be *tremendously* good!"

"Give over, pet, I've had enough of being made fun —"

"I never make fun. I'm absolutely serious, old girl. We could be like those Bloomsbuggers you like so much. Free love. No death by monogamy. Lots of *nimini pimini* all round. And in trad aristo style, after an heir and a spare, I promise to accept any other sprogs —"

"It's a great offer," Eleanor couldn't help giggling. "And I can't say I'm not tempted! Just to see our Mam's face!" She gripped his arm. "By 'eck, that'd show the bastards, wouldn't it, eh!"

Yet even as she gloated, she felt the loneliness of being among these people. Where she didn't belong. The unhappiness of the day woke again and took breath,

"But I won't take you up on it, just yet," she found herself saying. "I'm ever so grateful, Grenville love, but I don't think me and the country are quite suited some-how and you know, I want my own money, proper paid work and then, well... our relationsh—"

"Quite right!" he said. "The future, real theatre, real art! Let's escape to town!"

As the sun set, the air had changed from pink to blue. The snow gleamed cold and white again, like the bright moon that had appeared in the twilight.

Grenville positioned the sledge and looked down the hill, calculating.

"Right!" he said, "I may be no good on a horse but I'm bloody good at this. Jump on!"

"We're never going down there on that!" Eleanor put her hand over her mouth.

"You forget, dearest. I grew up here. On this hill. I know this land, every inch of ground, every stone, every path, every tree, as well as I know the Lord's Prayer. Come on, there's still plenty of light!"

She lay on Grenville's back. He pushed off and the sledge began it's descent, gathering speed, steel runners hissing over the snow, it's prow slicing through the icy air. In the silence, Eleanor's scream *eeeaaah!* streamed behind them in a long thin scarf of sound.

# Two years later

## i

## MISS

Since leaving home and coming to live with Grenville in London, Eleanor had managed to stay employed, though sometimes this meant taking work with touring theatre companies and living away from Grenville for months at a time.

"Terrible things happened while you were absent, Nelly, old thing."

"What?"

Eleanor had been in Edinburgh and Grenville had collected her off the sleeper at King's Cross. Having breakfasted, they were together in the bathroom and feeling unhurried because their work commitments were for later in the day.

"Missed you dreadfully for one thing." A naked Grenville searched for toothpaste among the tumbled mess of decapitated bottles, tubes and jars on the shelves by the handbasin, "And I had to be an usher at my cousin's wedding!"

"Oh aye, so you did." Eleanor paddled hot bathwater round herself. "How did it go?"

"*Monogamy!*" Grenville stabbed the word with his toothbrush. "How can people submit willingly to such a living death? Suppressing the mystery of sex and desire, turning it into drudgery and habit!"

He shoved a gout of toothpaste onto his brush.

Eleanor submerged herself in hot, frothy water. She had no boyfriend at the moment. The last one had survived on and off for about a year. Then the lad had fallen for someone else. Was getting married now. Luckily, it hadn't been very hurtful. When the romance and sexiness wore off, she still had Grenville.

"People want a home —" Eleanor began.

"And today's ceremonies!" Grenville turned the tap on. "At least the ancients understood the need for rites of passage, for meaningful rituals."

He spoke between bouts of brushing,

"The vigil, for example. This is now the stag-night with vulgar drunkeness and hearty hetero-sex," he spat. "Then this dressing up in the fossilised costume of a Victorian toff when, before crossing the threshold, one should *strip off*, discarding the old life!"

Toothpaste and spit spattered the mirror as Grenville went on,

"There is no ordeal, no trial, no grandeur. Instead, there is silly music and a new liturgy that a tabloid journalist would have been ashamed to write!" He sucked water out of his hand and rinsed out his mouth.

After all these years of living with Grenville, his body and its functions were very familiar to Eleanor. He never closed doors and would talk through a pee, and with only a slight pause in the voice when crapping. She still needed privacy in the toilet but could, like now, lie naked in the bath while Grenville stood naked at the handbasin.

Eleanor looked at him. She could see his back and, in the mirror, his face and torso. He was good to look at, always graceful, whether standing or sitting, clothed or naked, animated or in rare moments of repose. She could not see below his waist but knew that his cock hung straight and uncircumcised, backed by the furred, uneven shape of his balls. His skin had a warm tone and was smooth, apart from a light down on his legs and arms and the criss-cross of fresh red weals on his back and buttocks.

"One should purge the old self," he was saying. "Be washed, cleansed and dressed in the vestments of rebirth." He darted his toothbrush into a mug and picked up a can of shaving soap. "Weddings! Such a meaningless spectacle!" After squirting a cone of foam onto his fingers he dabbed his face with it. "Anointing with fizzy grape juice and the symbols of fertility made out of *paper*."

Picking up a razor he thrust out his chin at the mirror.

Even with his Father Christmas beard of shaving foam, Eleanor could admire the slender neck and the silky hair framing his lovely face... intense eyes, narrow nose and full mouth. Grenville was much more satisfying to study than the static studio nudes of the lifeclass. In spite of his restlessness, she loved drawing him. Liking to be naked and admiring her skill, he would pose for her. Because he never stopped talking and was never still, she had learned to catch his likeness at speed. The nipples, navel and penis — all the markers of his body were so familiar to her and their harmonies so rehearsed, he could be done from memory. His genitals were drawn without coyness, she depicted them as the dark core of his body, completing the image of male beauty.

"Marriage, as we know it, is wrong!" Grenville tilted his head and pulled his cheek taut. "All tied up with exclusiveness, the 'one and only'. Pah! A typically *bourgeois* illusion."

"You're so unromantic," Eleanor said.

"Me? Unromantic!" Grenville's outraged face with its foam goatee glared at her from the mirror, "Either you don't know the meaning of the word or you don't know me!" He agitated his razor in the hot water as he said, "I'm *all* for romance. It's a way of spiritualizing sex and making it erotic."

So beautiful and yet he was not erotic. Not for her.

From the start Eleanor had protected herself. Hadn't his first words been *I'm a faggot?* She pushed away all thoughts of him as a lover and never projected any romantic fantasy onto him. It wasn't difficult. He talked up a storm of fond words but there was never any glint in his eye. She was his pet lamb, his friend of the bosom, yes, and a constant witness to his never-ending lust for others. So many others. All her life compared to others and always found wanting, Eleanor knew how to protect herself now: she would not compete. She would not enter the arena. And the whip marks were a turnoff, a visible barrier to her fancying him or imagining that they could ever suit each other in bed.

"I had a most *romantic* time yesterday," Grenville waggled his eyebrows at her in the mirror. "Got Mistress Marty round and Jean Claude and so on. I'm rather in love with Jean Claude. I've given up on girls for the moment. So resistant to my ideas about unrestricted sexual congress —"

"Has it never occurred to you Grenville," she asked with heavy irony, "that you might be homosexual?"

"No, no! Too narrow!" he protested. "Too fixed! This idea that gender and sexuality are a field of play is so much more exciting, don't you think? If only you girls would *play* properly!"

In steady strokes and with terrifying speed, Grenville swept the razor upwards under his chin. He never cut himself.

"But perhaps we're just born one way or the other," she said.

"Why not born both ways!" Grenville peered into the mirror, turning his head this way and that, stretching his lips over his teeth.

"Maybe, but I'm sure nothing could turn me or Jean Claude onto women. Just like nothing could turn Sandra onto men. She says, deep down, she's always, always known."

"How boring and unadventurous," Grenville said. "Have you people no curiosity? Take Marty. Now there's someone *really* fascinating. God! He was wonderful yesterday. Took us right to the edge. One of the best... ceremonies... ever. And a blissful, dreamless sleep afterwards. I feel splendid today!" Grenville wriggled his shoulders to feel the welts on his back.

Eleanor sighed. She felt lonely. Had so looked forward to coming home to Grenville. But what she really wanted now was to go back to bed with a lad of her own, to kiss him and have a quiet, slow, comforting fuck, then doze in his arms and wake up to a loving smile.

"Family values! What does it mean?" Grenville discarded the razor as he answered his own question, "It means a licence for people to illtreat each other in the privacy of their own homes." He washed his face. "And when everyone is well and truly enslaved to the whole preposterous system someone breaks out —"

Eleanor closed her eyes. The job in Scotland was not going well. She'd been dealing with an arrogant prat and his boring costume designs. It was no-end frustrating. She could see so clearly how it could be done but no one was going to listen to a nowt-a-penny dressmaker. And she'd slept with the prat n'all.

"I wish I could afford to get a proper theatre qualification," Eleanor said. "I'm sick of having to make stuff from other people's crap designs. Half the time I feel I have much better ideas than —"

"What needs to be done?" Grenville asked, looking over the towel. "Is further training the answer? People break out because monogamy is simply not possible. Never mind affording it. Every time someone has to escape there are friends, family, masses of sprogs, all in a terrible turmoil of misery, not knowing who to side with. Ridiculous! And before you start on some feminist rant —"

"Rant! When do I ever get to rant with you around, Grenville!" she said.

"— about it all being organized to suit men, let me say that the present system suits nobody. I'd leapfrog all that qualification rot, Nelly. Put together a portfolio of designs and tart them round. I'll pimp for you, make sure you get looked at." He sprinkled his hands with cologne and patted his face. "Some alternative arrangement to the *nomini pomini* nuclear family must be found —"

"Chance'd be a fine thing." Eleanor sat up and pulled the plug out of the bath. She felt depressed and needed to escape Grenville's hammering voice.

He turned away from the mirror and faced her, propping himself on the handbasin,

"But we could lead the way!" he insisted. "Be in the vanguard of social reform! Renegotiate a completely new male-female partnership. Pioneer a new kind of marriage! What d'you think?"

She stood up and reached for a towel.

"Eleanor! What's the matter? You've hurt yourself!"

Grenville's shocked face made her look down in panic. The hot bath had brought on her period. She quickly covered herself and lowered her head. She felt ashamed and ready to cry.

"Sorry, 'sjust the curse. Sorry —" she stumbled out of the bath.

Grenville lunged across the room,

"Stop! Stop. Don't go. Please, please let me see." He gently pulled the towel away. Bright red blood flowed down her thigh from the dark pubic triangle. "*Blood streams from the firmament...* my God... what beauty," he whispered. "Dearest...?" He looked into her face.

The wonder in his looks and the softness of his voice seemed so personal, so like tenderness that all her defences were swept away in a storm of longing for him.

"Yoo-hoo, man!"

The front door thudded and Grenville's cleaner sang out the usual warning in her big, rolling, gospel-choir voice,

*"I'm on my way and I won't turn back
I'm on my way, O Lord, I'm on my way!"*

Eleanor snatched the towel from Grenville and ran off back to her attic.

# HIT

Grenville had been away in Oxford but Eleanor was expecting him soon. She had prepared a meal and laid one of the tables in the ballroom, knowing that he liked eating at home after days of performing and public dinners.

The front door sounded. Must be him calling her down to help with his bags. When she opened the door she was surprised to see Theo, Grenville's architect.

"I've come to see Grenville. He said sevenish."

Eleanor let him in and said as they climbed the stairs,

"I'm expecting him any minute. Let's go to the ball-room. I think you know the way?" Having supervised its restoration, he acknowledged this with a lift of his eyebrow.

Eleanor was "resting" between jobs and while Grenville was away, had enjoyed three quiet days, alone. Unlike him, she liked the solitude, even arranging to be out when the cleaner came. In between catching up with herself — seeing to her clothes, going to the dentist — Eleanor had spent the time drawing and, as Grenville had suggested, preparing a portfolio of theatre designs. Artists' materials were spread all over a table and sofa in her favourite corner of the ballroom. Eleanor couldn't stop Theo making for it.

He ignored the costume designs but was interested in a painting of the view through the french windows, taking in the balcony, its flowers and the trees of the square beyond.

"That's charming." He glanced up at the window and back at the image. "And skilful."

"Grenville won't think much to it. Not very *avant-garde*, is it?"

"Grenville is too uncompromising. May I?" Theo pointed at her other pictures and sketch books. "These are lovely." He picked up drawings of the ballroom plasterwork. "How clever of you to do it in grisaille. Very appropriate. Most authentic looking."

"Copying plasterwork is just therapeutic, restful. Pointless really."

"Not at all," Theo insisted. "I admire it. I like this, particularly." He'd picked out a pencil and wash drawing of a section of decorative frieze. "The anthemions alternating with the lotus and palmette design. You've captured the style perfectly. Cool greys, white highlights. Excellent!"

"Have it, if you're sure you really like it," Eleanor said.

"Really? That's very generous. Don't you want to sell it?"

"Don't be daft!"

"I'm serious. Neo-classical is *the* fashion." Theo snapped open the briefcase which he kept with him at all times. "Georgian pastiches are going up all over the place. It's definitely the style following the money at the moment." He took a folder from his case and carefully placed the drawing between hardcovers to protect it. "Thank you, Eleanor I shall treasure it."

Eleanor liked the way his large hands were set off by clean, white shirtcuffs. She found his courtly manners rather attractive too. Theo went on speaking as he closed his briefcase,

"Regency is all the rage. And Empire furniture, Georgian silver... all fetching terrific prices at auction. Dealers are doing a brisk trade in repro too, as you can imagine."

The phone rang. It was Grenville with a rigmarole about a puncture, about lateness and about his car getting locked inside the college gates.

"I would have rung earlier but I've been careering about getting it all sorted out. I'm still in Oxford. At Arnold and Jim's. The dear old queens have taken me in and fed me."

She heard Arnold's voice at the back, "Not so much of the 'old' if you don't mind and love to Eleanor."

"The silly young sissies send their love and are just about to see me off."

"Give them both a big hug from me. And Grenville! Theo is here to see you."

"Christ! I thought that was tomorrow. Hell! What a mess. Sorry, old bean. *Surely* you can find some use for him? Ungh? Ungh? Onwards and *up*wards ho ho etcetera? Put the blighter on."

"OK, love. See you later."

"Absolutely," Grenville made kissing sounds.

Theo returned from the phone, picked up his half-finished glass of wine and settled back into an armchair. He seemed in no hurry to leave, though his evening with Grenville had been postponed. Eleanor was getting hungry so she asked,

"Were you expecting to go out and eat with Grenville?"

"Ye-es, I thought we were going over to the proposed new gallery site, that I'd be indroduced to Mr Big, be sized up, possibly over a meal. Mainly, I hoped to land a further meeting. Fortunately Grenville gave *me*, not the client, the wrong date. It could be a deal worth millions so, needless to say, I left the evening free."

"And now I've got a dinner for two spoiling in the oven. Do you want to stay and have it? I reckon you'll find the cooking here's improved since those early days."

"That's extremely kind of you. Thank you. I'd be delighted. If you're sure it's not too much trouble."

"No trouble. Pity to waste it," she said.

Eleanor had always thought him handsome, even though he was so different from Grenville. Theo was larger, darker and bearded but she had always found him too stuck up to be likeable. Yet tonight, even though his suit, bowtie and restrained manners gave the meal a feeling of formality, he chatted easily to her about his work and ambitions. She warmed to him, responding to his compliments on the food and his interest in her drawings.

Over coffee, Theo asked her where she had trained as an artist or whether she had been to university.

"Just went to the local college and did dressmaking. So I've not been to a university, nothing like. Mind, I could say I've done better than that... that I've had four years —"

"At the University of Life."

"I wasn't going to say anything so pathetic," Eleanor said, feeling patronized.

"I'm sorry, it is a rather feeble idea, to be sure," Theo flushed.

"I've had four years with Grenville, was what I was going to say, and that's been an education second to none."

"I'll take your word for it. Very racy."

"Racy? I think Grenville would say he's disappointed in me in that area. You do realise our relationship is platonic?" Eleanor wanted to get that in. "No, I really mean an education like," she went on. "In art and literature and oh, you know, learning to think —"

Eleanor heard the thud of the front door. "That's him now." She got up and patting Theo on the shoulder, said, "And we'd better be ready for a bucketload of innuendo when he sees I've had you for dinner."

"Ah, if only…" Theo flirted,

"Don't *you* start, n'all!" But she gave him a jaunty look.

"Pet lamb!" Grenville threw his bags onto the landing and hugged her. "We had a fantastic time apart from the beastly *voiture* and the bloody college porters. I had to whore! Give them a flash of the old garter. Such a tugging of forelocks then, my dear. Deplorable. But I was desperate. And since you ask I was on tremendously good form at the conference and at the unscheduled hanky pankies after."

Grenville had taken something to keep him going, she could tell. His eyes were bright and his mood high.

"There were some really heavyweight *hombres* there. But I made their teeth rattle! Aha! Theo! You stayed on. I trust you two have been up to something disgusting?"

"Not disgusting at all." Theo and Grenville shook hands. "I had the most delicious meal and —"

"You were just choosing between the birch, the crop and the ruler!" Grenville flung his coat after his bags and led the way back to the ballroom as Eleanor and Theo exchanged "what did I tell you" looks.

"Sorry to disappoint you, love," Eleanor said. "Though I *was* singing your praises."

"She was," Theo said. "I'll vouch for that."

"I'm quite bloated with applause and adoration but always ready for more. Do tell." Grenville took Eleanor's empty glass and poured the remains of the wine into it.

"I was just saying," she began as they sat down in the armchairs round the coffee table, "that living with you has been better than going to university —"

"Oho! Well..." Grenville drawled, "Eleanor gets a first in Reeling, Writhing and Fainting in Coils but has failed Erotomania, *dismally*." He took a mouthful of wine. "So I'm witholding her degree!"

Eleanor and Theo shared another smile. Grenville flung his leg over the arm of his chair and ruminated,

"Perhaps I should have an Academy. Yes. A Uni*per*versity for those in need of moral improvement. I, Dr Delirium, myself a specialist in Victorian Values, guarantee a scurrilous curriculum, exquisite examinations and extr*ee*-mely languid passing-out ceremonies..."

Grenville was forcing laughter from Theo. He went on,

"Now, let me see. What shall we call this Crammer? Dr Delirium's *De*formatory? Deleterium? Derelictory? Depravatory for Debutantes? Hm. Such a lot of delectable words beginning with 'd': delinquent, debauchery, degradation and..."

Grenville's face remained serious as he made Eleanor and Theo laugh.

After their guest left, Eleanor cleared away the supper.

"How did you get on with thrusting Theo then?" Grenville asked. He was still drinking and following her back and forth from the kitchen. "Did Theo thrill you with his throbbing theodolite?"

Eleanor put dishes into Grenville's spare hand to stop him making obscene gestures.

"He's quite nice really," she said.

"I wouldn't go that far. Beware the worshippers of Mammon! Don't you find him awfully pompous?"

"He seemed very relaxed with me."

"Perhaps he's nicer with women. Brilliant architect but commonplace otherwise, don't you find? Not good enough for you, cabbage."

"He's very handsome and I —"

"Ho ho! *Now* we come to the nub! *Ungh, ungh.* I will allow that he is handsome... In a big, beefy, *hairy* sort of way. You like that sort of thing?"

"Mm," Eleanor admitted.

When she'd finished loading the dishwasher and wiping the worksurfaces, she interrupted Grenville who was darting round her, talking, buttering toast, rummaging through the fridge and opening cartons of juice.

"I'm bushed, love." Eleanor yawned. "I'm for my bed."

"And I'm for the wicked city in search of *adventure*... or perhaps —" Grenville pointed a carrot at the summer night, "I will hie me to the Forest of Arden... to Arcadia in Hampstead for a pastoral frolic upon the Heath!"

He looked at his watch,
"Good heavens! It's not even midnight!"

Theo sat back in the taxi taking him to his flat in Lancaster Gate. It had once been his parents' *pied-à-terre* in London till they had given it to him on his 30th birthday. Then he'd borrowed money, bought the apartment above and done an "architect's conversion", changing the property into a spacious home on two floors with views over Kensington Gardens. He often reflected that he was sitting on a fortune. And he could be in line for another if Grenville came up trumps tomorrow.

The evening had been alright really. Staying on had been the best option. Otherwise he'd have spent the time fretting about the postponement. Instead he'd had a very nice meal with Eleanor. Might be in with a chance there. Theo remembered Eleanor smiling, leaning towards him to recharge his wine glass. She'd nearly got rid of the vulgar accent but there was still that whiff of something common, which was rather sexy. Her touch on his shoulder coursed down his spine again.

The fact that Eleanor was close to Grenville would do no harm. Grenville might choose to live in a slum and decorate the ballroom like a fairground but he was still very grand. Theo had pumped her about the family and connections: a lot of army top brass. And Grenville was a great fixer, in close contact with new money... *real* money. London was awash with it. Best of all, Thatcher was back with a massive majority. Things were all set to go.

Moving the practice to Bedford Square had been a good decision. An excellent address. Theo thought of his expensively refurbished offices. That elegant drawing Eleanor had given him looked like an original. Could pass for a 19th century copy from the antique. She had talent, a real eye, no doubt about that. Nothing downmarket about her taste. He'd have the picture expensively framed, period style. Hang it in reception... strike just the right note with the clients.

Theo held up his watch to the passing street lights. Good, not too late. It was going to be a long day tomorrow. The dinner date with his current girlfriend would have to be cancelled. In fact, the whole day would have to be rescheduled. He drummed his fingers on his briefcase and put women and leisure out of his mind.

# iii

## DRIVE

"Eleanor! Not asleep or anything, are you? Nelly! I say old thing, are you awake?"

"I am now." Eleanor sat up and said through a yawn, "What's the matter?"

Grenville's shadowy shape moved across the attic room and she felt him slump down on her bed. Eleanor was suddenly wide awake and worried. In all their years together, he'd never done this, ever. She did not want to have to refuse him. Always dreaded this disruption of their friendship or anything which might lose her Grenville and her tenancy in his life. Always known that if they became lovers, she would soon be made miserable and jealous and that would put an end to everything.

"Thing is, after all, I'm not very fussy. I'm quite laidback really..." Grenville's voice was nearby in the darkness. "It's just I can't stand flies. They're tolerable outside where they belong and I understand that I have to share the world, with people and flies and slugs. But I can't cope with them in my bedroom. And it's not that they dip shit or bash themselves against windows, either. I can relate to all that. It's that 'Bzzz' business they go in for. Drives me mad."

"Does it, love?" Eleanor said.

"Bzzz. Silence for two seconds. Bzzzzzzz. Silence for eight and a half seconds. Bzt... bzzZZZzzz. Silence. Bzzz... bzt. Silence. BZZZZZZZ. And so on. I simply can't cope with the unpredictability, the dreadful *disorder* of it all."

"Turn the light off."

"It *is* off, dearest. Here we are in the dark."

"I mean *your* light. Then they shut up and go to sleep, like parrots."

"Parrots are perfectly all right, in spite of their feathers. But a fly? If I turn my light off, I'll still know it's out there... somewhere... waiting for me. *J'ai peur du sommeil comme on a peur d'un grand trou.*"

Eleanor heard Grenville shiver.

"Is it you want to get in? Do you want a cuddle?" she had to offer some comfort.

"Can't do cuddles. It would have to be sex."

Eleanor switched on the lamp. They screwed up their faces at each other in the light.

"I don't think that's —"

"On? Absolutely agree. Not after all this time," Grenville said. "Sex with friends. Too terminal. Not even as a last resort. Shall I make us a hot drink? Or is juice better?"

"What time is it?" Eleanor yawned and reached for her watch.

"The hour of the wolf. The hour when most of us are born and most of us will die."

"Midnight?"

"No, no, that's the witching hour. Don't you know anything? Thought you'd be an expert in all that folkloric gibberish."

"I'm starving."

"That's the wolf," said Grenville, getting up. "I'll make you a fresh-killed sandwich while you dress."

"Dress?"

"We'll go for a drive. That's the answer, don't you think?"

Eleanor put her head back in the passenger seat of Grenville's car and watched the dark city slide quietly round her and away. Lighted windows, shop fronts, street lamps, neon signs approached and then glanced off, out of sight. Jewel-bright traffic lights changed for no reason. The Belishas flashed faithfully at empty crossings. The on-off jostle of daytime driving was replaced by a swift possession of the streets. Occasionally a pedestrian or another car swung into view, rare enough in the deserted cityscape to be of interest. Who were they? Where were they going at this hour? But they too would glide away into the past. Tunnel lights flipped overhead, railings flickered by and the river lay still and heavy as they flowed past it on the Embankment.

"I want to ask," Grenville began. "You have lived with me for years. Are you warm enough? I've left the car roof on, spoils the view but I don't want us to be cold."

"I'm fine, it's very cosy like this."

"And I notice that you can go for long periods, weeks, without fucking anyone. Am I right?" he said.

"I suppose so…"

"How do you do that?"

"Well, I'm not like you…"

Since her supper with Theo, Eleanor had been in a lather. Wanting Theo to ring up. Wondering if he might come round to the house.

"Sex is important," she said, playing for time. "But it's not a priority, if you know what I mean…" She was keeping her feelings for Theo from Grenville. She couldn't face his *ho ho* and interference. "I mean, sex is not my religion, you know. I mean, for me there are other things that come first like —"

"I suppose sex *is* my religion," Grenville said. "What a clever thought! Shall we take Vauxhall or Chelsea? My insurance against cold obstruction. *Les morts, les pauvres morts, ont de grandes douleurs.* Better view from here. You have no consideration for the reputation of my house as a great bordello. A Cathedral of Sin. Always wanted to be a bishop, you know —"

"Well, you go to *Heaven* already," said Eleanor, hoping to distract him with talk of the club.

"But the whole purpose was," Grenville was not diverted, "to corrupt you, bring enlightenment. Look out there. Battersea Power Station. Such a wonderful building. Once crucial, now obsolete. Dead. What shall we do on the other side?"

"After death?"

"Kew or Greenwich? Life after death? That's what I fear. It might be awful. All earth and slugs. I want to be sure of oblivion. We'll go East. *Semper ad lucem.* Towards the dawn. *Entends, ma chère, entends la douce Nuit qui marche.* Don't you need sex? Why aren't you gibbering? How do you manage? I love cities, don't you?"

"Well, you might go to one, even after death. Slug-free." Eleanor, who felt she wasn't managing at all anymore, had to get him off sex. Death was safer.

"The Celestial City?" Grenville said before pouncing on her again, "I don't notice you taking cold showers. I see no instruments of auto-eroticism in your room or 'engines of lust' as our bedder used to call porn mags. We are coming up to one of *the* views. A city of the mind. Do you wank? Absolutely ordered. Would I like that? *And he that talked with me had a golden reed to measure the city, and the gates thereof, and the wall thereof. And the city lieth foursquare and the length is...* Too fixed, too obsessively controlled, perhaps? Even for a fetishist like me. Look, Westminster from this side of the river now. Don't you have a libido? You've sublimated it? *And there shall be no night there...* Tell me, my pet, I am concerned for your health."

"I've been happier living with you, Grenville, than I've ever been in my whole life."

"But this is extraordinary! Not much left of Blake's 'Lovely Lambeth', is there? Lets do the romantic destitution of Bermondsey and Rotherhithe. Happy! And so little sex? Here we are in Dickensville. I forgive him because he's a Londoner, an insomniac and a sado-masochist."

"Sadomasochist?" Eleanor was resistant, having enjoyed working on *Oliver!*

"Takes one to know one. So you're happy? You're not like one of his ghastly women, surely? Chastity, virginity and all that sort of repulsive, simpering prudery? Is that what women are like really?"

"No, it's how men... Dickens wanted them because —"

"How can heteros possibly *not* want women to fuck? That's really, really perverted. Dickens was tremendously mad."

"It was you turned me onto him!" Eleanor said. "He's ever so funny. Spot on about kids and really intelligent when it comes to —"

"I have always defined intelligence as 'wanting to know.' Sex is part of that drive towards knowledge, don't you think? We'll go back to Tower Bridge and into Jackthe-Rippersville. Knowledge of the world. Have you no commitment to self-discovery? No curiosity?" persisted Grenville.

She did not want to talk to him about her yearning for Theo. Specially not now... in one of his moods. She glanced at him. Was he on something?

"Yes, its true..." Eleanor looked out of the window at the river lights flitting in and out of the black swooping lines of Tower Bridge, "when I fancy someone, a big part of it is curiosity and —"

"Curiosity about what? The size of their... on my side Wapping... cocks? On your side Traitor's Gate..."

"I'm much more interested in the size of their brains," she said.

"Brains! This is the most terrible nonsense. It means you only want to fuck clever people. So few! And if my tutors at Cambridge were anything to go by, mostly old, bitchy and unkempt. Here you are, in the thick of every kind of erotic activity," he dipped his head at the rear-view mirror, "surrounded by eager boys and you do nothing..."

"You do it all. Spares me the effort like." Eleanor said.

She had always confided in Grenville and had always gone along with his funny moods. But just lately, he made her feel a bit tired and fed up somehow.

They passed through the narrow gorges of the City but were too enclosed and near the ground to see St Paul's and the tall office towers. The darkness had thinned, the sky turning from dirty yellow to blue-grey. The streets and buildings were more defined, the lights duller. There was some traffic now, vans and lorries delivering to newsagents, sandwich bars, cafes and restaurants. Empty buses, noisy road cleaners and rubbish trucks with twirling orange lights were beginning the occupation of the streets.

A kitchenboy in a white apron, one hand in his armpit and the other holding a mug, stood leaning in an open doorway. He looked at Eleanor before turning his head to speak to someone inside. Another lad appeared at his shoulder. She just had time to blow them both a kiss and see their faces light up, before the car swept her away.

"You're not traumatised, are you? Like Roland," Grenville started again. "Claims he was raped by our Head of House. Took it very badly. Never does anything with anybody now. Extraordinary! I remember being very jealous of Roland as you would have been if you'd seen our Head of House. An Adonis, my dear. Talking of doughnuts, you could have Pedro, I'm sure. He does it with girls too."

"I don't really want —".

"But he's so cute! Too dim for you I suppose. We will go round Piccadilly again, then down Whitehall to Westminster bridge and home. That way we will have described a figure of eight, the snake with the tail in its mouth, the symbol of eternity. London is the perfect city, don't you think?"

"You've taught me to love London and —"

"New York is thrilling. All right we will not insist on Pedro. But Marty the Mile End Masochist, how about him! He adores you and —"

"Forget it!" she said, "I don't like women's clobber at the best of times, so no, I don't want to be set up with a transvestite, thank you!"

140

"But you'd wear the trousers, my dear. He'd wear the little frilly apron and bring the breakfasts in bed! Seems like the ideal arrangement to me, old thing. Paris is the city of Beaudelaire. And if he burns the toast you can swish him. Berlin is wicked and tragic, Amsterdam, Madrid, Istanbul and so on, all wonderful but London... London has the best map and Marty has one of the most beautiful bottoms —"

"No, Grenville!" Always trying to get her off with Marty... Maps! A sure way to distract him,

"The Underground map, you mean, or the *A to Z?*"

"I mean that, like a poem, I can hold London in my mind in all its complexity because of the beauty of its structure. It is divided north from south by a river that runs from west to east — or left to right as we read — and the course the river describes across the page, so to speak, ends with that looping signature, that flourish round the Isle of Dogs which is so particular. Its streets, bridges, squares and parks are arranged in patterns, rhythms that always relate subtly to the line of the river. You can have all of these delightful boys. Yet you decline. I had thought to educate you. It's unbelievably frustrating. What's your explanation?"

"Well, it's difficult to —"

"Besides, what other city in the world has Eros at it's heart. You know that cock-teaser Jason asked me to put in a word —"

"Jason?" Eleanor looked over at Grenville. "He didn't!"

"He certainly did." Grenville leaned back to glance out of his side mirror. "Lucky, lucky you."

"But he's a rent boy!"

"So?"

"How can he want me. I'm a woman and years older and... are you and he having some sort of joke?"

"You insult me, Nelly! As if I would stoop to such vulgarity. You know I abhor jokes."

"All right. but I still can't believe it."

"Why not? Human desire is infinitely various. Changes with circumstances, with availability. Jason does sex for money. He might want to fuck you for love. I thought girls liked that sort of thing."

"I'm fond of him, of course. Poor lad. Needs a Mam. But we've nothing in common. Intimacy with Jason would be impossible."

"Intimacy? What could be more intimate. Carnal knowledge... up the arse or the cunt... the route direct to the innermost soul, surely? Lets stop off at Westminster Bridge and see the dawn. Then I could do with some carnality m'self."

"Isn't Theo coming round sometime today?" Eleanor had been planning this question as they left the car, walked up Victoria Embankment, past the statue of Boadicea and onto the bridge. "I thought you had some work for him," she tried to sound casual.

"Yes, but it was all settled on the phone. I'll drop us off at home and try my luck with a spot of cottaging in the station loo. It'll just be open. Got a cute night worker coming off shift last time. That way I'll be back for breakfast."

Grenville and Eleanor looked over the parapet at the sun rising over the river. After the warm confinement of the car they yawned and stretched, both shading their eyes as they took in the burnished water and the wide expanse of air and light.

Grenville had once made her a present of a book of poems about London,

"*Earth has not anything to show more fair,*" she quoted, to please him.

"Absolutely, dearest! And as true now as it was then. Just look at it." Grenville took a deep breath,

"*This City now doth, like a garment, wear the beauty of the morning.* God! I need a shag."

# AGE

It was Eleanor's birthday. Grenville had put the word out and friends had gathered, bringing food, drink, sounds and smokes. Uncle Archie and Rajiv contributed champagne and canapes. Yasmine had made an enormous tiered cake while Gail and Zeb gave her a homemade present and card. Also among the guests were acquaintances and the many itinerants and freeloaders who contributed novelty and gossip.

Grenville had given Eleanor a facsimile edition of Blake's *Songs of Innocence and Experience*, a lace dress and a leather jacket. The lace dress came from an antique clothes market and the leather jacket from a fetish shop. Eleanor was wearing them together with red tights, Doc Marten boots and her hair up.

"Ooh, very Goth. Give us a twirl then," Marty said. He'd come as a boy, with a card and flowers.

Sandra, who'd given Eleanor a book on Fred Astaire, said in her monotone,

"The top of Cyd Charisse's black lace dress in *The Band Wagon* was just like this." She parted the front of Eleanor's jacket for a better view. "Can I have a feel?" Sliding her arms under the jacket, Sandra hugged Eleanor and kissed her on the mouth.

"Shall I deliver you from the lubricious clutches of that lecherous lesbian?" Grenville shouted from his armchair. Eleanor already feeling high on Archie's champagne and all the fuss, called back,

"I'm a big girl now! And Marty will protect me."

"Y'wrong there, doll," Marty said. "I'm a lesbian I am, and I demand a feel as well —"

Eleanor tensed with excitement as she saw Theo arrive. He was unaccompanied. She went over to him right away and was given a gift-wrapped box of chocolates and a card in which he'd written "*love* from Theo". This gave her the excuse to lean on his arm and reach up to give him a thank-you kiss.

Gail was the only competition, she was eight months pregnant. Yasmine was happy, "Is magnificent! So big belly, big boobz! What for you hide? For why you not wear the pretty-pretty decolletages. Eh? More cake for mama Gail. I get."

"What about more cake for papa Zeb," Gail's husband said, grinning, "I worked ever so hard too, you know —"

"You watch I not batter the balls to eat with chips. Eh!" Yasmine made a chopping movement with her hand in front of his face while Zeb pretended to be scared.

When she'd gone, Terry, who didn't like women and was trying to pull Grenville, leant towards him and sneered,

"Fucking 'orrible dyke. Wot's that Yasmine got on you?"

"Nothing," Grenville drawled, looking at his slice of cake. Annoying Terry would spice things up a bit. He held up his plate and studied the delicate icing of frilly roses and sinuous ferns. "Actually, that's not quite true. Yasmine the Witch can wield the whip, did you know, with exquisite precision and —" Grenville took a bite of cake "— with feeling. Such accomplishment!"

"'Orrible fat slut."

"And that, too." Grenville licked his fingers. "Altogether superb."

When Yasmine returned to the ballroom, he called out to her,

"Fantastic cake, Mistress!"

Terry retreated as Yasmine came over and sat on the arm of Grenville's clubchair.

"Of course is fantastics! I make. Not for you chauvinists, for Eleanor."

"It is... magnificent. This icing. How's it done? These edible... um... fannies are so beautiful. As good as the real thing —"

"Pah! Porno poofty! What you know about the fannies? Ah? Nothing!" Yasmine, leaning over Grenville, explained in detail how she had placed the marzipan on the cake, rubbing it to get the air bubbles out. How she made her own icing, rolled it out, draped it over the marzipan and using dowling and wet fingertips created the intricate folds and frills.

Grenville, nodding and eating, looked up at Yasmine from time to time.

"And the sugar flowers," he wanted to know, "how did they get their delicate colours and shades?"

Eleanor, who was passing by, stopped to listen to Yasmine's answer,

"I paint like artist with the brushes and the food colour."

"'Slovely Yasmine, my cake, your icing 'slike the beautiful plasterwork," Eleanor looked up and Yasmine held her as she teetered. A spotlight cast the ceiling into sharp relief, dressing the wild mænads and dancing fauns in dazzling white. Their ecstacy was outlined in darkness and their open mouths and flowers were deep cups of shadow.

"This is my happiest birthday ever!"

Archie beckoned to Eleanor and as Yasmine watched her move away to join his group, Grenville asked quietly,

"What's she like, Mistress?"

"Sweet. So sweet."

"Really?"

"Aah…" Yasmine sighed, off guard. "And salty like the mermaid."

Grenville narrowed his eyes and nodded. On seeing this, Yasmine caught hold of his hair and jerked his head back,

"Ssss. No hanky-wankies with Eleanor. You stay the porno noses out! For make her sad I kill you. Eh!"

"Yes, Mistress."

The party had fallen into groups. Frankie, Jason, Jean Claude, hangers-on and gatecrashers, "the minnows" as Grenville called them, swirled and darted round the music centre and video. On the floor, Ollie, Grenville's old school friend, leant against Cathy, a local prostitute and drug buddy. Marty sat on the arm of Rajiv's chair, Sandra on a footstool within view of everyone so she could lipread and Eleanor, who had taken off her jacket was on a small sofa pressed between Theo and Archie. Theo had put his arm along the back of the sofa to make more room.

Music pulsed in the background, the front door thudded, people came and went and the room was full of voices:

— maybe like the gloves Rita Hayworth wore for *Put the Blame on Mame*

— Did you ever fuck mad Jasper?

— I saw a scary programme on telly recently, about gays in America

— What's so scary about shorts, lumberjack shirts and Fire Island?

— Did you ever fuck mad Jasper?

— Not that I remember. He's straight anyway

— it's typical of our times: irresponsible, self-seeking and contentless

— Nobody's straight

— Yes they are. Just like you're completely bent

— there's this new kind of clap now. But there's no cure for it and only gays get it

— marketizing every aspect of our lives is not going to strengthen the economy

— don't be so parochial. The real news is what's going on in Palestine

— they're dying like flies

While they were getting ready for the party, Grenville had put a record on the stereo, saying,

"As it's your birthday, I think we'll have *Death and the Maiden*."

"And you claim to have no sense of humour?" Eleanor had said.

Schubert had given way to Brian Eno and then to the latest club sounds brought by the boys. People came and went. Gail and Zeb left. Derek and his entourage arrived with Emerald the painter: a notorious ex-hibitionist, beauty, and Grenville's latest girl. Eleanor could see that Emerald was trying to play Grenville and Yasmine off against each other. Poor innocent, flirting with snakes.

As she laughed at one of Derek's wicked anecdotes, Eleanor leant back against Theo as if making herself more comfortable. Theo's arm slipped off the back of the sofa and rested lightly round her shoulders. People came and went and the room was full of laughter:

— Pull the other one! A disease that can tell if you're gay? Look, man! There goes a poofter, zap! You're dead!

— I couldn't do it with a woman if you paid me

— No women want porno dwarfy like you anyways. Yeach!

— There goes a guy in a leather cap. Must be a faggot, zap! Gotcher! Yee-ha!

— and she was one of the first. Went to Casablanca and had the operation and everything

— I'm ashamed of what is happening and I say that as a Jew

— these cruise missiles are all part of the megalomania

— I like going to the Zoo when they are feeding the constrictors. What does that make me?

— An 'orrible creep, dear

— and she said: don't do it. She said: you don't feel like a woman, you feel like a mutilated man

— But that's Thatcherism for you, an unholy alliance between the id and the super-ego

Eleanor was aware of nothing except Theo's body next to her. His dark, bearded head was close to hers, she could feel his breath on her hair and the tips of his fingers trailed heat along her bare neck and shoulder. Lying beside him like a sunbather by the sea, she felt hot with longing. The voices of her birthday reached her like the distant shouts of swimmers playing in the thundering surf:

— Last time I visited mad Jasper in the nick, he told me he'd met Beckett, years ago, in a club in Amsterdam

— this gay cancer sounds like a rightwing fundamentalist fantasy to me. Just the sort of thing barmy homophobics like to dream up

— "Oi've seen yer *Waiting for Godot*," says Jasper. At which point Beckett puts his head in his hands

— the Unions have only themselves to blame, they killed the goose that laid the golden egg.

— "Don't worry, sir," says Jasper to Beckett, "'twas all in French and Oi didn't understand a single feckin word of it."

— let's have no more witless babble about society and no more "can't do that"

— Beckett was highly amused by this and bought Jasper a drink. Or so Jasper claims

— Jeehovah, He knows who dey is, who is straight and who is bent and He will strike alladem per-verted cornholing cocksuckers dahn…!

— there'll be no stopping la Thatcher and her loadsamoney yobbos now

# V

## THEORY

Eleanor was lying on the sofa, smoking a joint. Rolling-papers and gutted cigarettes were scattered over the coffee table by her side. Autumn weather rattled the windows, the sound mingling with the clatter of Grenville's typewriter.

It had been a week since her birthday and the knot in her stomach had tightened as the days had gone by with no word from Theo. The dope would loosen it. Ribbons of smoke unfurled from the spliff into the great space above her. She tucked her shawl round herself and took another toke, slowly exhaling a shapeless blurr that joined the layers of smoke suspended across the windows. Not for years, since living at home, had she felt so depressed. She lay quietly, watching the illusion of water pouring over the plasterwork lozenges. This was a trick the room performed with mirrors, lights, reflections and rain. Today it was like lying in an under-water cave.

Grenville's voice echoed from the far side of the room, translating in jerks,

"*not all subjects... are subject to... to...* ah... *castration... yes... even when... even if there does not exist a subject...* bloody hell... *who is not subject to castration...* What! Holy Mother of God! There must be a better way of expressing thought than this! I blame those bloody Frogs, myself. What's happened to the lovely essay? And the French used to be so good at them! *Mon métier et mon art c'est vivre,* in the words of the immortal Montaigne."

Theo had been clamped onto Eleanor's consciousness for the past week. She could relieve herself of the pressure by telling Grenville. Not yet. Could not face knowing the worst. There might still be hope. Eleanor slipped onto the loop... perhaps Theo was on a business trip... not well... very busy... with his family... abroad on a business trip...

If she told Grenville, he would bring on a crisis. He would get in touch with Theo. Find out something definite. Not yet. It was Sunday afternoon. There was still time. The phone might ring and it might be Theo inviting himself round. She wouldn't tell Grenville.

"Grenville."

"Aha? What is it, my little cabbage. Shall we have some tea? Hang on. Hang on. *Lacanian formulas of sexuation,* fuck! Where's the *poetry* in all this?"

"I'm in love."

"Jolly good... the *signifying-language-user*... in lurve! Marvellous! Lucky you! Or not? Who is the fortunate creature?... *metonymy?* Let me guess! Male?"

"Of course."

"Has Marty struck lucky at last? Jason? No? It can't be Tinker-Belle. I hope it's not Freddie... he adores you of course, but he's tremendously queer and I really don't think —"

"Think straight," Eleanor said.

"Straight! Do we know any such people?... a *universal simulacrum*... David? Baptiste? Nick?" Grenville ran down a list of names of men he found attractive. Eleanor said no to all of them.

"Is it Foucault? Is he the *archaeology of epistemes*? Can we say that *art is meta-epistemic*? All theory seems to be about what is not, about absence, exclusion, castration, lack. So dreary. Is it Pedro? Christopher?"

"No!"

"Rumplestiltskin!"

"No!" Eleanor laughed, "It's Theo."

"Theo! I don't fancy him at all."

"I'm not you," Eleanor said.

"It's not good enough. All this *la valeur de renvoi de la signification* stuff just does not make the hair on the back of one's neck stand up. Doesn't make anything stand up, in fact. It is not sexy, is it? Theo? Christ!"

"I've got this miserable feeling —"

"Models of the mind are always so unsatisfactory. Why should the mind be like a landscape, a clock, or a building, or a computer? I'm getting a computer, I've got one on order."

"What do you want a computer for? You don't do maths?"

"Nothing to do with maths. It's a filing system and a wonderful sort of typewriter cum printing machine. But it doesn't think. Curious, this persistent fantasy about robots or rational humans, this fantasy of a mind unhampered by feeling."

"Well, I understand it," Eleanor said. "There's some feelings I could do without just at the minute."

"But what if thought *is* feeling? A unique *form* — the most flexible and complex. Maybe the way our minds work is the way the whole universe works." Grenville got up from his desk and began searching through his periodicals. "Perhaps our minds have solar systems, galaxies, planets, shooting stars, gravitational forces, what d'you think?"

"Do you know if Theo's away, Grenville? Have you been in touch with him this week, at all?"

"No." He rolled up a magazine and started swatting invisible flies on his desk. "I'm tired of institutionalized forms of discourse. These people are always setting up *associations* or *écoles* and chucking each other out of them."

"I thought you men liked all that argie-bargie and *I'm right and you're wrong.*"

"You women have some superior method I take it."

Grenville paced restlessly. He changed to using the magazine as an imaginary ping-pong bat.

"Happen women are not so obsessive," Eleanor said. "It's just that I did get the feeling Theo fancied me…" She sighed out sweet, herb-scented smoke, adding, "I do think women are more prepared to accept contradictions, changes of mind —"

"Oh *really*? You mean like our present *woman* prime minister. So flexible! So humane! Such a fine mind, full of infinite variables and possibilities. Yes?" Grenville threw the magazine aside, reached across his desk and drew the telephone towards him. The whirr of the dial punctuated his speech. "She's *incredibly* pervy, don't you think? So fixated. Never has London been more like Pornotopia. Rarely has the relationship of sex to politics, power to pleasure, eroticism to control been more evident!" He banged down the receiver. "I'm afraid there's no answer, dearest."

"I suppose not. Nothing changes, does it?" Eleanor said. "The boys at school were always like that, all macho argument and bullying."

"Of course! You went to school with the opposite sex. How extraordinary!" Grenville sat down at his typewriter again.

"Not extraordinary at all, love. Dead draggy, actually. I would have given anything to go to a single-sex place."

"Unbelievable! Why! Think of all the opportunities: bike sheds, bogs, dormitories full of throbbing adolescent wangers!"

"Oh yeah? What I remember is a no-win situation." Eleanor stubbed out her roach and brushed ash off her shawl. "You get bullied till you do sex and then you get called a slag. Put-downs in the classroom from male teachers and sexual harrassment in the playground from boys. Has Theo said anything to you about me?"

"Not as such. But he fancies you, *liebling*, I'm sure. I really don't understand this concept of sexual harrassment. He's probably out of town for the weekend."

"It's awful. So humiliating!"

"Nonsense!" Grenville began to type. "I'll keep ringing till I get an answer."

"You'll ring him? What will you say?" she sat up.

"I shall say *Eleanor is madly in love with you. Come at once. Stiffy at the ready*"

"Promise me you won't do that," Eleanor said. "It's all right for you guys, you eye each other up and... whammo!"

"Well, I realise it's a bit unromantic but I can arrange —"

"He'd despise me for a slut... it's different for women."

"I don't see why." The phone on his desk rang as he spoke. "These differences are all in the mind. Hello!"

Eleanor started up from her sofa but Grenville pulled faces at her and shook his head. She moved over to the windows, sighing to try and ease the lovesick feeling under her ribs.

"Who was that?" she asked, when the call ended.

"About Gerald. Old friend from the San Francisco leather-bar scene. His friend Caspar has just died of some horrible cancer thing. Gerry is in a bit of a state. He's in London, wanting a holiday from it all. Everybody over the pond is ill, it seems. Like a deadly flu epidemic."

Eleanor looked out of the balcony doors. The evenings were drawing in. Orange street lamps lit the yellowing leaves of the plane trees in the square and cast restless shadows through the railings and over the parked cars and wet pavements.

Grenville's voice came from the other side of the darkening room,

"Gerry's staying at the Clive and Ozzie ménage in Camden. They want us to go over. I think Clive and Ozzie and co. want a bit of moral support. Apparently Gerry just goes on and on and on about people he knows and their illnesses and symptoms... ulcerated throats, infections, blotchy things. Ugh!"

Grenville got up and turned lights on round the room. The view outside the window was replaced by a dark mirror.

"At my birthday party," Eleanor said, "I really thought, you know, I really got the idea Theo... I was sure. But you can't tell with men. I was reading an article, *Men are*

*Mutants*, in some scientific magazine, at the dentist's. It was all about biological differences and right and left hemispheres and men and women being fundamentally different. But why does different always have to mean inferior? That's what I want to know."

"Because —" Grenville broke off, "Eleanor! Have you no sense of history? Oh God, I really mustn't get into a discussion. I must write this bloody, bloody article but, in short, you women should just get on with it. Like those splendid hoydens of yore who burned their bras and ran about naked, shouting at policemen and sticking flowers down gun barrels —"

"They were embarrassing," Eleanor made a face.

"Yes! Yes! *Yes!* Absolutely! Wasn't it good. They were *brilliant*. But then they took to whingeing. They should have done what we poofters did. Organized 'tart-liberation' marches or something. Slut pride! Got women to wear *Glad To Be A Slag* T-shirts. Poor Caspar. He was a great old campaigner, you know? Would have died for the gay cause. Nearly did. Always getting beaten up. And Gerry. Used to be so positive but now it's all whingeing and conspiracy theories and paranoia."

There was a hammering on the front door.

Eleanor threw off her shawl and put her hands to her hair. As she rushed past Grenville, she saw him with his eyes crossed, his tongue out and his hand wanking the air. She shoved two fingers up at him and heard him hoot as she ran down the stairs to open the door.

It was Ollie, dirty and wet.

"What am I to say about this?" Grenville appealed to Ollie as soon as he entered the room. "Oh, the *boredom!*

Christ! I've only written two sentences. Both in pomodegook."

Ollie sat on the edge of Grenville's desk and blinked. He did not speak.

"Perhaps I'll ignore the topic altogether. Perhaps my silence might come as a refreshing change," Grenville went on. "I've tried following my golden rule: *whatever the topic, find the erogenous zone and bang on about it.* But I admit defeat."

"Why don't you explain —?" Eleanor said.

"Never try to explain anything," Grenville interrupted. "No use arguing with history. *Now* is what matters."

"Shall I make another joint?" she suggested.

Ollie turned his head towards her, like an owl.

"Nope!" Grenville slapped the desk making Ollie flinch. "Spoils the writing! Lose control. Don't like weed. Idiotic stuff for hippies. Charlie's the thing. Could do with a line right now. Get this dreadful thing written. Ollie? How soon?"

"Ten minutes if you give me the money." Ollie got off the desk. "I can score from the Havana on the other side of the square or maybe..." He scratched himself as he spoke in his junkie mumble, "...if you give me the money. Cash."


Eleanor reckoned Ollie would do a runner with the money but he came back. Giving Grenville a wrap he went over to a sofa, muttering,

"Got a little dab of something for myself."

Rather than watch Ollie stabbing around, searching for a vein at the back of his knees, Eleanor left for the kitchen to make a pot of tea. She returned to offer some to Ollie and Grenville.

"Don't interrupt, old fruit," Grenville waved her away. "Changing lives, *that's* what it's all about. Catch their souls by the tail!"

He poised his hands over the typewriter like a cartoon concert pianist. "Onwards and upwards!"

As Eleanor retreated to her attic, she heard the rattle of Grenville's typewriter and his voice calling out,

"God! I'm fucking brilliant!"

# THRASH

"Great party!" Troy screamed at Eleanor above the pounding music. The ballroom throbbed with sound. Waving arms and painted faces flickered in the coloured lights that swept over the crowded arena. Temporary scaffolding with steps had been constructed round the room, providing viewing galleries, platforms for exhibitionists and a stage for the band or DJ. The room had been cleared by pushing the furniture into shadowy dens underneath the platforms. Leaning over the scaffolding balustrades, Eleanor was with those resting, cruising, watching the dancers below and taking note of who disappeared with who into the dark lairs under the decks. The ballroom reminded her of a classical amphitheatre, where the laws of everyday life are suspended. Just that at this party, there was no difference between actors and audience: nearly everyone wore masks and costumes and was in the performers' state of rapture.

Eleanor had dressed in *travesti* as principal boy. She felt great. Only in this enchanted world of Grenville's could she make friends with strangers and give in to her love of extraordinary sights and sounds.

Vivid impressions registered like night scenes lit by flashes of lightening... Grenville, stripped to the waist, dyed-gold hair gleaming in the lights, weaving through a line of sailorboys in white. Emerald, raising a hooped skirt to reveal bright red pubic hair shaved into the shape of a Valentine heart. Frankie, stark naked except for fairy wings held on by a harness of studded leather straps and Getraud dressed as a Victorian child. Some were transformed by feathered masks, extravagant hats and heavy makeup. Others were faceless in leather, rubber, or leopard skin hoods but with the forbidden parts of the body exposed to view. Both girls and boys paraded in exotic frocks or dressed as cowboys, executioners, slaves or in travesties of uniform. Many of the famous were instantly recognizable but some wanted anonymity. Eleanor felt like one of the naughty cherubs on the ballroom ceiling as she peeped down from the gallery and tried to guess the identities of the deeply disguised.

"*Who* is that!" came a yell from one side of her.

"Don't recognize that bum at all," shouted Eleanor.

"Just boring old Bruno!" the boys on either side of her screamed in stereo as the masked dancer in the spotlight turned round, "Best party tinsel on the end of his todger!"

Eleanor felt her ankle being pulled. She saw Marty, in scarlet satin, beckoning her down. He reached out for her and as she dropped into his arms he shouted,

"Time you got stuck in, kid!"

They danced to a punk classic.

Marty looked fabulous, Eleanor could see. He stood square shouldered, flat chested and narrow hipped, sheathed in a tight, high-necked dress. Tonight, he'd left off the wig and his spiky blond hair, bright makeup and earrings gave the impression of a streamlined, irridescent insect.

When the band finished their set, the spotlight swung round to the disco and onto a figure in white who flowed like quicksilver onto the platform and took the mike from the DJ.

"Darlings..." he breathed.

"Wooh!" the crowd called back.

"We want a little glamour now, don't we?" There was a roar from the dance floor in which No! Yes! and laughter were mixed together.

"Gorgeous!" the tall star put his arm round the DJ who was adjusting the turntable. "Let us break free! Give us some *schmaltz*, darling! Some magic? Some romance, ple-eeze!" There were groans, cheers and more laughter from the dance floor as the strutting, swooping rhythms of a 70's hit came over the sound system. The dancers swayed or larked about but Marty shouted,

"Can you Tango?"

"Sort of," Eleanor nodded, puzzled.

"C'mon then. We're dressed for it... wrong way round but who cares!"

As they danced together Eleanor said,

"How come you do this, Marty!"

"Mum and Dad met at Ballroom dancing... mad about it. N'you?"

"Forced! To improve my 'deportment'. Hated it!"

"You're good, though!" Marty found her light and responsive to his lead.

Eleanor realised that they had been given the floor and the spotlight. She stared into Marty's eyes and said through her teeth,

"We are being watched by some of the most famous performers in the world. Oh God!"

"So what! They are so fucking stoned they'd be thrilled with dancing gerbils."

"This is so naff!" she hissed in his ear.

162

"It's our fifteen seconds of fame, doll. Bet we look great!" Marty just managed to keep a straight face.

"I can't do this."

"Course you can. This is a beautiful moment."

When the music finished the crowd clapped and cheered and forgot them. The party closed in and swept on.

Theo arrived late. Too sober, refusing to wear any kind of fancydress and with a dislike of dancing, he didn't know where to begin. He felt stirred by the sight of two leather-clad, bare-breasted women kissing and watched fascinated as one tweaked the rings of the other's pierced nipples. He looked away just in time to see Eleanor making for him through the crush.

"Theo!" she cried. "You look miserable!"

"I am! Grenville *insisted* I come but I'm not enjoying it —"

"I've had enough now, I must say! But my room is being used so I'm stuck with it."

"Do you want a break?" Theo looked at his watch, "We could go out to —" Eleanor saw Theo want to cancel the invitation as he took in her appearance.

"I'd love to escape!" she put her hand on his arm. "Will you wait while I go and change?"

He nodded.

Some rooms were closed off but Eleanor's attic gave onto the fire escape and had to be left unlocked at partytime. For a big event like this she was used to packing up and moving into her dressing room. She made for it now, picking her way through the people sprawled up the staircases.

163

Once inside, Eleanor transformed herself from Prince to Beauty in a moment. Wiping off the face makeup, the moon and stars patches and bright red lipstick left a fresh bare skin and lips to be redone in a subdued, neutral shade. The tight leggings, black jacket, buckled boots and wristbands were replaced with a simple dress and shoes. Her hair remained tied back... that could come down later, to good effect.

She grabbed her shoulder bag, tipped out pencils, *A to Z*, notepads and replaced them with her contraceptive kit, toothbrush and clean knickers. She scribbled a note for Grenville and bulldog-clipped it onto the mirror. Snatching her coat off the hanger, she checked that she had her purse and keys, turned the light off and locked the door again.

All the time she fretted that Theo would have changed his mind or been lured away by sirens offering zipless fun. Sure enough, a pretty but pissed tranny was chatting him up,

"Oi!" Eleanor put her hands on her hips. "C'mon, sister. This is my date!"

"Lola 's jus keeping'm warm f'yew."

Theo turned to Eleanor as Lola lurched away with a flip of her boa.

"This really is *not* my scene." He smoothed down his rumpled hair.

"Let's go then."


They were soon settled in a favourite club of Theo's where food and drink were served late.

"I don't know what possessed me to go to that party. Grenville was very insistent. But I just don't find those trashy people attractive or interesting. Anyway," Theo leaned across the table and looked at her, "I don't regret it, since I've come away with first prize."

Eleanor smiled at him, pleased with this hint.

"I suppose I thought it might bring me out of myself," Theo went on. "Take my mind off things —"

Eleanor took the chance for intimacy.

"What's on your mind?" she asked.

Theo talked about his work and his ageing parents. After the meal and as they were leaving the dining room, Eleanor made a speech she'd prepared,

"Well, I want to ask you back for coffee and Mozart, Theo, but I think all we'd get is poppers and punk."

"Do you want to go back to the party?"

"Not one bit! And —" Eleanor looked up at him. "I'm homeless till tomorrow. My room is full of ravers..."

As he helped her on with her coat, Theo said, "I have very good coffee at my flat. Or more soothing bedtime drinks if you prefer. Hot chocolate? All kinds of tea... herbal... fruity..."

"Ordinary? Straight?" Eleanor wanted to know.

"Buckets of it." Theo took her hand. "Let's get a taxi."


## AFTER

"Pussycat, pussycat, where have you been? Ho, ho!" Grenville, who was stacking boxes at the far end of the ballroom, took Eleanor's note out of his pocket and waved it in the air. "Naughty Nelly Nails some Nookie! Come now, tell the girls! Did you get your man?"

Eleanor had come back from Theo's to the usual scene of day-after devastation. The house had emptied out but there were some stragglers, some too drugged, drunk or hungover to be moved and some who, having nowhere better to go, were scrounging for afternoon breakfast. And as usual, the mates who could, had come back to help clear up and have a gossip about the party.

David was leaning on a broom, reading the Sunday papers he'd laid out on a table near the balcony doors. He looked up and said to Eleanor,

"We're debriefing."

"Y'know, talking about who got their knickers off!" Tinker called out.

"And remembering the big party of professional gatecrashers and *celebtitties* who had to be turned away —"

"I missed that. Tell us what happened," Eleanor said.

"Grenville was being terribly polite and reasonable... and long winded," David acted Grenville's posh manners. "Till Baptiste strutted past him onto the landing, cracking his knuckles and shouting, *Ah'm de Big Black Bouncer from Brixton an Ah'm bored wid dis!*"

Baptiste, slouched in an armchair, studying the financial pages of his newspaper, waved his hand and drawled in his real voice,

"They all melted away like ice cubes in the sun, my dear."

"Like you did," Grenville pointed at David and Baptiste, "when the police turned up."

"What happened?" Eleanor looked worried.

"Nothing," Grenville yawned. "They were very civil... *could you turn the sound down now please sir* and so on. Fortunately no one mistook them for fetishists. Now we want to hear about you, ducky."

Eleanor was telling how Theo had said, *I hope I can look forward to doing this again...* when she put her hands to her head and remembered, "Like a wet wellie, all I could think to say was, *yes please!*"

"Why didn't you say, 'Yes! See you tomorrow'?"

"Because it *is* tomorrow, if you see what I mean."

Grenville groaned.

"I know, I know, I've made a mess of it, haven't I?" Eleanor addressed the company, "Us'll feel like a blooming wallflower now..." She liked providing a comic turn. "I'll be in a misery of *waiting*. Will he? Won't he? Was it a one night stand, or what?"

"Such quaint hetero customs. Don't fret, my pet, if we haven't heard from the blister by next weekend, I'll ring him up, invite him round, hint at a juicy commission or something. Although beats me what you see in the pompous fart."

"Prodigious equipment, perhaps?" Baptiste said, turning a page of his paper.

"Yes! Yes, this must be the reason for your preposterous infatuation," Grenville said. "Is he huge? Of priapic proportions! Do tell!"

"No!"

"What then?" he insisted. "Come on, Nelly!"

"He's very nice. Very comfortable. Leave off, will you!"

Eleanor poked out her tongue and flounced away, leaving them all laughing.

When she'd changed, Eleanor went back downstairs to help with the clearing up. Already, quite a lot had been done: wine glasses and ashtrays washed and boxed, ready for return. The sound systems, the boyband and their gear were all gone. Hire firms would come and dismantle the scaffolding and lights tomorrow. Sofas, armchairs and a coffee table, cleared of party mess, were being brought out from under the scaffolding. The large table could not be moved as Ollie was asleep under it. Grenville had covered him with a blanket and wouldn't let him be disturbed. Yasmine had brought two enormous bags of her own freshly made muffins and was suggesting that it was time for a break. Eleanor volunteered to make tea but as she left for the kitchen, she turned and said,

"Some girly boys I've never seen before in my life, seem to have taken up residence in my room and I don't want to seem, y'know, all uptight and *boojwahr* but do you think one of you could move them on for me, like? I'm not in the mood to deal with strangers."

"Oh, I love strangers," David grinned. "As long as they are not armed fanatics or angry soldiers. After all, my dear, without strangers, what would we do for sex! Hm?" David rubbed his hands. "I'll do this favour for Eleanor if you all promise I won't miss any malicious gossip."

"O yes!" Yasmine said. "We tell all porno gossips about you, David, soon as you turn back your behind. Maybe we ring porno papers and dish the beans, eh?"

"Not even in jest Yasmine, please," David looked serious.

"Pouf! End of world-famous journo, eh!" She chopped the air in front of David's face. He put up his hands, as if taken prisoner,

"My career would be unaffected, it would be my family who'd be most hurt... my wife, the —"

"Shush!" Yasmine shook his arm. "What for you take me! You think the Witch is a traitor for my friend? Never! Eh! Never!" she patted David's cheek before turning to Eleanor,

"Come, we go and boil tea for the stupid poofties."

In the kitchen Eleanor found herself being nagged by Yasmine about work,

"Whatfor you do skivvy jobs, eh? In the sweaty shops?" Yasmine had found out that, at the moment, Eleanor was working in one of the big national theatre and opera companies' own in-house costume workshops. "Pah! they are driving slavers. Is waste of you. Time you make own 'shop. We are not competition. You like the history costume. History is porno. I like the pretty-pretty make beliefs."

"And where do I get the money to set up, Yasmine?"

"Grenville! Like he give to me for the starters."

"And how did you pay it back? I mean, I know you're the best, Yasmine, but there's no money in costume making. Nobody's ever heard of us, outside our little world. We're never even mentioned in the credits…"

Yasmine ignored this and stroked Eleanor's neck, saying,

"The Witch not pay back. Grenville give to me the moneys. He like for me to take. To be Mistress…"

Eleanor shook her head as she put clean mugs on a tray but Yasmine went on,

"Yes, yes he give for you the moneys. You his little lamb, eh?… his pet cabbage."

"I want to get into *designing*. But I don't want to take Grenville's money. It doesn't feel right. It would muddy the waters."

"Then what for you have this new boyfriend?" Yasmine murmured in Eleanor's ear, "Theo? He give you the moneys. The muddy-muddy not matter with him." Yasmine smoothed Eleanor's hair. "Tell me soon you wind him up the little fingers, this Theo, eh?"

Eleanor sighed and moved away to make the tea.

Her attic was clear. Eleanor unlocked the storerooms, filled a bucket of suds and as she washed the floor, Tinker's street-urchin face appeared at the top of the stairs,

"Aw, I hate vomit, don't you, El? Don't mind piss, shit and everyfink but vom! *Eugh*, Gawd!"

"Don't like snot either," said Eleanor.

"Nah, don't mind snot but vom! Turns my stomach. You done the worst, aint yer. Lemme start on the roof. Loads of glasses and mess out here." He'd brought a box and a binliner. "Oooh, bit of a naughty scene up here last night!" he giggled. "And then everyone pissing into the drainpipes. You finished with that bucket, El? Better wash down out here or it'll stink like a tramp's trousers."

Tinker kept up his usual stream of cockney patter as he busied himself on the roof. He was Grenville's latest "find" and referred to as Tinker-Belle the Stepney Fairy.

Grenville was not interested in people's histories but Eleanor liked to listen. Tinker had told her the usual renter's tale. The details varied but the plot was nearly always the same, she reckoned: Act I *Disorder and Violence*, Act II *Rejection and Runaway*, Act III *Drugs and Death*. When Tinker's nan had died he'd had to go back to his mam. She and her new boyfriend had actually locked him out when he was fourteen. He'd come home from school one day, to find two bags of his clothes outside the front door and the locks changed. It had made Eleanor feel sympathy for him and toned down her angry feelings about her family. They'd not done that. Nowhere near. She'd not spent time with people screaming and hitting her and throwing things either.

"There you go, then. All done. I'll take the rubbish down for you El. I want another of them cakes, wot they called?"

"Muffins."

"Yeah. Musn't let Yasmine catch me. Though her bark's worse'n her bite, innit?"

"Tell her you're hungry and she'll give you a plateful."

"Speak to the Witch, y'mean? Dunno as I got the bottle f'that!" Tinker rolled his eyes and vanished down the stairs.

Though grateful for his help, Eleanor was relieved when he'd gone as he never stopped talking and she wanted to be alone, inside herself, with Theo.

Now her room was cleaned up, there was not much more to do. She stripped off the cover from the mattress and took away the plastic sheet she'd put underneath.

She was sure Theo liked her. He'd said so.

After bringing out her bedding and pillows from the storecupboard and remaking her bed, she returned her lamp, clock, books and trinkets to the bedside table. She ran Theo's words through again... *you are very lovely... such delightful company*. And when he'd kissed her goodbye... *I enjoyed that very much*. Re-living Theo's kiss made a sudden space open up under her ribs.

It was getting dark but Eleanor had left the firedoor open for the evening breeze. Already, autumn leaves from the trees in the square were blowing over the parapet and round the chimneys. She watched them lift, spin and settle in a corner of the flat roof. Eleanor stepped out to look at the twilight sky over the city. It was a clear, neon green scored with pink lines of jet vapour.

She longed to impress Theo, earn his approval.

Lovemaking had been a bit jittery the first time. So desperate to please him, she'd had to fake it a bit. Too nervous to come. But this morning had been perfect...

Theo's place was so quiet and tidy, the rooms decorated in cool shades of grey and ivory. Half dressed, they had breakfasted on warm croissants and freshly made coffee. Theo had opened the blinds onto a view of Kensington Gardens and they had watched the distant panorama of the park: tiny figures jogging, strolling, walking the dog in the silence beyond the double glazing.

Eleanor ducked back into her attic, closed the firedoor and, leaving the lamp off, lay down on her fresh, clean bed.

Yes, when they'd woken up, everything had been relaxed and sleepy and Theo more familiar. She'd agonized over him for weeks. Waited, hankered, fantasised about him wanting her. Having her. And this morning it had all come true...

Eleanor closed her eyes. Her body plummeted as she replayed Theo's caresses and his tightening grip.

Distant noises came from downstairs. She heard the scrape of a pan lid, Tinker's whooping laugh, the loo flush and Grenville's voice calling *so glad you enjoyed my thrash!* Then came the good-byes and the sound of people leaving. The party was over.

# Three months later

i

## HIDING

It had been yet another evening of people in crowded rooms straining to be heard above the sound of their own voices. The director, cast, crew and friends had been celebrating after a film premiere. As she waited with Grenville while David rang for a taxi, Eleanor saw that Grenville was drunk. This depressed her. Over the past months he'd got more and more difficult. He seemed to be on a diet of pills and tranquillizers. To make him sleep, he said. She'd lost count of the times she'd asked him *what's wrong, love? Is it something I've done?* But he was just mardy and hurtful with her all the time. So unlike him. He didn't even tease her about being loopy over Theo. No *ho ho* or anything. She missed her old Grenville... full of himself, open and chatty, sharing his troubles, always her best friend. Was he just going through a bad patch? Was it something she'd done? She'd tried asking Yasmine, who waved it all away and ticked her off for *porno gossips*. Maybe, after five years, Grenville wanted her to push off. Theo had said she could move in with him...

"I got a bit bored with them all wandering about in that forest..." Leaning back in the taxi, David talked about the film. "Wanting to know the meaning of life? That's a hiding to nothing."

"What *issa* hiding to nothing?" Grenville turned a glassy look towards David. "What *hiding* 'sacly? Monly innerested if iss to do with floggin 'n flagellation. Bugger. Mma bit drunk." He grabbed the strap at the side of his head to steady himself. "Damn, don' like wooz... woo-oo!" The taxi took a corner. "World swirls bout 'l over the place." His hand slipped through the looped grip and dangled by its wrist in midair. "Out of control." He struggled to sit upright while handcuffed to the roof of the taxi. "N'point wanning to know meaning uv life. Like wanning to know what buff'los do on Sundays."

"That's easy," said David. "They do what they do the rest of the week. Eat grass... rut... you know, buffalo about. Not very interesting."

"Except ruttin."

"Except rutting."

"Buh meaning of life, David... that *is* inneresting, a'shally."

Grenville's trapped hand flapped infront of his face and he looked at it, annoyed, as if it didn't belong to him.

"Yes, but as you said yourself, it's not a sensible question."

"Like... what?" Grenville lurched forward and remained with his mouth open.

"Like what 'what'?" David asked.

"Like *wassa* sens'ble question?" Grenville quibbled but David yawned and didn't bother to answer.

They travelled in silence till Grenville, still trying to free himself from the strap, shouted,

"Where's the next shag coming from? Shagging! Thas the meaning of life, ol' boy."

The taxi braked suddenly and pitched David onto Eleanor.

"D'you want to shag Enelah?" offered Grenville, giggling.

"I'm a devoted husband, Grenville, I don't go with other women," David said, unsmiling. "That *would* be infidelity. Not that Eleanor doesn't have her attractions."

This last remark was addressed to Grenville, not to her, Eleanor noticed. They were treating her like a piece of goods. Sitting opposite them on the fold-down seat, she felt left out. Belittled. For the first time since meeting Grenville, resentment rippled over the surface of her love for him.

"S'what does the wifey think of your naughty beanos with the boys?" Grenville dug David in the ribs.

"Arrested development, I shouldn't wonder. We never discuss it."

"Does she know?" Grenville demanded.

"I'm not going to babble about my wife with you, Grenville," David said.

"Bet you lie to her. Marriage! Mog... nomony! Heterosoc... 's all about lies."

"Learning to lie and be lied to, is an essential part of family life. Of growing up. Of friendship. Lying in public office, now, *that's* a very different matter —"

"S'all lies... lies... women. Don' likem. Don' like any of it. All too foggy for me."

Eleanor looked out of the taxi window and wished she was going home to Theo.

After a meal and back at the house, Grenville seemed to sober up but he gave no sign that he wanted Eleanor's company. He would soon disappear up to his bedroom and shut the door. Time was, they would have gone into the kitchen, made hot drinks and with him sounding off, drifted into the ballroom to sit in the lamplight, gossiping about the film and the premiere and who he'd pulled into the bogs for a shag.

There was no point going to the ballroom now... too big and lonely and anyway Ollie seemed to have become a permanent resident, watching television all day from a repulsive nest of greasy blankets under the table. She remembered that huge table being brought in by crane over the balcony and how she'd been amazed at Grenville's driving determination to have what he wanted and at his energy for the work needed to realise his visions. Things had changed.

She was depressed by Ollie and wished he would go. He did nothing except watch television. He hardly spoke and his clothes looked as if they had been handed out, regardless of fit, size or colour, at a charity shop. His teeth were bad, his skin waxy and he never stopped scratching. He was contaminating Grenville with his junkie passivity.

176

As Eleanor waited for the kettle to boil, Grenville came to the kitchen for some coffee. She knew it was not the time to challenge him but felt too fed up to be sensible. She needed to assert herself,

"Grenville, is Ollie supplying you with drugs?"

"No. Well, charlie... occasionally. Bit of speed. But no. You know I don't much like drugs... booze. Awful this evening. Can't *bear* all that woozy... loss of control and so on. Why d'you ask?"

"Why is Ollie here all the time? I thought perhaps he had some hold over you."

"Not at all. Poor old Ollie."

"How did he get into this state?" Eleanor said. "He went to school with you, his family must be rolling in money."

"They are. Were. His parents, dear old Fleur and Bungo, died in a crash. Ol inherited a fortune... blew it all on friends, handouts, good times for all."

"What a waste."

"Waste of *what*, exactly?" Grenville snapped at her.

"He has no reason to take drugs —"

"That you know of. And now he has no reason *not* to."

"But love, why does he have to live *here*? Why do *you* have to take him in? He's thieving from you. He's past feeling grateful or caring about you or feeling anything for anyone —"

"We've both been sentenced —"

"I mean, why don't you just go down to cardboard city —" Eleanor, feeling confused and jealous let her voice rise in sarcasm "— and just ask them *all* to come and doss down in the ballroom. Eh?"

"Because it is *Ollie* who shared his Caramac with me on my first night at prep school —" Grenville gazed into the bottom of his cup, "— when I was seven and more wretched than I'd ever been before in my life. And he was the first person I ever wanked. That's why. And now, old fruit, if you don't mind..."

Grenville put down his cup and left the kitchen.

Sometime in the night, Eleanor woke up to the sound of shouting. She got out of bed and crept down the staircases till she had a view of the lower landing. She crouched and peered through the banisters. Grenville and a man she had never seen before were scuffling and arguing while a boy in jeans seemed to be crying. Was it Tinker? Grenville was trying to defend the boy but Eleanor was in time to see the stranger hit the lad. The boy cried out and put his arms up round his head. Eleanor couldn't make him out.

As she started down the stairs Grenville turned his furious face towards her. He was not wearing any mask or disguise but she did not recognize him. His eyes glittered and his face was set hard. His mouth opened,

"Get out!"

She ran back to her room and stumbled into bed, pulling up the covers for protection, panting and trembling like a child after a nightmare. But there was no one to come and tell her that it was only a bad dream. For a moment, a door had opened onto the wide landscape of human misery. She closed her eyes against it but the sound of the slap, the cry, the way the boy's head had jerked to one side when he was hit, would not be cancelled. She wanted to help, to know what was going on but Grenville was out of reach. She wished she could get up, get dressed and escape from the house. But where to go, at this hour? She thought of Theo and his life of order, of Yasmine and Sandra and the comfort always on offer there.

Eventually the voices calmed down and became muffled. There was coming and going. Doors slammed. Tense and shivering, she put on extra clothes and taking her smokes, went out onto the roof. It was cold but away from the disturbance below. She sat with her back against a chimney, rocking herself. The sky was its usual midnight yellow and Eleanor's imagination spread out underneath it, ranging over a city full of people in despair.

Sometime later she went back to bed and had a go at reading but couldn't concentrate even though the house had gone quiet. Turning the light off she tried to relax but needed to eat and make a hot drink to ease the sour grip of misery in her stomach. Raising herself up in the darkness, she listened. From the distance came the slow, rhythmic crack and cry of Grenville being whipped.

Eleanor curled up and hid under the bedclothes. Childhood terrors ballooned under her ribs. Pressing her hands over her ears, she shut herself in with her own heartbeat.

# A year later

## ONWARDS

"And what's Grenville up to these days?" Gail asked with a wink before pouring some tea and adding hot water to the pot. "Is he worried about this 'gay plague' thing, though?" she added, fetching milk and a jar of pureed vegetables from the fridge.

"Well," Eleanor answered from the floor, gently detaching little Lucy's hand from her earring, "I haven't seen much of him lately, since moving in with Theo. My life's a bit of a whirlwind *ad the boment.*" Lucy had grabbed Eleanor's nose. Eleanor widened her eyes and raspberried into the little fist. Lucy chortled,

"Agum!" she ordered, slapping Eleanor's face and hair with both her hands.

"Now then, Madam!" Gail lifted Lucy off Eleanor who got up and sat at the table.

Lucy struggled and complained, kicking her legs against her mother.

"Ooh! What's this then?" Gail distracted her with the parcel Eleanor had brought, tastefully wrapped with a hand-painted label. She settled Lucy with it on a rug among her cushions and toys. "We've got about four minutes to catch up on each other while she's busy unwrapping your pressie. Tell me about the whirlwind!"

"These last months at Theo's —"

"Classy! Me and Zeb did the plasterwork on his place. One of our first jobs and how we got to do Grenville's ballroom. I mean, Grenville's gaff is fantastic but in a grotty area. Theo's? Dead posh part of town! Surprised you come slumming it out here, girl!"

"Don't be daft! You've made this lovely." Eleanor looked round the kitchen-living room of Gail and Zeb's ground-floor flat in Putney, admiring the ragrolled walls, the stencilled cupboards, Gail's bright paintings and handcrafted cushions. Patchwork curtains were closed against the cold December evening and the gas fire and lamps made a warm light.

"You were never afraid of colour!" Eleanor said and they chuckled together as Gail looked down at her pink dungarees and orange shirt. "That's a gorgeous finish on the walls too, the yellow's perfect, such a hard colour to get right. And you've finished the mirror frame —"

"I used shellac over cutouts. Horrible stuff to work with but I wanted that, you know, muted antique look. It's all I've done. Lucy's such a full time job, somehow, and nobody told me I'd be knackered all the time. I'm in bed by nine!"

Lucy had finished tearing the paper off a red velvet dinosaur Eleanor had made and having taken it by the tail was beating it on the floor like a hammer. Then

182

the head with its sequinned eyes disappeared into her mouth.

"Me, I'm really into this decor thing," Eleanor said, "Theo's buying a listed wreck in the country so —"

Gail crouched by Lucy. Picking up a plastic ring she waved it in front of her. Lucy dropped the dinosaur and reached for the ring. Gail returned to the table with the soft toy and its dangerous eyes.

"So me and Theo, we find this place in a village," Eleanor went on, "The Old Rectory. It's not far, less than an hour out of London on the train and we're going to do it up."

Lucy had crawled over the carpet and pulled herself upright by Gail's chair.

"Theo will keep on with his practice in town. Keep the money coming in! And I will be set designer and site foreman like, out at the Old Rectory."

"That's excellent!" Gail said, "Make sure it's the sort of place where there's work for Zeb —" Lucy yanked Gail's clothes and whined to be lifted up. "Your Theo puts lots of work our way. He's ever so good to work for, none of this not getting paid for ages. Not like some, who don't seem to realise *we've* got a mortgage to pay n'all —"

Gail lifted Lucy onto her lap and went on,

"Things have got hard for people like us, what with London house prices going through the roof —" Lucy was patting her mother's face and trying to cover Gail's mouth with her hands, "— alright for the estate agents who want to play Monopoly and those yuppies who buy shares and fiddle funny-money in the City —" Gail dodged her head from side to side, evading Lucy's jealous little hands, "— but we need somewhere to *live*. The blooming mortgage is like a rock round our necks!"

Gail just managed to finish what she was saying by holding Lucy's wrists and leaning round her. Lucy started shouting with fury.

"Alright darlin'! Alright! Shall we get some dindins, eh? Look!" Gail had got up with Lucy in her arms and fetched a plastic bowl and spoon. She strapped Lucy into a highchair and put a bib on her. "We could have a *mansion* in Cardiff, near Zeb's family, for what this hole cost. But the *work* is in London, so…" Gail shrugged.

Lucy clattered the bowl and spoon together and chewed her bib while Gail quickly warmed some mush and put dilute juice and water into a beaker.

"Are *you* working at all?" Eleanor asked.

"Not much. I want to be with Lucy, don't I. I step in when Zeb needs an assistant and we can save the wages. But it's swings and roundabouts. Paying a minder would take the money I'd earn if I worked."

Gail spooned food into Lucy's mouth while Lucy banged her beaker on the table, sprinkling juice over a wide area. Eleanor was amazed at the mess but even more impressed by Gail accepting it.

"Aaah! Here comes Thomas, choo-choo-choo!" Gail angled a spoon at Lucy's mouth. "When she was tiny, Zeb wanted to take her to work in a sling but I wouldn't have it. All that dust and fumes and God knows what! Course things is better for women than what they was in our Mum's day but just you wait till you have a kid, mate. I warn you, it's back to the Dark Ages — wham! What are you working on?"

"I've been having driving lessons and running about with Theo, house hunting… I'm having such a good time, I can't tell you!"

"Ooh, you little pickle you!" Lucy had grown tired of her mush and had blown a mouthful out, spattering Gail with carrot puree.

"Good thing you're wearing an orange shirt, Gail! Doesn't show... *much!*"

Lucy clapped her hands and smeared mush through her hair as the women laughed.

Once Lucy was cleaned up, she was sat in Eleanor's lap. She was contented after her meal and showed Eleanor her farm animal picture book, patting it and turning the board pages this way and that. The two of them mooed, baa'd and quacked while Gail cleared away and began to prepare supper.

Then Lucy fell silent and sat still. She flushed and made grunty sounds.

"I think a certain small person has been busy..." Eleanor said. "There's a very warm *pong* sitting on my lap, now."

Gail came over, lifted Lucy up and rubbed noses with her. "Pooh!" Gail grinned. Lucy ran a hand inside her mother's shirt to feel a breast.

"Who dat!" Gail said as a key was heard in the lock, "Who dat! Hey?"

Lucy put her arms above her head and turned towards the door.

"Dah!" she shouted as Zeb came in, bringing a blast of cold air from the lobby.

Gail kissed his cheek and Eleanor said "hello" but he only had eyes for his child.

"Hello Scrumptious!" he crooned, bending his head down for Lucy to grab his knitted hat and pull it off, leaving his hair standing on end. She dropped the hat on the floor before pulling off her Dad's gloves and scarf.

"You're just in time," Gail said to him as he hung up his coat and slung his bag to the floor. "Scrumptious needs a nappy change."

Zeb took Lucy and nodded towards Eleanor,

"How are you, Ellie, alright?" Then he spoke over his shoulder to Gail who was taking the empty sandwich box and thermos out of his bag, "Gone six, is it? Might as well give Lulu her bath now she's done a poo."

Zeb stepped over the childgate and carried Lucy through their workroom into the bathroom. Soon the sound of splashing and gurgling drew Gail from the kitchen.

Left alone, Eleanor took over. Tying on an apron, she finished putting on the rice and vegetables, laid the table and opened the wine she'd brought. Zeb preferred beer. She drew out a six-pack from her bag and an expensive fruit flan bought from a patisserie in Queensway. Grenville had shown her that shop, years ago.

She'd been invited for supper but had taken Gail's hint about their early bedtime and as she gathered up toys from the floor into baskets, decided to leave after the meal and the washing up. Sitting back on her haunches she looked round with her theatre designer's eye. It was a tight little set, a bit like the inside of the toybox in *Petroushka* as it might be decorated by those Bloomsbury artists that she and Grenville disagreed about. Zeb was handy, he'd made all the cupboards and the fire surround and Gail, even now, had found the time to make the gold wire and tissue Christmas decorations that hung out of Lucy's reach.

Eleanor brooded on how she'd always envied them. True, they were exhausted and money was a big worry but they had each other: someone to work with, and they had Lucy: someone to do it all for. Eleanor shuffled across the floor and peeped through the bars of the childgate.

Framed by the distant doorway she could see Gail on the loo seat, elbows on knees, resting her tired head on her hands. Zeb, stripped to his vest, was kneeling by the bath which had been panelled in wood and painted with waves and sea creatures. Above the smiling dolphins, Lucy's head and shoulders could be seen. She was holding the side of the bath with one plump hand and pushing a wet sponge into Zeb's face with the other.

Eleanor looked in on them. It makes a lovely picture, she thought as it printed itself on her hopes for her future with Theo.

## PUNTERS

She'd not been this nervous since exams at school. For two days, dread had coiled tight under her breathing. Eleanor saw it as a test, never mind Theo's denials,

"It's just a few smart people I owe dinners to and some prospective clients. There's no need to fuss, Eleanor," he'd said. "If you can't manage it, I'll take them out but I must say I would prefer to entertain them here. These rich American types really appreciate being welcomed into one's house and given home cooking, specially after weeks of hotels and airport lounges." He'd persuaded her. "Besides what better way for them to get an idea of my style than to come to my home." That had clinched it.

Over the last two days, she'd shopped and prepared the food. The place was immaculate, there were fresh flowers in the hall and sitting room and she knew what she was going to wear.

But then she'd gone to lay the table and realised there was a problem. Her experience of posh hotels was minimal and her home life had not taught her how to set out a three-course dinner with cheese board, wines, dessert wines... Living with Grenville hadn't helped at all. There had never been any proper sets of anything. It was the luck of the draw there, anything from canteen plastic to Jacobean silver with the family crest. She looked at Theo's cutlery in its velvet-lined cases. Three kinds of knives. Bread knives? Fruit knives? Which was which? Same with the spoons... pointy ones, round ones and *four* different sizes and what were the forks with the wide outer prong for? The glassware cabinet was just as bad. What were the tinted glasses for? What to use for water? And flutes. What about them? Should she be putting them out? On the table or on the side? And napkins and bread plates, which side? Her head was full of questions.

And she only had a few hours. No time to go to the library. What sort of book was she after, anyway? Any problem and her mind went to Grenville, straight off. But Grenville wouldn't take her *boojwahr* fix seriously or if he did get interested in the ceremonial he would keep her on the phone with vague theories and barmy suggestions while time trickled away.

Eleanor clenched her teeth. This was why she had gone in for costume. Never wanted to be *in* the theatre. Never wanted to be involved with the nerves and hysteria of footlights and audience and actual performance. What she liked was to be behind the scenes, watching from a safe distance.

But where to get advice and some comfort? Now! Where? Eleanor had a vision of Rajiv. Maitre d' at a posh hotel. She ran into the kitchen and dialled his and Archie's Holland Park number. Nothing. Work number. Got through. He understood. He'd send someone over, no, he'd make time and come himself.

After twenty minutes of fidgeting, Eleanor let Rajiv into the flat and started to babble with stress,

"Oh tell me Rajiv, how did I *ever* let myself in for this? This is not my thing at all. I shall get found out! I feel such a fake!"

Unlike Theo, Rajiv was unembarrassed by her flapping hands and show of feelings,

"No-no-no! It is as you say in the theatre, first-night nerves only. Let us begin. You will feel better." He removed his suit jacket, checked his tiepin and rolled up the sleeves of his shirt. Out of his bag he took a spotless chef's apron, some cloths and a pair of white cotton gloves, asking, "How many people? What have you prepared? Show me." He calmed her with compliments on the menu and the appearance of the dishes, "Do not worry at all. It is balanced, fresh, not too complicated. You have good taste. This is most important."

In the dining room it was her turn to admire Rajiv's quiet confidence and expert handling of everything.

"You've such a talent, you know, cooking, all this... where did you train, love?" Eleanor asked, though she did not stop watching him. She would know exactly what to do next time.

"On the job. My family have always been in the hotel business. It was lucky. I got work straightaway when we arrived in England."

"So where did you come from?" Eleanor found chatting with her old friend calmed her nerves.

"Kampala."

"What part of India is that, then?"

Rajiv laughed softly and shook his head,

"It is in Africa, Ellie!"

"So it is. There I go. Must remember to keep my blooming trap shut, tonight, musn't I. What were your family doing in Africa, though?"

"Running hotels. Till Idi Amin?"

Eleanor nodded. She vaguely remembered it all on the news, years ago.

"Then we had everything taken away from us," he went on, "and we became no better than refugees. Unwanted."

Rajiv said he didn't like talking about childhood and schooldays in Africa. It stirred up memories of friends, first lover and a beloved teacher murdered in the atrocities. Instead, he told her about family in India and his ancestors. Eleanor was fascinated,

"Like Grenville, you know all about your family till way back and back, then."

"My parents, my grandmother, they remember," he said. "They go over the photos, the letters, the badges, the diaries, the medals. They talk always of the family and the past and better times."

"Really? Mine just want to forget that my Mam was a barmaid afore she were married and my Dad started out as a fitter's mate. We can't trace our ancestors further back than the Grans. Dad's lot were factory workers and Mam's lot ran a chippy."

Before Rajiv left they had worked out the seating as well, something Eleanor hadn't thought about and which he made her realise was vital. Without creating confusion by overloading her with information Rajiv gave her tips about bringing in the food and changing courses, how to manage her part and what to leave to Theo.

As she saw him to the lift Eleanor hugged him, "I definitely owe you one, gorgeous! Such a pity you don't want my body…!"

He grinned and looked impish as he murmured,

"Well, but we will think of something…"

Then he kissed her on the cheek and was gone, leaving her plenty of time to wash her hair, to dress and makeup before Theo arrived with his clients.

Eleanor could only half listen to the conversation at her end of the table, about a court case in the news. She was too worried about the progress of the meal to join in properly and anyway the tone of righteous outrage made her feel uneasy. She watched the vegetables being passed round and checked the level of the sauce boat.

"...and the worst offender turned out to be a gay, of course."

Eleanor frowned. There was something wrong in there but her attention was so focused on her role as hostess that she couldn't find it. She felt along the length of the sentence. It was the "of course" that was wrong.

She opened her mouth to protest. Surely the whole statement was suspect? She closed her mouth while she thought about it. What did "gay" have to do with it at all? This thought crossed over the "of course" and she became confused. As she began to speak Eleanor noticed that one of the dishes had lost its serving spoon.

"But thik spooffle —" she said.

What was it she needed to say? She groped for the words, for the point she must make but her mind was a whirlpool. With relief she realised that the conversation had moved on and nobody had noticed her silly gabble. What if they had all turned round and waited for her to speak? She would have let Theo down by making a scene. That is if she could ever have pulled what she wanted to say out of the muddle. Grenville would have grasped the argument and had a clever answer, straight away. And he had a way of delivering a ticking off without being offensive.

Eleanor fixed her smile, held a dish for her neighbour and felt like a traitor to her friends, to Rajiv, to Grenville and all that he had done for her.

The conversation continued to flow round Eleanor. The less she spoke the more difficult it became to launch herself back into the talk. She remained marooned in guilt, an exile from another world.

She thought of Grenville's visit last week to her new home at the Old Rectory. How he had set about cruising the workmen. Such a beautiful house she and Theo had found, walking distance from the station and trains to Kings Cross. Grenville had been impressed, not just with the house — approving the simple elegance of the Georgian building — but with her competence as Theo's deputy. She discussed plans with the district surveyor and listed-building regulations with the planning officer. She had mastered all the rules and systems very quickly. Out there at work, her real voice was an advantage and she was learning how to be liked while remaining in charge.

Eleanor forced herself back to the present as the food was being commented on. She was glad of the toffs' habit, which she had noticed at Theo's parents', of having the man of the house dish up, as she didn't know, as Theo did, how to offer second helpings, choices of dish and top-ups of wine without jarring the atmosphere with interruption. These days she could speak without a trace of her regional accent but it took concentration so she daren't drink. She remained taut with nerves.

Memories of her Uncle Arthur flickered on and off like an old home movie. His voiceover reeled through her head: *better say nowt and let them think tha's clever than open y'mouth and let them know tha's a fool.*

By the end of the meal she was cold, jittery and focused entirely on talking proper and passing the coffee cups without them rattling in her shaking hands.

After dinner, Theo suggested that he and Eleanor take his prospective clients to view the flat. They left the rest of the guests in the living room, enjoying coffee, liquers and chocolates by windows that looked onto a silent, double-glazed prospect of Kensington Gardens.

The American clients had bought a London *pied-à-terre* near Regent's Park and wanted it completely modernized and renovated but in keeping with its original style. The clients admired the streamlined modernity of Theo's chrome and white kitchen. Eleanor was used to her home being made public and she was a neat worker so the food preparation counters looked tidy and professional.

"Period style is all very well," Theo made his reassuring speech, "but not when it comes to kitchens and bathrooms. I don't think you'd want me to restore 18th century plumbing!" Everyone laughed and Theo continued, "And I do believe this quite elegant, rather minimal contemporary style is in keeping with a smart town house. I wouldn't myself have any of that fashionable country cottage nonsense. I had a client recently who wanted a Mediterranean farmhouse complete with Aga — which is a sort of old fashioned English stove — five storeys up in a Knightsbridge mansion flat! I ask you." There was more laughter as they walked down the spacious hallway with its cool ivory walls and bare oakwood floors. All the guests wore black and looked well in the glittering mirrors.

They went up the stairs and into the master bedroom. Theo had trusted Eleanor to clear away all signs of intimacy from his showpiece. There were no discarded clothes on the bed, makeup on the dresser or so much as a toothbrush making a spectacle of itself in the *ensuite* bathroom. He did not care for curtains or draperies so the windows had their original white interior shutters or fabric blinds of watered grey silk. Colour was provided by Persian carpets and the roses Eleanor had brought from the Old Rectory garden, though she knew Theo preferred more architectural flowers like white tulips or lilies.

As Theo and the clients discussed ideas for the Regent's Park residence, she withdrew into the privacy of memory. Had to suppress a smile as she imagined showing these people into Yasmine's soft, velvety bathroom or Grenville's bedroom. She could hear his voice echoing from the past,

"My bed looks wonderfully debauched. Bit smelly, though. Being such an expert on theatrical effects, you will advise me, dearest. Could one get the same idea but with clean sheets, d'you think? Could *untidiness* be my new art form?"

"One way for you to be a genius, love," she'd said, making him snort.

She inhabited the ballroom again, an instant of air and light, of her joy soaring up to join the dancers on the ceiling.

Eleanor fell from that other world as she heard Theo refer to her as his "interior design consultant". He always managed to imply that she'd been something important in the theatre and that famous actors she'd grovelled round, pinning their hems, were personal friends.

After the door closed behind the guests Theo said,

"That commission is in the bag." He clenched his jaw and punched the air. "They've made an appointment for tomorrow! I knew it was the right thing to entertain them here." He put his arms round Eleanor and praised her, "The dinner was excellent. Everything beautifully presented. I felt very, very proud of you."

"I felt very mousey and couldn't seem to get into —"

"Nonsense! You looked perfectly lovely. Quite the prettiest girl of the evening. I kept looking down the table and thinking: that's mine!" He pressed himself against her.

Eleanor felt cold and depressed but knew a warm bath and Theo's lovemaking would make it all better.

# iii

## MARTY

He was in his shirtsleeves, mounting children's project work. It was after school hours and the classroom was hot but quiet.

Through the post had come the offer of an interview for a position as deputy head teacher.

Through the underground pipeline of his secret life had come an invitation to Grenville's birthday party.

The party and the interview. Two sides of his life and no crossover. Nothing new there, then.

Looking at a child's painting of a Roman soldier in a red cloak, he chose a piece of red sugar paper. The kid had called her soldier Felix Maximus and given him strappy sandals and bright pink toes. Marty smiled... perhaps Felix had been a transvestite and worn pink nail varnish. But Felix was not the right name. Despisus Maximus, more like. His smile faded.

All the windows were open because of the heat. Taking off his tie, Marty undid the top button of his light summer shirt.

A deputy headship outside London would mean a rise in salary and an affordable place to live. Somewhere to have better disabled facilities for Dad would transform both their lives. And it would mean respect, self-respect and a chance to make a difference.

The guillotine sliced through the coloured paper, straight and clean — *ssshum!* Done. If only decisions were that easy.

Most times, teaching, being with kids, managing them, helping them to unfold, satisfied him to his very soul.

But sometimes that secret self, sewn into his being, tore at his seams till the shame and agony left his reason in rags. Then he fantasised about chucking it all in and becoming a bartart in a tranny club. Go where *she'd* be appreciated. No more hiding. Live among his own kind. Dress up every day and be out on the town every night.

He'd go fucking nuts, longing to be in real work, be with real women, have a relationship like he remembered his Mum and Dad's. To have children of his own. To be a father.

That tasty looking single mum had been in again today, hanging around as she collected her boy. Marty was getting the message loud and clear: she fancied him. Tempting. Till the other day. Her kid had been larking around in a girly sun hat he'd got from somewhere and she had snatched it off his head with a — *don't want you growing up a poof, do we!* Made you want to give up and run away, howling. But then, on the other hand, it was another reason to stay, to resist from within, change things, make a difference.

To and fro. To and fro. Like a driver at a busy crossroads, just as it cleared one way there was something coming up the other.

And teaching was not compatible with a girl's nightlife. Anybody's nightlife. A teacher's nightlife was marking tests, writing reports and making lesson plans.

Marty chose blue paper to back another child's picture. So good. She'd copied the details of battledress and siege engines accurately but the ambitious panorama of purple hills, pine forests and galloping horses was all her own. The kid did nothing but draw. Wasn't interested in anything but drawing. Might be a way out for her. Not a happy home... alcohol problems...

Marty glanced at his watch. He'd staple all these pictures to the display board and get off. This was the evening he stayed in with his Dad. They had takeaway, played cards and watched their favourite sitcom.

The new job would mean leaving London and the gay scene. Only, the scene was in meltdown. The sickness. The nightmare.

But he'd tested negative. He had a future. *What was he going to do with it?*

A task for tomorrow was to get the kids to put the old display work in their folders and put their folders back in the right places. *Runs a tight ship*, bet it said that in his job reference. Security and respect... that's what all children should have. He was respected and loved back, and he knew it.

So was he really going to throw away everything he'd worked for because once in a while he craved some fast sex in silk knickers?

What about a compromise. Turn down the interview. Stay on here in London. Go to Grenville's party. It was an opportunity to be in drag. And see Eleanor. Didn't like being dressed up around her, though. Too confusing, his two selves criss-crossing like that.

Marty breathed deeply, trying to displace the unhappiness that lodged below his ribs. After putting the stapler away, out of reach, he went round the classroom locking the windows.

Not sure he wanted to see Eleanor. It would just give him heartache, since she'd gone off with that big architect bloke. A real man. Bet he couldn't dance the tango, though... the bastard.

It was a vivid, floodlit memory. Everyone at Grenville's party watching him and Eleanor. She was the principal boy and he was the slapper. Cross-dressed but man and woman, all the same. For a few moments, as the dance demanded, they had been alone together, held tight in each other's gaze.

Marty sighed as he picked up his jacket and bag to go home.

Nothing in his life was ever straight or simple.

## CHORUS

Suffocated by the idea of travelling by bus or tube, Eleanor was walking from Theo's Lancaster Gate flat through Kensington Gardens. She was on her way to Grenville's but would much rather have been at the Old Rectory, in the shade of its tall ash trees or moving through its cool, stone-flagged rooms, looking, thinking, planning. It was nearly a year since she'd left Grenville's and she had a "ballroom" of her own now.

Eleanor strolled through the heat. The city beyond the park faded into the sun-bleached sky and sections of the Broad Walk ahead vanished into lakes of light. The heavy air pressed down onto the Round Pond and it gleamed flat like a sheet of steel. People moved slowly, wobbling into view, distorted by the wavering heat haze as if in a funfair mirror.

As soon as The Old Rectory had running water and a habitable room, Eleanor had moved in. Theo came every weekend and during the week, if he could get away from his London practice. London, less than an hour away on the train, seemed remote to her now. The Old Rectory was her home and her work. She never wanted to leave it. And this weekend, the stifling July weather was another reason she would not be in town except for the invitation to Grenville's birthday tea party.

Eleanor walked along the tree-lined path. The trees had pulled everybody, except her, into the circle of their shade, leaving an empty desert of scorched grass. There was some activity near the lake. Children sailed their boats, nobody caring if they got wet as their clothes would dry on their backs in the time it took to walk to the park gates.

Her work on the Old Rectory had started with ordering skips and clearing rubbish from the buildings and garden. One day, after flinging a shrivelled pot plant into a barrow, she had paused, full of yearning. Grenville tugged at her. She had looked round, expecting to see him. He was not there. Only his scent. Snuffing the air then sniffing her paw-like workgloves she'd searched for him. Tracing his scent to the discarded potplant, she'd retrieved it from the barrow, decided to replant it and see if it wouldn't perk up.

Today, a totebag over her shoulder held the rescued plant, it was bushy again and sprinkled with tiny pale flowers. Having taken cuttings, Eleanor thought she'd give the original to Grenville for his birthday. Feeling that a scented-leaved geranium was too mingy a present, she had made Grenville a peacock-blue, crushed velvet scarf backed with black silk. But it still didn't seem right. The scarf was daft in this weather and would vanish into the chaos of his wardrobe. If he ever found it again he might get to wear it once before losing it. And he'd neglect the plant. Forget to water it. The best present would probably turn out to be the parcel of homemade shortbread and the packet of ordinary teabags she was taking to make sure of a decent cup of tea.

"I thought you might like its scent. If you rub a leaf —"

"Lovely, dearest. Sujata! Brian and...? Asadullah! So glad you could come!" Grenville was distracted by new arrivals.

Left by the open door of the balcony Eleanor put her plant on the decking, noticing that it was tidy and that one or two pots of herbs and an evergreen bush in a tub were looking well tended. All three balcony doors were wide open and she could tell by the faint movement of air round the hem of her dress that windows at the far back of the house had been opened to create a slight stir in the afternoon heat.

She stood outside and looked into the ballroom. It was a wild, tempestuous sea of disorder. Waves of books, clothes, magazines, records and tapes tumbled over the furniture. Guests with presents, birthday cards and plates of biscuits tossed about in the surge avoiding the tangle of computer leads, lamp flexes and telephone wires that swirled dangerously underfoot, round chairs, across the floor and even through a tray of used coffee mugs.

There had always been a fast tide of people flowing in and out of Grenville's life and since she had been away, engrossed by Theo and their renovation project, she expected to see some newcomers and changes.

The wheeled scaffolding platform was still there. Grenville had never had it removed, claiming the ballroom was a "work in progress". But there was a new piece of decor. A huge, purple brush stroke was splattered across one wall and its plasterwork. Commissioned graffiti. Eleanor appreciated the humour and the skill but was relieved Theo wasn't here to see it.

Ollie had gone from under the table. Into her attic? And there were some new lads with Troy, bobbing round the stereo, sorting out sounds.

She leaned her head back and looked up high to where the plaster dancers still floated serenely in their calm, blue heaven. Voices rose around her, out of the tumult below:

— this Stockhausen shit is not what you need at a party

— the exploitation of third world countries is the great evil of our times

— Cixous is brilliant yes, cool, very French, the very latest in feminist chic

— Archie, "there is no such thing as society", remember?

— but I still prefer the sadomasochistic frenzy of American feminism

— and put some kind of brake on the grotesque obesity of the West

— I didn't recognize the pictures of Rock Hudson. He looked like a little old geezer. Scary. I mean, he was a hunk

— Pretty-pretty for Lulu? You like? Yes, come to Tata Yasmine. Upa! Upa! Do walks

— They think because I'm a nigger I have to like Rap. I'm middleclass for fuck's sake. I'm a city lawyer. I fancy nice white boys

— You're a bloody snob, Baptiste

— Agum! Agum Tatayummy... legol ligol ligoh...

— You bet I'm in the fucking closet, man. It's bad enough nobody sees past the black face... and you want me to be black and gay? Black and a leper now! Jesus!

As usual, Grenville had invited everybody he wanted to see and relied on them to bring interesting people and fill the gaps in the catering. It was typical of him not to have made any preparations for his party except to decorate the room. On promontories above the storm stood tin buckets, waste paper bins, silver pitchers, jugs and old jam jars blazing with flowers. On the mantlepiece, garish blooms billowed out of a gigantic and hideous soup tureen. Eleanor knew it was Grenville's doing because the flowers were carefully colour coded in accordance with their position in the room. Blue in the North, Red in the West round the fireplace, Yellow in the East and, as if on cue, Grenville was wading his way towards her in the South, calling,

"What have you done with your plant, Nelly?"

"Put it out here in the sun."

"Quite right. Green and white at this end. What's its name?"

"It's some sort of *Pelargonium* but —"

"Heavenly pong. Want to talk to you about Tinker. So many delicious grades of niffyness. Lavender, I love — Wyvernden laundry room. Eucalyptus... Nanny in medicinal mood. So what have we here?"

"Lemons. What about Tinker?" Eleanor asked.

"Wants to set up a sandwich bar near South Ken tube. Good pitch. Needs a bit of moolah. Shall I give him the money? Mint is marvellous. You're a good judge of these things. Can I smell floor polish? Fresh ginger?"

He looked at Eleanor as he stroked the plant and sniffed his fingers.

"I like Tinker —"

"Do you!" Grenville, always pleased for people to get on, lit up. "Perhaps there is just a touch of Jeyes Fluid... school bogs? The whiff of transgression. And then there is pine... or even, let's see... Rosemary? Why do you like him, specially?"

"Tinker's clean for one thing... no drugs and really quite sorted under all that dippy camp and screechy laugh. He'll make a go of it and... well, I just like him. Never a drag. Amazing, considering the life he's had. He was brought up by his Gran and everything was OK till she died and he was forced back to his Mam who —"

"Mouthwash or cologne? What d'you think?"

"Your aftershave."

"So it is! That's very helpful, dearest and I — ah, Helen! Marvellous performance piece last night! And Lauren!" Grenville broke off to greet his agent. Plunging back into his party, he left Eleanor stranded.

She didn't seem to know many people. There was Tinker, already gathering up dirty coffee cups and emptying ashtrays. Archie opening bottles of white wine. Rajiv coming in from the kitchen with bowls of chopped fruit and ice cubes. Yasmine and Sandra cutting a spectacular cake. Gail and Zeb busy with little Lucy and all the attention she got. David, ever the journo, chatting to a famous aid-raising celebrity. They were all out of reach, busy, with a part to play. She must leave the balcony and get back in somehow. Go to the kitchen and make tea, maybe? She felt unconfident, an outsider. Where was Marty? Such an old mate. He'd come and chat. Or had he drifted away like her?

Eleanor leaned against the doorpost and looked out at the plane trees in the square, breathless in the heat, still as a painted backdrop. Occasionally she turned and looked back into the ballroom and listened to the talk. Living outside London and rarely seeing these old friends, their anxious voices sounded to her like gunfire from a distant battlefield:

— they won't let us gays give blood anymore

— it's definitely in blood but it could be in saliva as well

— Moh num-num, me moh yumyum

— So you're not a "home-owner"? My dear! You can't be a human being

— just don't get in an accident and need a blood transfusion

— property buying and shopping is the value system now

— seen Jason or Marty? People keep disappearing

— but you try getting insurance or a mortgage if you're "out"

— Lulu's making words like bikit-bikit for biscuits. An old greedyguts, like her Da!

— that guy who came in the club the other night? He'd obviously got it, you know, his face... really disgusting. Nobody'd talk to him

— Barman served him but didn't really want to

— bloody lemmings, the voters have given la Thatcher *carte-blanche* now

— When the guy left, the barman picked up his glass with a cloth and threw it in the rubbish. Yeah. You bet.

— so I said, "well, would *you* hug an AIDS victim?" I mean, would you?

Grenville, sitting in an armchair, suddenly clapped his hands above his head and shouted,

"Stop! Stop talking shop. This is my party and —"

*"I'll cry if I want to"* came the chorus.

"But that's just it! I don't want to cry! I want no more sickness and despair. No more of the 'A' word. The subject is *banned*." He looked round and lifted up his hands like a priest,

"Let us..." he intoned, "Let us now remember the lusts of our youth. Our first loves..."

"Oooh piss off!" Tinker made a face and jerked his shoulders, "first time was 'orrible."

"I said first *love*... didn't I? Let me see. I will tell you —"

By now Eleanor had managed to edge in and join the group of old friends round Grenville. He picked up his wine glass from the floor and drank before continuing,

"He was called Jim and he came one summer in the school hols... 1960? for the fruit picking at Wyvernden. He had a motorbike and —"

Sandra who was sitting on the floor next to Yasmine and Lucy, leaned forward and tugged his trouser leg.

"Ah! The bikedyke! Hm, a *Norton Matchless*, I think. Anyway, I adored him. We exchanged many looks. We knew. I badgered and badgered him to give me pillion rides —"

Grenville was interrupted by Tinker leading another chorus of *oooh!*

"Yes yes, har har. But he was rather shy and thought he might get into trouble. On Jim's last day there, old

208

Gosse, our estate manager, told Jim to *go on, give the young master a turn about*." Grenville gazed into the faraway. "I remember a late-summer evening, roaring down the empty lanes, my cheek on his back, my arms round his waist and..." Grenville turned back to his listeners and leant forward, "my hands in his pockets."

When the group around him had finished teasing, Grenville turned to Yasmine,

"Do you remember your first love, Mistress?"

"Yes, of course I am remember. Even it is a time I like for forget. We have nothings and live in one room altogether. So much hungry and afraid. Mama... all days and night my good-good Mama —"

Yasmine let her tears fall. They splashed on Lucy's arm and the child looked up, mystified.

"Mama make the dresses for important wifes. For the dresses Mama can get food for us, moneys, papers for escape. Mama send me to do fittings. I only a little girl but I know already everything for the sewing. Is hot-hot sun outside like today. The streets everywhere with soldiers and broken with the bombs but inside rich womens house is all sssh quiet and dark with the curtains for shade. She make me drink with the real fruit and sugar. Sugar! Ai yai yai! Sweetie-sweetie! I have orgasms to think of it!" Yasmine was laughing now and wiping her eyes.

"Is that it, Yasmine? The sugar?" David asked.

"No." She sniffed and wiped her nose upwards with the palm of her hand, "We go to her bedroom for try her dress with the mirror. In her bedroom she take all away my porno peasant clobbers and give me pretty-pretties for try on too. She make bath and wash me. She brush my hair. She ask me all the time if I like. I like.

209

Then she is kissing me... I like also very, very much and soon... ah, she make the love for me. Is the first. So, so good with the more lemonades after!"

But not even Grenville's efforts, the laughter or stories worn smooth by memory could prevent the sinister tide of dark rumour turning and seeping back into the voices of that afternoon:

— I'm fine, just a bit of a summer cold, I think. Silly really, in this weather

— Have you had the test? Do you have to go private?

— You must come and visit the Old Rectory. I'm there all the time, in charge of the whole project

— London is the pleasuredome no more, alas!

— I so wanted to get into design and the Old Rectory is like having a whole real-life set to work on

— I heard Jonny'd got it

— it's magic to see what you've done on paper come to life in the real world

— we're all afraid, dear. Trouble is, nobody knows what of exactly...

— Mad Jasper tried to top himself when he got his test result

— then we found this amazing place full of antique doorknobs and fingerplates

— He'd heard you get blisters, go blind, go bonkers and die. Thought he'd skip all that and make a dash for the end

— But they found the poor bastard. Pumped him out

— You have to go out to the woods and do it. Alone. Where you won't be found.

# Two years later

## i

## OUT

Eleanor stood in her workroom at the Old Rectory and looked at the postcard in her hand. She had worried about the village postman seeing this "California Guys" picture but had at least managed to snatch it out of the letterbox before Theo saw it. It was from Grenville. Who else. From the States and eye-poppingly vulgar: all dark glasses, leather jackets and enormous cocks. She turned it over,

"Nelly, dearest..." There was this cheery message insisting that he wanted to meet up with her when he got back from America.

Their friendship had faded with her leaving London. She had wondered sometimes, why that had happened. Her and Grenville. What had it been about, then? It had been about her living with him, her being there and him not liking to be alone. She couldn't help resenting the way her space in his life had been filled so fast and how

211

Grenville showed no sign of missing her. Out of sight meant nonexistent with him. And, from her end, she didn't see why she had to put up with him being sneery about Theo and about her living "out in the sticks". It was not as if she hadn't tried phoning. But he was always hurtful or annoying, asking her *how are things in Much-Bottom-on-the-Bidet* and suchlike. Often hearing laughter in the background she felt mocked and could not bring herself to ask, *do you know? Have you had the test? Have you got... IT?* Somehow she had lost the right to ask and he was so offhand with her, it was hard to demean herself and beg him to be friends again. Anyway there were other reasons. She'd been working flat out on the Old Rectory and on interior design commissions for Theo's firm. There was so much interesting work and hardly a moment to spare. Not much time to read the papers or watch television. All the same, she was aware of the terrible shadow hanging over Grenville and all her old mates. And felt a bit guilty. Though most of it was media hysteria, surely. She tried not to think about it. And Theo's attitude didn't help any. He had always wanted her to leave Grenville and that whole scene behind. He'd almost made it a condition. And now, with the AIDS thing, he didn't want her having contact with those people at all. It wasn't safe. She might catch something.

"Nelly, dearest..." Eleanor looked at the words and heard his voice... "*dearest...*" She couldn't resist. Theo didn't have to know. She wanted to see Grenville again.

"How's *your* Old Rectum getting on, dear?" Grenville asked as he stood by the stereo in the ballroom, squinting at a record sleeve. "Of course records and all this equipment are obsolete now, the compact disc thing is set to take over. Marvellous sound quality and so on. But, you know, I have this atavistic need to hear these old recordings, they are part of my... past. And the past is all —"

"It's really come on. The major exterior works are completed: roof, plumbing, foundations all sound. Working on a listed building is so slow! So many regs. Now it's the interior, like. Floors, plastering... Zeb's working in the entrance hall. The outbuildings and landscaping has started too. All to my designs. You haven't been for ages, Grenville! I wish you'd come. It's getting really interesting. I'm choosing colours..." Eleanor tried to tempt him.

"Nelly, I have to tell you. I have not been too well lately. Is this the moment for the E minor? I think I'm in the mood for Chopin. Someone doomed."

"I've collected lots of yummy colour charts and samples and I want us —" Eleanor stopped as the thousand fears she had chopped off like snake heads suddenly burst out and coiled tight round her voice. But still she struggled with the brutality of fact. "Not well?" she whispered, refusing to see the weight loss, the shake in his hands, the fact that he had become an old man since she'd last seen him.

"I have *converted*," he said with a snort.

Eleanor snatched this up and hacked at the monster, "You've joined a sect? Who are they? Do you have a special diet? It's making you ill! Who are these people?"

"The dying."

Grenville's bark of laughter and next words were drowned by the piano concerto. This made Eleanor frantic and she lurched towards him across the room, shouting over the barricade of music,

"What's all this? What have you done?"

"What d'you fucking well think, Nelly!" Grenville drew back from Eleanor and put his hands up as if to fend off any attempt to touch him. She registered this unconsciously and stopped by an armchair, letting it act as his shield.

"But not you, please. No! I can't believe it, love. I can't stand it!"

"You must. I have to," he smirked. "At least it's the wages of sin, my dear."

Without looking at her, he lowered the music volume, moved over to his sofa and sat down. Eleanor's dread, suppressed for so long, converted into anger and erupted into the space of the ballroom between them,

"Why didn't you tell me! How long have you known? Ages! Since before I left, I'll bet! When did you have the test?"

"Look, old bean —"

"*Why* didn't you tell me? You pushed me out! What did I do wrong, eh? Because I'm a woman, I suppose. Not good enough! Not one of your upper-class gang of —"

"Nelly! Nelly, stop. You're running amok."

"But why didn't you tell me?" She was so giddy she couldn't tell if she was really shouting or whether the sounds of her rage were roaring in her own head.

"Please let me off," Grenville pleaded. "Go and make us some tea or —"

"Didn't you trust me? Didn't you ever love me? You don't need me!" The echoing *me, me, me,* made her quiet at last. Looking over at the back of his head, which

214

rested wearily on his hand, she spoke again, dry-eyed, like a robot, "I'm sorry, love. It must be terrible. Terrible for you."

"It is. Will you do something?"

"Anything."

"Spare me your feelings." He looked round at her, "Please."

"Yeah. Yeah, anything. Yeah."

"And please spare me the awful tedium of explaining. It is such an ordeal. I know it all and the boredom of having to communicate it again, and then have people misunderstand and question *again.* Or worse. Make suggestions! Urging me to try garlic pills or Flying Futon therapy. Trying to argue themselves out of the reality."

Grenville's face lit with a smile.

"What!" Eleanor snapped. "You never laugh. Except now of course, when it's not at all flamin' funny."

"It is funny," Grenville insisted. "It always amuses me. Listen. Chopin's made his principal theme reappear... but a semitone flat. He won't 'correct' this till... *there,*" he chuckled.

Eleanor couldn't grasp any of this but remembered a time when Grenville had swept her off to new galaxies of art and thought, urging her to lay claim to the stars. Now his talk made her feel weightless, abandoned in space.

"It's so lonely —" she managed to say.

"Not at all. I have masses of company."

"Who?"

"You want news from the Front? Troy. Gerald in the States went last month. Peter. Neville, the gym dandy. Frankie died a blistered skeleton in hospital being treated by people in moon suits. Bernard. Helmut.

215

Dennis. Jean Claude. Kevin Naughton's dead. 'Kujie' Kujan. Sean from Riverside. Bruno —"

Grenville's voice hammered on,

"Mad Jasper accomplished his deliverance at last, *person under a train* at Leicester Square tube. Jolly brave. Bit messy. Willy Weirdo did one better. Went over the top at 8.40 a.m at Bank Underground station, thereby causing maximum inconvenience to yuppie commuters. He gets the VC. Garcia. Marlon. Cazz. Bambi. Marlene. All so young! And old Cambridge chums Lloyd-Bates and Steven. Graham and poor Ollie on their last legs. There's Robbie, Channel 4 Robbie, you know? And Rob Murray. Scores of people in the States you've never met. Drugfiends Sandy, Josh, Cathy and Juan Gonzales *and* his friend Nick. And we must spare a thought for all those 'conshees' in the closet. We've got such a complexity of closets now —"

"I can't take it in, Grenville."

But like relentless bursts of machine-gun fire, his voice rattled on,

"Adrian in Bristol. Derek. James the Poet. James the Actor. Freddie. And there's Terry, you never liked him, a deeply unpleasant person so perhaps we don't mind terribly about him. But Doughnut Adonis, Pedro and Jason, they joined the 'plus' ranks recently while —"

"But what are you... what I meant was —"

"I'm linked in with a whole system of tests, drugs, pills, placebos, guinea piggery, routine clinic visits and so on. Nelly, do you think we could leave it at that? Dispense with it all, dearest? Will you do that for me. No having to talk about it. No more questions. Spare me your love or... concern or whatever it is. The vulgar psychodrama. I just want your —"

The phone rang twice. Bleeps and Grenville's recorded voice blared *...and I'll get back to you...* over the closing chords of Chopin.

More bleeps were followed by, *Pick up the phone you lazy cunt. It's Simon, honey. Just checking about tomorrow. 2.30. Ring me if there's any problem. Bye-eee.*

"Fascinating things these answerphones..." Grenville said. "One's friends talk to one but talk to themselves talking to one. The return of the monologue. I find myself rehearsing little speeches. Soon we'll hardly have to go out or deal with real people at all. Is that a good thing? What d'you think? Bodies are deadly difficult but what else is there?"

"Poetry? Art?" Eleanor's voice was sour, repeating his lectures.

"Answerphone Art? I feel very little enthusiasm for it. The pornographic possibilities seem very limited. This new technological revolution which they are predicting will have the effect of fast-forwarding everything, which is exciting, of course. But I can feel the past shrinking rapidly and people like myself with very long pasts, their minds forged by the Classics and moulded to the music of Shakespeare, the King James' Bible and the Book of Common Prayer are obsolete already. And it's no use, that as heir to a long line of soldiers, I know that new technology also brings more sophisticated ways of killing —"

Eleanor wanted to pick up the soup tureen on the mantlepiece and smash it down on his head,

"You said no questions but who did you tell first?" she interrupted.

"A woman, Yasmine. So there. Then Tinker. Wasn't very difficult. Felt perfectly well for ages. Cure always a possibility. It's the witch-hunt atmosphere that's the most dreadful thing. It's either that or terrible soap-opera cliches and soppy religiosity. Now I've told you, I will do my moral duty, stick to my principles and come out about having the plague."

"How's Tinker?"

"Refusing me certain cruelties. Insisting on condoms and *safe sex*. Safe sex! Defeats the purpose, my dear. I'd rather be dead. Ha!"

"Tinker is in the clear, then."

"And determined to survive, the traitor!"

"Marty?"

"Vanished. Other side of the wire. Can't get any news of him. I think we have to report him as *lost presumed —*"

"Rajiv and Archie?"

"Silence from that end of the trench. As with David. And I never ask. I don't agree with court martials. Interrogations."

"I know. I know. Sorry. I've had my head yanked out of the sand... Just let me get my bearings."

Eleanor moved away from his end of the room and over to the balcony windows. She tried to order her thoughts but was suffocated by the pounding in her head and chest. Was she going to pass out? She leant on the doorframe and looked down at a table covered in houseplants. She stared into the heart of a white flower. Her mind emptied out into the whiteness.

"What's this flower, Grenville?"

"Makes me think of Caravaggio's *Lute Player*. He was good at boys... and flowers. Such beauty." Grenville came over and stood beside her. "*Gloxinia, Mont Blanc.*

Feel the leaves... smooth, velvety things with frivolous edges."

"That's nice too."

"Easy-peasy, *Catharantheus roseus*, good for the air. Aunt Pod gave it to me. And like her, likes to be permanently moist."

Eleanor smiled, remembering his Aunt Pod's weakness for gin and it. She wanted to ask about his family — did they know? How had they taken it? Did they want it kept secret? — but put aside her questions. She said instead,

"This is very bright but not in the right place in the room for the orange colour, surely? According to your scheme it should be over there between the red and yellow walls. And what about this one —"

"Yes. *Susan, Black-eyed.* The red papery one is *Hibiscus* and this gorgeous creature is *Temple Bells.* Well, I should have liked the colour symbolism but I had to give it up. Plants will not be imposed on in that way. And I do so like to see them bloom. Such drama queens some of them. The sulks, my dear. The fussiness! She likes to be hot with a bit of sun and not too wet but she likes to be warm but gets a headache in the sun and so on. I like listening to them, though."

"Listening to them? I thought *you* would do the talking," she tittered with nerves.

"I do that too, of course. A great deal. I listen with this."

He picked up a small wood and metal object which she presumed was a tuning fork and flourished it like a baton. Eleanor, whose resistance to emotion had been tried to the limit this afternoon, began to giggle,

"Whah? Whoh! Whah? What is it?" she gasped.

"A water hammer."

Eleanor clutched his arm as the laughter spilled out of her,

"You wave that at them and they sing to you d'they? Don't tell me!"

"A charming idea! But no, I'm not spending the time left to me upon this earth conducting an inaudible choir of potted plants."

"Go on!" she snuffled.

"This is ancient technology. Tremendously practical. All it takes is a good ear. Gardeners of yore tapped the pot with the hammer thus... and depending on the note they knew if the plant needed watering or not. So you see, flowers do have a voice. And very individual wants."

"I never knew you liked gardening." Eleanor calmed herself.

"I don't. This is all right though. No slugs!" Grenville put down the water hammer and stepped out onto the balcony. "Just weevily things, the odd *virus*... and lots of complicated little bottles of medicine. I can sympathise with all of *that*."

As the sun spangles and leaf shadow flickered over the balcony and across the floor, Eleanor remembered her first sight of the ballroom on that other summer afternoon, long ago.

"The trees have grown since I first came here," she said.

"It's a bloody 'conservation area' now and they won't prune the trees. People complain! And the square's garden is being tidied up and made into some 'designer' horror. I came here ten years ago because it was a slum, full of riffraff: decayed artistes, lavatory attendants, *hors de siècle* eccentrics, barmy Bohos and refugees. And *now* look what's happened! All done up. Awful, respectable people have moved in with their neighbourhood watchery and children and *you can't have parties or loud music.*" Grenville sat down on the balustrade and shaded his eyes with his hand as he mourned, "Remember Frankie 'working' from The Havana? And Miss Whippy's dungeon?" He waved across the square at a done-up set of offices, "I could step out and meet someone interesting, in seconds. Old Wally. Gladys, the business girl's maid. The business girls! All been moved on. Jamal's is a pine furniture shop now. He couldn't afford the rents. There's no real *people* anymore. Just money-making yobs, proclaiming wealth as a good in itself. They are the real whores, these 'executives' with their paltry aspirations. They take no thought for their souls but fuss about rubbish in the square or graffiti. Or their cars getting scratched. Their *cars* for God's sake!"

He was furious but Eleanor noticed that his voice had lost some of its old edge.

"And a really hateful class of people have moved in, following the money. Organised drug barons. Ruthless pimps. As a reward for my life of purity I shall petition to go to Hell and be put in charge of their punishments."

Seeing him shiver even in the warm breeze, Eleanor suggested they move back indoors, saying,

"You look tired, love. I should go and let you rest but I don't like to leave you alone."

"Tinker will be back soon. Don't worry about me, dearest. I've made a decision this afternoon... about dying." He drew himself up, "I'm going to be terrifically brave and dignified."

"You can't decide that, can you?"

"Most certainly you can. It's grand, it's aristocratic and it's romantic, all of which I like. It fulfils certain family expectations, *semper ad lucem* and all that. Best of all it gives me something to focus on... a project. I shall concentrate on putting in the best possible performance. You, of all people, whose true heart lies in the theatre, should appreciate that."

After Eleanor left, Grenville went to the bathroom. He examined the plants but avoided his image in the mirror. Then he looked at his watch, filled a glass of water and took some pills before returning to the ballroom to sit quietly listening to the pain in his stomach ebbing away. His mood lightened but he was exhausted. That naughty *Flamingo Flower* needed potting on. Tomorrow. Eyes too tired to read. Must latch his mind onto something. Ring someone. Someone silly and undemanding. He thought of Simon with gratitude.

Grenville was about to return Simon's answerphone message when, better still, he heard Tinker letting himself into the house.

"How did it go?" Tinker asked, bringing Grenville a cup of herb tea and lighting a cigarette for himself.

"Got it over with."

"You look knackered, mate. Did she give you a hard time?"

"Yep."

"I don't blame her. Ages ago, I told you to tell her, didn'I. So how was she?"

"She was hurt. Furious!" Grenville puffed out his cheeks.

"Is only 'cos she loves you, y'stupid berk. Wish somebody cared about me like that."

"Do you? Awfully tiring."

"What do you feel about her, then?"

"Sorry," Grenville said.

But the truth was, he didn't feel anything for anyone. Sadness rolled like a stone onto his chest. Leaning his head back on the armchair, he closed his eyes over his tears. Nothing for anyone. His withdrawal from life had begun.

# ii

## TELLING

The door was closing on a dream in which she was begging Grenville's forgiveness, taking his face in her hands and kissing him. She had the sense of being humoured... he evaded her even as the dream withdrew. As she stirred, Theo reached out for her and was pleased to find her so turned on.

After breakfast, as on most Saturday mornings, Theo and Eleanor did the rounds of the Rectory and she filled him in on the week's work.

"This feels like a kids' bedroom."

"Your instinct is right, as usual," Theo said. "Considering its position in the house I'd say it was almost certainly the nursery with Nanny's room through this doorway we've unblocked. Make a nice upstairs sitting room with library cum study attached."

"Why don't we restore it as a nursery with —"

"Waste of the view and I think we'd best leave the disposition of the rooms to the people buying the house. It's a good idea to keep the spaces as neutral as possible. Let the buyers decide what they want the rooms for."

Eleanor did not like to be reminded of the strangers who would come and live in this house that she had worked on so hard, thought about so carefully, bringing out its beauty with such care. She liked coming to the nursery with her cup of tea when she needed a break from the army of builders and inspectors. Through one window, beyond the tall trees cluttered with rookeries, she could see the church. From the other window she could catch the sunset and a glimpse of her neighbour working in his vegetable plot. She had allowed herself to take possession of the house, even to thinking that this room might one day hear the voices of her and Theo's children.

"I like to think of our own children in here one day," she said.

"Not in here. And anyway not yet, I hope." He looked straight at her, "Eleanor! Eleanor?" She shook her head. He breathed out again, "Not ever, if it was up to me."

"You don't want kids," she said.

"Not really. But I know I shall have to give in on this sooner or later." He smiled. "Just make it later, sweetheart, alright? And now, what are you doing about the windows in —"

"Why don't you want kids?"

"Well, my siblings are all breeding like rabbits. The women are always preggers and the oldies are awash with grandchildren, which lets me off. Secondly, I don't find my nieces and nephews at all life enhancing. Noisy, messy, time-consuming and for what? They're fantastically expensive, grow into rude and indolent teenagers, take to drugs... I really can't get interested. And you know my sister's house near Oxford, a lovely property, or could be, but it's a disgraceful mess. And she used to be jolly pretty but look at her now! Fat, dowdy and running about in a rusty old banger."

Theo put his hands on her waist.

"I don't like the thought of you blowing up like a balloon or having to share you with a bunch of squalling brats. I want you to myself, sweetheart." He kissed her and murmured, "I must say, you were extremely delectable to wake up to this morning..." This was so true that after a pause, he took the opportunity to tack on a little fib "...after a week of abstinence."

But Eleanor registered that pause. She heard the bat squeak of betrayal.

Theo smiled down on her,

"You're the golden girl with everyone at the moment." He did hidden penance. "The Middletons? You did their Voysey interior restoration, remember? Well! They have praised you to the skies and given our name to their friends the Pritchards. None other than Pritchard and Pearce! And they've got in touch!"

Eleanor was pleased. Theo took her arm and they began to move out of the nursery. "The whole office is holding it's breath," he went on, "as, among other things, they own a sizeable chunk of prime London warehousing. Rumour is, they want it converting into state-of-the-art Dockland apartments. That is a very, very big fish swimming towards us, sweetheart, all thanks to you!" He kissed her again. He had learned that his attentions and praise for her work were the most effective secret atonement, much better, with Eleanor, than presents, chocolates or flowers.

They continued round the house together, talking about another project that was ready for her interior restoration input. Theo was in good spirits. His reputation was high after a prize-winning redevelopment. Other architects were going to the wall, his practice was thriving... Eleanor was a brilliant addition to the team. Very pleased by the outcome of the general election, too... a decent Tory majority and most of his carefully cultivated contacts still in place.

The work Theo was talking about would mean Eleanor staying in London more often. Normally she would have been reluctant but was drawn to the idea of visiting Grenville. Seeing him more often. Before he... Her thoughts drifted away. Spending more time in London would help wean her off the Old Rectory.

After the tour of the house, Theo had gone into the room they called the site office, to do work he'd brought for the weekend. Alone, washing up the breakfast dishes, Eleanor thought about Grenville. During the years of living and working with Theo, Grenville had receded but now he surged forward into the front of her mind. Since her visit to him last week, he'd filled her head and her dreams. But she still couldn't face what he'd told her. It was as if she was walking backwards, gazing into the distance she'd just come from, going over and over past conversations and memories. Forgotten moments and their minute details came back to her. The sound of the balcony door tapping against its wedge in the breeze. Grenville holding out bits of cheese to the area's feral cats... Atonic and Astrophe, he'd called them. And that face he pulled as he squinted down to do up the top button of his shirt. The teeth marks on his pencils. The way he twirled his signet ring with his thumb...

She'd tried telling Theo about Grenville but though he listened, he would not sympathise with her misery. He wanted to get on with his work. When Eleanor pushed him for a response he'd said that it was very unfortunate but only to be expected with that lifestyle. A lifestyle that disgusted him. He was glad to have rescued her from it.

"Didn't you like Grenville?"

"Well, same as you, I was rather taken in by him. And he was very useful, I'll say that. But I never approved of the way he treated you — like a little dog, taking you about with him everywhere. And his beautiful house, some of my best early work and look at the state of it!"

So Eleanor spoke to Grenville privately in her thoughts. She put aside his death, like everybody's death, like her own, it was sometime in the future. For now, she must find a way to be in contact, see if she couldn't tidy things up between them. What would she say? How to kick off? Musn't be heavy. "How are you?" was useless. "How are you *today*." That was it. The *today* admitted the terrible situation but left him free to choose between moaning or denial. Eleanor went upstairs to make the bed and, on impulse, picked up the cordless phone Theo had left on the chest of drawers and dialled Grenville's number. She was about to put it down again having got the answerphone when Grenville's "He-e-ellope!" interrupted the recorded message.

"Hello pet, it's Nelly."

"Ha! Hello, yes. Hello!"

He'd tensed up, she could tell. What was that phrase she'd prepared?

"How's the stiff upper lip, then?" she said.

"Stiff as anything," she heard the relief in his voice. "Only goes for the lip, mind you, so don't raise your hopes."

"Aw, I had a sexy dream about you n'all."

"Did you? I'm very flattered. I hope it was filthy. My dreams are bland unmemorable rubbish and not doing their 'wish fulfilment' stuff as Dr Freud promised.

By rights I should be murdering people, inflicting unspeakable refinements of torture on polititians and pimps, ordering floggings of celebrities, tee-vee personalists — TV in quite the wrong way — and gutter journalists. Hypocrites! Self-righteous moralists spreading suspicion and darkness. God Nelly, I'm so *angry*. Being brave is actually more difficult than I thought —"

Eleanor made a sympathetic sound as she settled herself on her and Theo's unmade bed.

"I veer from anger to self pity," Grenville went on, "neither at all conducive to calm self-command in the line of fire. Can't make up my mind whether to set a good example, as befits my ancient lineage, or make a spectacular nuisance of myself."

"Make a nuisance, go on," Eleanor said.

She heard Tinker's voice in the background, shouting, "...you're a fucking nuisance already, mate."

"Well, that's my instinct," Grenville said, "— but the thought of storming the barricades of hypocrisy makes me feel tired rather than sexy, I fear. I'm just an impotent, armchair Jeremiah."

"Who's Jeremiah?" she asked.

"You see! I even speak a dead language," Grenville sighed before going on in a lighter tone, "Tinker has just spilt some salt and is now chucking it about over his shoulders. It's *too late* Tinker Belle, dear! Or perhaps you're like Madame Pompadour after the Lisbon Earthquake: giving up rouge for a week *to placate the Demon of Fear.*"

In the background Eleanor could hear the distant sound of Tinker speaking.

"Hang on, Nelly." There followed a muffled discussion about domestic arrangements, prescriptions and food shopping. Grenville came back with, "Tinker sends his love. He's such a fan of yours."

"Send him mine," Eleanor said.

"He's just gone out but I will, with pleasure."

Grenville's disembodied voice seemed to be his essence. It made her conscious of how well she knew him still. She could hear him saying to Tinker later, "Eleanor sends her love. She's such a fan of yours."

"How's Tinker?" she asked.

"Sandwich bar doing tremendously well. A terminal combination of people and food, don't you think? But he loves it. There was a bit of a 'sandwich war' with the local mafia —"

"Was that exciting?"

"Not in the least. I got Baptiste to sort it all out for me. I've never had any interest in criminals. They're insufferably banal, they just want money. The fantasies of psychopaths are a bit more interesting, although even they are rather robot —"

"Where's Tinker living?" she fished.

"Poor Ollie has been moved to a hospice. So Tinker's living here now, with me."

"And the libido?" Eleanor tried for their old intimacy.

"Hm. Comes and goes. I still feel madly randy in warm weather. The drugs affect it. Mama Morphine kills desire... as mothers do... in return for other sorts of bliss. The very oddest thing is feeling the desperate need for the chase, the flirtation, the nod, without the desire to follow through..."

"Sounds a bit girly —"

"Does it! Is that what makes you all so confusing? But *I'm* tired, wobbly, itchy, hideous, falling-to-bits-unmentionables... but women! What's your excuse?"

Without waiting for an answer he asked, "How's life with Theo?"

Eleanor wondered whether to treat him as an exhausted invalid and say "fine" or to confide in him. The phone enabled her to speak the truth into space,

"Not great, at the moment."

"What's wrong?" his voice shot back immediately, "Tell."

"He does nothing but work. Eats, sleeps and dreams work. I know I'm luckier than most women, at least I'm involved. We work together a lot and I'm so happy about that. I'm an employee of the firm, earning proper money and everything. And appreciated! Clients ask specially for me to do their interiors now. I mean, you know how important work is to me, Grenville. But I want time off. With him. To be together. But he never lets go. Except in bed and even there…"

"What?"

"It's all a bit predictable —"

"Predictable! My dear, that is easily dealt with. Naughty underwear! Sex aids! Come and choose! Whole cupboard full of saucy accoutrements. Tink and I will give you a demo, show you how they all work! Some of them are really quite dangerous. *Un*predictable enough to satisfy the most jaded sensation junkie! There's one frightfully amusing gadget for the bath which you put up —"

"I don't mean like that. I mean… It's all a bit mechanical. He needs sex. I'm available."

"Make yourself unavailable?"

"He'd get angry and maybe go elsewhere, besides, I quite like, you know… *it*, myself. I still fancy Theo like, a lot." She knew she could count on Grenville's sympathy for any kind of erotic attachment, whatever its object.

"So what's the problem, exactly."

"I just want the odd night out, the odd talk, the odd weekend away —"

"That's a lot of odd things, certainly."

"I mean. Like this morning? We've been apart all week," she dropped her voice, "He does it, right? Lovely! No complaints about that at all, only I'd like to lie around, have breakfast in bed, chat, have a bath together, do it again even but —" Saying all this on the phone made it seem less disloyal. "But immediately after, he's up and off into the office with his bloomin' briefcase!"

There was silence from the other end of the line.

"Grenville?" she called into telephone nowhere.

"I'm afraid loneliness is a terrible problem, dearest. You should have married *me* when you had the chance. But you had a lucky escape. Although I do think Death can come in many forms: a hubby, a bourgeois life, monogamy and —"

"Kids." Eleanor finished for him. Theo wasn't the only predictable one.

"Well… I wanted an heir for Wyvernden but that's not the same as wanting sprogs, I suppose. But just think, you might have survived to be a rich widow. Terribly grand in a gloomy sort of way. Anyway, too late now, old thing."

"Shurrup, yer mekin' me blub."

"Good-oh! That's the idea. When are you coming to see me again? My beautiful gardenia is about to bloom. Do come. Yes. I should like that."

Hearing tiredness starting to slow his voice, Eleano made an arrangement to visit and they finished the call.

Putting the phone aside she curled up on the bed, rocking in agony. She had to turn her face into the pillow to smother the sound of her crying.

# iii

## WORK

On the following Monday morning, Eleanor came into the Old Rectory office in a furious mood. The builders' merchant had delivered a lorryload of the wrong sort of paving cobble. As she went for the telephone she noticed that a message was waiting on the answerphone. More crap about some petty planning regulation or those suppliers giving her the run around. It was going to be a morning of listening to Vivaldi. She stabbed the "play" button,

*I was hoping to be excited moved turned on... something! They're all up in arms about it... so I heaved myself off to the exhibition... well my dear it didn't deliver at all... no pain or terror... it was just kinky kitsch... emotionless pornochic... harmless... no urgency at all... completely ineffective... doesn't deprave or corrupt... changes... nothing! How dare they call it Art! Advertising is the really effective pornography of our culture now... don't you think? I have to write about it... Oh God...*

There was a long pause followed by a sound that might have been a sob.

*... are you there?... Thoughts from the Bog... I've been sitting here for ages... I can't deliver either... Nelly... old thing... would you — ?*

Grenville's voice was cut off, the machine had run out of tape. The message changed her mood. Having dealt with the cobbles problem she rang Grenville.

"I detest this fashion for irony," he began at once.

Eleanor could never remember what irony was or how it worked. She shuffled papers on the desk, looking for an invoice.

"You're having trouble with constipation? What about Allbran? Figs?" she suggested.

"It's not radical. Irony. It's smug. I've eaten every fig in London."

"I try to understand it because of Theo," Eleanor said. "I look up 'irony' in the dictionary and I think I've got it but I can't see how it can be applied to pictures or buildings. Have you tried putting lots and lots of sugar in a bit of warm fruit juice, love?"

"It's pastiche. Irony. An emollient. It's so bankrupt. The cure you suggest might set up a whole set of other problems. I hate copies. Remixes. All that sugar might start a war in me innards. I can't see where all this rehash of culture is leading. It's all plunder. No originality."

Eleanor had wedged the receiver into her neck so she could sift through a filing tray with both hands. Grenville's voice was fuzzy under her ear,

"I really don't want to die on the lavatory. Like Elvis. Whenever his name is mentioned, that's all I think of. If I'm to die I must be allowed some glamour. Not Allbran. The margin between art and beefburgers is getting very, very narrow now. All is shopping and consumption. Perhaps it's time art left the gallery altogether, what d'you think?"

"You could try massage," Eleanor suggested. Having found the invoice, she held the phone properly again.

"Whatever happens it will be right for the culture, whether I like it or not," Grenville said, "but I feel so impatient with it all. Strange to think that you will see how it turns out. But I try not to be resentful of survivors. Hm. Massage? As long as the masseur is not too cute... putting me to shame. Sorry! Slight wobble of the upper lip there. I don't mind admitting to you, on the phone, that I'm a bit depressed, Nelly."

"Tell..." She was looking over the description of goods on the invoice.

"I should like to have left some account of myself."

"But your books and articles, love. They're very highly thought of, specially by those progressive types." She began to search for the paving catalogue.

"Yes, not bad. But I'd only just begun. There's so much I wanted to say."

"What?"

Mr Sudbourne, the hard-landscaping contractor, was signalling at Eleanor through the office window.

"We only properly realise that through the process of saying," Grenville began.

Eleanor reached out for her pocket calculator.

"But I have ideas I want to explore about morality, art, sex, politics. Hm. The beauty of fourteen year old —"

"Make that twenty..." she was muttering.

"Certainly not! Besides the issue of consent is a dark and complex matter —"

She gestured at Sudbourne and mouthed "two minutes."

"And one of the things I most wanted to talk about. The politics of it. As a sado-masochist I fancy I'm supremely well qualified —"

"Go on then, get to your desk," she said.

"I'm too tired now. I shall have a rest before Simon comes by with lunch. He swears by hand-reared corn-muffins with organic giraffe pellets or something. O Lord! What we endure for the sake of friendship. Though it might work, I suppose? Outward and downward!"

From that day, Grenville developed a habit of phoning her. Sometimes he rang three or four times a day. They sorted out methods for regulating the length of the calls and signalling their need to ring off. He said that often, the very briefest exchange was enough to nudge him off the treadmill of despair.

Her relationship with Theo improved, too. She didn't feel so fed up. No longer put pressure on him to do things that he couldn't see the point of, like holidaying or going out together. Didn't need Theo to sit about nattering anymore, either. Tucking away her daily thoughts and comic anecdotes, she kept them back to amuse Grenville, to distract him and while away the time when he needed her company. He became her secret, inner other. Her own special friend again.

Eleanor never had any trouble being alone at the Old Rectory, her rooms were secure and she was in friendly contact with the neighbours. In the evenings she was relieved to be rid of the builders and get on, uninterrupted, at her drawing board. It was only that without Theo, bedtimes and breakfasts could be a bit flat. Now, she didn't mind so much, as they were accompanied by chats with Grenville. Returning to an empty house was always lonely but now she didn't mind that either; Eleanor went straight to the answerphone, knowing she was coming home to Grenville's voice.

## STAY

Two days ago Theo had announced that he was going to Milan. Short notice. Tight schedule. Would have loved Eleanor to go with him but it would mean delaying Zeb's work on the sitting room plasterwork and cancelling his family's visit. He'd smiled. She'd seen that smile before. She pushed away its full meaning.

"Do this for me, sweetheart?" Thinking he could distract her with his gratitude, "My sister annoys me, her husband's a windbag and their children drive me round the bend. Whereas you like them…"

Resentment edged in closer but she shouldered it away.

"Go on," he'd wheedled, "you'll enjoy it!"

True enough.

After Theo left, Eleanor took hold of the arrangements. How to keep off brooding about him? Do a Bloomsbury. The nowt-a-penny nobody was going to have a country house party. She remembered that Gail and Zeb, while on a job for Theo, had been lodged with his sister and they had got on. Eleanor pleased everyone by inviting them all to stay for the weekend.

"I think she's settled down now —" Zeb came into the Old Rectory kitchen from trying to put Lucy to bed. "I'm glad you borrowed that cot, Eleanor, or she'd be swarming all over the house. Oh man, I need a beer!" He helped himself from a jug brought over from the village pub.

They were waiting for supper till Theo's family arrived. Eleanor had prepared the dining room by converting Zeb's work trestles into a large table. There would be Gail and Zeb. Theo's sister Imogen and her husband Carlo plus four kids spaced about among the adults. Lucy upstairs in her cot, asleep. No Theo. The cutlery and chairs were a bit random, reminiscent of Grenville's in a way but at least she had brought in blue flowers from the garden to match the blue paper napkins.

In the kitchen Zeb checked the baby intercom as Eleanor cut quiches and Gail sat stroking her pregnant stomach.

"How's Thrasher, my lovely?" Zeb crouched by Gail's chair and put his ear to her belly.

"Thrashing." Gail gave him a tired smile.

"Here comes the dropkick! Come and feel this, Eleanor!"

"Don't mind me, Zeb," Gail said.

"I know we've been through it all before with Lucy but I still can't get over it! Come on," he beckoned to Eleanor, "what d'you think of that!"

"Have you ever felt...?" Gail put a hand out to her. Eleanor shook her head.

"Feel."

Gail took Eleanor's wrist and planted her hand just above the groin.

"Eee 'eck!" Eleanor gasped. "It feels like... like puppies on a trampoline! And your tummy, it's so hard! Doesn't it hurt?"

"Oh no! No. Not this bit."

"That's them now!" Zeb had heard the crunching sound of tyres on gravel. Eleanor followed Gail and Zeb out to the entrance portico. There was a tootle on the horn and the raking crash of the orange campervan's sliding door.

"Oh my God!" Zeb shouted, "It's like the bloody Trojan Horse, isn't it!" as children, dogs, bags, toys and sweet wrappers erupted from the van.

Before long, the hall was full of mattresses, sleeping bags, clothes, boxes of food, dog bowls, shoes and wellingtons. Bedding, towels, pillows, clothes, toys, rolls of lavatory paper and a potty had broken out of their plastic binliners and were making their escape up the stairs. Greetings, barking and excited laughter echoed up to the landing and soon Lucy could be heard crackling over the intercom,

"Me down! Me down! Upa! Upa! Dadda? Dadda! Me down now!"


Eleanor showed Carlo the sleeping arrangements, apologising for the lack of proper furniture.

"Stop saying sorry!" Carlo said. "It's just fine, honey. The empty rooms are so restful... makes a real change for us! I like it. The get-away-from-it-all of summer camp but with proper sanitary arrangements and *privacy*! It's great. I'll start bringing up our things and get the kids pumping up their lilos."

When Eleanor went back downstairs she was stunned by the complete scene change. Her tidy kitchen had been transformed into a chaotic canteen. It was as if her and the visitors' belongings had been mixed together, flung into the air and left wherever they landed. Gail, pregnant and eating lightly but often, had started on a quiche. Seeing this, the children said they were starving and Imogen had begun to hand out food, insisting they sit down properly at the kitchen table. Being sent on a hunt for chairs, the kids discovered the dining room and ransacked it for chairs, cutlery and blue paper napkins. Eleanor was in time to see a packet, which was being pulled open by a nine-year-old, come apart suddenly, creating a ceiling-high fountain of salted peanuts. The dogs went berserk. It was now a race to see how many peanuts could be salvaged before the dogs gobbled them up. Above the noise Theo's sister called over to her,

"I've opened some wine we brought. Here's yours, darling!"

After supper the adults sat among the ruins, drinking and passing round a joint while the children, who had been put to bed, could still be heard in the distance.

"They're so excited those kids, they're still racketting about up there!" Carlo yawned.

"How do we amuse them if the weather breaks?" Eleanor asked, worried.

"Darling, stop fretting," Theo's sister patted her arm. "If it's raining they'll play football, Batman and princesses up and down the corridors and if its sunny they'll do it outside. Live for the day! You have to with children!" Imogen leaned back in her chair and took the spliff from Zeb. She inhaled the smoke, "Oh heaven!" she breathed, "the children are happy *somewhere else*. It's the end of the day. I've got some wine and some dope and I'm not bothered about the meaning of life.

I'm sorry Gail, darling, I forgot, you can't drink or smoke. But it's extraordinary how when one's in pod one doesn't want any of it, actually."

"Yeah, and being pregnant is the one time..." Gail sliced banana onto a piece of bread and marmite, "I'm not bothered about the meaning of life, either."

"That's because you *are* the meaning of life, honey, and —"

Carlo was interrupted by his daughter who'd come down to the kitchen in her pyjamas to complain that her brother had taken her Sad Rabbit because he couldn't find his Silky and she and her friend wanted to be in the same room and the baby wanted to be in with the boys too but was a bit smelly...

Zeb switched on the intercom, bringing the upstairs hullaballoo into the kitchen. In amongst it, his Lucy's furious voice could be heard, yelling,

"Me down! My done poo! My done poo! Want noo napnap now! Me down now!"


When the children and dogs had finally settled to sleep, the adults began a drift to bed. Eleanor, the last to leave the kitchen, hesitated tipsily in the doorway,

"By 'eck! I don't think I've ever seen such a mess..."

Gail put her arm round Eleanor and looked at the kitchen with her,

"Yeah, mate. I'll admit, it's impressive and what's more we're going to leave it all till the morning, eh."

"Good thing Theo isn't here to see it —" Eleanor giggled as she switched off the light. "I think Grenville'ud be proud of me, though, don't you!"

# CONVERSE

Zeb set up his trestles in the garden and the kids dragged out chairs. They helped Carlo construct a barbi and agreed to guard the food from dogs and flies in exchange for ice lollies. Eleanor worried to Imogen that in spite of doing an enormous shop, maybe she had not provided enough.

"Don't fret, darling," Imogen said. "If I brought a trailer full of breakfast cereal and fruit juice it still wouldn't be enough. And as for loopaper! What *do* they do with it?"

As the hot day passed Eleanor began to relax. Bloomsbury was never like this. But she thought of Grenville instead, of his parties and how he'd stood back and allowed them to take on a life of their own. She decided to let go and found that housework turned into kids' games and really good food arrived somehow out of the chaos.

That afternoon, the adults sat in the shade, round the remains of lunch. Behind them, the lime tree hummed with bees like a generator. Another adult had joined the party. This was Lauren, Grenville's agent. Eleanor had always liked the older woman, finding her sensible, straight and reassuring. A day or so ago Lauren had got in touch on a professional matter. The business concluded, and made bold by Theo's absence, Eleanor had invited Lauren and her two teenagers to come for the day. The impulse had paid off, Lauren fitted in and her kids were a great childminding asset. Away from their peers, the teenagers had reverted to childhood and were romping in the grass, gathering handfuls of hay, chucking it about, stuffing it down each other's shirts and chasing the younger ones who screamed with excitement.

Eleanor shaded her eyes and looked over the wide swathe of new-mown grass, through the twinkling gnats, to where children and swallows darted in and out of sunlight and shadow. Her guests were laughing again, this time at the puzzlement of the dogs who raced around yapping, jumping up to catch flying handfuls of grass and snapping at the air when the bunches disintegrated round them.

"We want drinks!" one of the children rushed up to the table. Her friend followed slowly, his eyes goggling through his thick glasses.

"Tell us about the little friend, then," Zeb said when the two children had gone back to the others.

"He's her classmate," Imogen said. "We've offered to have him at weekends. Give his parents a chance to sort things out. They're having a terrible time. Marriage trouble. That little chap's special needs are part of it. They offload him on anyone who'll have him."

"Its wicked!" Zeb licked the paper of his roll up. "Poor kid! How can they do that! The family, for better or for worse, it's everything, isn't it?" There was no doubt in his voice.

"Well, they want to have an 'open marriage'. The boy's Dad has fallen for another woman and there are problems with sex —"

"Sex! Sex? What's that?" Zeb frowned, "O ye-es! It's coming back to me now! We have very happy memories of it, don't we Gail?"

"An open marriage...?" Lauren looked round. "As a divorcee and older woman I'd be interested to hear the opinions of the younger generation."

244

"Open marriage? Great idea. Never works." Carlo sighed out smoke from his after-dinner cigarillo.

"No," Lauren said. "But why? Why not? My ex wanted an open marriage. It worked for him. I didn't like it at all. Well! Didn't have time for it either, I was so preoccupied, exhausted, juggling my career and those two —" She looked over to where her teenagers were giving rides to the young ones by sitting them on an old shower curtain, pulling it across the meadow and down a grassy slope. "But then I came through the motherhood tunnel, hit the roaring forties and met someone I fancied. My husband couldn't cope with that, at all. He was stunned."

"Typical! There's men for you!" Imogen looked over at her husband, Carlo, *"It's all right for me but not for you."*

"What happened?" Carlo asked Lauren.

"We had a foul time for a while. He wanted to try again. Said he loved me. People urged me to stay for the children —" Lauren raised her eyebrows at Zeb. "But I felt like a sacrificial lamb and in the end I couldn't face the idea of living with him. I just couldn't be bothered with him. So we split. Now I live blissfully as a single parent, with visits…" Lauren smiled, "from my fancy man."

"And your ex-husband?" Imogen wanted to know.

"He found a young woman in two minutes, and having become a father again, I predict he will shortly be petitioning his new wife for an open marriage," Lauren said.

"I don't think I'd cope very well with the open marriage thing," Eleanor said, waving a wasp away from her wine glass.

"No, no! That's not marriage at all!" Zeb said. "Don't get married if you want to mess about. Fidelity is an essential part of marriage, in my opinion."

"I think fidelity is quite a thing to demand from the red-blooded male," Carlo said.

"I don't have any trouble. Why should I?" Zeb pulled a face at Gail who looked amused.

"C'mon, how can you say you don't have trouble, man, with all these beautiful girls in the world," Carlo gestured round the company. "You women are such a torment. You have no idea. There isn't a woman in the world between the age of sixteen and sixty that I don't want to unwrap and enjoy —"

"Marriage," Lauren interrupted him, "can be quite a long slog for both parties."

"Thing is," Zeb said "you make a decision don't you. And you stick with it."

"Ah, but can you decide about that sort of thing? About feelings?" Lauren turned to Zeb.

Eleanor remembered Grenville's decision to be brave. She wanted to think about him but realised that, as hostess, she must say something to interrupt; the atmosphere was getting edgy.

"Grenville," there was relief in speaking his name, "has made a decision. A decision about dying and he is —" her voice wavered. She must not cry. She must not cry in front of visitors. But grief lurched awake inside her and the tears came, "Sorry! I'm so sorry —" she got up.

"No, darling. You cry." Imogen put her arms round Eleanor and stopped her going. "Nobody minds. We're your friends."

"Poor Grenville... it's a terrible thing to happen," Gail spoke from her lounger.

"Of course we've heard of him, in the media and through my brother Theo but never met him. What's he like?" Imogen asked.

"As his agent, I only really know his work," Lauren said, "which is uneven, perhaps, but always extraordinary —"

"A mad genius," Zeb put in, "very extreme, you must admit, Eleanor."

"Extreme? I don't know. His curiosity, his energy, his daring, I just thought it were wonderful!" Eleanor groped for a tissue. "And after my home life, which was so mean minded and all about getting-one-over, Grenville was so generous and open! Tell him anything." Her voice was firmer, "There was nothing, but nothing he wouldn't talk about or think about. I loved that about him."

"There wasn't much he wouldn't *do*, either. God!" Zeb rolled his eyes.

"And none of us admire that?" Lauren wanted to know.

"Admire him? Not at all." Zeb said.

"Are you sure this isn't a class issue?" Lauren spoke to Zeb.

"Class issue, is it? I don't think so," said Zeb. "My family hassle me about politics but I tell them I can't be bothered with class war. Can't afford it, see? If there were no rich buggers doing up posh houses or rich tourists going round stately homes, where would I get the work I trained for? I'd be plastering back extensions, like my Da. Or bloody unemployed, like my Da."

"And we don't envy Grenville his lifestyle, hm?" Lauren was still at Zeb.

"No! Hell, no. Couldn't handle it at all!" Zeb said. "You need a steady hand and a head for heights in our work. The clubbing, the noise, the drugs, the late nights wouldn't do at all! Anyway, I like going out with the family, like —" Zeb glanced at Gail who was looking over to check that the older children were still minding out for their Lucy. "I'll get wrecked with the boys after a rugby match, once in a while, but —"

"You're not mates with them much," Gail said, her eyes still on Lucy.

"Right. And I'll tell you why," Zeb said. "Take our team's fly half. On the field, I'd trust him with my life. I play wing forward, you understand. He's magic. Always there when you need him, knows just what you're thinking. Off the field? Now, there's different —" Following Gail's gaze across the meadow, Zeb stood and stubbed out his roll-up as he finished, "Bore you to death. Cars. Smutty jokes. 'All men' is *not* my idea of social life at all." Zeb stroked Gail's shoulder and loped off to check on the little ones.

Carlo had been indoors, made coffee and brought it out to the women. "What about the orgies, the anonymous sex-on-tap gays are famous for?" Carlo brought back the topic of conversation.

"Anonymous sex wouldn't do for me," Eleanor said, stirring her coffee. "Too scary! I like to get to know people, you know, be intimate. Orgies are so unromantic."

"Maybe as an older woman, I just don't need *that* much sex anymore?" Lauren said. "Quality not quantity is what I enjoy these days!"

"If Carlo didn't want sex, it would mean he was dead." Imogen patted her husband's knee.

"I would not want gay-style sex. Too violent and gladiatorial. More like assault than sensual pleasure. And *now* look what's happened..." he said.

"All that instant sex is very empty," Imogen said. "I should be sorry to see our boys turn out that way; gay relationships are so cold and ruthless. But I expect this terrible AIDS thing will put them off —"

"Just a minute!" Eleanor cut through this. "Being gay isn't a choice, you know, and I can tell you there's all different kinds, like. Long term couples and ever so many not out clubbing every night and anyway they all have just the same struggles with love and sex and jealousy and living together as straights do. Even Grenville. He would never allow jealousy, because he believed in sexual freedom, but he needs people and gets upset by rejection, just like the rest of us. Sorry, I don't mean to be rude or anything but I must stand up for my friends —"

"Sure, sure, honey," Carlo put up his hands, "and I'll support their rights and everything *but*, and I know its politically incorrect, I've got to say... I never met a gay I liked."

Lauren and Imogen sucked in their breath.

Eleanor was unmoved. She remembered Grenville's lessons: political correctness was alright as a form of good manners but sexual fantasy was beyond its reach and, most important of all, *discussion should never be censored.*

"Go on. *Out in the open with it!*" Grenville's words came out of her mouth.

"Well, they seem real vain to me and dumb, you know?" said Carlo. "Sure, I remember comparing cock sizes, seeing if you could pee further than the other kid and having jerkoff races —"

This made the women laugh.

"Yeah, but I grew out of it, for heavens' sakes! And I guess I'm the kinda guy who just can't understand anyone who isn't —" Carlo put his arms out and smiled at the women, "just crazy about girls!"

Eleanor and Lauren began to clear the table while Imogen and Gail looked away from him to their children playing in the meadow.

After the washing up, Imogen and Carlo disappeared to their bedroom while Lauren and Eleanor went back to where they'd left Gail snoozing in the shade. Lauren settled into a garden chair and said,

"I'm so grateful for your invitation, Eleanor. It's bliss to escape from London and come to this paradise of yours. Life is getting so tight, so pressured these days! My office is filling up with new machinery and ferocious young things drinking bottled water. Gone are the days of dog-eared manuscripts and boozy lunches with dotty authors. I'm having to completely reinvent myself..." Lauren looked round at Gail and Eleanor, "But do tell me... relationships, the lives of you young women... these things are altogether better now, surely?"

"Dunno," Gail's voice was sleepy. "Win some, lose some, I'd say."

Lauren put on her dark glasses and took out a book.

"I thought I might read, but it's too much like work. Much more enjoyable,' she said, putting the book down again, "to sit back and watch the sports."

Zeb was running about with Lucy in his arms. He seemed to have organized a chaotic form of rugby played with a frizbee. The dogs were bounding after him, worrying his ankles and barking hysterically while everyone else was useless with laughter.

Eleanor had joined in the game till she reckoned it was time to go and make some more drinks. Alone in the kitchen, she rearranged the muddle, enough to bring a feeling of order, before setting out the ingredients for lemonade. She thought of Yasmine as she squeezed the fruit and stirred in the sugar.... missed her... Mama Yasmine... always so warm and approving. Another of her friends Theo couldn't stand...

After putting the jugs in the fridge she moved through the cool of the house, piling up books and toys, putting scattered jigsaw pieces in a bowl, hanging up towels. It did not bring contentment. She stopped half-way down the stairs. The entrance hall was the Old Rectory's glory. Mellow afternoon light dropped softly from the glass dome onto the wide, curved staircase, gilding the banisters and warming the worn stone floor below. Eleanor paused to admire it, to see it as she hoped her guests would. She heard soft endearments from behind the door of Imogen and Carlo's bedroom and shouts of laughter from the meadow. The house was just as she wanted it: beautiful, scented with lemons and full of her friends. But she felt so lonely.

A swallow swooped through the front window, flashed round the dome and vanished into the sunlight of the open door at the far end of the hall. The shock of its swift intrusion left her gasping, gripping the banisters, her heart pounding in her chest.

# V

## CALL

"Hello!" Eleanor yapped.

"Old bean!" came Grenville's startled voice.

"I'm just *so*, so angry," she shouted down the phone, "I've had it with Theo!"

"Bound to happen! Stopped cutting the mustard in bed, did he? Shaved off his beard?"

Eleanor had expected Theo to come home, to talk, to try and sort things out. She had prepared a meal and tidied herself up but he'd rung to say he couldn't face it and was going to stay in town. After an hour since his call spent sobbing and tossing angry arguments around in her head, she pitched her frustration at Grenville,

"I just know you won't see it my way but Theo is cheating on me!" she said. "The bastard doesn't even bother to deny it anymore. And I can't stand it! I'm so hurt and humiliated, I feel like I've been burgled! And all my belongings, our relationship, all smashed up and scattered about all over the place. And by him! How could he! Oh, I've heard all your blooming theories, about openess and fulfilment and free sex but I can't put up with it and that's that!" Her anger, and the phone, made shouting at Grenville possible. She half expected him to cut her off, as Theo had.

"It's all beyond me, old thing. I thought you fancied him. It's the only excuse."

"I do. I did. He really has it for me. I could never resist him —" she clamped her hand over her mouth to hold in her feelings.

"Poor old you. And to no avail. Terrible when that happens. Particularly when he's so disagreeable. I do sympathise dearest. I too have boiled in the cauldron of concupiscence in my time, and for some pretty dreadful people. So, Theo has gone off —"

"No, Grenville! I'm the one going off! Me!" her fury burst out again. "I have had enough. Theo still wants me, if you want to know. He says that the other women don't count. He says 'it's just sex, sweetheart'. And don't bother defending him. I know you're on his side!"

"Not at all! What does he mean, *just* sex! I don't hold with *just* sex. I won't have sex reduced in that way. Specially now I'm to die for it. I could take on the role of martyr, what d'you think? St Grenville of the Virus?"

Eleanor's rage evaporated at this reminder, "It's not your style, love."

"Quite right. Too pathetic. Always thought martyrdom a euphemism for defeat. Mind you, the essence of martyrdom is to be absolutely unrepentant and I'm certainly that! Particularly in the face of the moralists who have not heard the Good News —" He began to sing-song like a priest, "Hear these comfortable words spoken by our saviour Friedrich Nietzsche: *Go-tt ist to-t.* Therefore all you fuck-witted imbeciles AIDS is no-t a mo-ral pheno-men-on."

"How are —"

"Heard that Douggie Sert has died. *Defectus per pestilentem,*" Grenville swept on. "We always used to call him 'Dead' anyway, remember? Ran that awfully good bookshop in Warwick. Poor man. Hated being queer. Aghast to be gay, you might say. He was one of my failures. Never managed to persuade him to a life of joyful depravity. Skulked about for hours in changing rooms and bogs. Nothing wrong with that, except he was so dreary about it. Full of shame and guilt." The cheerful voice had a cracked edge. "Will have to go to his funeral. It will be all family and cover up. Spend my life now, going to fucking funerals —"

"You're being very brave, my love," Eleanor managed to cut in.

"Well, you know, the situation isn't altogether irredeemable. I shan't have to be old, for one thing. And I realised last night that I needn't bother flossing my teeth any more... flossing... always such a bore, don't you think?"

"What are you —" she tried again.

"Uncle Archie was here this morning. Brought me the news about Dead Sert. Then Miles the Militant Queen, turns up. At first there's jolly talk about enormous cocks and pretty arseholes and then, my dear, the most cataclysmic row! Hang on a minute. The front door again. Tinker's getting it." Grenville dropped his voice, "God! Not *more* people!"

Eleanor stretched the telephone line across her desk and changed to sitting in her workroom comfy chair. Wanting to be distracted, she listened to Grenville's story.

"Miles the Militant said something frightfully right on about feeling that every time he stuck his cock up somebody's arse, he was asserting the right to be queer and that even his illness was a source of pride. Sharp intake of huff from Archie the Ancient. It pains me when people don't get on, as you know, and I was just about to return the conversation to boys' bums when madam Militant added some burble about 'outing' people for the sake of the 'gay community'. Archie la Closet didn't like this at all. Hang on, Nelly. Just giving Sandra a little wave —"

Eleanor heard the sound of a kiss being blown and watched a blackbird eat berries in a bush outside the window.

"*What gay community!* Archie was apoplectic. *No such thing unless you mean a ruthless clique of heartless exhibitionists!* Archie roared on, *The only thing that unites you people, that stops you tearing each other to bits, is that you are persecuted and facing catastrophe.* I wanted to shut Closet up but then Miles started shouting back. I think the excitement brought on a fit of infantile regression, because all that came out of my mouth was Matron's voice saying, 'Now, now boys —!"

Eleanor laughed at Grenville's falsetto,

"— you know we are *never* at home to Mr Rude!"

"What happened, then?" she asked as the blackbird flew out of the bush and landed on a patch of bright green, sunlit grass. A need to get away from the Old Rectory began to weave itself into her thoughts.

"Finally, in an attempt to lift us out of the mundane squalor of politics I bleated something about the sacred aspect of Eros. *Trahit sua quemque voluptas*, Archie said —"

"What! He said what?"

"Latin for 'it's just sex, sweetheart.' I've never seen Archie so livid. *Steady on!* I managed to squeak in the end, *or you'll have a stroke and beat me to the pearly gates.* But Archie will survive me though he is even more obsolete than I am, with his Virgil and his liberalism and his demands for privacy," Grenville snorted. "And for queers to be respectable. Must forgive the old poof I suppose: a total conformist and patriot forced to spend most of his life as a criminal."

"I wish I was with you. I'd love to see Archie." Eleanor fiddled with her hair, lifting strands round in front of her face and examining the ends.

"No, no. I'm completely exhausted," Grenville complained. "Fortunately the Witch turned up on her broomstick, turned Archie and Miles into frogs and they've hopped off."

It made a good story but Eleanor could tell Grenville was upset. He would have wanted Archie and Miles to flirt, not fight. She knew she ought to move the talk on but said, flipping her hair away,

"Well, I think Archie's got a point." Her mind, like the needle on a compass, swung back to its grievance, "I might have been able to manage your free love thing if Theo hadn't made me feel like... like one among many, an interchangeable piece of goods." She repressed the anger in her voice, "I don't want to compete with others. I'm sick of being compared! Always found wanting by my family —" She could hear that Grenville was being spoken to and knew he wasn't listening but it relieved her to talk. "I want something that's just mine. I want to feel special. Intimate. And for that, you need privacy."

"Privacy!" Grenville picked up the last word. "Gawd! Not another one! Secrecy. Privacy. Repression by another name. Think of the transformation if everyone *came out*. Said what they were. Imagine it! An end to hypocrisy. No more exclusion," Grenville's voice was insistent, "no more guilt and shame. Ah then, I would not have lived in vain!"

"Did Rajiv come with Archie?" Eleanor felt a real need to be with her old friends. "How is he? It's too long," she hinted, "since I came —"

"Ah! Hm…"

Eleanor waited and then said,

"Oh Grenville, no. Don't tell me. Please. No."

There was silence between them.

"Oh God. Not him, too," she whispered.

"Nothing definite, dearest…" his voice dragged, "but Uncle Archie does seems very angry or very downhearted these days. It may be that young Rajiv just wants to spread his wings. Leave the old boy? Archie was sixtysomething this year. Anyway haven't seen him. Haven't been asked round for ages. I can only suspect Rajiv doesn't want to confront his destiny in my increasingly repulsive form."

"Just ask Archie. Come on! It's unlike you not to just ask —"

"Much though I disapprove, indeed, violently disapprove of secrecy, good manners requires that I respect Archie and Rajiv's closet. Besides, Archie is family —"

Eleanor was going to ask what that had to do with it when —

"Nurse Tinker has come to bully me about pills. I'll take them! I promise! *And when will that be?* says the Belle of Stepney. Excuse me. Don't go Nelly!"

Eleanor knew she could not face the weekend alone at the Old Rectory. Hearing sounds of swallowing she took the chance to ask,

"Would you like a visit?"

"Well, perhaps." He did not sound keen. "Thing is, Archie and Miles have worn me out. I don't cope with real live people anymore," Grenville raised his voice, "except useless bits of fluff like Tinker."

"He is not the useless fluffy! Tinker is good boy."

Eleanor heard Yasmine's voice calling across the ball-room, followed by rude banter. She wished she was there. With her friends. Where she belonged.

"The Witch is besotted with Tinker," Grenville returned to her, "since he plucked up courage to tell her that her cakes were the best thing since sliced bread!"

The pleasure in his voice made Eleanor miss him.

"The Witch and her familiar are just off. A moment, my dear, while I grovel to the Mistress. The lesbians send lascivious greetings!"

"I should so like to see you all," she pleaded.

"But talking to you on the phone, Nelly. I like it awfully. I can reach you from my bed, from the bog, from my soul."

"Where are you now?"

"By my plants. Archie brought me a Passion Flower. Rather apt in a grim sort of way. Talking of martyrdom. Nails. Crown of thorns. Purple. Gorgeous thing —"

Dread gathered in her guts at the prospect of being stuck at the Old Rectory. Alone. Tearing herself to bits over Theo.

"And I can reach out to that lovely geranium you gave me, dearest," Grenville was saying. "Such a delicious pong. I've got quite a little collection of scented-leaf geraniums now. There's *Lady Plymouth*.... she has a strict sort of whiff... school prize-giving... and —"

Where to go? Who would accept her at such short notice?

"*Fragrans*... for a walk in the forest and *Peppermint*... ah... hot summer days with Nanny, catching tiddlers in the moat at Wyvernden..."

Eleanor heard the sigh of his breath.

"I miss you so, Grenville."

"Nonsense! I look hideous. You really don't want to see me. The blower's the thing. Real live people are too exhausting, don't you think? Can't put the receiver down on them with any grace."

Eleanor, realizing that she was not going to be allowed at Grenville's, was impatient to get away and start making arrangements. She must find someone to take her in. She moved back to her desk and reached for her address book.

"Archie also gave me Dante's *Paradiso* to read. Rather tactless, I thought, and not my idea of heaven at all, more like a giant corporation. Too neurotically systematic, even for me. But the conclusion. I'd forgotten. Such poetry! So sublime yet so simply worded..."

There was a rustle of pages at both ends of the line.

"At the climax of the poem and the soul's long journey, there is a vision of God," Grenville explained, "light, rainbows, squared circles and so on, the usual mystic caboodle. But at the centre of all this, for a second, the soul sees *itself*. A moment of complete acceptance, don't you see?"

Eleanor began to make a list of telephone numbers.

" 'And then at last'... listen, listen, a rough translation," he began. " 'My will and my desire were set in even motion like a wheel... by the love... *l'amor che move il sole e l'altre stelle…* by the *love* which moves the sun and all the stars.' "

After a silence, he said in a voice full of longing,

"Oh that it might be so."

But Eleanor wasn't listening. Her mind was elsewhere, wondering where on earth she could go. How she was going to find a home for the weekend. Who would want her?

# Six months later

## i

PART

Tinker had given her one of Grenville's old shirts for measurement and it hung, like a ghost, in Eleanor's Old Rectory workroom. She was stitching, hand finishing a garment. She tried to concentrate on the minute weave of her needle, binding and tucking frayed edges, smoothing out and unpicking any knots or catches in the machining and secreting loose threads under the seams.

At her last visit, Grenville had waited till Tinker was out of the room before leaning towards her,

"What shall I wear to meet *the* Queen?" he'd asked, pointing heavenwards. "Tink won't let me speak of my departure but it's very important. My last ritual. Advise me, dearest, on my costume." It had been almost like old times, that long, rambling discussion about clothes and colours and symbolism.

Eleanor stopped sewing because she could not see to work. Tears blotted the cloth. Exhausted with weeping, she laid her head on the worktable.

This morning, Theo had left the Rectory for London, though she had pleaded that he stay and talk.

"No more talk," he'd said. "Enough now. We've been round and round it all hundreds of times and I've told you my position. It's up to you, sweetheart, but I can't take any more of this. Of this going on and on and on. You women. The same old ground, day and night, over and over. It's mountains out of molehills."

She smoothed the soft fabric, turned it, carefully examining the sleeve and shoulder seams for gathers or wrinkles. The neck of a garment needed special care, even with a simple robe like this.

Grenville had returned to the subject of grave clothes many times during their calls. He'd favoured green for a while as the colour of Epiphany but then said, "Green is no good. I don't feel at all enlightened."

Tinker also contrived moments alone with Eleanor. She never forgot to ask how he was coping. During one of their recent chats, he'd mentioned that Grenville had few clothes he would wear,

"Everything itches, dunnit, apart from that old Moroccan thing what I can't hardly get off of him to wash," he'd complained.

"Leave it to me! This one's mine," Eleanor had clutched Tinker's arm. "Oh, at last, love! I've got a part to play. Something I can *do*."

Since most clothes were torture on Grenville's flaying skin, she hoped that her careful choice of cloth and virtually seamless work would bring warmth without torment. She had made two djellabas, in different shades, one in a weave of blues, the other in warm pinks.

"I should like white, really," Grenville had said one day, "the colour of light and the liturgical colour of Christmas. But," he'd worried, "white represents innocence of soul. Do you think I'm allowed...?"

Yes. Eleanor had made that decision for him. Here, in her hands was a third robe, soft and warm, of the purest white.

Laying aside her work she went to wash her tear-stained face again. The house was winter quiet. The day, being still and overcast, made the light from the dome so soft, it cast no shadow. Such a lovely space. So much room to be unhappy in.

Could she and Theo live together as friends, without sex, she'd asked. Have their own bedrooms? He could have as many "casual affairs" as he liked then.

Theo had rejected that idea, straight off. Couldn't see the point of it. Pleading. "But you are my sweetheart! My partner! We work brilliantly together. You are the person I care about, live with, come home to. Those other women, they don't mean anything." Exasperated. "You're living in some romantic never-never land! I never expected a friend of Grenville's to believe in monogamy. Time to wake up to modern life, sweetheart." Defensive. "I really can't see what's so dreadful, it's only a bit of fun. Casual sex. Women can do it too, now. You've done it yourself."

Eleanor confronted her puffy face in the mirror,

"Only because *you* did, Theo," she argued aloud at her reflection. "To pay you back, you bastard, and because I felt so lonely." She stooped and splashed her face with cold water. Made me even lonelier.

"Time to leave the Old Rectory," he realised. "I've missed you. We'll live together properly in London. I shan't be tempted to stray then," he supposed. "Deep down this is all about you wanting sprogs," he understood. "Go ahead. I'll come round to it. I'll do whatever you want."

Eleanor wanted back whatever it was that had made her in love with him. She'd fancied him so much. So manly. Big, dark and impressive. Bit like her Dad, in a way, but not a pig-ignorant bully. Theo was famous and admired, even Grenville rated his intelligence. Theo was cultured and treated her work with respect. It had been that... work and sexiness put together. Swept her off her feet. She'd felt close to him because he was part of her work. Nothing could have made her feel more involved, more attached. And then, on top of that... finding him *so* attractive. But with his bits on the side showing for all to see, had come a reaction. The humiliation of it! She'd shut down. Gone off him. From finding him a turn-on she'd switched to feeling insulted by his lovemaking. His cheating made him vulgar. Unromantic. Her idea of him had been eroded, exposing layers and layers of resentment.

She held her face, eyes shut, in the darkness of the towel.

If only Theo would let her withdraw from his sex life. No involvement. No feeling compared. Just friendship. Like it had been with Grenville.

Theo had asked, "Don't you want sex?"

"Oh aye," she'd said.

"But not with me, is that it?"

Right. And there, at last, she had managed to pay Theo back. Hurt him like he had hurt her. Trouble was, revenge wasn't sweet. It tasted like dust butty.

Having made a hot drink, Eleanor wandered through the empty rooms of the Old Rectory. She looked out of the tall sitting room windows at the silent garden and motionless copse beyond. The winter stillness of the view was interrupted; two squirrels rippled along the bare branches so fast they looked like silk ribbon whipped through the trees.

Eight years ago she'd escaped from her family. Not three years with Theo and she was slipping back into that state of perpetual unhappiness she associated with home. Home, that place where she had always felt most desolate.

The Old Rectory was finished, ready to be inhabited and on the market for a great deal of money.

"Spacious period house of outstanding beauty..." read the brochure.

Eleanor went back to her warm workroom.

She took up the robe again. One of her long, dark hairs had caught on the soft material. Picking it off the white cloth, she threaded it into her needle and began to weave a minute, coiling pattern. She worked round the open neck of the gown, where her discrete decoration would not touch or chafe his skin. The hair was springy and difficult to manage but she pulled out another from her head, and another. The roots acted as tiny, anchoring knots in the fine fabric. Soon the collar was delicately embroidered with the dark threads of her hair.

Grenville's garment, the one he would wear forever, was finished.

## CLOSE

"Here you are..." Eleanor took the parcel out of her bag and handed it down to Grenville, who was in his armchair.

"My dear! What's this?" He looked over to Tinker for support.

"We noticed how you're always wearing that djellaba from Morocco and that it was getting a bit past it, like —"

"Yes, so warm and comfortable but —"

"But. I know. Tinker told me," Eleanor reassured him, "you've tried to get replacements but the new fabric's too scratchy. So I made these three myself in the softest, equivalent weight cloth I could find. They're ready to put on, all washed out, no chemicals or enzymes or anything."

Grenville fingered the material and put a thin hand out to Eleanor,

"What kindness..." he closed his eyes as she leant over and kissed him on the forehead.

"I hope you like the colours. The white one..."

"Oh yes..." he unfolded it slowly and then looked up at her, "Yes Nelly, we shall keep this one *for best*."

As Tinker gathered the garments off Grenville's lap Eleanor said,

"And I've brought a lemon cake and teabags. I know the only way to get decent tea in this place is to make it myself."

She followed Tinker out of the ballroom. Going upstairs, she leant against the wall with her eyes tightly closed and her hand clapped over her mouth. "O God," squeezed out from between her fingers.

"Yeah, I think he's gone down a bit since you last saw him…"

Eleanor opened her eyes at Tinker and nodded.

"Bit of a shock is it?" Tinker moved towards Grenville's bedroom, "I don't notice it so much, see, cos I'm with him all the time, n'I"

"He's lucky he's got you."

"Yeah, well. Dunno as his relatives think so. I have to make myself scarce when they're around."

"I'm surprised at Grenville wanting that!" Eleanor helped to put the djellabas on hangers.

"It's not Gren's idea. He wants me to face 'em out. All right for him though, innit. He don't have to put up with them staring like I'm an alien with two heads or something. His Auntie's all right but the rest of them give me the heebie-jeebies. I can see what they're think-ing: *fucking little rip off shit*, that's what they're thinking."

"They're not, you know. Nobody rips them off! Likely they're fascinated by your piercings, love. And if it's aliens from another planet you're on about, that's *them* not us!"

"Y'right!" he burst into his nervous, shrieking laugh.

"How's the sandwich kiosk?" she asked, when Tinker had got his breath back.

"It's going great. Sold out by two o'clock, even now, out of season. Making a pile of money. I work for it, mind! Rushed off me feet."

As they went down to the kitchen Tinker said,

"Only it's getting so Gren could do with me here. He don't say nothing about it, but I can tell. Know what I mean? I'd like a chat with you about it, El, but not now, later." He made the "on the phone" sign, adding, "Give me the cake and everything. I'll do the tea. You get back to him El, go on. He hates being alone, doesn't he, eh?"

Grenville was over by his plants, examining a collection of auriculas.

"Do they cry when you pick them?" she tried to sound lighthearted.

"Don't be silly. The whole point is that they're not human. They're a completely different order of being."

"But you say they need to be talked to —"

"Yes, but I don't know why or what aspect of my language is effective. It could be some unknowable-to-us particle of human speech they need or simply the displacement of air caused by my voice. Besides I need to talk to them."

"Why's that?" Eleanor, miserable and at a loss, was using questions to fill the space. She found it hard to look at him. This champion of difference was fading into the anonymity of the dying. He looked like all the others, with ears too big, hair close cropped and the gaunt grimace of skin pulled taut over the skull.

"That sense plants give me of other worlds," he said, "The possibility of other forms of consciousness, even. Consciousness is the great mystery, not love. Love is just lust and sentiment, a form of dependence or addiction, what d'you think?"

"It's too terrible. I can't live with that."

"No, all right. All the same, I'm much more interested in consciousness."

Before he died Eleanor knew she wanted to find a way to say how much she loved him. She had thought about it a lot. She musn't leave it too late.

"We tend to think of consciousness in terms of sight, and thought in terms of speech, when neither are anything of the sort..." his voice drifted by her.

A splinter of dream about a mirror nagged at her memory. Somehow Grenville had stepped through into Looking Glass Land and she could see him in there but between them was this invisible barrier.

"I'm hoping that consciousness is some sort of element at large in the universe," he continued, "which we host during our lives. A sort of parasitical energy? Perhaps consciousness is hosted by many different forms in many different ways, even by my lovely flowers. Art might be a sort of very clumsy, secondary host form that we humans have managed to make."

"Ghost form?" she misheard, preoccupied with how to make her declaration.

"You're right. It's not very original. Just a different way of talking about the same old stuff. Ghosts. The soul, migration of, and so forth."

Eleanor looked round the room, searching for something to say to stop her blurting out the words "I love you." She must prevent herself. He'd hate it. He'd ranted on, often enough, about lazy minds and soppy cliches.

"It's much more tidy in here than I've ever seen it," she said.

"That's Tinker's fault," he said loudly as Tinker came in and put down two mugs of tea covered by plates of Eleanor's cake.

"Aw, get lost!" Tinker stuck out his tongue at Grenville before flouncing away.

"I'm too exhausted even to make a mess. What is it with you people and tidiness? Is it, after all, that the feminine tends towards stability and order? I thought I was going to find out about women from you, Nelly. What *is* it you want. Hm?" Grenville stooped over his plants again.

"I want to say..." But he seemed so out of reach she lost her nerve and mumbled, "Well I... well, I want Theo to love me."

"That's wet. An excuse to be indolent. You can do better than that, surely."

"I want to say..." she mumbled. Even though he looked round at her, sharp as ever, it was as if he had turned away down the dark road and was already out of earshot. She had left it too late. He was indifferent to the demands of love and beyond the need for it. Still, she tried to call after him,

"I... I want to tell —" she broke off again.

"I know, of wanting there is no end but go on, try. You want —?"

"A home, family —"

"Yeuch! Well, if you must. Get on with it."

"Theo doesn't want it."

"Leave him then, for fuck's sake! Just stop whingeing and get on. On, on! Onwards and upwards!" He was suddenly very angry. "It's as I always suspected," his voice was furious, "what women want is the domestication of sex, a truly deadly idea and I don't like it or them."

To stop herself shouting that she hated him, Eleanor moved away. Again, she searched for something to put in the space between them. The ballroom swivelled round her. Nothing caught her eye. She looked down at the table by his armchair. The usual glass of water, pillbox...

"I've been reading up about AIDS and there's —"

"Aha! I deduce that you've been to the dentist's again, Watson, reading magazines there —"

"— these new therapies that —"

"No, Nelly. I told you. I have decided to concentrate on the metaphysics and a good performance."

Her gaze continued to rest on his table. The familiar still life: his watch, worry beads, old leather bookmark. Would they go with him? Into his coffin? She shut off an image of the iron grille over the vault at Wyvernden and came back to chewed pencils, sharpener, shavings, notepaper and an open book,

"What are you reading?" she asked.

"The divine Donne. While I can still read. My eyes get so tired."

He came over and sat in his armchair. "I could get tapes but often I don't like the voices. You read to me. Will you? Nelly?" He picked up his book and turned the pages.

"I don't think..." she perched on the arm of the sofa near him.

"Go on, go on, this one," he handed her the book.

She took it, shaking her head.

"I want to hear you read this one," he tapped the page before settling back in his armchair and closing his eyes.

Eleanor took a breath,

> *"Sweetest love, I do not goe*
> *For wearinesse of thee —"*

"Stop! Stop! That's dreadful. Use your real voice and not that deracinated noise you've learnt to put on."

Eleanor glanced down the page at the unfamiliar language,

"I don't understand a word of it."

"Nonsense. 'Course you do. Stop being so impressed. Get on."

She looked at the poem again and took charge of it. Using the commas to guide her from one phrase to the next, she read slowly and smoothly to the end,

> "... *But thinke that wee*
> *Are but turn'd aside to sleepe;*
> *They who one another keepe*
> *Alive, ne'r parted bee.*"

"Beautiful, dearest," he said, opening his eyes. "I could hear you searching, caressing the form. It was like the first time for me, too."

"Go on!" Eleanor felt flustered so she grinned. "Bet John Donne didn't have a clog-dancer's accent."

"Pooh! He's just as likely to have sounded like you as John Gielgud. Donne was the son of an ironmonger. Lived in the Strand and Drury Lane and, proving that it doesn't do to live in suburbia, was miserable in Mitcham. A true Londoner. He may well have sounded like Tinker. Of course! *Ev'ry thy 'air for love to worke upon Is much too much*. Perfect!"

"Here, wossat about me?" Tinker came in rattling a little tub of pills.

"I was thinking, me old china, of getting you to read to me," Grenville pointed at the book. Tinker looked down his nose at the open page,

"Oooh, piss off! All that poetry bollocks 'slike being back at school. Does yer 'ead in." This brought a yelp of laughter from Grenville. "Wot? As if I don't do enough for you already, eh?' Tinker put his hand on his hip and shook the box of pills at Grenville. 'Come on dear, time for your next hit. And you should have a rest as you're going out tonight."

Eleanor, took the hint and got up to go. "Somewhere nice?" she asked as she picked up her bag.

"Concert with Archie. Where I shall be arrayed, like the lilies of the field, in one of the lovely robes you made for me, dearest."

Grenville was exhausted by Eleanor's visit. She made it difficult to maintain the small circle of light around himself, beyond which he must not look. He knew despair waited there in the darkness... like a wolf in the forest, prowling, just beyond the firelight. He must not catch its eye. He must concentrate on the light.

"What are you doing this evening, Tinker Belle?" Grenville asked, as he took his pills.

"Well, there was this guy in The Boltons last night... trying it on. Said he'd be in again tonight, so-oo...! But I won't be late. I'll be here when you get back," he reassured Grenville.

Preparing to light a cigarette, Tinker looked down at the untouched mugs of tea and cake commenting, "Didn't get round to it, I see."

"No..." Grenville said absently. He would have to find a way of telling Eleanor that there were to be no more visits. Just the phone from now on. On the phone, death was just a figure of speech. He did not discuss this decision with Tinker because they never referred to his illness. They lived as if the present would continue indefinitely. The reverses, the shrinking circle of his world, the closures were accepted without complaint or comment.

"Mm. I could really fancy some now," Grenville reached out for the cake. "Go on, you have the other bit."

"I will. I love cake... and *fags!*" Tinker let out his screeching laugh.

"Yum," Grenville agreed.

# iii

## MOTHER

"You can't put a Victorian fireplace in here. This is a 1930's house. It would look all wrong," Eleanor said.

"How can it be wrong," her mother said, "it's all the fashion."

Eleanor was at home. Her family wanted her there for the christening of her sister's latest. They had insisted — it would look peculiar in the photos without her.

"When is the money coming through from the Old Rectory? Why don't you get on with it?" her mother nagged. "You're not living in it any more. It's just sitting there. Must be worth a fortune!"

It was after supper, Eleanor and her mother were in the dining room wrapping presents and making table decorations for the party the next day.

"It's not that simple, Mam," Eleanor tried to explain, "now the bottom has fallen out of the property market. We can't break even, you know, sell it for what it cost us to restore. Let alone make any money. And after the stockmarket crash, Theo is still trying to recover… his firm is on the edge."

The glass and gilt chandelier cast its cold light over a room fussy with ornaments. Curtains shut out the twilight and Eleanor felt suffocated by the cloying scent of the air freshener her mother always sprayed round after a meal, not wanting her house to smell like the works' canteen.

"How much is Grenville going to leave you?" her mother went on. "You must get something out of these men."

"I haven't thought about it. I'm not hanging about waiting for the sale of the Old Rectory or for Grenville to die. I need to keep going. On my own two feet. Making a life of my own and that means building up a reputation at work." Eleanor opened out a roll of decorated gift wrap. "*Work*, that's what matters now!" she said.

Her mother sniffed. In that sniff Eleanor heard the disagreement about the fireplace proving that she knew nothing about interior design and heard contempt for women who had to work because they were not attractive enough to get a man to look after them.

"And I'm leaving Theo —" she might as well get the story of her failures over with.

"What? Now! Before you've got your money? That's mad! You put yourself in the wrong if you leave him. You must stay till you've got what you can out of it. Wouldn't blame you going off, after. Never liked him!" her mother said, scissoring through a sheet of tissue. "Not a patch on our lovely Grenville. Here! And another thing..." she paused with the scissors. "Where do you think you're going to live? I don't want to sound unfriendly but I can't have —"

"Don't worry! I'm not going to try and come back here," Eleanor said. Sometimes she could bring herself to the edge of panic wondering what would have happened if she'd not served Grenville at the theatre bar that night, all those years ago. Would she still be stuck here? Among people who thought nothing of her? Working for her Dad? Watching the lads watch football?

"You can go back to Grenville's, anyway. Plenty of room!"

"That's out of the question." Eleanor tried to think of something to distract her mother, "Where did you get these silver rosettes, Mam? They look expensive!"

"Isn't he leaving it to you? The house? You must come in for something. He's worth a bomb."

"What! What are you on about? It all goes back to his family! His money wasn't a lot of doubloons kept in a sock under the mattress, like."

"He made you no gifts? Didn't he give you any presents?" her mother's bracelets jingled against the table.

"Grenville gave me everything I wanted. Gave me a life! Talked to me. He —"

"He would have married you, if you'd been sensible. But you wouldn't go to bed with him. It's beyond belief."

"Sex with him would have spoiled everything," Eleanor tried to explain. "It wouldn't have worked. He had all kinds of... fantasies that I —"

"Rubbish! What d'you think marriage is for? Sex and romance for ever? Once you'd had a family you could have amused yourselves elsewhere. You're so simple! How could your Dad and me have had a daughter who's so bloody simple."

"I could never have been what he wanted, Mam. I'd have been unhappy. You don't understand." Eleanor was trying not to get into an argument.

"Don't come that w'me. I know he were a bit of a... funny one but perfectly capable..." Her mother paused. "I'm sure. He would have managed, even with you."

At this, Eleanor stopped folding paper and looked up. Though only on the other side of the table her mother seemed tiny, like someone seen from far away.

"I'll never understand why you didn't marry Grenville when you had the chance. You and your kids could have lived like royalty..." Eleanor's mother snipped pieces of sticky tape, "Had your picture in the papers. Been a celebrity! Had everything you wanted!"

"Had everything *you* wanted, you mean." Eleanor picked up the scissors. "Likely me and my kids would be dying by now. Have you thought of that? You haven't, have you?" Eleanor's voice was savage as she added, "But you wouldn't care about that! Would you? Just so long as I was Lady Grenville!"

"How dare you say that!" her mother gasped. "That's a terrible thing to say to me!"

"The truth *is* terrible —" Eleanor jabbed towards her mother with the scissors. "And those two blues don't look well together at all!"

"Oh!" her mother was blinking, shocked by this Eleanor she had never met before. "You don't think they go?"

"No! Put the blue ribbon with the white paper and the silver ribbon with the blue paper," Eleanor said.

"Mm!" her mother agreed. "That does look better!"

"I can get some things right, then."

For once, Eleanor had the last word.

## NOCTURNE

Tinker always contrived time alone with Eleanor when she visited. Usually they would have a smoke in the kitchen and chat about daily problems but this time they talked about his future. Grenville had bought him a flat a few streets away.

"He offered to leave me this place but I said nah." Tinker screwed up his face. "Don't like it, do you? That great big room! Gives me the heebie-jeebies. With all of them creepers what he's got growing up the walls as well. And he aint fixed nothing since he first come here. Nothing works. It's a fucking mess." Tinker drew on his cigarette. "So he's given me a bit of money." He dived forward and gave Eleanor a little push. "I got a bank account, would you believe!" he hooted. "And this other place, waiting for me when..."

"Have you thought what you'll do all day when...?" Eleanor off-loaded some of her own worries into the question, "I mean, you gave up your work to be with him..."

"I owed him, El. He was the only thing stopped me putting an end to myself!" Tinker shrieked with laughter.

"So what will you do? It's going to be very... You know... when..."

"Well, I got this friend..." Tinker darted Eleanor a nervous look and turned away to fill the kettle. "Do you think it's wrong?"

"What?"

"Well, you know. Kevin might come and live in my place, when…" he flicked the switch on the kettle. "I aint told nobody but you, El. Gren knows, sort of, but we don't say nothing about it. Do you think it's bad of me?"

"No, Tinker, no. I'm glad. I'm glad you've got someone. If anything, I'm a bit jealous! So will you set up the sandwich bar again with this Kevin?"

"Nah, looking after Grenville is what I really likes. Don't want to go back to no sandwiches. I got used to vomit aint I and Kev's a nurse, right? We meets him at the hospital where I goes with Gren, yeah? So Kev says I should be a nurse and I says it's mad, don't I!" Tinker waved his cigarette and shrieked, "I says what hospital would want rubbish like me!"

"Of course they do!" Eleanor said before putting out a hand, "Kevin's so right! You listen to him. They do want you. They need you! Really. Please tell me you'll go for it. You will won't you, love?"

"Well, Kev says I can start as an auxilliary, you know. No problem, you know, when. Whenever…"

As Tinker carried a tray of tea and biscuits into the ballroom, he spoke to Eleanor over his shoulder,

"Kev's a bit… different, what I mean is he don't like the 'scene' at all. On his days off, he flies kites! Me and Gren, we goes to the park with him!"

"Aha, Belle!" Grenville peered round in their direction. "You are talking about my new paramour. We are very, very in lurve."

"*Hello chicken!* That's what Kev says to Gren when he first meets him!"

"She is an angel from heaven, my dear," Grenville confided to Eleanor, "and so cute."

"So you've got two angels to look after you," she smiled.

"Ah yes," he turned to Tinker.

Thinking him incapable of such tenderness, Eleanor was amazed to see Grenville reach up and bring Tinker's hand to his cheek.

The trees in the square were gauzy with spring. A cloudy day with no shadows brought a soft light into the ballroom to blur the outlines of its disorder. The milkiness muted the boldly coloured walls and blooms of Grenville's strange bower. It had been a warm afternoon and the balcony door nearest the plants was open. The scent from a large tub of tawny wallflowers edged in on the breeze. Tinker made a move to close the doors saying, "Can't have you catching cold."

Grenville stopped him,

"Don't, Belle. Listen!"

Tinker sat back on the cushioned arm of Grenville's chair. A needle-sharp trill of birdsong pierced through the blanket of city sound. Grenville sank his head onto Tinker's chest and his eyes closed. Tinker gently stroked the hand that lay across his thighs.

"Adagio for blackbird and heartbeat," Grenville murmured as he and Tinker rested in each other's arms.

Since he had no regard for privacy, during her time with Grenville, Eleanor had caught sight of most types of sexual activity, either in the flesh or in the pornography that lay about the flat. But this she had never seen. She shifted her gaze but kept very still, wanting to be included in the quiet embrace of the moment.

The three sat without talking till Eleanor signalled to Tinker that it was time she slipped away. But Grenville opened his eyes and ignoring her protests, got up and shuffled across the room with her.

"Nelly?" he said, his head turned away from her. "Nelly? Are you listening?"

"Yes, love, yes. Of course I am."

"Will you be very good and do as I ask?"

"Yes," she promised him. "Anything! Anything you want. You have only to say."

"Don't visit again."

"Y'what!"

"Don't visit, dearest. I don't want you to see me any more."

Eleanor blinked and blinked but could not speak.

"We will talk on the phone," he said. "Good-bye, Nelly. Kiss me and go quickly now."

As she went down the stairs she heard the ballroom door close behind her.

In a trance, she walked into the square, negotiated the evening traffic in the high street and travelled on the underground to Embankment. In good time to meet Yasmine at the National Theatre, she began her walk across the Hungerford footbridge.

The evening had thickened into blue. Eleanor stood looking over the iron parapet towards the stiff arcs of Waterloo bridge and the sudden skyline round the gilded bauble of St Paul's. It was always a wonder, after the confinement of the Underground and streets, to come out into this vast atrium of sky and water.

At her back, she heard the rumbling of a train out of Charing Cross and the come-and-go, come-and-go of footsteps and voices. Winking lights moved slowly across the sky. On-off. On-off.

*Was that it? Had she seen him for the last time?*

The heavy chunks of the South Bank were perforated with light and began to float behind the illuminated swags that edged the embankments.

*What did it mean? What was it he'd said?*

The black river was restless with rocking strokes of reflected light, irridescent scribbles and glittering dots of white and gold. Among the spatter and stipple were tiny flickers of red and green. Stop-go. Stop-go.

*Was that all? Was it really over?*

It was here, on the way to a concert, that Grenville had talked to her about music and painting. She understood the ideas now. She hadn't understood much then but had been full of happiness just to be there. There. Then. So long ago.

Below its shimmering surface of colours, the dark current of the Thames swept on, dragging at its banks, at the piers and bridges. And here she was. Now. At this moment. On the bridge. She couldn't see the point of it.

*What did it mean without him? What was the point of it?*

Eleanor turned away from the view and went on with her walk to the other side.


## MOURNING


Like an anxious mother, Yasmine sat at her kitchen table watching the food go from the plate to Eleanor's mouth and nodding whenever anything was swallowed. After the theatre, Eleanor had been invited to Yasmine and Sandra's house to have supper and stay over till she got herself sorted out.

"This is so good, Yasmine," she said.

"Yeah!" Sandra agreed. "My favourite too."

"Eat! Eat!" Yasmine said. "Too much bones. No boobs. What for you not take care with yourselfs, Eleanor. Eh?"

"Too right, love," Eleanor said, trying to control her jittering. Though her cheeks were hot, her hands, feet and underarms were cold and clammy with stress. "I've been living on coffee and cigarettes."

"I make for puds the hash of it. Much better. Smoke is porno." Everytime Eleanor tried to thank them for taking her in, Yasmine interrupted, "Not talk please. Make too much windy. Eat. Eat is good. Talk about our life and the porno fuckups for afters."

When she was full of food, wine and Yasmine's spiked cakes, Eleanor was encouraged to tell her troubles.

"I feel like a refugee," she shivered with tension. "It makes me feel so scared. I must get this next job. Thank God for work! It's all I've got. No home. Don't belong anywhere. Can't stand Theo's flat —" Eleanor spoke through her teeth, her hands curved into claws, "— where he had his other women."

"Pff!" Yasmine rolled her eyes but Eleanor was not sure whether this expressed impatience with her or with Theo.

"I don't think he ever loved me really. My family don't rate me either. I've just had the most bloody horrible visit with them. I felt like a foreigner, as usual. Don't know why I bother. Really, I don't." Eleanor couldn't hang her head and mumble because of Sandra's need to lipread. "Just at the minute," she said, rocking in her chair and rubbing her cold legs, "I don't need any more reminders of how useless I am!"

"Eh? Who is useless, please? You Yasmine and Sandra's best baby. We boast always, *Eleanor is our baby!*" Yasmine polished her nails on her bosom. "We teach her everything!" She looked over to Sandra for agreement and put her arms round Eleanor, "You famous now, everybody see your houses in the magazines. Is magnificent. Is cap for our feathers!" Yasmine waggled her head with pride. "Your name droppings bring many, many works for us. We love you for always, Eleanor." Yasmine kissed her and smoothed the hair off Eleanor's hot face.

"You're the only people who do love me, then." she said.

"Aaawoh" Sandra drawled, miming mawkish self-pity before reaching out to pat Eleanor's cheek.

"Grenville. He love you. You forget him already?" Yasmine said.

"Forget him! I think of him every hour of every day. But he's thrown me out as well!" Eleanor dropped her head and her speech was slurred behind her hand. Sandra got up to clear away the dishes. "I want to go back to him so much," her grief spilled over Yasmine's shoulder.

"Is good to cry, it let porno out." Yasmine rocked Eleanor in her arms. "He is finish. Is very sad. Sad for Grenville. Sad for the world. He was magnificent." Yasmine's tears fell. "He save us. He make country for the refugees. For the belong nowheres." Yasmine wiped her own and Eleanor's face and made her drink from a glass of water Sandra had put on the table,

"Is good. Good for body. Make wee-wee." Eleanor's teeth rattled on the edge of the glass. "Grenville make you, Eleanor. Also you his baby. He love you for always."

"I wish I could wind the clock back and him be well. For this terrible thing not to have happenend!"

"You know is never the go back, Eleanor. Is cry and go on."

"I can't stand it!" Eleanor rocked herself.

"She is knackers. No more talk," Yasmine spoke to Sandra, "We make bath, we go for relax and for sleep."

Eleanor did not resist when Sandra took her through the bead curtain into the bathroom, undressed her, sat her on the loo for a pee and ran a bath.

Having lit some candles, Sandra knelt by the bath gently bathing Eleanor's feet and hands in the hot frothy water. Eleanor lay and drowsed in the warmth, wondering at the intricate pattern of tattoos on Sandra's bare shoulders. Thorns. A lizard. Then she watched the wavering shadows on the painted night sky of the ceiling.

Yasmine joined them and the two women washed her hair, Eleanor moaning with the pleasure of Yasmine's kneading fingers and the heat of the shower rinsing through to her scalp and down her back.

"We make good the relax, eh? Not ouf! ouf! ouf! and alls finish like porno chauvinists."

She was helped to stand up and be dried. Wrapped in candlelight she was brought onto the soft, pillow and duvet-strewn mattresses next door. Her hair was combed out and pinned up by Sandra whose toneless voice was further blurred by the hum of the drier and the slow swish of the brush past her ears.

"Mmm, lovely stuff," Sandra murmured when the drier was off and she was laying dried tresses over Eleanor's shoulders.

"Always she have the pretty-pretty hairs but too much bones. Sss. Like a... eh? It *ri-ki-kri* all the hot nights. Away far, in my country... in my childtime..." Yasmine reached out and touched Sandra's cheek, "The little hop-hop in *Pinocchio*. What is?"

"Jiminy Cricket," Sandra said.

"Eleanor... she is the little sleepy crickets!"

"The fairy in *Pinocchio* is the best," Sandra said. "So beautiful. She was my first love."

The women's voices were like a lullaby. Eleanor sank into the warm cradle of Sandra's arms and opened her limbs to Yasmine's caresses.

Bliss slowly gathered at the core of her body till it flared and died away into the darkness of sleep.

# Six months later

## DARK

Eleanor had moved in as a lodger with Theo's sister and her family. It was a good solution for the time being. She'd always got on with them and their house was driving distance from the big project Eleanor had landed in a town west of London. Living with Theo's family muffled the fact that she and Theo had separated. She would no longer return to the flat in London and he, though evasive about it, was already seeing someone else. Soon they would have to consult properly, untangle their finances and reach a settlement. For the moment though, she was concentrating on her work.

Eleanor finished making notes and put her plans, colour charts and drawings into their folders and looked at her watch. Past midnight. She must get to bed and try and get some sleep.

The guest room was under the eaves of the old house. A narrow turning stair took Eleanor up and away from the family rumpus and chatter. The low space with its bed, beams, bare boards and one window reminded her of that other attic and the wonder of moving in with Grenville. Nearly ten years ago... The memory made her aware of her present misery, of the tightness in her stomach that prevented her sleeping. This time, the lumber in the attic was hers: boxes which she would be allowed to store here till she sorted out a place of her own. She still had Grenville's voice, at least. In this homeless period of her working life spent on trains, in hotels and at other people's houses, his calls were where Eleanor came to rest. There was a new-style telephone on the bedside table and earlier in the evening Grenville had rung her on it. Eleanor wished she could talk to him again now.

She lay in bed, stared at the gadget in the gloom and willed it to ring. Nothing happened. The phone by his bed would be switched off but she could just leave a little message on the ballroom answering machine. She tapped out the numbers.

"Is that you, Nelly?" Grenville's voice came right away.

"Oh love, sorry! Did I —"

"Can't sleep. The drug cocktail is not up to speed tonight. It used to be simple insomnia. But now there is pain to contend with. Soon, of course I shall have all the sleep I've ever wanted. What are you doing, your end? Too much to hope that you're in a leather corset being rogered violently by four sailors and a shaggy goat?" his voice was weary.

"Don't be disgusting. I'm lying in bed, alone, in the dark —"

"Ditto. Sadly, no filth this end either. And?"

"There is moonlight from a little window which is kept open, just enough, for the cats. They come in through the trees and over the roof.

'Ah, you are in the country, of course."

"And wondering how I could have ended up in this mess."

"Are you in any physical pain?"

"No."

"Rejoice, dearest. Nothing else matters. It is pain that drains the ichor from the veins. Bludgeons one over the threshold."

"It must be very lonely," Eleanor knew her lines. Her role was to give him permission to despair.

"You'd think so. But it's not, actually. Uh. Complete self-absorption is the therapy for dealing with that. Along with huge doses of anger. I think anger is keeping me alive. I'm on a life-support system operated by fogey fury. Uh. I must stop caring soon, surely?"

Eleanor could hear his breath edged with effort.

"I've spent all my life trying to detach sex from the abomination of bourgeois morality only to see it become a meaningless sport," he paused, "uh, and the whole world in the grip of greedy swindlers and uh —" he paused again and Eleanor turned a yawn into an encouraging,

"Ahum?"

"Gradgrinders! Where is the vision? O God! Even the question is obsolete, the model of the mind being the computer, these days. Marvellous things but not like my mind at all."

The sound of Grenville's voice comforted Eleanor. It had loosened the knot in her stomach that stopped her going to sleep. She closed her eyes.

"What will be the fate of the imagination?" he wondered, his voice slow and quiet. "What questions will people be asking?"

"Grenville, love, people will just be struggling along like they've always done." She yawned again.

"Of course. But what will they *want* as they struggle on?"

"I wish you'd let me come and comfort you," she mumbled.

"You know I always liked to talk to you, dearest. But," he sighed "I'm afraid I have no deathbed words of wisdom for you. I understand nothing. I can't make anything of it, however hard I try."

Eleanor was losing the fight to stay awake. She forced her eyes open and looked over at the moonlit casement and blinked at a sudden movement. It resolved itself silently into a cat, silhouetted against the night sky. It vanished with a soft thud. In a moment Eleanor felt a gentle pummelling as the cat settled itself beside her.

"...what I valued..." Grenville was saying.

Eleanor stroked the cat and tried to concentrate.

"...the things I fought for all my life have become irrelevant..."

Her eyes had closed again.

"...I have been left, brandishing my sword on a deserted battlefield..."

She drifted in and out of his voice.

"...but I must keep smiling through. What else is there? I must do it for the others..."

"But why can't I..." Eleanor tried to form words out of the cat's purring.

"You will help me by not coming... because you're not here... I can speak to you when I want to be a coward..."

"What about me and what I want?" Eleanor was appealing to a figure in shining armour standing against the moonlit windows of the ballroom.

"That was always too difficult," it answered.

"I love you, Grenville," she said in her dream.

"I was never going to understand that."

Grenville's voice sighed out of the receiver as it slipped from her grasp.

He had been cut off. Grenville put the phone back on the bedside table, careful not to disturb the drip stand. He leant back on his pillows and remained sitting up. Lying down was no good.

*Semper ad lucem*, he fingered the crest on his signet ring but did not turn on the lamp. The light hurt his eyes and besides he could no longer see enough to read or write.

He folded his hands in his lap and concentrated on keeping above the pain.

"Please let it all be over soon," he whispered into the darkness. "I can't take much more of this."

## MEET

Marty usually tried to get a break after the end of the school day. He needed it. The job was very demanding. Too busy for lunch, he caught up with a teatime snack before walking back to his office. He seldom left work or got back to his Dad before seven. In four years of hard work out here in this town he had all but lost touch with his old life. He allowed himself the occasional secret flit up to a London tranny club but saw none of the old crowd anymore. That was gone. Closed. But he thought about them. It was why he liked this recently opened cafe with its metropolitan decor, capuccinos and continental food. Reminded him of London.

Eleanor was walking down the town high street on her way back to her present job when she stopped and glanced at her watch. Would she make herself late by going into that cafe over there? Needed a break. Could do with being alone for a bit...

This place was popular but not with the sort of locals or parents who might want to talk to him about their kids. In here Marty allowed himself the first cigarette of the day. He would light up and people-watch. He was an expert, using the mirrors to study others unobserved or pretending to read the paper if he wanted to eavesdrop.

Alone for a bit. They must manage without her for two minutes. Eleanor would take a break here, away from the clients, technicians, decorators and the endless questions. Yes. A quick tea and a sandwich. Nice modern looking cafe. Reminded her of London...

Today Marty had found a window seat. This was best really, the most restful. He could treat the passers-by as a spectacle without the torment of wondering if there was any way he could enter their lives, as himself.

London... This morning Tinker had called Eleanor from there to say that Grenville was being admitted to hospital. Both of them knew what that meant. They were into countdown...

Marty started up as he recognized her. He sat down again and hid his face as Eleanor turned to enter the cafe. Where the fuck had she sprung from! His heart hammered in his chest. Of all the towns in all the world...! How come she's out here? Sparks of memory flew up through his head. A happy girl on the top deck of a number 30 London bus. His red satin shift and studded leather choker. Their tango at Grenville's party. Grenville... the cigarette in his hand trembled slightly as he pulled on it.

Countdown. The photo shoot for that colour supplement was the next thing on her agenda. Another magazine coming out to this provincial town to do a feature on Eleanor and her restoration work. Great and everything. But she was talked out. And all the time, thoughts of Grenville seeping between the cracks of her concentration. Dampening the lively impression she wanted to give her interviewers. This next time she must do a better self-promotion job. Keep up the work...

It must be years since he'd seen her. Years! But it was her. No mistake. Before knowing the decision was made, Marty was planning his approach. He would wait till she'd finished eating in here and then solicit her in the street where anything revealing she might say would melt away into the traffic noise. It was a risk but he didn't bother to calculate it. Take it. Couldn't stop himself. She knew his secret self. Her power and the danger she represented were part of the excitement. He was in the grip, already past the point of no return.

Work. Eleanor checked her watch again. Must get back to the job now. *Onwards and upwards.* She went to the till, paid, put on her coat and stepped out of the cafe into the chill September street.

"Excuse me —" a fair, sharp-featured man in a dark suit accosted her. "Eleanor, isn't it?"

"Ye-es. Wh-?"

"Sorry. It's Marty. Do you remember me? Grenville's —"

"What! Oh my God! Marty! Is it really you?" Afraid the shock was going to make her cry, she let go her feelings by flinging her arms round him. "Marty! Oh Marty, it's so lovely to see you!"

He responded to her, his face softening as he held her in his arms.

"Marty, I've *got* to go! Please can we meet up. Oh God, don't say you're just here for the day!" she said.

"I live here," he answered, grinning.

"Do you! That's brilliant, love! Where can we meet? When? I'm not free till nine tonight." She tried to calm down.

"Too late for me! I can't handle late nights in my present life."

"I don't believe it! A wicked girl like you! What are you up to, eh? You look the part in that suit dear, whatever it is!" she held his arm.

"I'm head teacher at Market Street County Primary School," he said.

"Bloody Hell! What! You? How?" Eleanor said. "You're having me on!"

Marty's look reproached her.

"Oh fuck! Fuck. Sorry!" she babbled. "I'm impressed, I really am! Marty love, I'm being an idiot because I'm desperate to see you again but I've got to go. Give me your number," she ordered.

"What are you doing out here in the sticks?" Marty asked as he scribbled down his school and home numbers.

"Just rounding off a heritage commission — the old Assembly Rooms, supervising the restoration of the 18th century interior. I will see you again?"

"You've done a great job," he said.

"You've seen it?"

"Certainly. Opening Recital. Complimentary ticket because —" Marty raised his eyebrows, allowing himself a whiff of camp, "I'm an essential part of the cultural life of this town..."

Eleanor said as she began to leave,

"I'll ring you tonight. Just after nine. You'll be home?"

"I'll be waiting," Marty called after her.


## TALK

Marty had suggested meeting at a new winebar and restaurant. The ceilings were high, the decor contemporary and the atmosphere provided by a lively clientele. Dinner parties, premieres, and new wave restaurants weren't part of his background but hanging out with types like David the journalist and Grenville the toff, he'd soon got the idea. It was all a matter of performance. Learn your lines and wear the right costume. And he liked it, at least he felt more at home in it than anywhere else. Sex and talk — nothing better. He must remember not to wave his fork when he got going, that's all.

"You've done well in the Thatcherite 80s, then," Eleanor said, looking at Marty's clothes. Plain. The sort of plain that costs a bit.

"No. I've done well in spite of them."

"So what's it like being a teacher?" she widened her eyes. "Headmaster, no less!"

"A nightmare," Marty replied. "Except I'm good. Good at it. I pulled that school round. It's not bad now. And I'm popular. The Head before me was a bully so —"

"So you're a softie," Eleanor said.

"No way. It's a social priority school. I've been taken on as the hard man from the East End. Plus, I've got a good head for figures and I don't mind that three quarters of the job is politics. You need to accept that these days but —" he shook his head, "I feel sorry for those people who came into the profession to educate and care for children…"

This irony was lost on Eleanor. Marty noticed she'd stopped listening so he said,

"And you, Eleanor? You're looking good." This was flattery. He could see too much makeup covering up strain, sleeping pills and overwork.

"Wrong side of thirty," she made a face.

"We made it, anyway." He waited and then forced himself to ask, "And Grenville? I drifted out of that scene. Four years ago, is it now? Hm. Just as the AIDS bomb went off. But I hear rumours…" He cringed, waiting for the blow.

"Not long to go," she mumbled.

"God!" He rubbed his forehead. "Shit! *Shit!*" he hissed.

Their talk turned to the ritual of mourning. They remembered their dead friends, adding names to the casualty lists and to the roll call of the dying, the mortally wounded and the survivors.

"And you, Marty…" Eleanor wrenched the question out, "Are you… OK, pet?"

"Yes. Yes I am. Though sometimes I feel like I'm the only one left." From long habit, Marty's eyes darted round making sure he could not be overheard. "I've been spared, I'm over the moon of course. Sort of… *fouf!* that was a close one! But then, what if so many of us have copped it, eh? I feel guilty. Feel I owe them. I must do something brilliant with my life… direct action, join the campaigns, nurse the sick." Marty's voice was low but Eleanor had the impression of a dam bursting.

"But I was always careful..." he checked again that no one was listening. "Did safe sex before it was invented, didn't want to be seen down the clap clinic, didn't have time to be off-colour, didn't want any of that, couldn't risk it. I've got... I've got responsibilities."

"What? You've had a kid or something!" Eleanor said.

"If only."

"You mean your work —"

"Work! Nah. Everyone's replaceable, even me! No. It's my Dad." Marty spoke slowly now, playing it down. "He's disabled. Work accident. He lives with me." Before Eleanor could comment he went on, "Sometimes, when I'm down, I catch myself wishing I had the right to be in it with them, it would be simple then, I'd be outside Parliament in me slap and pelucca *telling* the fucking bastards. But as it is... I love my job. Despicable, eh?"

"No!" she said. "Be glad to be alive! Grenville is so angry and desperate. You'd be so angry to have your life snatched away. Forget all that morally improving shit! And... and it's a... a terrible death."

Wanting to change the subject and trying to sound perky Eleanor asked,

"How d'you cope with being respectable, Marty!"

"I've never been anything else," he answered back. "And I'm not tormented by wanting to take morning assembly in a chongsam and red stilettos —"

The thought of this set them off giggling together.

"But I'm in the closet, it's true. And that is where that part of me has to stay," Marty went on. "Specially as most people think drag means gay means paedophile."

"And you work with children. Jesus!"

She began to realise how much Marty was trusting her. Responding to his low-key manner, Eleanor kept her voice down, "Seriously, your secret is safe with me."

"And you?" he asked. "How are you? Not happy."

"How d'you know?"

"Feminine instinct."

"I'm all right it's just…" Eleanor's voice trailed off. She looked miserable.

"Hey ey ey…" he said gently. If they had not been in the restaurant, he would have put his arms round her. He went to take her hand across the table but was interrupted by the arrival of their food.

"Go on, tell Marty all about it," he said as they began to eat.

"My life's a *mess* —" Eleanor talked about her time with Theo, summing up,

"…So I finally left him six months ago. The money thing is still all over the place. My gear is in cardboard boxes at his sister Imogen's. I'm trying to go freelance. I'm dossing about with whoever'll have me. You say you feel guilty? Try this one! My best friend, the person I owe everything to, who I love most in the world, is dying, and I'm not even helping to look after him. I've really lost it, Marty, really I… Sorry! This is one long moan, isn't it?"

"It's all right, all right, I mean it, I want to hear all about you. Moan on!" he said.

Eleanor felt sure Marty liked her and was enjoying her company. Even though she was down. A great change from Theo who'd always given the impression that he was being patient while wanting to get away. Away from anything emotional.

"I haven't been able to talk like this to anyone for ages," Marty said, echoing her feelings. "I can't tell you how much it means to me."

"I could never get Theo to talk," she said. "Work? No problem. But anything personal? Emotions? He thinks it's unmanly. Effeminate, he called it."

"Yeah, he's dead right. It's pathetic. So let's carry on. What was it you liked about him?"

"I suppose I'm a sucker for the big, dark, masterful man," Eleanor said.

"Aren't we all, dear. But there must have been more than that, to keep you together for so long."

"First off, it felt good to be taken notice of by someone so impressive, you know? And then, he liked my work. Liked everything of the best. He's the sort of boss not easily pleased but appreciative when you deliver. Great to work with. And after Grenville, Theo was, you know, organized and he really liked women —"

"Eh?" Marty stopped eating. "Really liked women? Explain!" he said.

"He was hetero, straight, what d'you think!"

"Being hetero is *not* the same as liking women. At all." Marty wanted to be on her side but could not let that pass.

"You know what I'm saying!" Eleanor was annoyed at having to spell it out to Marty. "He was *not* gay, in other words, he fancied me, properly. And I never doubted it. And he... in bed... he took trouble. None of this getting drunk," she wrinkled her nose, "and wham bam, like you get with most blokes."

Eleanor broke off to eat and when Marty didn't say anything she added,

"Oh I don't know Marty, he turned me on, what else can I say?"

"So what went wrong?"

"Like Grenville, Theo believed in free love."

"Well, who wouldn't? *I can be randy and selfish but don't you dare try it.* It's a great idea!" Marty said.

But Eleanor wasn't amused. Talking about her failure with Theo was making her feel upset, "Theo was unfaithful to me and it put me off him. But I don't expect someone like you to understand that."

"Here! Hang on! Someone like me? What's that? A rampant faggot? A slut?"

"No. Just male."

"Ooh! What an insult!" Marty sucked in his cheeks. "Definitely below the belt!"

Eleanor caught that and couldn't help smiling. "Marty! You are a tonic, love. Seeing you again has really cheered me up."

"Good. It'll do for a start. I've been thinking about sex —" he went back to eating.

"You never!" Eleanor said.

"Give over will you," Marty leaned towards her, his face full of humour. "I'm trying to have a serious girly talk, here."

Putting down her glass, she rested her chin on her hand and looked attentive.

"Sex is an instinct," Marty began. "A compulsion, you might say. Certain times, you can't think about anything else. Well, I can't, anyway." He took some food before going on. "There's this incredible pressure, right? A long term relationship is good for dealing with some of that. As long as your partner's got the same needs. But the catch is, men and women are very different. I should know. They have very different... requirements. It's a big compromise. For both sides."

"And what about love?" she asked, going back to her meal. "I suppose you're like Grenville and think it's a lot of romantic rubbish."

"I'm very romantic, if you want to know. I am. I'm full of... ooh... impossible dreams." He made a restless movement with his fork.

"Like what?" she asked.

Marty frowned. "I'd like kids for one thing."

"Really? It's tough on gays, that," Eleanor said before going on, "I tried to make it better with Theo. More intimate. Spend more time together. But he just said if I was lonely I could have a baby. He said I didn't need to work. We didn't need my income. He thought he was being generous, making a big compromise, as you call it."

"Doesn't he want kids then?"

"That's not the point," she stabbed her salad.

"I know!" Marty didn't remember her being so touchy. "I can see all that. That the kids idea is to keep you busy, get you off his back and everything. But its like he doesn't want them for himself."

"I don't think he's thought about it," Eleanor said.

"In my experience straight blokes have never thought about anything," Marty waved his fork again.

"What d'you mean?" she asked.

"They don't have to think, do they. Straights! They haven't a clue who they are, because they fit in, don't they. The world's their oyster." Realizing that he'd finished his food but was still holding his fork, and waving it, Marty put it down before explaining, "Me, now. I'm a bit, well... peculiar? So I've had to do some thinking..."

He looked at Eleanor and spoke slowly, "I've had to work out who I am, what I want and how I'm going to get it..."

She held his gaze and said,

"So how's about a pud, then?"

The strangers at the next table looked round at Marty's loud, "Yes!"


## WALK

Marty was getting ready to go out. It was the weekend and Eleanor had agreed to spend the day with him. They might go to a country house that was open to the public and which Eleanor wanted to visit. He'd been there, accompanying classes from school. Music and movies were more his thing but his special subjects at teacher training had been history and drama, so he liked old houses well enough. He hoped the weather would be good, there were walks all round there. Autumn. Start of the school year and he was up to his lugholes in work. But perhaps they could talk, out in the fresh air, away from it all. He needed to move things on.

Marty looked at himself in the bathroom mirror. He was not that much taller than her and not the big, dark type at all. Thin, pale and ratty, more like. But at least with women looks weren't always the priority.

"You wish, mate!" he said out loud, jabbing his finger at the Marty in the mirror.

"The oldest part of the house reminds me of Wyvernden, Grenville's place," Eleanor said to him as they stood side by side on the terrace overlooking the park.

"He was a mad bastard," Marty said.

"Who? Grenville? He was wonderful! He is wonderful," she said. "I can't bear it. I can't. The thought of life without him. Even if I've only the phone left now. You know he won't let us see him?"

"Why's that?" Marty noticed Eleanor's voice slipping out of its fancy dress. She was sounding more like the Eleanor he remembered. Good. It must mean she felt at home with him.

"I tell myself it's nothing personal, but it upsets me, Marty. I miss him so much! I tell myself that he wants to be with his own kind, what d'you think? Anyway it doesn't hardly matter what I feel next to what he's going through, does it?"

"He is wonderful," Marty said, "you're right. But I was never comfortable with his politics. His instincts were not democratic."

"Really? But he wanted a genuine Depravity Party promising sleaze for all!"

"Not just the lucky few," Marty chimed in.

"He was an aristo into SM," Eleanor went on. "It was bound to be a murky area. But I never had any problem with it, did you?"

"Well we wouldn't. He was an elitist and we were part of his elite. And he had a head full of all that stuff. He belonged in some other era." Marty tilted his head at the historic house behind them.

"There was nothing he wouldn't talk about," she reminded him. "Or think about or look at. It's such a loss! All that energy and curiosity gone out of the world. I can't bear it…" her voice faded.

Some tourists had gathered close by them. They were preparing to pose and change places for each other's photos. Marty stepped forward, gestured at one of their cameras, pointed to himself and mimed taking a picture. They understood him at once. Eleanor watched them freeze frame their smiles three times as Marty took the same group photo with three different cameras. The delighted group thanked him, putting their palms together and nodding to fill the language gap.

"No problem. My pleasure," Marty said.

As Marty and Eleanor went down the wide stone steps of the terrace and onto the gravel between the elaborate parterres, she said,

"Grenville tells me I'm in the business of turning the whole country into a theme park for tourists."

"No use thinking that. Anyway, I'd rather have tourism than war." Though he liked to talk politics, Marty nudged the conversation towards intimacy, "Did you ever get to have him? He did women for a while."

"I adored Grenville but I never wanted him." Eleanor could see that Marty didn't believe her. "OK, I did and I didn't," she said. "I know he was gorgeous but I was sure it would mess up our friendship. For me that is. I couldn't stand the idea of him fucking me as some sort of experiment or 'interesting experience'."

She and Marty strolled side by side between an intricate pattern of lavender enclosed by low box hedges.

"And," she went on, "I think I must have sensed he preferred the lads. There was some governor on me... stopped me wanting him. I was protecting myself, maybe? From rejection? For all he wanted to *be* everything and *do* it all, I'm sure he was gay, really."

"Yep," Marty agreed. "Though he never accepted any labels. Too tidy. *No labels! No limits!* Wanted people to *use the abuse!* Take it on. Poof! Slag! And he'd go on and on about hating ghettos and tribal factions—"

"You must remember," Eleanor laughed, "that time he said: I won't have these *camps!*"

"Yeah," Marty said, "he never stopped telling you what he thought. But you never really found out what he felt. Or if he was serious. Though he cared about you, Eleanor, a lot, I know... the way he talked about you."

They passed under an arch of clipped yew and into a wide roofless corridor of dark evergreens. The outline of the hedge walls was sharp against the blue sky and down one side of the long green gallery ran a straight slab of deep shadow.

"You talked?"

"Like you said, Eleanor, he was good at that. He got me to accept myself. He'd listen to me, you know, fascinated... like I was really interesting. It helped me to face it all. Take it on. Funny thing is —" he lowered his voice as some people strolled by, "I told him all the filthiest stuff about me but I never confessed that I was a teacher and wanted to get on —"

"Whyever not!" Eleanor said. "He liked ambitious people."

"Nah. It would have been *yuppie* this and *bourgeois* that." Marty shrugged. "Can't see what's wrong with *bourgeois*, myself. Foreign food, good clothes, decent education, me own gaff instead of a drug-trashed council estate. Nice holidays for Dad and trips abroad for me. I love travel. The Continent. They can't build that Chunnel fast enough for me."

"Oh aye. I got the *boojwahr* lecture n'all. But what he meant," she defended Grenville, "was petty values. Repressive. All that narrow-minded prejudice —"

"Fff!" Marty cut in. "That's not *bourgeois*. That's everywhere! Plenty repressive where I come from and pig ignorant with it."

"You liked that Grenville was upper class, then."

"No. Most toffs are pig ignorant yobs n'all. The worst beating I ever had was from a bunch of hoorays outside a posh West End club. Nobody likes trannies. We're still fair game. Figures of fun..." Marty paused and his voice slowed, "What I liked about Grenville was the talk. The complete acceptance. He never judged. And the sex. About certain things, like... his rituals, he had high standards. So when he... used me, and I... got it right, it made me feel good. Like I was the business. And I liked his manners. I don't like 'old fashioned' anything, except I've got a thing about good manners."

They had reached the end of the yew walk and having made way for other visitors, passed through a deep arch and onto a lawn. They were alone except for their long shadows flung out across the grass.

"I once told him sex was his religion," Eleanor went back to the subject of Grenville.

"What happened?"

"He seemed quite pleased with the idea."

"Mad!"

"You keep saying that, Marty." She sounded grumpy.

"Sorry. Call me Martin. No don't."

Their shadows stretched out before them towards some wide descending steps.

"Grenville liked to be taken right to the edge," Marty said. "It worried me sometimes. I think he was hooked. I think it was a habit like any other. Like Ollie's habit. Like I was David's habit. Like my cigs and my... Did you ever read his books?"

"I tried but I couldn't get the half of it," Eleanor said.

They had come down to the lakeside. The wide expanse of water was mirror-like in parts and ruffled in others, reflecting sharp and blurred the blue of the open sky, the dark trees and the curve of yellowing sedge far away on the other shore. A creaking call echoed over the water. In the distance a bird emerged from the reeds and drew a slow line across the surface of the lake.

Marty went on,

"He was full of... ideas. Theories! Couldn't tell the difference between fantasy and reality, if you ask me. It wasn't enough for him that I'd learned to manage myself and my life. He wanted me to go for it. Show everyone. Change the world. Force society to accept the real me. Thing is, I wasn't even the real me with Grenville." He picked up a stone and leaning down skimmed it over the water. The air snapped with his movement. A complex pattern of interweaving circles spread out across the lake.

"Well, he felt so passionate about changing the world he could bang on a bit," Eleanor said before asking, "Didn't you agree with him about the need to protest?"

"Of course I did! It's just that he would've had me walking the streets in fishnets, blowing truck drivers every night. Fantasy stuff, Eleanor! What would I do with the rest of me, eh? What would have become of my life, I'd like to know! He was a fantasist, like I said. And I couldn't help thinking — it's all right for you mate, with your advantages but I'm unprotected... I've got to try and get on, out here, in the real world."

He skimmed another stone before speaking again,

"What was it Grenville used to call us? *Aristocrats of the gutter*, that was it." Marty hunched his shoulders and tucked his hands into his armpits as he talked. "When my Mum died, my Dad went to pieces. Took to the bottle. I reckon that's why he had his accident. Then I was taken away from him and put into care. I spent three years as a nobody. Dumped. Unwanted." Marty's eyes narrowed in pain. "The gutter is a *very real place* to someone like me."

They strolled on round the lake, crossed a bridge and began to walk slowly up the grassy slope to the folly. It was late in the afternoon, the house and gardens would be shut by now and the grounds too, had almost emptied of people. As they stood at the foot of the tower, Marty looked back over the view, shading his eyes against the low sun. Eleanor, admiring his slender neck and wide curving mouth, said,

"But you always looked fabulous in drag. Not like some. Remember that tango we did?" She took his arm and leaned her head on his shoulder.

Marty breathed in sharply.

"It's so good talking to you about Grenville..." she murmured. "About old times."

"I want to talk about *now*," Marty said. "About the other me. I want to talk about Martin. Martin who made it to head teacher by thirty-five. Who managed to get his Dad back." The restless movements he made detached him from her. He spoke fast, "Who likes to go to the flicks with his girlfriend. Who really likes women. Wants a family. Be a husband and father."

"Martin?" Eleanor was confused. "Who?"

311

"Yes! Martin! Me!" he beat his chest with his fists but reminding himself of Tarzan and feeling a berk, put his hands in his pockets. "Oh God, this was not how it was supposed to be. It's all gone wrong!"

"What?"

"Coming out!" he shouted.

"I'm sorry. I'm not with it. What are you telling me?"

"Eleanor, listen!" He put his hands on her shoulders. "I'm mostly a straight bloke, who likes women, prefers them to men at all times except that I have this... thing. When the fit comes over me, something triggers it off, I don't know, I want to dress up as a slapper, be caned on the bum and fucked up the arse."

"Oh aye. So you're not gay..."

Marty snatched his hands back into his pockets and looked away from her,

"Come on!" he said. "Didn't Grenville teach you anything!"

"Don't you come the schoolteacher wi'me!" she snapped. "Give us time to adjust, won't you. Until yesterday I only ever knew the slapper, remember?"

They moved round the tower. Marty recalled failing his first driving test and feeling if only he could do it again, immediately, he'd get it right. He swore under his breath. He was sweating with nerves. Had an erection. Must try to calm down.

"But you fancy men," Eleanor said.

"Never. I want them to fancy me. I, I fancy women. All the time."

"And you don't really wish you were a woman?" she asked.

"It's not that I don't want to be a woman. It's that I like being a man. And I like being a man because I like making love to women. Women turn me on."

*And I could prove it to you right now, doll!* The words shot through Marty's head. He clamped his jaw shut. Folding his arms, he leant on the wall of the tower.

Eleanor stood away from him.

"You want me to call you Martin? You're saying Marty isn't the real you?"

"She's not the real me, she's a part of me. Not even a constant part but, and Grenville did get me to see this, I musn't try to pretend she doesn't exist. She's a bloody nuisance but she's been coming back, on and off, ever since I can remember and I've learned that if I try to ignore her, she turns nasty and makes my life a misery."

It was getting late. Eleanor started to move down the hill. Marty came away from the wall and followed her. He must bloody shut up. He was in a state. Still had a stiffy. Gabbling on now would only make things worse. The breeze fanned Eleanor's dark hair across her cheek. It made him ache to touch her. It was all so simple, really. Why couldn't they just sort it all out with a fuck? But he knew he must wait. Knew all about cat and mouse. His only chance now, was to pull back and give her space.

They had walked back across the meadow in silence and were rounding the corner by the visitors' centre when a woman's voice called out,

"Martin? Martin!"

They turned towards a family group. The woman was a member of his staff. There was an exchange of greetings and time for everyone's eyes to flicker over Eleanor with interest.

"Well, anyway," Eleanor whispered when everyone had moved on, "I'll be good for your image."

"Nothing wrong with my image," Marty said as they continued towards the car park. "I'm not some sad creep, you know. I've had plenty of girlfriends and proper long-term relationships."

"What went wrong?" she asked, thinking of herself and Theo.

"Came unstuck over the tranny thing. I couldn't tell them. With one, I knew she'd go off me completely and anyway she found my Dad a problem. I risked it with my next long-term girlfriend but she couldn't hack it. Emerald loved it. You remember her? Painter. Met her at Grenville's. But she got bored with me... wanted a full time pervert."

It was time for them to return to their own cars. They stood together in the nearly empty car park.

"You shouldn't have tried to talk to me about it all, Marty," she apologized, "I'm just not up to it at the moment. I'm really sorry I was such crap to talk to."

"You still don't get it, do you!" Marty said. He squeezed his eyes shut and clenched his fists. "I want you, Eleanor! Always have. Since I first met you."

"Aoh," she looked down, biting her lip.

"I'll leave you to think about it," he mumbled. He needed this scene to end before he said or did something demented. He held her elbows lightly.

She glanced up and saw his wide, curving mouth as he pleaded,

"Please be in touch. We can still be friends, hm?" He kissed her on the forehead. "Yes? Friends? Something. Anything. Let me know. Bye now."

314

They turned from each other and got into their own cars. As Eleanor drove away, Marty banged on his steering wheel with his fists, shouting self-abuse in language that would have amazed even Grenville.

# iii

## FATHER

Though she was familiar with the town from working there, Eleanor had difficulty getting into Marty's street from the one-way system. It should have been easy on a quiet Sunday afternoon, only the heavy rain made it hard to read the signs. But eventually she was driving into the visitors' parking bays of some residential courts built on the site of an old brewery. Now the silver birch trees had grown in front of them, the flat-roofed, horizontal lines of the buildings blended in, but Eleanor could imagine the resistance to this modern style when they first went up.

Marty appeared by her car with an umbrella and together they ran down a wide ramp to Marty's father who could be seen waiting in his wheelchair just inside his front door.

"Don't you worry none about Trixie's barking," Marty's father said as he led the way through a widened doorway. "She's as soft as butter. Don't mind dogs, do you?"

"Not at all," Eleanor stooped down and put her hand out for the little terrier to examine.

"I never had no dog till we come here. But I wouldn't be without her now," he addressed Trixie. "Even though you're a menace, girl! Aint yer, eh?" He signalled permission to the dog who jumped into his lap, then swivelling his chair round to look up at Eleanor, he said, "You'd like some tea, I expect, after your drive."

316

"I always want tea," Eleanor smiled and moved towards the kitchen alcove, "I'll put kettle on for us, shall I, Mr —"

"No darlin', none of that 'Mr' here. Just Ron will do!"

Marty's father, who was used to home helps coming into his house to bustle around, was put at ease. He was relieved she was not the type to sit on the edge of the settee making polite conversation and trying not to stare at his scars.

For Eleanor, there was something about Marty's father that reminded her of Great Uncle Arthur, the only family she'd ever got on with. Ron's manners, the style of his furniture, the smell of bacon, cleaning fluid and dog, all made her feel at home.

Marty took charge of the tea-making while Eleanor chatted to his father.

"My Uncle Arthur had a little dog just like Trixie, you know, called Pip. He used to take Pip everywhere with him in his bike basket. One of the very first things I can remember — I used to love going with him to his allotment — he'd put me and Pip together in the bike basket and run us down the hill. He'd have to wait till we were out of sight of our house before he did it, mind. He and my Mam and Dad didn't get on. At all!"

"All families are like that," Ron waved a hand. "I remember regular doorstep ding-dongs between my old Mother and her sister-in-law. And then there was others not speaking for years on account of something nor nothing. The something is always money. It's always money, aint it." He pointed a finger. "And you girls stirring it up! Keeping it all going on and on, like dogs with a rat. I know. Bet it was with your family. It was, wasn't it?"

Ron crossed his arms. Though his energies were con-fined, Eleanor had the impression of a forceful man. He'd been handsome, she could see that, and still had a burly, confident style.

Marty was embarrassed by his Dad's old-fashioned tone with women. Patronizing. But he waited to see whether Eleanor would withdraw or take him on. She took him on.

"It wasn't about money, actually, Ron."

"What then!" Ron leaned forward.

Challenging, aggressive even. But not like her Dad. In this face there was a warmth and good nature which no scars could erase.

"The way I see it," Eleanor said, "Uncle Arthur had been a working man all his life and didn't want to change his ways. And he could tell he was being looked down on by our family. He'd mutter on about how we'd gone ever so 'lah-di-dah' as he called it. He used to say about my Dad, *he's nobbut jumped-up delivery boy* and about me Mam," Eleanor imitated an old man's toothless grumbling, *"she's all fur coat and no knickers!"*

This performance made Ron and Marty laugh. Marty's father flapped his elbows like a big, heavy bird trying to take off.

"It's good to have a laugh. Specially at the relatives! You're just what we need on a wet Sunday, darlin'! Aint she Martin? Dear oh dear!" Ron wiped his eyes behind his spectacles.

"I've always remembered it," Eleanor said, "though at the time I didn't have a clue what he was on about —"

"It's obvious, girl!" Ron shot into the air with the gun of his hand. "Class war! With your poor old Uncle. That's what it was. And him all cloth cap and no teeth. He knew he'd lost. Class war. It was!"

Trixie kept her balance in Ron's lap, through the turbulence.

"I suppose, yeah, you're right," Eleanor said. "Thing is though, at the time, all I knew was that I loved my Uncle Arthur to bits because he was the only person in the world who preferred me to my sister. I was on his side because he was on mine."

"Well, I have to be glad to see my Martin going up in the world. He might as well. There's nothing left for the working man now!" Ron banged the arms of his wheelchair. "The Tories have destroyed us! What they done to the miners is disgraceful. I can't believe the country can put up with that Thatcher for much longer. Half the people," his broken hand chopped the air, "with far more than they need and the other half," he heaved up his big shoulders, "with nothing at all! We've gone backwards! To the bad old days. All grab, grab, grab and never mind who gets trampled to death in the rush."

Ron emphasised everything he said with mime, as if he spent his life among the deaf.

"And don't get me wrong," the gun-hand shot out again. "I'm ever so proud of my Martin, doing so well. He's slaved for it, he has! College. Studying. And we've got this lovely place, now. But the mortgage! I know this house has gone up and up since he bought it. Worth funny money. But what good is that? I ask you," he appealed to Eleanor, "you got to live somewhere, aint yer? And anyway that can't go on neither, can it!" He turned to his son, "Where there's boom there's bust. A blind man in a mist can see that."

Eleanor wondered what Marty had told his father about her and Theo and the Old Rectory. Ron might not be very sympathetic. The whole thing depressed her. She wanted to get off the subject of class and money and buying and selling. She cradled her mug of tea and searched round the room. Marty stepped in,

"Did I tell you Dad, Eleanor did ballroom dancing when she was a kid?"

Eleanor snatched this up, "O yes! I've been eyeing those cups." She left her chair and went over to a trophy cabinet on a wall of framed photographs, "Are they all for dancing?"

"They are indeed. All with my beautiful wife."

"This must be her," she pointed at a heavily framed, filmstar style photo, hung at waist height. "May I look?"

"Of course darlin'. Be my guest."

Eleanor stooped and looked at a lively eyed woman with elaborately dressed hair and Marty's wide curving mouth. "She's gorgeous!"

"Oh she was! She was. I never looked at another woman. You can see why. And never a cross word." Ron stroked Trixie. "She was the only one for me. It's twenty-five years now since she passed away but there's not a day goes by..." his voice had dropped. "I was glad to leave London when our Martin got his promotion. There was nothing left for me there. I'd gone down so low. Pleased to leave it all behind, I was. The only thing I mind is my darling's place of rest being so far away... can't visit her as often as I'd like. But musn't grumble, eh?" he addressed this apology to Trixie who nuzzled his chin.

Marty was impatient to get Eleanor away. He had not sat down and she had been aware of him all the time, in his dark cotton pullover and black jeans, prowling up and down.

"Musn't grumble," Ron repeated. "I'm lucky. A man couldn't have a better son." He reached out and touched Eleanor. "Only one thing I don't like about him..." He winked at her. "The girls lose all interest in me when he's around!"

Behind his father's back, Marty struck a wildly camp pose. Eleanor's nostrils flared with supressed laughter as Marty pounced to take her arm and say,

"So, Dad! I'm going to drag Eleanor off to my cave, now. All right?"


## HOME

The visit could not last long. Eleanor was on her way back to London as she had a meeting with clients early the next day.

"If it wasn't for this rain we could've had a ramble through the town, the river isn't far from here," Marty said as they walked through a carport and ran up an outside staircase to his front door. "But I want you to see my place anyway."

"It's completely separate from your Dad," she said as they flurried in from the wet.

"Oh yes." He put the open umbrella aside to dry. "Having my own front door has definitely improved my life. I could never stop Dad staying awake till I came in. He finds it hard when I go away. He's not lonely, he's very popular and out all over the place... clubs, socials, charity work. It's just he worries something will happen to me." Marty led the way into his sitting room. "Once

321

when we were going through a bad patch, I lost my rag and asked how come he didn't worry about me for all those years when I was dumped in the home. But he started to cry and say sorry. I couldn't stand it!" Marty bared his teeth. "Not a good moment."

"Has the move out of London been all right, then?"

"For Dad, yes! He's transformed. Set up a life of his own. He says it's because it's all new people, people who don't know every stupid thing he's done. I'm the one who finds it hard, I hate not living in London, I feel like a refugee, an exile," Marty talked fast. "But you have to go where the work is, don't you? And I'd rather live in the middle of this town than in some fucking nowhere at the end of the District Line," he sighed. "That's what I have to tell myself, anyway. But I'm rabbitting on, sorry. Pay you back for that time on the bus, donkey's years ago, when you told me all about yourself!"

"What bus? I don't remember any bus!" Eleanor shook her head.

"I do! I had my eye on you even then." Feeling he'd sounded smarmy, Marty struck out quickly, "Do you miss your home town?"

"Not really. I associate it with being unhappy. All my happy memories are of London... though I've had to put up with a lot of *Eee by gum have you joost come oop from t'pit!* rubbish and people thinking I'm ignorant the minute I open my mouth. So I do miss being a local, I suppose, and the moors and fried egg butties..."

"Butties?" he asked.

"Sandwich to you, y'ignorant Cockney!"

They stood together looking out of the wide window,

"It's a nice view, even through rain…" she said, "All those little courtyards and higgledepiggledy chimneys and rooftops. But your back garden's a disgrace, Marty!"

"No time! No money!" he said. "Wouldn't know where to begin anyway."

Eleanor automatically began to design the space in her mind's eye… paving for the wheelchair, seating area, scented shrubs…

"Can I get you anything?" Marty cut across her visions.

She turned and looked into the room and took in fresh paint, armchairs, books and a big desk with one of those new home computer things. It was bare, functional and the only colour was provided by children's artwork pinned to the walls. She moved over to look at the pictures.

"I love their stuff," Marty said. "And the early writing they do which looks like runes. As for that goggly-eyed mutant with fluorescent yellow hair —"

"It's you! To the life!" she nudged him. "But why are you holding a toilet roll?"

"Search me. It must be the latest government White Paper on Education."

"Choo-choo trains! I used to do those," Eleanor pointed. "So countryfied. It's all flowers, smoke coming out of chimneys and tigers in the jungle. No high-rise. No telly —"

"London kids do it too. It's an inner world," he said.

"Is it very different down here from what you're used to?"

"Kids are better behaved, compared to what I've known. But I still had to sort out a fight last week. One of the boys is a horrible little weasel and the other isn't a nice kid either. Wouldn't be missed, either of them. Tempted to leave them to it, I was."

"How do you sort out a fight?"

"Meaning I look like a wimp. Eh?" he put his head to one side. "Drag-Queensbury rules," he went on. "Don't let them wind you up. Don't look afraid. Keep a sense of humour. All easier said than done. Only I've had lots of practice dealing with morons. It does help I'm wearing a suit and not four inch heels and lace gloves. And that the morons are not big and drunk."

"You look good in a suit," she said.

"That's lucky," he pointed at his hairline, "because it's getting harder to look cute in the other kit. You still haven't said whether I can get you anything."

Eleanor accepted the offer of a snack. Marty went into his kitchen while she went to use the bathroom.

She could tell that no reference would be made to what he'd come out with last weekend. They were shy with each other now. She'd been so free with him when she thought he was gay. But things had changed. All kinds of springs and levers had shifted inside her, creating a different rhythm to her feelings for him. She had started to think of him as a man instead of an exotic spectacle. In the bathroom, she looked at his toothbrush and men's deodorant, noticing that he liked expensive soap. She began to feel curious about Marty. About the private person behind the performance.

After leaving the bathroom she glanced round the rest of his place. Modern. So different from the soaring space of Grenville's ballroom or the impractical but graceful passage from room to room at the Old Rectory. Good of its type, though. Well designed.

She sneaked into Marty's bedroom.

Plain but not so bleak. Big, warm-coloured duvet. Matisse repro in hot colours. A real painting on the other wall... one of Emerald's? Of a sleeping girl. Television and video. Postcards from friends. Framed photographs... one of a little blond boy with his young Mum and Dad on a seaside promenade.

Bedside books... Eleanor tiptoed over to take a closer look. A recent novel by an African writer, poems for children, satirical magazine, film listings... Nothing creepy. Nothing to put her off or shut her out. Eleanor returned to Marty, happy to be alone with him.

Marty cut bread while Eleanor stood by the kitchen counter. Having noticed his newspaper open at an article on a gay celebrity, she commented,

"I think gays really changed the agenda about sex. Grenville says they forced people to be more open about it."

"I have a sad feeling," Marty shook his head, "that AIDS is what changed the agenda. And in bad moments I think nothing ever changes. Like stupid parents who want to protect their children from gays but who never think their kid might *be* one."

"Can you tell how kids will turn out?" she asked Marty.

"Not really. My lot only go up to eleven. Sex shouldn't have surfaced yet. At this age, girls think boys are totally pathetic and the boys' idea of a relationship is to hit each other round the head with their sports' bags. No, my main concern is kids coming to school in the clothes they've slept in and from a home where they are slapped about and shouted at. Or worse."

"Were you hit? Or worse?"

"I was knocked about a bit after Mum died and Dad went on the bottle. In the children's home run by the Godsquad there was no 'worse'. I was never raped. Lucky by all accounts. But I did get walloped."

"Were you damaged by it?" Eleanor asked, wondering if this might be a clue to Marty's darker side.

"I don't know what harm it did me but it did me no good." Question after question. Marty could feel her examining him. He could sense her curiosity like sexy little fingers searching under the covers. He must keep still. He must wait for her to find him.

Eleanor leaned in the kitchen doorway taking in the layout and atmosphere of Marty's place. As she always did with any interior, she treated it as a stage set, reading off from it a Marty she was only just beginning to know. Compassionate. Dedicated. Lonely.

"Have you forgiven your Dad?"

"Nope. Don't really believe in it either. Like David said, forgiveness is just another word for letting them get away with it. But I do believe in letting things go... if, big if, you can. Do you remember David? Journalist. Jewish. Older guy. Introduced me to Grenville —"

"Course I do. Did David's wife know about his other side?" she asked.

Marty could see now what Eleanor and Grenville had in common... why they'd got on. Their curiosity never slept.

"David was always very careful to keep me well out of his family's way," Marty said. "Very discreet. Don't know what he told his wife or anything at all about his private life."

"He used you like a prostitute!" Eleanor sounded like she didn't approve.

Marty paused as he took the milk out of the fridge. "That was the whole idea," he said.

"I was never introduced to his wife, either." Eleanor began to arrange the cutlery and mugs Marty had put on the kitchen table. "Peeved me the way Grenville went to their dinner parties but I was not invited. Not good enough, nyuh!"

"I saw David's wife once..." Marty said. He wanted to grab Eleanor. Yes. Or kneel at her feet. Yes. Fuck! No! Grabbing. Grovelling. Women didn't like either. Dickhead! Must not screw up again. "David's wife was..." he tried to concentrate, "not my type at all..." Why the hell were they wasting time talking about this irrelevant old bat? From a previous life? That neither of them had ever met? He was feeling randy. It made him irritable. Watch it. Musn't get into an argument. "She's not our type." Marty tried to get rid of her. "Super-clean. Headscarves. Big brooches —"

"There's more to people than the way they dress," Eleanor said.

"Is there, though?" Marty argued.

"You should know!" she answered back.

"OK, lets hope she has a secret life as a lipstick lesbian." Marty puffed out his cheeks. He was getting into an argument. He was all jittery. Like with his first love. Jenny Mills! She sprang from his memory like a cuckoo out of a Swiss clock.

"Does your Dad know about you?" Eleanor started up again.

"No-oo." Marty looked at Eleanor who had sat down at the table. She looked exhausted, ill. Perhaps all these questions were just to keep her mind off Grenville and her misery.

"Why can't you tell him? I'm sorry, am I being very nosey?" she frowned.

"It's all right," Marty said. "Never wanted to tell him. He'd be so embarrassed. When you think about it, there's something pitiful about *anyone* dressed as a tart. And trannies... even gays despise us. I don't feel any need to put me and Dad through all that just because I take a little walk on the wild side once in a while. I need my space. So does Dad. He's full of blokey shit, as you might have noticed. But he's not a racist, misogynist, queer basher. That, I couldn't stand."

"You wouldn't like my Dad. He gets all bulgy eyed and hysterical about shirt lifters."

"Very suspicious," Marty tapped the side of his nose. "Sounds like he's got something to hide."

Eleanor gave a tired shrug and her attention slid away.

Marty yearned to comfort her. Be given permission. To be the one to give her pleasure.

"How d'you like it?" he asked.

"Eh?" she looked up at him.

"Your butty," he said with a sly smile.

Eleanor looked at his mouth and felt the first rustling of desire.


FIRST

After the meal they took their mugs of coffee into the darkening sitting room. It was still raining. Marty put on a lamp which softened the light. As he sat down opposite her he said,

"About telling my Dad. Or telling anybody. Don't you think I might be ashamed?"

"Ashamed! No! It never occurred to me. I'm used to Grenville I suppose, who never apologised and never felt shame and never hid anything, ever."

Marty, who had been sworn to secrecy by Grenville about that romp with Eleanor's mum, wanted to argue. But he sucked in his bottom lip. Each to their own version, he decided. There was a limit to what could be shared. Eleanor's romantic view of Grenville annoyed him. But he wouldn't do himself any good by destroying it. And he was the same. Wouldn't let anyone interfere with his memories. His Mum and Dad. Together. Happy. Always loving him.

"Hm," was all he said.

"Thanks for looking after me Marty," Eleanor looked at her watch. "I'll have to start shifting along soon."

"So what *did* you feel about Grenville?" he asked.

"I adored him."

It was her phrase. He was already a legend. Marty understood then, that he was not competing with Theo, the big dark masterful man, but with Grenville. It was Grenville he would have to live up to.

After Eleanor had driven away Marty dropped in on his father to say goodnight. He would do this before his Dad's mates arrived for their evening card game.

"So I get to meet her at last. From what you told me about her job I thought I was going to meet someone," Ron waggled his head, "all hoity-toity. But she's one of us, aint she. Lovely girl!"

He wheeled over to the kitchen counter and fetched some glasses. Marty leant against the wall.

"I'd grab her with both hands, if I was you, Martin. And you knew her years ago, you say?" Ron prodded his son as he wheeled by. "Don't hang about no more!"

Marty rolled his eyes but was glad that Eleanor and his Dad had got on. It made his hopes seem less lunatic.

"Well, I'll just —" Marty thumbed towards his exit.

"*All fur coat and no knickers*, eh! Tell you what, I should like to meet her Ma n'all!" Ron chuckled. "Bit of a giggle your Eleanor. I like that. Me and your Ma had a lot of laughs." He swivelled round to face Marty. "You're mad about her, aint yer. I can tell."

"How?" Marty said. "Anyway I —"

"Give me some credit, son. I may be dead from the waist down but it don't mean I can't remember. I can tell, I'm telling you!" He turned his chair away and began to get packs of cards, ashtrays, beer glasses, a pad and pencil out of the sideboard. Sensing that Marty was not listening he spoke to the photograph of his wife, "Mad about her! For all you wouldn't have thought she was his type. Bit of a plain Jane. I like a bit of glamour, myself."

Trixie's barking signalled the arrival of the card party and Marty escaped out the back.

He stood on his outside staircase and grinned into the gloom...

By the car, holding an umbrella and determined not to rush it, he'd gone to kiss Eleanor on the cheek. But she had lifted her hand to his face, her lips had parted and she had kissed him on the mouth. It had been so soft. So brief. Like being crashed by a moth.

Marty closed his eyes and breathed in. First kiss. A whole new life.

# LAST

Glittering lines of light streamed through the darkness, converging on London after the weekend. Since Eleanor had left Marty's house, the rain had cleared and the night turned cold. But she was insulated inside layers of car warmth, music tape and thoughts of Marty. Likely he was thinking of her too. Sexy feelings flickered round inside her body.

Suburban landscape, industrial estates, cars on the motorway were laid on her windscreen in an ever changing pattern of gliding and winking lights. As the huge, pink, autumn moon appeared on the horizon she thought at first it must be the dome of a leisure complex or supermarket. A sign for a motorway service station edged past. She glanced at the digital clock on the dashboard. She hadn't made her daily call to Tinker at the hospital yet.

Eleanor turned into the service station and parked. The music cut out with the engine.

She stretched and heard herself yawn inside the sudden quiet. Grenville had sent her one of those new mobile phone contraptions, insisting that for his sake, she learn how to use it. The thing was on the passenger seat. It was temperamental at the best of times. But she might be close enough into London for it to work. Wanting to stay in the warm, she'd give it a go. She pulled her bag off the floor, took out her Filofax and having checked the number, rang the switchboard. Eventually she was through to Grenville's ward, to the staff nurse on duty and then to Tinker,

"Wotcher El. All right, mate?"

"Oh aye. M4's been a bit slow. Sunday evening, you know. How's things, flower?"

"As usual. Sometimes, he goes off. With the *fairies*, Kev says." Tinker sniggered.

"Let's hope so!" she said.

"He's always talked funny, anyway, aint he," Tinker said. "Does it all the time now. In his sleep and everything. Last time his Uncle Archie come, I says to Archie, 'it's rubbish, yeah?' But Archie says it's Greek. And Gren has a giggle as if he's been having us on, know what I mean? Don't like it. Does me head in."

"Don't worry, love," Eleanor said. "I felt like that when he was talking English." She could tell Tinker was feeling low. Worn out, poor lad.

"And he's been talking to you, El. Thinks you're listening. Today he's going on about his funeral. Dunno why. It was all sorted ages ago. Yesterday he was driving me mad over his food. Today, it's his funeral. And you know how he wants me and you to go with him, in the car? When. You know. When they come to fetch him back to that place. Whatsit?"

"Wyvernden."

As if on old film footage, Eleanor saw a little boy, heir to a great estate, being given strawberries by an ancient tenant, an old labourer who pointed to names on a war memorial. The memory camera cut to a stone dragon and a grille set into the dry sandy walls of Wyvernden church.

"I wouldn't never go out there to that country place with him. He wanted me to but I wouldn't. But I got to go now, aint I? And I don't want to go to no funeral. Wasn't let go to my Nan's," he laughed. "I'm dreading it —"

"You are doing everything right, Tinker love," she said. "Keep your pecker up, eh?"

"I aint never been out of London in my life, El. Don't like it. And all his family there. They give me the heebie-jeebies."

"Don't worry, love. I'll be there with you. We'll have each other."

"Yeah. Thanks, El. I'm all right really. And a lot of the time his mind's all right. I only gets upset when he talks cobblers. Though he told me this morning that he loved me! So maybe he has lost his marbles!" Eleanor had already lifted the bulky mobile away from her ear, anticipating his screeching laugh.

"He never has! It's good!" Sure of Marty, Eleanor felt only a pin-prick of jealousy. "I think it's the best thing Grenville's ever said."

She looked out of her car. The moon was edging clear of the saplings by the petrol station. It was smaller now, paler.

"Makes me want to come and be with you," she sighed. "But I've given up asking."

"I wish you could, mate, but... nah. He aint looking good, know what I mean? You'd only upset yourself and him. He didn't never like being seen once it got bad. And he won't have it no more."

"Everybody else visits," Eleanor made her old complaint. "You'd think I'd be special but —"

"He won't do the phone nor nothing now. No one is to come. Since last week. Not Yasmine, not Archie, not his Auntie, not no one. Its just down to me and Kev now. But you is special, El. He always wants to talk to you. And you called at a good time, tonight. He's quite chirpy. Have a go at talking to him, will you? It always settles him."

She agreed to try.

"Wait a bit and I'll go over and set it up. Ready now? Hang on."

Eleanor rested the heavy mobile on her shoulder and gazed out onto the yellow-lit forecourt of the service station. Silhouetted figures hurried in and out of the automatic doors. After a few moments of blankness she heard crackling and muttering at the other end.

"Hello? Are you there?" she tried.

"I think so. Still. *Dum memor ipse mei,*" came Grenville's thin voice. "Alive enough to worry about my um. Last ritual. Bach? Hm? What d'you think? Then I thought of The Kinks' *Waterloo Sunset,*" he spoke very slowly. "One of the angels here brought it in for me to listen to. Such kindness. Hm? But not with the Bach. The word..." he hesitated and Eleanor strained to hear as a group of noisy lads trotted past the car. "The word um? Bathos comes to mind. Bathos no good. I want people to cry... not corpse... that will be my privilege, won't it..."

Eleanor put a finger in her ear and closed her eyes, the better to concentrate on the wheezing voice,

"...um Purcell? What d'you think? Dido's lament? Always made me blub..."

"I know it," Eleanor said. "I once made a *Dido* Act 3 cozzie. *When I am laid in earth, may my wrongs create no trouble in thy breast —*"

"Oh no, my little seamstress. No earth... no slugs for me."

The memory footage flickered again... dry walls, stone coffins, the church on a hill. She must think of something quickly, to pull Grenville back.

"Do you remember Marty?"

"Mistress Marty! Mm. Such a beauty! Such a talented um? Disciplinarian..."

Silence again but before Grenville could retreat too far, she spoke clearly,

"I've met him again!"

"Always fancied our pet lamb. Mm. In lurve. Madly in love with it."

"Really?" she fished.

"O yes. Mm? Told us all about it. O yes. Bored on and on. Nothing we could do because..." his voice lapsed again. "Nelly went off... off with..?" Was there really a loss of memory? "...left us all for some..." Or was Grenville still playing? "...some ridiculous creature," he trailed off.

The silence made her anxious in case he'd had enough. She didn't want it to end there. She leaned into the rustling gadget, as she had as a child, when trying to hear the ocean in a seashell. From far away she heard Grenville speaking to Tinker,

"Nelly's seen Marty. We are very, very jealous, aren't we Belle," his voice receded even further.

She tried to draw him back, "I bumped into him and he's —"

"Have you fucked him?" Grenville's voice returned suddenly, quite clear.

Confusion scissored through Eleanor's mind. What could she say? Could the difference between the past, present and future matter to Grenville, now? She could not fail him. She must not. She must lie.

"Yes!" the word leapt free from the tatters.

"*Nunc dimittis!*" Grenville breathed. "And... and was it? Um. Splendid!"

"Aye. Aye it was." It would be true. "Heaven!"

"Ah, dearest." She heard a distant voice full of sadness.

"Please let me come to you," Eleanor could not stop herself. "Please!"

"I will come back and haunt you if you do." He seemed to have gathered strength.

"Why? At least tell me why," she pleaded.

"I must have someone. Mm? Nelly? Someone to remember me as I once was..." he hesitated.

Eleanor shut her eyes tight and reached out for his words,

"Do you remember me?" the fading voice was doubtful.

"Yes, of course I do —" she could hardly speak.

"Promise me?"

"Yes, my love, yes. I promise."

"I want you to remember me, dearest. Remember me... Forget my fate..."

iv

## LIGHT

Eleanor walked slowly into the park. The last few days had been cold and wet... the usual grey November weather, but today of all days, when it should have been dark and miserable, the sun was shining in a clear blue sky.

She had received the news on the phone this morning, just before a meeting with clients. It didn't affect her much. Made her feel a bit light headed, that's all.

Long tree shadows cast by the low winter sun passed on either side of an empty bench. The meeting had gone well, she'd pleased the clients and been given the go-ahead on her plans. Feeling weightless, Eleanor moved towards the sunny bench and sat down, gripping its arm to stop herself floating away. She closed her eyes and turned her face towards the light. Always towards the light. His motto. But there was no warmth in the sun at this time of year.

Beginning to feel cold, she got up and walked in the direction of the ICA. Go in. Get warm. Look at some contemporary art. Grenville would want her to keep up with the latest thing. No back sliding. No resisting the present.

She paused by the lake. Ducks. They went on as usual. Eleanor felt light, as if her bones were the quills of a bird. Fly away. People walked past her. Nothing terrible had happened to them that day. Ordinary people, chatting, arguing, laughing inside the bubble of their own lives. Float away inside a bubble.

Eleanor cried out as a crowd of office boys shouldered past, knocking her off-balance. They'd been drinking and found her shock hilarious. Mimicking *eeooh!* and exchanging crude remarks, they went off, pushing and shoving and yelling with laughter. Lucky for them she wasn't carrying a machete. Grenville was dead and those worthless morons could take up space and waste their lives. She stared at their backs, hating them. The St James' Park Massacre. But Grenville would not have approved of her angry fantasy. That peaky looking blond one, Grenville would have found him attractive. She knew his taste. Eleanor made towards the Underground. Not so floaty. Under the ground.

She travelled out of London to where she'd parked her car. It was twilight by the time she drove away. The short winter day was over. The sunset pulled her with it to the earth. Home. She must go home.

Hour after hour she drove, following the road, taking exits, taking another road, any road, filling up with petrol, going back on the road. Driving through the night, changing tapes, changing lanes, holding on to the way ahead.

Sometime after midnight she happened upon the sea and came to a stop on the edge of a deserted beach. The moon lit the vast empty space and made a bright pathless way to nowhere. Fear crawled over her. Terror. Breathe it in and go mad. Eleanor teetered on the edge of herself before starting the car quickly. She turned inland again. On and on, she followed the road into the early hours. Seeing a sign for Marty's home town, she took the direction. Something to aim for.

She came to rest under Marty's dark windows. No lights on. Late, too late. Eleanor dozed over the steering wheel and woke up as the car got cold. Too cold to sleep. Must go. Must move. She tried to use the mobile phone Grenville had given her but it wouldn't work. A telephone box stood on the street corner like a giant lantern. Taking her purse, she went over to it, rang Marty's number then propped open the heavy door of the booth with her body so she could see out across the road to his house. After a few rings she saw the light go on behind his bedroom curtains.

"Eh yeah?" came his sleepy voice.

"Marty, I'm sorry, it's Eleanor. I'm so sorry. I've woken you up."

"Eleanor?"

"Is there anyone with you? You know. Are you in bed with... have I —?"

"With me? Where? Course not... blimey!" he yawned. "Fat chance —"

"Are you sure? I'll go —"

"Nah, I'm a sad bastard," he mumbled. "I go to bed with a cup of cocoa and reports. Shit! Is that the time! Are you all right?" He struggled to wake up. "Are you all right?"

"No," she began to cry.

"Where are you?" Marty sat up, wide awake. "What's happened!"

"Grenville's gone and I've..."

"Oh God! Where are you? Are you safe?" he flung out of bed.

"I'm here..."

"Where! At the hospital? I'll come, I'm coming! I'll drive —" he grabbed his keys off the bedside table.

"I'm here. Outside. Are you with anyone —?"

"No! I said *no* for fuck's sake! Outside where?" he shouted.

"Your window... the phone box across the road from you."

"Jesus!" The bedroom curtain swept open and Marty's naked silhouette appeared against the light, the cord from his bedside phone spiralling into his head.

"I'm sorry I woke you up, Marty." She could see him. "I'm sorry. Sorry! It was so stupid. I should go. You'll have work tomor —"

"Bugger work! Bloody hell! Get yourself up here *now* —!" Marty squinted out of the window and then at the receiver in his hand. "Hang on! Why am I talking to you on this? Get out of that phone box and get over here!" Afraid that she'd vanish if he rang off, he threw the receiver on the bed. Rushing over to his underpants and hopping past the bed as he put them on, he leaned over the phone, calling, "Don't go away, Eleanor! Hold on! I'm just going to the door, now. Now!"

But Eleanor had already left the phone box. She locked her car and remembering the way from her visit, crept, careful not to rouse Trixie, round to the back of the house. She climbed the steps. Marty, standing in the light of the doorway, opened his arms to receive her.

# Two years later

## London — November 1990

### i

## RETURN

It smelt different. Cat pee had been replaced by varnish and fresh paint. The tidiness began in the hall — no cardboard boxes, trashed bicycles or discarded furniture. Gone were the ancient deposits of junk mail tramped down into layers. The local archaeology of takeaway menus, small business advertisments, newspapers, flyers and free offers had been removed to reveal a marble floor. As Eleanor and Marty went up the stairs, the heavy door did not slam behind them but slid shut with a click. The hall and landing where the fashion journalist waited were now brightly lit and an enormous glass chandelier glittered in the stairwell. The journalist's name was Natasha. She and her husband had known Grenville socially, and after his death had bought his house. His name had been a big selling point. Natasha, preparing a magazine spread about Grenville, had arranged for Eleanor to come and be interviewed and photographed in the ballroom. She leaned forward and kissed the air next to Eleanor's cheek saying,

"How pretty you look. You've filled out a bit —" reminding her that she was back where weight-loss was the standard of worth and where low-status people talked too fast and smiled too much. Forgetting that she came with her own glamour now, as well as Grenville's, Eleanor fell into the old habit of losing her accent.

"I've brought my husband," she said. "I hope you don't mind, he so wanted to see —"

"Of course you're married now!"

"I'm Martin," Marty introduced himself.

"Should we know you?" Natasha asked.

"Nah," he answered, knowing that people don't see beyond their expectations. "I'm one of these New Men: Mr Slouch hitched up to Ms High Flier."

Natasha looked at Marty and his good suit with approval. She did not recognise him.

Eleanor avoided Marty's eye and fixed her smile.

"And what a beautiful top! One of yours?" Natasha chatted as she hung Eleanor's coat in a newly built cupboard. "We all match! Black is the colour! When are we ever going to wear anything else? I simply can't think of us all in pink or blue or green, can you? But colour has to come back to the high street someday. It's a law of nature —"

Eleanor remembered Grenville saying he'd lusted after this woman. *What a bottom! And a shoe fetishist! Ungh!* Grenville noises pulsed through her head. Did he ever make it? Did he bother? Or did time run out on that heterosex recce?

"We can't go on wearing black forever, can we?" Natasha was saying.

"'Snot black a new colour —" Eleanor babbled.

"That's what I say!" Natasha led the way to the ballroom.

As it always had, the heavy door opened slowly. Eleanor gasped as she had the first time she entered the great space. But today, the shock was at seeing the ghost of a room she had once known so well.

The rich colours had drained off the walls and been replaced by shades of ivory. The three tall windows were shrouded with curtains and deeply swagged pelmets. The view of the square was fogged behind white muslin. Only the white stucco dancers on the blue ceiling remained, frozen in the sunless light. The rampant jungle of plants and creepers that had flourished as Grenville faded had been swept away as if overtaken by a new ice age.

"I simply can't imagine myself in colour," Natasha was saying to Marty. "Seems so vulgar! Strictly for the royals and the working class, don't you think?"

Eleanor took in the tightly stuffed furniture round the fireplace. The damask was correct for the period but with the bulging silk cushions, pale, deep-pile carpets and the glazed finish on the curtains, the effect was a queasy mixture of fussy and cold.

"We would've had you do the room for us, Eleanor, but we heard you'd gone back to the theatre," Natasha said. "We all think it rather funny and old fashioned of you —"

*Real art, Nelly, that's the ticket!* Grenville's voice played in her head.

"No future in the theatre, surely?" Natasha went on. "But I defended you, said it's more fun."

The room felt unused despite the glossy magazines laid open on the gold and glass coffee table. Everything looked new and clean. The warm presence of thousands of Grenville's books had been replaced by ornaments bought from antique shops: cabinets, clocks, Greek urns and gilt framed mirrors.

"And a little bird tells me that Eleanor is hot favourite for the top job at the —"

"Nothing certain yet —" Marty, realizing that Eleanor was in meltdown, spoke up. "But it does look like I might fulfil my ambition to be a kept man."

"Will you wear a loincloth and peel grapes?" Natasha purred at him.

Eleanor left her to Marty while she read the room. She knew from her work in period drama that to make a set look authentic and give it the charm of habitation, furniture had to be brought over from a previous era and surfaces distressed. The ballroom, full of an imported past, was a perfect expression of the present, of this couple's aspirations.

"My hubby says we've a talent for spotting winners," Natasha said. "We had Cassandra do this before she became famous. She's become quite the celebrity since. Worth loads of money now she's on the telly. We told her we didn't want anything changed at all, just the decor."

Eleanor, stunned by the changes, could not switch off her radiant smile.

"The colour scheme Grenville had in here was so-oo wacky!" Natasha was telling Marty. "Every colour under the sun and put on with no design sense at all! Really! Too, too much!"

But then, Grenville's colour scheme had not conformed to any notion of interior decor. It had been an expression of his private mythology.

"This Grenville was quite a *handful*, from all accounts," Marty said.

"*Yiih!*" Eleanor squeaked and looked up at the ceiling. Was she going to have hysterics? At least the ceiling was still there. Grenville had wanted a blue sky, painted dawn-pale at one end of the room deepening subtly across the firmament into soft dusk. He'd employed scene painters from the theatre, friends of Eleanor's, to realise his vision.

"We fancied a more Jane Austenish style." Natasha was saying. "Really light and pretty. I'm such a terrible romantic."

"O aye, yes." Eleanor, who judged by appearances, was finding it all impossible. The interview was going to be a nightmare. Shouldn't have come. Had come, not for Grenville's sake but out of curiosity. Serve her right.

*Nonsense! Always give in to curiosity, dearest, for desire is holy,* Grenville's voice played back approval. But she must get control and stop grinning like a daft ha'porth.

"Grenville is such a huge celebrity these days," Natasha said. "Programmes. Articles. You must be busy Eleanor, even though he's dead. It's the James Dean-Marilyn Monroe effect. Car crashes, suicide, AIDS — all glamorous ways to —" A telephone rang and Natasha, apologizing, hurried out of the ballroom to answer it.

When she'd left, Marty puffed out his cheeks,

"Being a girl isn't wasted on her, is it. I feel sexually harrassed, I do."

"Do you find her attractive?" Eleanor breathed out and tried to relax her stiff shoulders.

"Not quite. Too stupid. In the wrong sort of way. Nice shoes. If she wore those and not much else, I might manage."

Eleanor was giggling with nerves, "I should never've allowed you to come, Marty!"

"After all the trouble it cost me to get the day off," he said. "I didn't dare tell them it was for the wife. I really can't take any more nudging and winking. Every time the dinner ladies bloody see me, they start sniggering, 'Your lovely young wife keeping you busy, sir... *Decorating!*'" But Marty couldn't help liking it, feeling that part of him at least, was allowed to belong.

"How am I going to get through this! It's terrible!" Eleanor was shaking now. "Me being interviewed about Grenville. Here! And for a fashion mag!" She supported herself on the table where a pad, prepared questions and a recording machine had been laid out. There was an open portfolio of pictures sent by Grenville's agent. In them, Grenville was young and beautiful but bland... studio pictures taken before Eleanor knew him. Not her Grenville at all, really. "I can't imagine why I agreed to it! Why did I agree to it? Why!" she felt close to panic.

"Because you couldn't resist coming back to see this place and anyway he'd have loved it. Here, look at

346

this —" He handed Eleanor a copy of one of her own drawings. "He wouldn't let you see him because he wanted you to remember him like that..." Marty pointed at the picture. Even though Grenville's nude pose was languid, with head turned away, Eleanor's strong lines had captured his restless beauty. "He trusted you with his image, he made you its guardian. You've got to do it!"

"But what if I'm delivering him up to the *culture crunching jaws of journalism,* as he called it? And they just turn him into media mulch. A style icon. Another tragic leather queen who had it coming. He hated all that celebrity crap. And Oh God! Why did it have to be now?"

"Because it *is* now — the anniversary of his death and there's a flurry round the publication of his biography!" Marty answered. "And if he's a style icon, more people will buy it."

"It's too much, Marty. It's overload. I can't cope. My head's full of this new job. What if I get it? Do we move? What about your work? And your Dad? I'd want him —"

"Oioi, hang on! One thing at a time. Let's get through this first. I'm wound up enough as it is," he said. "This is my past too, you know."

Despite the glacial effect of the decor Eleanor felt hot and faint. They moved over to the balcony doors.

"What am I going to say in this interview, love? You must help me!" she said.

"Remind them of his anger," Marty said. "How angry Grenville was about people being isolated or ashamed or shut out, for whatever reason."

That's your agenda, she thought but didn't interrupt him.

"Don't let them forget his belief in sexual freedom and having everything out in the open. And, *and* how he did not repent or regret anything."

She lifted back the muslin curtain and looked at the trees in the square as Marty continued with his list,

"Tell them how gorgeous he was. How you loved him —"

"Oh no," Eleanor had to contradict this. "I'm not going there! That's private. They'll make me out the sad fag hag."

"And you mind that?" Marty startled her by tapping the window frame next to her head. "Well? Do you?" he persisted.

The balcony doors had been double glazed; the branches of the plane trees jostled silently. If the blackbird sang, it would not be heard.

"I used to think," she began slowly, "that I liked gays because it was a way to be friends with men, flirt even, without being put upon or made responsible for all that sex they want. Anyway," she sighed, "I'd rather be ignored by a lot of screaming queens than have the attention of most blokes. You know?"

He didn't know. Not his perspective at all. So he nodded without saying anything.

"But there's more to it, really." Facing Marty, she said, "You go on about queer girls and boys growing up confused, despised and all? I'm straight but I can identify with that. You've met my family —"

"Aargh!" Marty waved his arms.

"There you go. See what I mean! It was like living under a rock. Like having your soul crushed out of you. Just like you, I don't feel comfortable in straight-world," her movements became nervous again, "where everyone is always some flamin' thing or other before they're a human being. In my case, a girl, with all the rubbish that's supposed to mean. I can't stand all those assumptions." She pressed her hot forehead and palms onto the cold glass.

"*Smug, classbound heteroshit!*" Marty said. "That's what Grenville called it. Gawd, he could rant for England!"

"He hated England. *The fucking flag, fucking football and the fucking Falklands war!* He said the only country he'd ever fight for was Bohemia. He said at least it's full of awful people because nobody's ever denied entry —"

Eleanor and Marty jerked away from the balcony doors as Natasha hurried into the ballroom, calling,

"The photographers are running a bit late. I'm so sorry Eleanor. Bear with me, I've nearly got it sorted. I do need them to shoot you here, and me and everything. Good publicity for all of us."

Eleanor realised that this interview was a self-promotion exercise. This woman, having bought a dead celebrity's house, would, while Grenville was fashionable, be a celebrity herself. Would Grenville have minded?

*I can hardly hold it against such a wonderful bottom. Wuff!* Eleanor swallowed another gadfly giggle.

"I hope being here doesn't upset you. It must be very nostalgic. Reminding you of him so much." Natasha looked sentimental and Eleanor knew that she was expected to be human and show some emotion.

*Soppiness is forbidden! Humbuggers will be flogged! Buggers too, if they like.*

"Poor old Gren is absolutely the man of the moment. And Mrs Thatcher being given the push is perfect timing. He'd be dancing on her grave, wouldn't he!" Natasha said.

"O aye. Likely he would. Yes," Eleanor managed.

*It's just that I'm the one in the sodding grave, dear.* Grenville was haunting her now. Was he going to make her do something deranged?

"It's curtains for Thatcher, all right!" Marty said. "But the big question is... who will inherit? Will her dodgy ideas live on?"

"Everybody I talk to is obsessed with it... can't get them to concentrate." Natasha complained.

"Being working class, my Dad won't have her name mentioned —" Marty spoke about his Dad with deliberate pride. "Only, I suppose you've got to admire her bottle! D'you know, I reckon she might have got away with it but she made a fatal mistake, eh! Didn't she, though!"

"Yes, love," Eleanor said, trying to quell him. "She wore those big brooches and pussybow blouses you don't like."

"Bleagh!" he grimaced. "And I always said her 'orrible handbag would bring her down in the end." Natasha laughed but Marty wagged his finger and became serious again. "Thought she could do it on her own, didn't she. That was her mistake! Okay, she's the Prime Minister and I'm only a two bit teacher in a one horse town but I know I can't bring in the changes I want if I don't have the support of my team —"

"Natasha, love," Eleanor interrupted. "My rooms were on the top floor when I lived here. Could I...?"

"Of course! Do go up." Natasha said. She was relieved, it would pass the time and keep her guests amused. "I'll go back and chivvy the photographers and leave you to show Martin. I warn you though, it's still a mess. We've not started up there yet."

## PAST

"I've never been up here," Marty said as they stood in her old attic. There was no furniture, only a coathanger and a discarded lampshade on the dusty floorboards.

"It held me close..." Eleanor said, "like a chrysalis. I was so happy but also..."

She stood still while Marty moved through the deserted room, in and out of the shadows, disturbing the motes that floated in the slanting shafts of sunlight. Seeing this abandoned place made Eleanor think of her home with Marty. She looked at him as he traced his finger over an empty shelf, drawing initials in the dust.

"My bed was in this corner and over here —" she tried but her voice trailed off again. Somehow she couldn't be bothered to tell Marty how this place had been furnished. Instead she thought of their bedroom. Sleeping together. The comfort of his body. Eleanor watched as Marty's hand entered a square of light on the bare floor and picked up the discarded coathanger.

"Your clothes probably hung on that," he twirled the wire skeleton. "You were happy here. You'd come back?" he asked.

"No!" she jerked out of the shadows with her answer. "Bring Grenville back, yes. But I want us, you, our home —"

Marty nodded, before slinging the coathanger on the naked curtain pole. He tried the firedoor, opened it and stepped out onto the flat roof.

Eleanor was about to follow him when she noticed some cardboard boxes left behind in the storeroom. Her old stuff? Grenville's? She went to see. Letters... photos... and gay porn from a time of innocence. Leave it. She had enough grief.

"Come and get some air, mate," Marty called from the roof.

As always, autumn leaves from the trees in the square had blown over the high parapet and were spinning in a corner. Eleanor and Marty stood out of the wind and leaned their backs against the warm, sunlit bricks of the chimney.

"Grenville always used to have bad dreams before he went home —" Eleanor said.

"Like you did, last night," Marty said. "All muttery and twitchy, you were."

"I dreamt that —" Eleanor broke off.

Marty was curious now. "Go on," he said.

"I can't. It's too..."

"Who was in it?" Marty changed tack.

"All of us. All our friends who've died as well. Grenville... it was a bit of a wild party."

"One of his orgies, you mean."

"Yeah, sort of. Everyone in the weirdest costumes. Real baroque opera, commedia dell'arte style. Powdered wigs. Fetish gear and feathers. Whiteface, the lot."

"And Grenville?" Marty felt a jab of jealousy.

"He was wearing a gold, *innamorato* mask. But I knew him. I'd made his costume, I think."

"What happened? He shagged you." Marty couldn't stop himself.

"No..."

"Don't worry. It's a dream. I'll understand."

"He peed over my hands," Eleanor said.

"Blimey! Interesting. Did you feel abused?"

"No I didn't. Not at all. It was all gold and shimmery... and silky. It was beautiful. Very loving, somehow." Eleanor turned towards Marty and he took her in his arms. She hid her face in his neck, "I can't believe I told you that," she mumbled. "It's so shameful —"

"You can't be ashamed of anything with me," Marty said. "Anyway dreams are nothing to be ashamed of."

Eleanor pressed herself against him for comfort and put a hand up to stroke his face. "Marty? This time of year... it reminds me..."

"Me too, doll. The way *I* remember it..." Because it was rustling round his ear, Marty took Eleanor's hand and held it against his chest. "You took advantage of me under an umbrella." This comic version of their story was still the only safe crossing to the past. "November..." he said, "It's always going to be the month when Grenville died and we got together and did nothing but fuck and talk and go for walks in the rain. What a time of love and death, eh?"

Eleanor rested against Marty.

"It was strange," she said, "I was so happy with you... but it made me feel guilty about Grenville."

"I know," Marty sighed. "I couldn't find room for him. Not even to talk about it."

"Grenville said he wanted people to cry at his funeral," Eleanor edged them towards the unvisited past. "We didn't cry at all."

"The whole thing reminded me of Grenville's um... kinky rituals," Marty said. "All of us held in tight by the ceremonial."

"Well, I wouldn't know. But yeah, the only person who cried was Tinker —"

"Who's usually the only one laughing," Marty said.

"We had to go off and hide so Kev could hold the poor lad —"

"And the rest of us could have hysterics. Can't remember what was so funny, now..."

"It was Tinker being asked about Grenville's last words," Eleanor lifted her head from Marty's shoulder.

"Yeah!" Marty remembered. "And he said it was *bollocks!*"

Eleanor sniffed back her tears and imitated the superior accent of one of Grenville's in-laws: "*I think we must have some advance on 'bollocks' for the sake of the press.*"

Marty slipped into Tinker's voice: "*Aw all right, then. Nimini pimini. Eh? Nimini pimini. Them's his last words. Like I said mate — bollocks!*"

Marty and Eleanor's jittery laughter scattered over the rooftops.

"That day was just the beginning for Tinker," Marty shivered. "Poor guy, it was like his whole life started to catch up with him. And how! We didn't get it at first, did we?" Marty tried to think it through as he spoke. "Because by rights, he was the lucky bastard. He'd defied all the odds: been on the streets, then Grenville's lover but not got sick. He'd survived! That's amazing! Plus he'd got a home now and money —"

"A job at the clinic and Kevin the new boyfriend —"

"Tinker Belle's in clover and…? He goes off his head!" Marty blinked back his own feelings. "Cracked up enough for all of us. Oh God. It was like when my Mum died… Tinker was like my Dad all over again."

"Your Dad was brilliant with him," Eleanor said. "And I'm so glad Kev stuck by him. I don't think he would have pulled through without Kev and Yasmine and coming to stay with us —"

"You've brought me back to them. Brought me back to our old mates, Tinker, Archie, Yasmine and everyone." Marty tucked Eleanor's hair behind her ears. "It's good. I'm ever so grateful." He wiped away her tears with his thumbs, "Friendship… that's what counts in the end."


ON


Marty returned to the ballroom and as Eleanor paused outside the bathroom, Natasha met her, saying,

"Give me ten more minutes and I'll be ready. I'm so sorry you've had to wait. Your Martin is being very nice about it too. Isn't he sweet!" she chattered. "Just right for you! You'd need someone safe after Grenville. Have you noticed how everybody's jumping on the bandwagon now? Claiming to have known him. And to have been fancied by him! But I said I wanted to go straight to the horse's mouth…" Natasha looked at Eleanor with respect. "Because you really *did* know him."

"But he really *did* fancy you, pet." At last, Eleanor had found something positive to say to Natasha.

"Well, I don't like to brag…" she responded, putting her hand on Eleanor's arm. "My husband is the jealous type and, Heaven knows, Grenville was one of *the* most divine men on this planet. Anyway, nothing came of it…" She pouted with regret. "But then, if it had, I might not be alive to tell the tale." The women exchanged sad looks before Natasha waved her hand, "No more doom and gloom! I'll make us all some coffee and we'll get started."

"I'd much rather have tea," Eleanor said with sudden confidence and in her real voice. No more cover-up. Grenville was right. From now on she was going to be herself.

"And why not! I'll make you a pot, no-oo problemo," Natasha said. "You just chill out, darling. Get back into the atmosphere. I won't be long now."

Though the view from the window was the same, the bathroom had been changed round. Being back here was like wading through one of those dreamscapes, mutations of the familiar, where school corridors were castle ramparts or the toilet on a floodlit stage. She grounded herself by thinking about home: Marty… and Marty's Dad… and Trixie the dog… who greeted her without barking… because she was family now.

As she dried her hands, easing the towel round her wedding ring, she experienced a new sensation… belonging. She was no longer a tourist, wandering in and out of other people's lives.

Not that her marriage was all plain sailing or anything. There was a suitcase in Marty's wardrobe. He'd shown her where he kept it. His box of tricks. She knew it was there and knew what was in it —

"Do you want it out of our home?" he'd asked.

"I'd rather it was where I can see it," she'd answered.

So, there it was. This bit of Marty that did not belong to her. But after all, it didn't cause her any trouble. Why should it? She had what she wanted.

Eleanor took a hairbrush from her bag. Their intimacy was what she wanted — the privacy of it. Eleanor brushed her hair, tilting her head at the reflection in the mirror. Sometimes, in public, she would catch Marty's eye. They would exchange secret looks. It always made her yearn to be alone with him. Have him touch her.

*So it's boring old nomini pomini for you after all.*

Eleanor stopped brushing her hair. Go away. It isn't anything. Except my life. What I want. She waggled her brush at thin air. Isn't that what you believed in? She dropped the brush, like the last word, into her bag. But there was no satisfaction in outsmarting the dead.

Eleanor took out her lipstick.

Grief shadowed her still… as she walked through Grenville's beloved London or calculated the effect of a colour or caught the scent of flowers. Today it had even followed her into the toilet. He'd never had any regard for privacy.

Eleanor's face in the mirror was like the mask of Tragedy as her mouth opened taut for the lipstick. Would he ever leave her? Did she want him to? Where was he?

Her drawings of Grenville hung in the studio where she worked, stitching, sketching, dressing thought in a costume. When it was going well, she missed his praise.

But it was when she was stuck that she missed him acutely, his endless questions and nutty notions... so often the key to a new idea. Then she might turn to his picture for inspiration but be overcome with rage, mourning the loss of his being and the loss of her young self.

Eleanor peered into the mirror.

Where was that girl? *Nelly... dearest...?* Grenville had gone off with her. Taken her with him. That young Eleanor belonged to Grenville and he'd snatched her away into the past, swept her away with him down to the kingdom of the dead.

Eleanor closed her eyes and placed her hands on the cold washbasin as she took time to steady her breathing and fold up her feelings.

Marty was standing by a large, state-of-the-art television when she returned to the ballroom.

"Do you think Natasha would mind if I turned it on?" he asked, looking for controls on the monitor. "I want to know what's happening. It's the end of an era!" Marty picked up a gadget lying near the television, "How do you work these things now?"

"But what if I get that job?" Eleanor wondered out loud. "There'll be questions about —"

"No there won't," Marty, preoccupied with reading symbols on the remote, misunderstood. "The article is not about you, this time. Today... can we get a news channel? Today, the rap is about Grenville..." he trailed off as he tried pointing the gadget at the screen.

"I know that!" Eleanor said. "The trouble is I still haven't decided how to play it —"

"I told you already," Marty said. "Remind them of what he stood for and — yes!' The television flashed into soundless life. "Say you loved him. Say it for both of us."

"Then they'll ask if he was my lover. What do I say to that, eh?"

"You answer, 'if only'. And if that makes you the discarded woman, I'll be the husband you put up with in your disappointment."

"But that isn't how it is at all!" Eleanor was shocked.

"So?" Marty stopped fiddling and turned to her, "It doesn't matter about us. Spread his message. Adore him. Make him a saint. He's as qualified as anyone. He did good, Eleanor. And we owe him." Marty pointed to and fro, at her and himself, "We know what we've got *in here...*"

An image of the deposed Prime Minister appeared on the television.

"Now! Let's find out what's going on *out there*, shall we!" Marty pressed the volume key on the remote control,

*extended news coverage of the latest events... and here in the studio with me are*

Eleanor moved away to the other side of the ballroom. What would happen if she was offered that job? What would they do? Where would they live? And what about the kids Marty wanted? Must get on with it... not leave it too late. And then whose career would come first, hers or Marty's...?

*just ask whether they want to see those people back in power, holding us to ransom, go on, ask them if they propose to reverse the achievements of*

But today was going to be all right. She stood alone in quiet rehearsal. Preach Grenville's message of openess, lots of talk and no secrets etcetera. Remember how he'd always tried to bring people together and been passionate about everything and so generous.

*the victories were achieved at a terrible cost, we are now a more unequal society, dangerously divided*

And she would underline it by saying she'd loved him. Love. An everyday word she would not be asked to explain.

*the disparity of wealth, the north-south divide, the appearance of beggars on our streets*

Eleanor looked up at the ceiling. It was the only place she might find Grenville now, in that blue sky above the furniture of the world. Up there, where naked babies tossed flowers and tumbled through ribbons, where the followers of dawn and dusk swayed past

*this inequality is reflected across the globe. It's a dreadful legacy and there will be*

Where the boys and girls, the fauns, the nymphs and wilful creatures danced on, their plaster eyes searching the invisible, their mouths open in silent song

*when we will be bringing you the main stories from around the world*

Onwards they trailed, singing the O of longing.